TRIAD MAGIC

Praise for the Triad Blood Trilogy

Triad Blood

"'Nathan Burgoine is a talented writer who creates a fascinating world and complex characters...If you're a fan of demons, vampires, wizards, paranormal fiction, mysteries, thrillers, stories set in Canada, or a combination of the previously mentioned, do yourself a favor and check this book out!"—*The Novel Approach*

"*Triad Blood* was a fun book. If you're a fan of gay characters, urban fantasies, and (even better), both of them, you'll enjoy *Triad Blood.*"—*Pop Culture Beast*

Triad Soul

"'Nathan Burgoine's *Triad Blood*, the first book in this series, was one of my favourite books of last year and *Triad Soul* is, if anything, even better...what sets it apart, and makes me genuinely love this book (and series) is the depiction, both in fact and in allegory, of queer community. The prose is generally crisp and cleanly written, but there are also flourishes of creativity that elevate the writing above the prosaic. It has heart, imagination, and skill. Like *Triad Blood* before it, I suspect this is going to be one of my favourite books of its year."—*Binge on Books*

"'Nathan Burgoine really excels at creating a fascinating and unique supernatural world full of interesting politics. If you are a paranormal or a suspense fan, I think there is a lot here that will appeal to you, particularly if you are looking for a unique take on the various supernatural beings. Burgoine has really created something engaging here and I definitely recommend the series."—*Joyfully Jay*

Reviewers Love 'Nathan Burgoine

Exit Plans for Teenage Freaks

"Burgoine has created a gay teen protagonist who is a bit goofy at times but who is comfortable in his own skin…Overall, a feel-good, contemporary read with strong LGBTQIAP rep and an unusual fantasy subplot."—*Kirkus Reviews*

"READ THE BOOK. NOW. IT IS AMAZING."—*Book Princess Reviews*

"The plot was a great deal of fun, and the characters were wonderful. Cole is gay and most (all?) of his friends are in the school's Rainbow Club – but that's not the plot. No one's queerness is a plot point… Because this book is about teleporting and teenagers graduating high school and awkwardness. It's not about queer tragedy."—*Almost, Almost: Queer librarian blogs mostly about books*

"This is a character-driven story with very little angst and a smooth writing style that is easy to get caught up in. The seamlessness of the inclusion was really impressive to me."—*Boy Meets Boy Reviews*

"*Exit Plans for Teenage Freaks* by 'Nathan Burgoine is a fun queer rom-com sci-fi novel set in present time Canada. From Cole, our bullet journal loving protagonist, his ace BFF Alec, and Malik, the hottest guy in school, you will find someone to relate to or fall in love with in this Queer YA novel."—*Lara Lillibridge*

"It's rare I read a novel with a MC so clearly realized. 'Nathan writes Cole so 3-dimensionally, you swear you know him from the moment he speaks. That clarity along with a kick-ass story makes this my favorite YA novel for 2018. Nathan mixes Sci-Fi with budding male/male teen romance and the combination works perfectly."
—*Philip Bahr, Librarian, Fairfield Public Library*

"Burgoine uses science fiction elements to explore homosexuality, pansexuality, bisexuality, and gender nonconforming identity… Burgoine's immersive writing excels in the details, from the precise sensations Cole experiences at the onset of a teleport to the overwhelming intensity of his feelings for his friend Malik… VERDICT: A definite purchase for any library collection."
—*School Library Journal*

"Cole's narration is sardonic and adorably self-deprecating. His habits of mind: list-making, signing in ASL, extensive planning, all helped create a fully-developed, slightly goofy, teen boy...It's a fun and sweet read, with a collection of realistic characters whose details I wanted to discover and figure out further."—*V's Reads*

Of Echoes Born

"Burgoine assembles 12 queer supernatural tales, several of which interlock...The best tales could easily stand alone; these include 'The Finish,' about an aging vintner whose erotic dalliance with a deaf young man named Dennis gets complicated, and 'Struck,' in which beleaguered bookstore clerk Chris meets Lightning Todd, who predicts his future wealth and romance. A pair of stories set in 'the Village,' a gay neighborhood, feature appealing characters and romances and could be components of a fine *Tales of the City*–like novel."—*Publishers Weekly*

"The best short story collections are treasure chests that sparkle—not from the gems they contain, but with a light greater than the whole as the reader is left knowing more about life. In such work the mysteries aren't solved, but the questions get redefined. And so the tales in *Of Echoes Born* shimmer like gold, and not the kind you'll covet. This is one of those books that, when finished, you hurry to buy copies for friends."—Tom Cardamone, Lambda Award winning author of *Green Thumb*, *Night Sweats: Tales of Homosexual Wonder*, and *Woe and The Lurid Sea*

Lambda Literary Award Finalist *Light*

"What's stunning about this debut is its assurance. In terms of character, plot, voice, and narrative skill, Burgoine knocks it out of the park as if this were his tenth book instead of his first. He, along with Tom Cardamone, has the considerable gift of being able to ground the extraordinary in the ordinary so that it becomes just an extension of everyday life."—*Out in Print*

"*Light* by 'Nathan Burgoine is part mystery, part romance, and part superhero novel. Which is not to say that *Light* emulates such 'edgy' angst-filled comic book heroes as the X-Men; if you'll pardon the pun, it is much lighter in tone."—*Lambda Literary Review*

"*Light* is an enjoyable, light superhero story that was a lot of fun to read. With an openly gay and proud main character and events taking place over the course of Pride Week, it will find a welcome home with readers looking for LGBT characters, especially in science fiction and fantasy."—*Come Hither Books*

"Burgoine's initial novel is a marvelously intricate story, stretching the boundaries of science and paranormal phenomena, with a cast of delightfully diverse characters, all fully nuanced and relatable to the reader. I honestly could not put the book down, and recommend it highly, as I look forward to his next novel."—*Bob Lind, Echo Magazine*

"*Light* manages to balance a playful sense of humor, hot sex scenes, and provocative thinking about the meanings of individuality, acceptance, pride, and love. Burgoine takes some known gay archetypes—the gay-pride junkie, the leather SM top—and unpacks them in knowing and nuanced ways that move beyond stereotypes or predictability. With such a dazzling novelistic debut, Burgoine's future looks bright."—*Chelsea Station Magazine*

"Engaging and hard to put down, *Light* speeds along at an incredible pace in a mixture of humor and urgency. A great narrator, Kieran is forced to juggle his new relationship, his hidden powers, and his ongoing battles in a plot that mixes drag queens, giant dogs, astrally-projected mentors, superhero-style battles…This book is recommended for libraries of all types as well as anyone interested in dipping a toe into the waters of m/m romance."—*Mack Freeman, GLBT Reviews: ALA's Gay Lesbian Bisexual Transgender Round Table*

Three Left Turns to Nowhere

"Three short stories, three chances to enjoy unique and unusual stories with LGBTQ characters that aren't your typical. Not only are the stories different but the geek in me loved that all three characters are on the way to a science fiction convention…But there truly is a lot to love in these stories…If you like friendship and unusual romances, this is the novel for you. The stories are short but are complete, well paced, and engaging."—*The Nameless Zine*

Praise for the Village Holiday Novellas

Felix Navidad

"I'm jumping all over the place reading this Little Village novellas series but having a blast doing it. I love the found family, the rep, the care with which the characters are treated and how they treat each other. If I were willing to brave a Canadian winter and live in Ottawa, I would enjoy calling these people friends. I definitely want to go back and read the other two novellas and hope that there will be additional ones to come."—*Dear Author (Recommended Read)*

Faux Ho Ho

"The setup is simple: fake boyfriends for the holidays, started as a lie to get someone out of a dreaded family event, but snowballs into a more elaborate ruse. A tried-and-true formula really. But *Faux Ho Ho*, 'Nathan Burgoine's new holiday release, is anything but formulaic or contrived. The execution is original, and the story is an utter delight. It's charming, fun, and sweet, everything a Christmas romance should be. And it's also a little bit nerdy! Which, in my book, is a bonus."—*The Novel Approach*

Village Fool

"I absolutely adore the Little Village novellas, they're short and sweet in all the best ways. *Village Fool* is no exception. 'Nathan Burgoine has once again lured me in and kept me hooked for the less than 200 pages it takes to tell his stories."—*QueerBookstagram*

By the Author

Light

Of Echoes Born

Exit Plans for Teenage Freaks

A Little Village Blend

Three Left Turns to Nowhere

Triad Blood Trilogy

Triad Blood

Triad Soul

Triad Magic

Village Holiday Novellas

Handmade Holidays

Faux Ho Ho

Village Fool

Felix Navidad

Visit us at www.boldstrokesbooks.com

TRIAD MAGIC

by

'Nathan Burgoine

2024

TRIAD MAGIC
© 2024 By 'Nathan Burgoine. All Rights Reserved.

ISBN 13: 978-1-63679-505-8

This Trade Paperback Original Is Published By
Bold Strokes Books, Inc.
P.O. Box 249
Valley Falls, NY 12185

First Edition: April 2024

Credits
Editors: Jerry L. Wheeler and Stacia Seaman
Production Design: Stacia Seaman
Cover Design by Inkspiral Design

Acknowledgments

Is it poor form to begin your acknowledgments with an apology? Ah well, too bad. For everyone who has asked me over the years when the third Triad book was coming out, I'm so sorry it took this long. While I'd intended to take a wee break by writing *Exit Plans for Teenage Freaks*, the plan was to come right back to *Triad Magic* thereafter, but then… Well. A rescued husky named Max came into our life, and on one particularly icy day in Ottawa, noticed a squirrel, lunged, and basically between falling badly and not having been able to brace for impact, I all but destroyed the tendons in my left arm, all the way down to my wrist. Months and months of physiotherapy followed, and I could only type in short bursts, and so if I was to release anything, it needed to be shorter. Hence the stream of novellas and my single Hi-Lo novel, *Stuck With You*, none of which broke much over thirty thousand words.

I kept working on *Triad Magic* as I could, though, and after finishing physiotherapy (or at least, getting to the point where I think I'll be for the rest of my life, which isn't back to normal but is pretty close) I finally, finally got to finish it.

So. I'm sorry. Thank you for waiting. I hope you enjoy Anders, Curtis, and Luc as they face down this final adventure in my supernatural version of Ottawa.

Thanks as always go to my editors and proofreaders: Jerry L. Wheeler and Stacia Seaman are magic, and Jerry especially had to hold my (good) hand through a lot of the struggles in this one, given how long and protracted my path was to getting it done. Also huge bushels of love once again to my cover artist, Inkspiral Design, who worked some, uh, magic with this cover (sorry) to bring about a real progression and sense of finality to the third cover, even though he had nothing to do with the first two.

There are also a tonne of readers, fellow authors, and just plain awesome human beings who've been with me along the journey of this one. If you find your name inside these pages, it's on purpose: naming characters after you is my way to say thank you. You rock. (Sorry if your namesake also happens to die.)

Most importantly, all my love to my husband, Dan, without whom none of this would be possible. And I do still adore our rescued husky, Max, with whom this almost became impossible. He's got me wrapped around his paw anyway.

For Richard Labonté, who told me Curtis needed a book after he accepted "Possession" for an anthology.

You are missed.

ONE

The café on the upper floor of the University Centre wasn't one of Curtis's usual haunts, but after finishing his final exam of the year—scratch that, he'd just finished his entire linguistics degree—Curtis found himself wandering the campus. When his stomach gave a half-hearted rumble, he decided on a cup of tea and some poutine.

The first forkful made it clear he'd had the right idea. He'd already been well acquainted with the reality of tea as magic, but it turned out curds, fries, and gravy might merit a close second.

He had most of the place to himself, and the screens were muted in deference to the exam period. A few other students were studying in the corner booths. Many of them looked like they hadn't slept in days. One guy was even in a bright blue furry mouse onesie. Probably a tunnel rat, one of the students who lived in residence and used the underground campus tunnels to get to and from his classes. All the power to him, given the typical Ottawa April weather cycle of rain, damp, and even more rain.

"There you are."

Curtis turned, Mackenzie's smile growing as he sheepishly worked to swallow his mouthful of poutine. And she wasn't alone. Rebekah stood to her left, and to his surprise, Dale and Tracey were with her, too. It was almost the whole Craft Night gang, minus Matthew.

"Hey," he said once his mouth was almost entirely empty. Mackenzie was a year behind him in university, though they'd shared a prof or two. Rebekah and Tracey went to Ottawa University. He had no idea if Dale attended post-secondary school or not. The guy wasn't exactly forthcoming about, well, *anything*.

"So, you're done. Bask for us." Rebekah took the chair across from him, then eyed his poutine. "Oh. I'm going to need some of that."

"Grab a fork, there's way too much here for me," Curtis said, nudging the basket into the space between them.

"I might get something myself. Anyone want anything?" Dale said.

"A whole poutine of my very own," Rebekah said.

"Coffee, please, if they have dark roast," Tracey said. She looked dubious. Curtis had the distinct impression Tracey held strong opinions on the quality of, well, everything.

"Green tea, if they have it?" Mackenzie said.

Dale nodded and was gone.

"Did you have an exam today?" Curtis asked Mackenzie, surprised they were all here.

She shook her head. "No. We're here to congratulate *you*." She pointed at him. "You finished your degree!"

"Yay," Curtis said, wiggling his fingers. It came out flat and false.

"Ouch," Rebekah said. She'd had her hair redone, he realized belatedly. The tight braids had threads of a deep red in them. It suited her and matched her lipstick, which was as rich a red and completely flattering her already gorgeous dark brown skin. The combination made him think of the fire magics she so effortlessly commanded. Frankly, she looked amazing.

"Okay, loving the hair," he said. "And the lipstick."

"Thank you." She smiled. "I'm carving time for self-care among my new...*duties*. Lippy is an important part of my ability to handle the Mitchell bullshit."

Curtis tried not to wince on her behalf at the mention of her new role among the wizards of the city. Rebekah Mitchell had received her Family inheritance a few months ago—a magical one—to "see magical truth." Since she'd inherited the gift, she could see through any illusion as well as the workings of magics usually not visible to the naked eye. He knew she'd been afraid it would completely curtail her life, as her Family, the Mitchells, relied on the gift to be mediators in the complex inter-Family workings that kept the supernatural side of Ottawa running smoothly.

Still, she seemed more determined than ever to stay in control of her own time, and it was a good look on her. It likely helped her mother was the new coven head of her Family, and according to what Mackenzie had told Curtis, the two seemed to have buried much of the anger and resentment of their past, too.

"I'm glad." He did wince now. He hadn't sounded completely confident.

"Did the exam not go well?" Tracey asked. She'd changed her hair, too. It was shorter, and the highlights seemed more subtle. Had she gone to a tanning booth? Her pale, creamy skin seemed to have a bit more color, and her makeup seemed even more elegant than usual. Tracey always looked like she'd walked off the cover of a magazine, but the changes made her seem a bit more approachable. Or maybe he was projecting. He often felt like the fifth wheel.

"No, it went fine." Curtis shrugged. "I'm sorry. It's a whole different thing."

"What thing?" Mackenzie asked.

When Curtis looked at her to answer, he realized Mackenzie's usually haphazard waves seemed perfect. "Hang on. Did you three do a ladies' spa day or something? You all look amazing."

"Pay up." Rebekah held out a hand to Tracey, who blew out an annoyed breath. But she dug into her purse and dropped a loonie into Rebekah's palm.

"What's happening?" Curtis said.

"Dale didn't notice, and you did," Mackenzie said. "Rebekah won the bet."

"I believed in you," Rebekah said.

"I'm not sure if I'm flattered or stereotyped," Curtis said. "But you're all catwalk ready."

"Thank you," Rebekah said, pocketing the loonie. "What thing?"

"Huh?"

"You said there was a whole different thing."

Curtis swallowed. Dale was still waiting at the bar, which helped. He could never quite get a read on him, and Dale's bland poker face was a bit intimidating. Mackenzie, on the other hand, he found himself blabbing to whenever she gave him her big brown eyes of concern, and Rebekah put up with zero shit whatsoever, so he'd learned over the last few months not to even *try* to hold back with her.

"I *maybe* gave Luc and Anders a deadline," Curtis said. "And *maybe* it's today."

"A deadline for what?" Tracey said. "Is it something to do with the house?"

Curtis was midway through having a new house built. It was slow going. He wanted it done right, and he also wanted to build the best magical protections he could from the foundation up. Doing so meant slowing down construction so he could visit the house and work magic on it. Binding runes into the foundation had taken three days. The construction crew were convinced he had some sort of anxiety issue and needed to triple-check everything himself. He'd decided not to argue with their assumption. To his surprise, they'd been really accommodating. He paid well, and he wasn't holding them to tight deadlines, so they didn't mind. Or so he hoped.

At least now school was done he could get there whenever he wanted.

"Not the house," Curtis said. And then Dale was there with a tray, handing out cups and divvying up two basket bowls between himself and Rebekah. He'd also ordered a poutine. He sat, and Tracey gave him a quick kiss.

"Wait. A *deadline* deadline?" Mackenzie said. Her eyes were wide. She'd totally gotten it.

"It was Valentine's Day, and I'd nearly died. Y'know, *again*." Curtis sighed. "I wasn't in a good place confidence-wise, and I just sort of blurted it out." He stabbed at some fries. "The next thing I knew, I was Mr. Emotional Confession, handing out deadlines."

"What are we talking about?" Dale said.

"I think Curtis proposed," Tracey said, taking a sip of her coffee.

"Aww," Dale said, and the cheerfulness in his voice was a solid surprise. Huh. Maybe he'd misjudged the guy. Then his smile faltered. "Wait. Proposed to Anders? Or to Luc?"

"Yes?" Curtis said.

Tracey arched her eyebrows. Dale blinked a couple of times. Rebekah grinned. But it was Mackenzie who gave him a look of understanding.

"So. you put it all out there, and you're regretting it?" she said.

"Not regretting. I'm twenty-two. They're…older than twenty-two. If I can admit how I feel about them, they can tell me how they feel about me. It's more I'm dreading the answer."

"How does that even work?" Dale said.

"Well, Dale, when three people really love each other…" Rebekah started.

Dale rolled his eyes. "I meant proposing. You can't marry two people."

"I didn't actually *propose*," Curtis said. His face burned. "It was more of a declaration. I told them I loved them. And I wanted to know—*want* to know—if they love me."

"Aww," Dale said again, and Curtis glanced at him, not bothering to hide the surprise on his face.

"He's a shipper," Tracey said, patting Dale's shoulder. "He wants the whole world to be as happy as us."

"That's really sweet," Curtis said, and he meant it.

Dale shrugged.

"And?" Mackenzie said. "You're killing me, Curt. What happened after you dropped the L-bomb?"

Right. That. Curtis took a sip of his tea, then admitted the truth. "Anders looked like he wanted to jump out a window, and Luc got all clumsy and tongue-tied."

"You're shitting me," Rebekah said. "Luc? Butter-wouldn't-melt, duke-of-the-city, my-suit-has-never-seen-a-wrinkle? That Luc?"

"Yep." Curtis stabbed another load of fries, gravy, and cheese onto his fork. "And then they got all dressed up—well, Anders did, Luc is always dressed up—and fed me torte and cheesecake. But they didn't *actually* answer. Though, in fairness, I told them they didn't have to. I didn't want them to rush. I wanted them to think about it and said they could tell me after my exam. This exam. The one I just finished."

"Way to steal your own thunder," Rebekah said.

Curtis had to admit she had a point.

Silence fell around the table.

"I don't suppose Matt is coming?" Curtis said. "Because I could totally use someone who can see the future before I go home. Maybe I could shake his hand, and we could all watch his future-seeing tattoo and see if it shows me in a happy puppy pile with Luc and Anders, or if I crumble into tiny tattoo pieces."

"Okay, first? You will not fall into tiny pieces, regardless." Mackenzie squeezed his arm. "Second, Matt was supposed to meet us, but he didn't show. I'm sure something came up."

"Jace." Rebekah coughed Matthew's boyfriend's name into her hand.

"Probably Jace," Mackenzie said without blinking.

"Are we worried about how much time he's spending with Jace?" Tracey said, a small line between her eyebrows. "Because it feels like a lot. Their trip to England was one thing, but he's missed a few Craft Nights, too."

"They're prioritizing. It's still new," Dale said. "I don't think we can blame him for looking for more time with Jace, especially while he's juggling being the Stirling oracle."

Huh. Again with the shipping from Dale. Dale noticed him looking and lifted one shoulder again before diving in for more of his poutine.

"That's…fair enough," Curtis said. Hell, it was more than fair. Jace was a hunk. And a werewolf. "Well, even if I can't get a quick prophecy from Matt, I'm kind of wasting time because I don't want to go home before the sun goes down. I'd rather Luc be up so he and Anders can…" He waved a hand. "Tear off the Band-Aid in one go, I guess?"

"So when you say 'torte and cheesecake,'" Dale said, leaning forward and lowering his voice. "Is that…Is that a gay thing?"

"It's just dessert." Tracey laughed, though fondly. Then she eyed Curtis as though she was second-guessing herself. "Right?"

He nodded. He was trying not to laugh at Dale himself.

"Well," Dale said, and for the first time ever in Curtis's presence, he was blushing, "that sounds good. A good sign, I mean." He looked back down at his poutine and dug in again. "This is really good."

"Agreed," Tracey said. "About the good sign, I mean."

"How about we finish up here," Mackenzie said, "and then we go hang out somewhere. Until, y'know, sundown."

The tension in Curtis's shoulders unwound a fraction.

"You people are the best," he said. "Thank you."

"Can I try some?" Mackenzie said, looking at his bowl.

He handed her his fork.

TWO

Now that work was underway on their new house, coming home felt oddly dissatisfying. Curtis idled in the driveway for a moment. Luc's Mercedes was in one garage, Anders's SUV in the other. He turned off his car but stayed seated. He'd spent years here with his parents, and while it had memories, he found himself more than ready to start something new somewhere else.

Thank you for this. Curtis aimed his gratitude to the negligible somewhere he hoped his parents might hear him. *If you hadn't left me this, I have no idea where I'd be.*

The last of the sun's rays were fading, and he didn't have to check the dashboard clock to know sunset had gone by.

Funny the sort of things you could get used to. Curtis had never been particularly conscious of sunrises and sunsets before Luc had come into his life. Now the time for both was one of the first things he looked at in the morning on his phone. That first sight of Luc, coming up the stairs from the basement, usually impeccably coifed, gave him a sense of being more *complete*. Also horny, because impeccably coifed was hot on Luc, in his whole dark French Canadian way. Curtis almost felt bad for how often he jumped on the man to undo the clothes Luc obviously spent such care donning in the first place.

Almost.

No, Curtis didn't like the daylight hours when he could feel, deep in his chest, how in a fundamental way he and Anders were on their own.

Not that Anders was a fan of the early daylight hours himself. The demon was more of a crack-of-noon kind of guy. And he didn't wake up impeccably anything, unless it was possible to wake up sexily rumpled. He did sexy rumple very, very well. He also tended to grab Curtis and drag him back to his bed, turning crack-of-noon into something more like crack-of-one.

After much, uh, *cracking*.

Curtis loved them. In different ways, but he loved them. And he'd told them.

Since then, there'd been a lot less jumping and cracking, and a distance between the three of them he knew was his fault. He'd made it happen. He had used his mouth words and turned the fun and sexy part of their arrangement into something awkward.

And that needed to stop. Now. Tonight.

"You've got this," he said, but he didn't move.

Feeling even more ridiculous, he slid his sleeve up, exposing his left forearm. There, on the inside near his elbow, a triskelion divided a circle into blood red, sky blue, and golden yellow on his skin. The tattoo wasn't large, about the size of a loonie.

Curtis brushed it with his fingertip. Luc was awake. Anders, too, though that wasn't surprising. They were both inside. And the tattoo strengthened their connection enough for him to feel their emotions, even out on the driveway.

Anxious. Worried. Tense.

He let go.

"Liar," he said to his reflection in the rearview mirror. "You *so* don't got this."

Still, he put a smile on his face, forced a confident rise to his shoulders, and went inside.

They were waiting for him in the kitchen. Somehow, this felt like another bad sign. The living room was where they gathered to work things out, to share the events of their time-shifted day-and-night cycle, or to watch movies or TV shows in Curtis's ongoing attempt to educate them in all things geeky and cool.

The kitchen, on the other hand, was where things exploded or tried to kill them—he wasn't even exaggerating, that happened *twice*—and not nearly as comfortable a place to talk.

Also, there was nowhere to cuddle like on the couch.

"Hey," Curtis said. He was aiming for casual, but it came out choked and he cleared his throat.

Anders was wearing his long-sleeved brown shirt buttoned almost all the way up, and his nicest jeans, which was practically suit-and-tie for the demon. The color played well against the same bronze-brown tone of his skin, and although he hadn't shaved, he'd obviously taken some time to tidy up his neckline. Or he'd shape-shifted the hair away. Whichever.

Luc was more formal, which was no surprise. A crisp blue shirt, shiny grey pants, and every dark hair on his head just so. Luc was entirely clean-shaven, and his whole "I could be a runway model" thing was dialed up to roughly eleven.

In their different ways, they both looked amazing. It was so cosmically unfair, because as good as they looked, Curtis could tell how they felt. Face-to-face, he didn't need the tattoo. Both men pulsed regret and sadness.

"How was your final examination?" Luc said.

"Let's..." Curtis had to clear his throat again. Damn. That was annoying. "Let's not do that," he said.

The two men eyed him. Anders barely made eye contact. Curtis had never seen the demon anything other than cocky. It was as telling as the flood of warring feelings surging around their bond like a three-way tide.

Finally, Luc nodded.

"So it's a no, then," Curtis said. It hurt more than he expected, even as it struck him he wasn't surprised. Every day neither Luc nor Anders had approached him to say they didn't need more time to think about it, that they loved him and would figure out a way to make what they had into something more than just a mystical bond of supernatural convenience, it had chipped away at his optimism. If you loved someone, surely saying so didn't require months to think about it, right?

Right.

"*Lapin*," Luc said, and the nickname sent another stab through Curtis. He saw Luc flinch and knew the vampire felt it as much as Curtis did. He wished they could figure out a way to clamp down on their emotional connection. The tattoo was a great way to reach each other when they were apart, and it allowed them to draw on their bond when they needed the power their triad unlocked in all of them, but maybe they should have found a way to include a dimmer switch for when they were face-to-face.

At least enough to be able to deliver white lies.

"Sorry," Curtis said, instantly annoyed at himself for saying it. He *wasn't* sorry. He was many things—confused, let down, frustrated, and pissed off—but he wasn't sorry. "I mean, go on."

Luc glanced at Anders, but Anders still stared at the ground. Anger of a sort radiated from him, but it was turned inward, and Curtis couldn't quite figure out what or who might be the target.

Yeah, Curtis was definitely more *confused* than *sorry*.

"We can't be this for you," Luc said.

"We." Curtis could hear some anger in his own voice now, and tried to bite it back. Wizards and anger didn't mix. Not well, anyway. Magic liked anger a bit too much, and spells tended to spike and flare if he let his temper get the better of him.

Anders finally looked up. He managed to look pissed off and sad all at the same time. Maybe it was a demon thing. "We," he finally said, in a voice like gravel.

This didn't make sense. Curtis took a deep breath. The problem was, it didn't matter if it made sense or not. It wasn't like he could argue them into admitting they loved him. Plus, at the moment he wasn't sure he wanted the love of either of these damn men. But their triad bond told him daily, in a million little ways, that they *did*.

He knew it. Viscerally. They loved him. Both of them *loved* him. Hell, they even had similar feelings for each other he'd been picking up on for months, which was a miracle of the highest order given how Luc and Anders had felt about each other when this had all started, but...

"It's not enough," Curtis said.

Anders raised his hands, eyes wide. "Wait. Don't. Think about what would happen."

"He's right. Don't be rash," Luc said, shaking his head.

"What?" It took Curtis a second to clue in. "Oh, no. No. I told you both. The triad stands. It keeps us free, not to mention Luc's dukedom, and it's not like we have other options. Well, *I* don't. You two do, I suppose."

That last part came out a bit harsher than he'd intended, but he didn't dial it back, and a tiny, petty part of him didn't much mind the way both Luc's and Anders's eyes widened at his delivery. Besides, it was true. Luc had the position and power to join another coterie now, and Anders had an open offer with at least one pack willing to accept him. It was Curtis alone who was stuck. His Craft Night wizards were great, but they all belonged to their own Family covens.

No, if their triad broke, only Curtis had nowhere else to go.

He took a deep breath and regarded them. "No, I meant...I meant how we—how I—feel. You're saying it's not enough to give it a shot." He looked at Luc. "Which is what you're saying, right?"

Luc's nod came with a pulse of regret so biting Curtis had to lean into it.

And it *still* didn't make sense. How could they feel this bad about it, and so strongly for him, and still not want to even *try*? He deserved to know that much, at least. To hell with their feelings, he wanted the *reason*.

"Well, okay. But can I ask—" Curtis started, but then his cell rang. Of course. "Hang on."

People didn't call him, for the most part. His friends texted. So, if the phone was ringing, either it was going to be a telemarketer or it was going to be something important and probably awful and maybe the kitchen would end up trying to kill him again.

He'd never hoped for a telemarketer before.

Instead, he frowned at the name on the screen. *Jason Parsons.* Who the hell was Jason Parsons? It took him a second. Jace.

Matt's werewolf boyfriend.

Why would Matt's werewolf boyfriend be calling him? Every scenario he could think of was worse than the one before.

Curtis answered. "Jace?" he said. He nodded to Luc and Anders to let them know it was okay to listen in. They had predator hearing. They'd be able to hear whatever was said on the other end of the phone. If this was something bad—and Curtis couldn't think of another reason for the werewolf to call him—it would simply be easier if they listened in, rather than trying to remember and repeat everything after.

"When was the last time you saw Matt?" Jace said. His deep voice was tight, his words clipped.

"A couple of days ago," Curtis said. "We were—"

"And the last time you heard from him?" Jace cut him off. "A call or a text?"

"Uh…" Curtis had to think. "He texted me yesterday morning, I think?" He tried to remember.

"And you're *sure* it was him?"

Whoa. Curtis frowned. "I think so. Jace, what's going on?"

"No one has seen him in the last two days. He was supposed to meet up with Aaron, but nobody can get in touch with either of them."

"Aaron?" Curtis didn't know who Aaron was.

"They're missing," Jace said. "He's missing."

"Where are you?" Curtis said. "I can come to you." He saw Anders frown and shake his head, and stared him down. If Matthew's boyfriend needed help, he'd damn well offer it. Anders's preference of not getting involved in other people's problems didn't rank high on Curtis's list right now.

Jace exhaled into the phone, though whether from relief or anxiety Curtis couldn't tell.

"I'm going to Aaron's. He's not answering, but that's where Matt was supposed to be, so I guess meet me there. Only I'm out in Merrickville, so it's going to take me forever. I need to get going."

"Jace," Curtis said firmly. "I don't know who Aaron is or where he lives."

"Right. Sorry. Right." Jace's voice had taken on a distinctly dark rumble. Almost a growl. That wasn't good. Werewolves had a "protect the pack" instinct. They watched out for each other, protected and cared for each other in a primal, driven way, and Jace wouldn't do well if he couldn't find Matthew.

"Hey," Curtis said. "Listen to me. Slow down. Take deep breaths. Don't get all…y'know…furry on me. We've got this. Let me reach out to Mackenzie and everyone else. We'll be there. Now, tell me where I'm going."

Luc had gotten a pen and notepad. He wrote when Jace gave Curtis an address.

"Okay," Curtis said. "I'll call the others and—"

Jace hung up.

"And he's gone," Curtis said. He looked up. "I have to go."

"We're coming with you," Anders said.

"No thanks." Curtis took the notepad from Luc.

"*Lapin*," Luc said, his voice taking on the slightly patronizing tone he had when he thought Curtis was being foolish.

Which helped Curtis's resolve immensely.

"I'm going to have a bunch of wizards with me," Curtis said. "I'm good. I'll call you if I need you. And while we will *definitely* finish this conversation later, the last people I want to see right this second are you two."

He was already dialing Mackenzie as he turned his back, but he saw the widening of their eyes as his words landed, as well as the way both of their mouths snapped shut.

Good.

THREE

"We're going after him, right?" Anders said.

"Of course we are." Luc paused, looking at the now-empty notepad, frowning in concern. He remembered the address, though, and could put it in his own phone easily enough. It wasn't the address bothering him but rather the name the werewolf had given Curtis. "That name. Aaron Young. It's familiar."

"I don't know it." Anders shook his head.

"I can't recall how I do, but I'm sure I've encountered it." Luc tried to pull up something more than familiarity from the name, but it didn't work. Maybe it was a trick of his memory. As he'd lived over a century, something often seemed familiar but was instead a parallel of something similar he'd previously encountered. Quite likely he'd met an Aaron Young at some point in his long existence.

Anders rubbed his chin. "So, Ducky, that…didn't go so good."

Luc sighed. As affected gestures went—he didn't breathe other than to speak—it was still one of the most eloquent nonverbal statements at his disposal. Especially when Anders trotted out his oft-used moniker for Luc's title.

"No," Luc said. "It did not."

"I didn't say anything," Anders said. "You told me to shut up and let you do the talking. I did that."

Luc eyed him. "Is this your way of suggesting you think you could have handled it better?" The truth was, he wasn't sure the demon could have done worse. It galled him, but there it was. Every word felt ill chosen the moment it had left his mouth, but with the awful feedback loop of their feelings racing around the room through their bond, all his carefully considered speeches hadn't felt right.

Improvisation, it appeared, was not his forte.

Anders reached out and squeezed his shoulder. "Are you kidding? I'd've fucked that up royal. Six different ways. Do I look like the feelings guy? I am so not the feelings guy."

Oddly, the gesture and the contact brought some comfort to Luc. "Well, I suppose I should be glad to have 'fucked it up royal' only one way, then. At least it's done," he said, and he tried to tuck his anger and frustration and—yes—disappointment away. He tilted his head. "As is the hum of his silly little car. Ready?"

"Let's take mine," Anders said.

Luc didn't bother arguing, which was a measure of how poorly the evening had gone, really. And he'd barely been awake an hour yet.

The silence of their drive lasted barely out of their neighborhood.

"He's gotta know it can't work," Anders said.

"I agree. But I think he forgets, sometimes, what we are," Luc said.

Anders grunted. This was ground they had covered and re-covered so many times in the last few months Luc could have had it alone. He knew all their lines.

"It will be okay," he said instead.

Anders spared him a brief glance before turning his attention back to the road. "You think?"

"In time."

"Because to me it felt like we kicked him in the stomach. Or did you not get that feeling?"

"I did." Vividly.

"And his face? I couldn't even look at him. I mean, I knew he was into me. Us. Probably mostly me. I mean, look at me. But—"

"Anders."

The demon glanced at him again.

"You are in danger of being 'the feelings guy.'"

"Fuck." Anders gripped the wheel.

"Indeed."

After a few more surges of frustration and annoyance flared between them through their link, Luc reached forward and turned on the radio. The assault of noise blooming from the speakers made him wince.

"Good idea," Anders said, already bobbing along in time with the "music."

❖

They drove for nearly an hour, the buildings and suburbs of Ottawa long replaced by alternating trees and farm fields. Aaron Young's house was more of a cottage. Small, only a single floor, it appeared to be tidy and well-maintained from the outside. Beside the cottage a series of small container gardens ran the length of the yard, each surrounded by chicken wire, capped with lids to be as animal-proof as they could possibly be, Luc assumed. Curtis's hybrid was parked along the curb with a black Jeep, and a cherry red muscle car took up the driveway.

"The Camaro is Rebekah's," Anders said, turning off the SUV and pointing at the sleek red vehicle. "We like her, right?"

"Yes," Luc agreed. Rebekah was one of the wizards Curtis knew. Luc had only met her a few times, months ago, but like Anders, she'd struck him as being at odds with the Families, which only spoke to her credit. And she'd been handy in a fight.

"So, he said not to come and we came anyway. How do you want to play this?" Anders said.

"As a future opportunity to apologize," Luc said. "Come on."

They got out of the car and started for the small house.

Luc's phone rang. It was Curtis. He showed the demon, then answered. "Hello."

"Hey," Curtis said. "Look. I, uh—"

"We're right outside," Luc said.

There was a long pause.

"Well," Curtis said. Luc couldn't tell if there was relief or annoyance in his voice. He'd be able to feel it once he got close enough, he supposed. "I'll see you in a second."

"Can someone invite us in?" Luc said.

"There's no need," Curtis said.

Luc and Anders shared a dark look. "I see. We'll be right there, *lapin.*"

"Thank you."

At the threshold to the small house, Luc opened the door and stepped through. No hint of resistance pressed against him whatsoever at the threshold. The law of residency, one of the strongest magical conceits, did nothing to stop him.

Whoever had lived here was no longer living.

Anders followed him through.

They didn't have to go far. The interior of the cottage was much like the outside: simple, well-maintained, and tidy. A small kitchen opened into the main living area, a bed lay tucked in the far corner, and above them via a ladder, a half-loft appeared to be devoted to storage. Luc assumed the single visible door meant a bathroom set in the far corner. Mostly, everything was made of polished wood, with accents of cloth—mostly in greens—to soften what might otherwise be too much of a single thing.

The body on the floor was perhaps the most obvious object in the room.

Curtis, standing with three others, met Luc's gaze, and the relief Luc felt at seeing the wizard wasn't angry was almost visceral. Luc recognized Rebekah and Mackenzie, but not the tall, stocky blond man standing with them.

"Dale, this is Luc and Anders," Curtis said. "Guys, this is Dale." He looked down. "And this, we're assuming, is Aaron."

The body lay in the middle of the tiny living area.

"He was a werewolf, yes?" Luc said. If he'd been in wolf or wolf-like form upon dying, the body would have reverted back to its human state. When it came to lycanthropes, only a few telltale indications for those in the know remained, but it would take a scalpel to find traces of hypermobile joints and minor odd variances in the eyes and ears. Then again, the body wore a pair of what appeared to be comfortable jeans and a T-shirt, so Luc assumed the man had died at least somewhat in his human form.

"We can't figure out what killed him," Curtis said. "Nothing obvious. Time for a Postrema Visio spell, I think."

"Are you sure?" Mackenzie said. She sounded worried.

"I see no obvious wounds, but I can smell a hint of blood…" Luc crouched low to the body. Aaron was on his back, facing the ceiling, eyes open and unseeing. Without touching him, Luc drew as close as he could. There, again. The faintest trace of blood. He was nearly lying on the ground now, but he caught sight of something on the back of the dead wolf's neck.

"A small wound. On the back of his neck." He frowned at the feel of the wood floor beneath his hands. "Also, the wood here is damp. It was recently wet."

"A small cut to the neck snuffed a wolf?" Anders didn't sound convinced.

"Poison maybe?" Dale said.

"The strike could have been precise." It seemed unlikely, but Luc could see no other unusual marks. He rose. "Matthew Stirling is not here." He didn't want to dismiss the dead body, but this wasn't why they were there. If Matthew Stirling was also somewhere on the property—*especially* if he was also dead—it would be a much more significant problem. Malcolm Stirling was the head of the Families. The death of his great-grandson would be...*unfortunate*.

"We've checked up there, and the bathroom," Curtis said, gesturing up to the loft. "No sign of him. And Matt's motorcycle isn't here."

"Does Aaron have family we need to call?" Mackenzie said. "I've never met him. How does Matt even know him?"

"No idea," Curtis said. "Jace said he was *helping* him. No idea what that meant. I guess we could call Taryne? Or should we maybe call David?"

Annoyance hummed through their bond. Luc tried to ignore Anders's typical reaction to mention of the demon police officer.

"If we call David, even with his more elevated position, we risk getting the Families involved. He's surrounded by sorcerer spies, no?" Luc said. He flashed an apologetic smile to Mackenzie, Dale, and Rebekah, but they didn't seem to take any offence.

"You're right," Dale said. "My family has at least three sorcerers watching him."

"Do we have Taryne's number?" Anders said. It was a clear vote against calling David.

"The knack," Luc said. Finally, he'd remembered.

Curtis frowned at him. The others looked with varying amounts of interest.

"What?" Anders said.

"I couldn't recall why Aaron's name was familiar. But last winter, when we were looking for the demon killer, signs originally pointed toward a werewolf with some level of magical ability. Speaking about Taryne reminded me. Denis gave me a list of wolves with magical ability, and Taryne was on that list, of course. But an Aaron Young was mentioned, too."

"Matt's been helping a werewolf with the knack? Why?" Dale said.

"It might be nothing," Luc said. He pulled out his phone. "But I do have contact information for Taryne. If this is one of her wolves, she'll want to deal with it."

A twist of uncertainty hummed in Luc's chest. It took him a second to realize it came from Curtis, and he met the wizard's gaze.

"I think I should do Postrema Visio first," Curtis said. "While we still can."

"What is it, exactly?" Luc said.

"It lets him see the last thing Aaron saw before he died," Dale said.

"Just in case it's something we need to know," Curtis said. "Or if it'll help us find Matt. Once we involve the werewolves, I don't know if they'd let me."

Luc took a moment with that, but he couldn't find fault. "All right."

"Good," Curtis said.

"I should do it," Dale said.

Curtis turned to him. "Pardon?"

"Ever done it before?"

Curtis shook his head. "No, but—"

"Then let me." Dale crossed his arms, and Luc noted the way the fabric stretched across Dale's chest and biceps. He might have had a rather forgettable, bland face, but Luc imagined the body beneath the clothing might very well be impressive. "It can be bad. Postrema Visio isn't fun. But I know what to expect. My Family…Spirit is our element."

Luc noticed neither Mackenzie nor Rebekah seemed surprised this Dale was volunteering to recover the final visions of the dead man on the floor. Curtis, on the other hand, was staring at Dale, forehead creased, an unspoken question in his open mouth.

"Okaaay." Curtis drew out the word, leaving the question unasked. Luc, who could feel the curiosity thrumming in the wizard, was impressed with his restraint.

The spell itself didn't take much time. Luc watched Dale crouch before the body, and though he sharpened his predator senses, he could see no outward signs of magic at play, even when Dale reached out and held his hand over Aaron's unseeing eyes and spoke quietly. The subtlety of magic was one of the reasons it was so dangerous to his kind. A power you couldn't reliably sense coming was a power you couldn't prepare for.

Dale closed his eyes and opened them again.

Luc managed not to react, but it took conscious effort not to jolt at the change. All hint of Dale's irises and pupils had gone, and the white of his eyes no longer retained its healthy pale color but something slick and vaguely yellowed, as though infected.

Or rotting.

The whole manner of the man seemed changed. It took Luc a second to realize Dale had stopped breathing.

"Oh," Curtis said in a tiny voice. Mackenzie shivered.

Dale turned in a slow circle, frowning and tense, each movement of his head seemingly more jerky and difficult than the last. He stumbled before he finished the full circle, and Rebekah stepped forward to take his shoulder. This seemed enough support for him to finish, and with a trembling hand, he covered his eyes and clenched his fist. He then yanked his fist away, the resulting explosive inhalation dropping him to his knees despite Rebekah's efforts to keep him upright.

Dale sucked in breath, coughing and shaking. Luc caught the briefest whiff of something foul and rotten in the air before it vanished.

"You okay?" Rebekah said, rubbing his back.

Dale nodded, still coughing. He reached over to the corpse again and opened his hand above its eyes. Something too quick for even Luc's senses to catch seemed to *flow* from the wizard's open palm into the unseeing eyes.

"Holy crap," Curtis said.

Dale, pale and obviously laboring to get his breathing under control, offered Curtis a weak smile. "Yeah," he said a second later, coughing again. His voice seemed almost strangled. "Necromancy. Like I said. Not fun."

They waited until Dale seemed more or less ready to continue. Rebekah helped him back to his feet, and he finally took a deep, even breath. Luc could hear Dale's heart hammering in his chest, and although this Dale was somewhat plain of face, the combination of vulnerability and rapid pulse was more than a little enticing.

Fear. It often appealed to the baser part of his nature, and most of the time he tried to be better than his inclinations, but he could very nearly taste it. He clenched his jaw when he saw Anders glance his way, the demon's lips turning up in an amused smirk.

"Okay," Dale said. "Matt was halfway out the door when this guy died. He was running, I'm pretty sure. And there was ice everywhere." Dale gestured at the wood floor.

Luc frowned. "Ice?"

"Ice is Matt's go-to for sorcery," Mackenzie said. "If he's defending himself. Did you see the murderer?"

Dale shook his head. "There was no one else in the room."

"So," Anders said, and everyone looked at him. "Are we gonna ask the obvious?"

The wizards—Curtis included—all frowned as though they couldn't fathom what could possibly be obvious.

Luc forced enough air into his lungs to sigh. Raised by the Families, they might have been exposed to the harshness of the world around them, but they were still all so young. "Is it possible Matthew murdered this man?"

"*What?*" Curtis said. "No!"

Mackenzie was shaking her head, and Rebekah scowled at him.

"It didn't look like it." Dale, to his credit, took a few seconds to consider. "I don't think so."

"Dale," Mackenzie said. "Of *course* he didn't."

Dale shrugged. "There was no one else in the room."

"But Matt—"

Dale raised both hands. "I agree. I'm not saying it's him. It's just…strange."

"Matt wouldn't ice the floor and run away if he'd done it," Mackenzie said firmly.

"Okay," Anders said. "So where is he?"

More silence.

Curtis pulled out his phone and dialed. They all waited, and heard when the call went to voicemail and Matt's voice asked him to leave a message.

"Hey, Matt," Curtis said, in a decent approximation of his own casual voice. "Just wanted to talk for a sec. If you get this, give me a call, okay?"

Luc waited for him to hang up. "I think now we call Taryne."

No one argued, so he dialed. He looked down at the body of the werewolf on the floor and waited for the druid to answer.

FOUR

Now what? Anders thought.

The wizards hadn't wanted to stay inside with the body—kind of squeamish, for flicks—so they stood outside the small cabin in a circle. Luc's call to Taryne had been brief. Anders had heard her terse promise to be there as soon as possible, and that had been that.

Now they waited. At least it wasn't raining. In fact, the sky was clear for once, though the drip-drip-drip from all the trees around the cabin reminded Anders April wasn't done yet. If he'd given a shit about stars, Anders might have considered it a nice night to watch them, but he'd never understood the point. They were stars. They didn't *do* anything.

Also, it reminded him of someone who had watched the stars, which wasn't worth thinking about.

"Are we absolutely sure we shouldn't maybe also call David?" Curtis said, breaking their silence.

Anders swallowed annoyance. "We can't trust David not to have it leak back to the Stirlings," he said.

"He's right," Dale said. "My family's people watch everything he does."

Plain-faced or not, there was a lot to like about the lug, Anders decided.

"Would the Stirlings help us look for him?" Rebekah said after a moment. "If they knew Matt was missing, I mean?"

Mackenzie, Curtis, and Anders all issued the same snort of derision in unison. If it wasn't for the corpse in the building behind them, Anders might have laughed.

Instead, he stood there under the damn stars and shoved his fists into his jacket pockets.

Rebekah sighed. "Right."

In the distance, Anders caught the sound of gravel under tires. "Incoming," he said. Luc nodded, though the wizards didn't quite get it.

"We can hear a car approaching," Luc said.

"Predator ears," Curtis said to the others.

"Must be handy," Mackenzie said, regarding him with curiosity.

"It is. And whoever it is, they're speeding," Anders said, cocking his head a little.

"Indeed," Luc said.

By the time headlights were visible, it was obvious whoever was driving the pickup truck knew the path well, and the pickup barely slowed down as it cornered onto the tiny bit of driveway Rebekah's Camaro hadn't already taken up, skidding to a stop with a jerk of slammed brakes and a spray of gravel.

The figure who got out was not, however, the slight, lean frame of Taryne Rhedey, wildlife veterinarian, werewolf, and druid. Instead, a large man in a black leather jacket threw open the door and all but leapt out. It took Anders a second to place him.

The boyfriend.

Large, rough-and-tumble looking, and definitely pissed off, the dark-haired man sniffed at the air, then started for the cabin.

"Jace," Curtis said, stepping forward. "Crap. I'm sorry, we should have called you right away. Matt's not—"

The next part happened too suddenly for Anders to react. The boyfriend—Jace, right, that was his name—barely paused. He shoved Curtis hard in the middle of his chest, and Curtis flew back and landed on his ass in the gravel. The jolt of surprise and pain ricocheted through the bond Anders had with him, and then Anders was moving.

Luc beat him there, of course. Demons were fast. Vampires were faster.

The werewolf barely had time to blink before Luc was in front of him, and Anders grabbed the back of Jace's neck with one hand, already letting the heat of his hellfire rise through his palm.

"Stop," Luc said.

Jace trembled beneath Anders's hand, but it wasn't fear. Anders could smell a muskiness coming off him, and there was *motion* beneath the skin of his neck. Muscles and tendons and bones undulated beneath his palm.

Well, shit. The boyfriend was about to wolf out.

"Where is he?" Jace said. The words were as much growl as voice. Anders spotted a ripple of movement under the skin along the back of Jace's neck, and the neatly trimmed line of hair at the back of his head began to spread downward, toward Anders's grip.

"You need to calm down," Anders said, squeezing hard enough to be felt. "Your guy isn't here."

"I smell death."

Ah. Fuck. Of course. "Not your guy." Anders squeezed again. "It's the other one. Uh…What's his name?"

"Aaron," Luc said.

Jace shuddered once, then took a deep, shaky breath. "Matt's not here?"

"Matt's not here," Mackenzie said. Anders glanced over and saw she was helping Curtis get up.

"If he's not okay, you're fucked," Anders said, giving the back of Jace's neck another pulse of heat.

"Stop it. I'm fine," Curtis said.

Jace lowered his shoulders, rolling them. Anders let go of his neck, and Luc took a step back. The hair Anders had seen grow down the back of Jace's neck faded back into his skin. Good.

"Sorry," Jace said, aiming the word at Curtis.

"It's fine, really," Curtis said. "I get it. We already called Taryne."

Invoking Taryne's name seemed to help calm Jace down even more.

"Matt was supposed to be here," Jace said. He was shaking his hands out, like they were cramping or something. Anders watched. He'd never really gone head-to-head with a werewolf. One time he'd fought a wizard pretending to be a werewolf, but he'd used a necromantic dagger to change his shape, turning himself into a looey-goop or something. He'd gotten the drop on Anders thanks to his magic, as well as having the strengths and abilities of both a werewolf *and* a demon, so that ass-kicking didn't count.

Besides, Anders had still snapped his damn neck. With an assist from Luc, sure, but that *definitely* counted.

Anders saw the way Jace struggled his way back under control, and decided if he ever needed to take a werewolf down, the time to strike was definitely when they were changing. Jace looked like most of his attention was turned inward. Good time to gut someone.

"He *was* here," Dale said. "And he was running away from whatever happened in there."

"What happened?" Jace said. "You said Aaron is dead? What happened to him?"

"A small wound to the back of his neck," Luc said. "It looks to have killed him without much of a struggle at all."

"No struggle?" Jace frowned, like that didn't add up. Which, fair. "And Matt?"

"We used a spell," Curtis said. "To figure out the last thing Aaron saw before he died, and it was Matt leaving the cabin. He'd iced up the floor behind him, so he was definitely getting away from someone. Or something."

Jace looked at the cabin door. "I'd like to go see Aaron."

"Of course," Curtis said. "It's not bad." He flinched. "I mean, it's awful, of course, but...he doesn't look..." He sighed, shaking his head. "Go right ahead."

Jace went inside.

As soon as the door closed, Curtis put a hand to his chest. "Ow."

Anders went to him. "You said you were fine."

"I am. I mean, I will be. He's strong is all." Curtis shrugged. "You two looked like you were going to rip his head off."

Anders scowled. "Offer is still on the table."

Curtis rolled his eyes.

"Good Lord, smell the testosterone," Rebekah said.

Curtis coughed into his hand, though it sounded suspiciously like a laugh to Anders. He wrapped one arm around Curtis and pulled him in close. "You can be a fucking idiot, you know that?" Anders said.

"Excuse me?"

"You stepped in front of an angry werewolf," Luc said. "You often don't stop to—" He tilted his head.

Curtis waved a hand. "I don't stop to what? Please, do continue the lecture. Surely it won't be patronizing."

This time it was Rebekah who cough-laughed. But Anders caught what had made Luc stop talking now, too. Another car.

"Taryne?" he said.

"I assume so," Luc said.

❖

Inside the cabin, Taryne took a moment to look over Aaron's body, then put the green blanket Jace had covered him with back in place. Dressed for comfort in a blue cardigan-style sweater and faded jeans, she'd arrived with her long brown hair tied back in a functional ponytail. She looked young and fragile.

Anders knew she was neither.

"I assume you took a look around," Taryne said, rising. Her voice had an edge, and though she was doing an admirable job of looking calm, Anders would have bet real money she was fucking *pissed*. He liked that. All too often big players of the supernatural world didn't give a shit about the little guys.

Taryne did. It was a mark in her column he'd willingly credit her with.

"Rebekah and I did," Curtis said. "And Dale here did Postrema Visio."

Taryne looked at him, dark brown eyes sharp with interest. "And?"

"Matt was running away. He'd laid down ice." Dale gestured to the floor near the door and around where the body lay. "But I couldn't see an attacker. They might have been behind Aaron, which means Aaron wouldn't have seen them, so I couldn't see them."

Magic. Anders crossed his arms. It was just fucking weird.

But Taryne nodded like it all made some sort of sense to her. Maybe it did. She was a druid, which despite Anders's admittedly near-zero understanding of what a druid was, did mean something magic. Or at least she'd said as much when they'd first met her last year. Something about the sun being a part of her magic and how she could knock Luc on his ass if she'd wanted to.

Right now she certainly seemed to want to knock *someone* on their ass.

"What happened?" she asked, to no one in particular.

"Matt was supposed to be working with him today," Jace said. He'd been leaning against the wall, as far away from the rest of them as he could be.

"What do you mean, exactly?" Mackenzie said.

Taryne looked at her.

"It's just…" Mackenzie held out her hands. "We have no idea what you're talking about. It might be helpful if we did."

Taryne took a breath. Anders would have put even odds on her to give them some shit about "it's private" or "it's personal" or some other variation on "I don't want to tell you, but I'm going to make it sound like a polite fuck off instead of a blunt one."

"The knack?" Luc said.

Taryne frowned at Luc, but eventually, she nodded.

She does not like he knew that, Anders thought.

"So Aaron could do magic?" Rebekah said.

"In a limited way," Taryne said, after a moment. She looked around the room again, as though taking everyone's measure. Despite himself, Anders straightened. Ugh. He hated it when he had the urge to give a shit about what people thought of him.

"Limited how?" Curtis said.

"Aaron's a coywolf. He isn't—" She paused, looking back at the still form under the blanket. "He *wasn't* a member of any of the local packs. He was a good man, though, and I think they might have accepted him if he'd wanted to join, but he preferred to be alone, in part because of his knack." She eyed Luc. "It was strong but narrow. He was prescient. He could catch glimpses of the future. Possibilities. He had trouble controlling it, though, since he'd never really been taught. It tended to evade his conscious control, and being around other people made him see things. But it also kept him out of trouble."

Anders had no idea what the fuck a coywolf was, but that last part was bullshit. The dead man's gift did *not* keep him out of trouble, or he wouldn't be dead. "Except someone murdered him."

Taryne swallowed. "Yes."

"And Matt was helping him with it," Mackenzie said. "Because Matt's also prescient."

"Yes."

"How did Matt even *meet* Aaron?" Mackenzie said. "I mean, this is kind of the middle of nowhere."

Jace cleared his throat. "I asked him if he'd help."

"As a favor to me," Taryne added. "Aaron was struggling with something. I have no gift for prognosticative magics, and while Aaron wasn't a member of any of the local packs, I offer a form of leadership to all of the weres in the area, and I knew of Matthew's skill set."

Rebekah frowned. "You mean Jace told you," she said, aiming a not-so-pleasant look Jace's way.

Jace, though, lifted one shoulder like sharing the secret of Matt's gift wasn't a problem. "Matt wanted to help," Jace said. "He always wants to help." The words didn't quite sound like a compliment. More like a pain in the ass.

Anders caught himself glancing at Curtis, who stared right back, his chin rising. Probably not the time to tell Jace he completely got where he was coming for on that front, then.

But then Anders frowned, because something massive wasn't adding up here.

"Wait," he said, and all eyes turned to him. "So, you've got this guy who can see the future, but he's kind of not in control of it, fine. And you've got the Stirling kid, who can also see the future and is damn good at it. Stirling comes here to help this guy fix his antenna or whatever." Anders waved a hand. "So they're both here, working on seeing the future together."

Taryne frowned, but raised one shoulder. "More or less."

"Then somebody fucked up." Anders shook his head. "Because neither of them saw this coming."

"Anders," Curtis said, annoyed, but Anders held up a hand to cut off whatever bullshit "don't be mean" speech was coming.

"No," Jace said, pushing off from the wall. "No, he's right. Matt *always* knows before there's trouble."

"Oh." Curtis blinked. "Like at the bar."

Anders nodded. Now they were getting it. Last year, some demons had tried to jump Curtis, Jace, and Matt at the Village Pub, and they'd been prepared thanks to Matt realizing something bad was about to happen. It had saved their lives, though Jace had been torn up some keeping the group of demons at bay.

"Right," Anders said. "And if you're saying it's *impossible* to get the drop on Matt—and I'll buy it, it lines up with what I know of the Stirling kid—how the hell did someone get the drop on *two* people who can see shit before it hits the fan?"

There was silence in the room.

"I need to find Matt," Jace said.

Curtis bit his lip. Anders wanted to groan out loud. He could feel the welling of concern and compassion from Curtis in his own stomach, thanks to the bond he shared with the other two.

"I don't suppose you have any of Matt's blood?" Curtis finally said.

And there it was. Curtis getting them even more involved. Anders exchanged a glance with Luc, spotting the same resignation there.

"His blood?" Jace said.

"You want to try scrying him," Mackenzie said.

Curtis nodded. "I've had luck using the pendant you gave me."

Right. They'd used it a few times. Curtis could track someone down with their blood and a crystal on a chain. Something about things always being connected on some level if they'd ever been a part of each other. It was just more magic fuckery to Anders.

"What about hair?" Dale said, looking at Jace. "Any chance he left a brush at your place?"

Jace frowned, thinking. "Maybe. I think so?"

"Hair is almost as good as blood," Curtis said.

"Is there anything else you can try here?" Taryne said. "I'd like to take Aaron's body. I can see what I can learn from his wounds, and also try a few divinations of my own."

"If we knew exactly the moment we were aiming for," Curtis said, "we could try a Memento Loci, but we don't."

Anders hated it when Curtis sounded like he was apologizing for something when he'd done nothing wrong.

"If there's nothing at Jace's place, I could go to the Stirling chantry," Mackenzie said. "I'm pretty sure I could get in to his room if I told them I needed something he borrowed from me. We hang out enough it wouldn't be too suspicious. But it'd have to be soon, before they realize he's missing."

"Maybe go right now anyway," Curtis said. "Just in case?"

Mackenzie nodded.

Anders frowned. It was one thing to get involved with whatever the fuck was happening here, but it was another to take the lead, and Curtis was starting to sound like he wanted to do just that. Anders opened his mouth to say something, but Luc touched his arm.

"It's not worth trying," he said, voice pitched low enough Curtis wouldn't hear. "And it will only further aggravate him."

Fuck. He *really* hated it when Luc was right.

"Okay," Curtis said. "Let's figure out what we're going to do, then." Fuck. Yeah, they were helping these people solve a murder that had nothing to do with them.

Again.

Anders sighed.

FIVE

The drive to Merrickville gave Curtis more than enough time to second-guess everything he'd done, not done, and maybe should have done. And, added bonus, it wasn't just his personal life he was stressing over this time.

The biggest thing was how wrong it felt to leave Dr. Rhedey to deal with Aaron's body, but she'd all but demanded to be the one to handle it. Curtis wondered if she'd involve anyone else—like, say, the police, given it was a murder—but he doubted it. The urge to reach out to David struck him again, but he remembered what Anders and Dale had said about David being watched by the sorcerers who worked for Dale's family, and tried to let it go.

At least Dale had promised to try and find out if the sorcerers watching David knew anything was going on yet.

They'd all agreed the longer they could keep Malcolm Stirling out of the loop, the better, but now even that made him wonder. Malcolm Stirling wasn't a good man, but he was Matt's great-grandfather, and though there was no love lost there, Curtis knew Malcolm Stirling absolutely cared about Matt's gift of seeing the future. It passed down along the Stirling bloodline, and having access to Matt's gift was fundamental to Malcolm Stirling keeping himself as top dog among the covens of Ottawa.

Was it right to keep him in the dark? The man had resources Curtis couldn't imagine. Rebekah had offered to drive Mackenzie to the Stirling chantry, which felt like a disaster in the making if the truth came out for the real reason for her visit, but if Mackenzie was right and she could get into Matt's room, it might very well be worth it. Or so Curtis hoped.

Ahead of him, Jace's pickup made a left, and Curtis followed suit.

His chest still hurt from where Jace had shoved him out of the way. He really hoped there wasn't a bruise. He understood the man's urge to get inside the cabin—even if he hadn't enjoyed being the speed bump—and hoped wherever Matthew was, he was safe, as much for Jace's sake as his own.

Jace clearly loved him.

Which brought Curtis's thoughts back to his own love life.

The men in question, Luc and Anders, hadn't been pleased when he'd offered to follow Jace home. They'd been even *less* pleased when he'd told them he'd be fine on his own.

"I'd feel better if you checked in with the other coteries," he'd said to Luc. "Make sure they haven't heard anything." As the duke of the city, Luc had sway over the other vampire groups, and while Curtis was pretty sure it would be a dead end, it got Luc out of his hair.

Then Anders had wanted to ride shotgun for the trip to Jace's, and Curtis hadn't had it in him to be trapped in a car with the demon, given their earlier discussion, so he'd come up with something else.

"Or, instead of babysitting," he'd said to Anders, projecting as much "leave me alone" energy into his voice as he could, "you could check in with your people, too. See if they know anything."

Anders had backed down, too, after a glance at Luc. There'd been palpable tension and anxiety and worry and a bunch of other feelings Curtis couldn't have named if you'd paid him in cash money, but at that point, he was out of crap to give.

Curtis didn't even feel guilty about it, even now. He'd earned a little space and some time to think.

Of course, now he was overthinking, but that was more or less his default.

They do love you.

He sighed for at least the dozenth time and gripped the steering wheel tighter. He wasn't going to solve the problem of Luc and Anders today, so he needed to let it drop.

They totally love you. You can feel it.

"Shut up," Curtis said to himself. "Please shut up, brain."

They crossed the locks into Merrickville, and Curtis followed as Jace took a left at the main intersection of the town. It wasn't a big town, and from what little Curtis knew about werewolves, it seemed the kind of place they liked: enough comforts to be human, but a short drive—or four-legged run—to some real green space available nearby in nearly every direction.

A few turns later, Curtis pulled in behind Jace in front of a small house. Jace was already unlocking the door by the time Curtis got out of his car, and he heard Jace call out Matt's name as he crossed the threshold. There was no response.

Curtis approached the door, feeling a pressure against his chest and a sudden, almost threateningly cold breeze against his skin. He paused, and Jace turned to look at him from inside.

"What's wrong?"

"Did Matt put extra wards on your house?" It was nothing like the powerful barrier erected around a chantry, one of the old homes of the Families, but it was nothing to sneeze at, either. Whatever was making its presence known felt greater than the basic, natural protection of residency, which also pulled at Curtis's magic and let him know this house was not his.

Magic would be harder here, especially if he tried to aim it at Jace, the rightful owner.

Still, Curtis was fairly sure he *could* have walked in, if the cold air hadn't made him want to stop. The coldness felt…predatory? Ready to spring at him? Something like that.

"Oh. Right. Sorry," Jace said. "You can come in. I invite you until the next setting of the sun, as long as you do me no harm."

The pressure parted, though it didn't vanish. The wards pulled back, striking Curtis as nearly alive, their presence coiled and waiting, rubbing against his sense of all things magic with an almost slithery sensation, as though to remind him they'd happily throw down with him at a moment's notice. What remained of their power teased his skin like a coolness lingering in every corner of the room, but at least in the meanwhile it wouldn't be like having one eye closed and one arm tied behind his back.

Matt did good wards.

Curtis entered Jace's house. It wasn't large, but Curtis got the sense everything had a place, from a little table inside the front door set up with small bowls where Jace tossed his keys, wallet, and sunglasses in quick succession to every wall on the ground floor, which was painted a soft yellow and filled with simple black-framed photographs of people at regular intervals. The light wood floor, polished and occasionally broken up by tan rugs, had been swept and cleaned, and while it had the dents and scratches of a place long lived in, there was no denying it appeared to be cared for.

All together, the space felt pretty, homey, and warm.

Well, except for the cold magic in the corners, glaring at him.

"You have a nice home," Curtis said, trying not to shiver.

Jace didn't seem to hear him. "His stuff is in the bathroom," he said, already leading the way. He'd hung up his coat, revealing lines of ink wrapping around the biceps on his left arm, a chain of phases of the moon done in an intricate spiral.

❖

They found a brush in the ensuite of the upstairs main bedroom, and Curtis took as many strands of Matt's short hair as he could tug free from the bristles. Jace got him a sandwich bag, and Curtis rolled it up and put it in his pocket, the hairs safely stored inside.

"When will you try?" Jace said.

"As soon as I get home. I'll need my pendant and a map to make it work."

Jace rubbed his chin. He swallowed. "And it'll tell you where he is?"

Curtis took a breath. "I hope so, Jace. I'm going to do my best." There. He hoped he hadn't oversold it, but he did believe it was worth the attempt.

Jace closed his eyes. "This is all my fault."

"Hey," Curtis said, touching Jace's shoulder when Jace didn't open his eyes. He might not know what was going on here, not exactly, but he believed Matt wouldn't want Jace blaming himself for any of this. "No. It's not."

"I asked him to help with Aaron." Jace shook his head. "I knew it put him in a bad place with his kin."

"To be fair," Curtis said, "his kin are morally bankrupt, and he can't stand them, so I'm sure it wasn't a hard choice on his part."

Jace laughed. "Morally bankrupt. Nice. Yeah, that's the Families."

"Anders says they're more like a mafia," Curtis said.

"That works, too." He stared at Curtis for a long moment.

"What?" Curtis said. Werewolf stares were *intense*. Jace's way of not blinking made Curtis want to take a step back.

"You don't work with the Families, right?"

"Not if I can help it." Curtis stood by the whole "morally bankrupt" assessment. The Families did what they did for the benefit of themselves and maintaining their own hold over everything and everyone else. Some individuals were better than others, of course. He'd met

Mackenzie's mother a couple of times, and Katrina Windsor seemed far, far less awful than the rest of the coven heads. And Rebekah's mother was a coven head now, too, come to think of it. Things might change. But Kendra Mitchell and Katrina Windsor were still outnumbered three to two by Malcolm Stirling's sort. The Families hadn't changed so much that Curtis was going to ask to join the club.

Jace was still staring, dark eyes measuring him in some way, and it struck Curtis he was alone in a werewolf's house with the werewolf in question, who'd already hit him hard enough in the chest to probably leave a bruise, and was now staring at him, standing very close, close enough to emphasize how big Jace was and Curtis wasn't.

"Is there something else?" Curtis said. *What big eyes you have.*

"Matt was working on something," Jace said. He crossed his arms, which emphasized his strength all the more. "Did he talk to you about it?"

Curtis thought about it. "The last thing we worked on together was my new glasses." He pulled out the pair of glasses from his pocket, in their carrying case. They weren't prescription, but rather plain glass lenses which the whole Craft Night group had help him enchant, and Matt had been a part of it. "The whole group helped me enchant a new pair after my old ones got traded for something. Is that what you mean?"

Jace shook his head, glancing at the glasses case. "No. Not that."

Curtis waited.

They stared at each other again. More watching. More of the sense Jace was measuring Curtis in some way.

"You're going to have to give me a better hint," Curtis said, fighting the urge to take a step away.

"We went to London," Jace said.

"Right. In December. I knew that," Curtis said. It had been during his previous exams, but he remembered Matt talking about it at one of their Craft Night meetings. "Matt said he needed a break, and you two took a trip to England, right?"

But Jace was shaking his head. "No. It wasn't for a break. He'd been dreaming. Of London. Almost every night for over a month." He let out a short breath, rubbing the stubble on his chin with one large hand. "So we went."

"Okay," Curtis said, but then he got what Jace was saying. "Oh. You mean *dreaming*." When Matt had inherited the Stirling bloodline gift for prescience, it had started with prophetic dreams, and had begun with learning which of the other people in the five main Families of Ottawa were on a similar path to inheriting their familial bloodline gifts. Matt's initial dreams had been the reason he'd gathered Mackenzie, Tracey, Rebekah, and Dale in the first place.

In Matt's case, he hadn't particularly wanted the gift. The Stirlings tended to use whoever had the inherited gift as a personal family oracle, determining ways to keep their Family on the top of the social pecking order among the five Families of Ottawa, as well as the dozens in other cities.

But instead of allowing his ability to see the future to be bound into runes or tarot or any other method the Stirlings could also interpret from the back seat as he used the power, Matt had found a way to bind his prophetic gift into a tattoo on his forearm.

The rest of the Stirlings—Malcolm Stirling in particular—saw only images and pictures as they bloomed across Matt's skin, images that made sense on an instinctual level to Matt, but not always the rest of his family.

Matt hadn't wanted to be at their beck and call, and he'd wanted a way to potentially keep whatever information he saw of the future out of their hands. And it had worked. The tattoo focus put Matt in charge of his own ability in many ways, but Matt's precognitive abilities weren't completely leashed and under his control. He knew when he was in danger, for example, which happened when it needed to.

And sometimes, Curtis knew, Matt still dreamed things. *Important* things.

"So you went to London to follow up on one of his prophetic dreams?" Curtis said.

Jace nodded. "It was something to do with the Families. Matt thought it was something they were going to do, but when we got there, he said he was wrong. It wasn't something they were going to do, it was where *something they'd already done* had started."

Curtis waited, but Jace didn't go on.

"That's…a little vague," Curtis said.

Jace snorted. "I know. But when we got back, he kept working on it. He said it was important. He kept dreaming about it, I know that. He'd wake up sometimes and sit in the dark. I caught him a few times." Jace shook his head. "I asked him, but he said it was better if he figured it all out before he said anything to me. I should have *made* him tell me. I was hoping he told you, or the others he met with?"

"He didn't say anything to me," Curtis said. Which bothered him.

Did it mean Matt hadn't trusted him? It stung. He liked Matt. He liked all of the Craft Night crew. They worked on magic together, taught each other, and flew in the face of what the Families would strictly approve of. Which was why they didn't let the Families know their meetings even happened, if they could help it. They weren't a coven, they were a group of friends.

Or he'd thought they were. Matt might have told Curtis what was going on if they had been. They didn't have the binding of a coven to force them to have to be around each other. They only had their mutual desire to work together outside of the Families.

Then again, maybe that explained why he hadn't. Their arrangement didn't allow them any real protection at all. After all, as much as they liked each other, he barely knew anything about them, when it came right down to it. They stuck to magic most of the time and rarely spoke about anything that might compromise themselves or each other.

"There's a notebook," Jace said. "He wrote in it."

"If it might help, I'd like to see it," Curtis said. "If nothing else, I promise I won't say a thing to the Families. I won't even talk to the rest of the group, if you don't want me to. Even Luc and Anders, unless it's really important."

Jace took a few more seconds, but he nodded. He led Curtis back into the main bedroom. Like the rest of the house, it was warm and inviting and looked comfortable, with a deep green blanket and pillows on the large king-sized bed taking up most of the room. Jace went to the farthest bedside table and opened the top drawer, then stopped, frowning.

"It's gone."

Curtis crossed the room. Inside the drawer, he spotted a couple of pens and scraps of paper, and also some lube and condoms, a handkerchief, and a small box of cough drops, but no journal.

"He must have taken it with him," Curtis said.

Jace nodded, still staring into the drawer, like maybe it would offer up the notebook if he glared at it hard enough.

"It's going to be okay," Curtis said.

Jace closed his eyes. "It's…hard for us."

"I'm sorry?"

"Weres."

Curtis still didn't follow. "Hard."

Jace rolled his shoulders in a very deliberate motion, and the cracking noise it produced made Curtis cringe. "I want to protect him. All the time. It's worse because he's not a wolf himself. I know he's got his magic, and I know he can take care of himself—I've seen him do it—but…" He tapped his impressive chest. "I can't make myself *believe* it when he's not around, when I'm worried about him." He shook his head and laughed. "This must be what it's like to be an Alpha. Always wanting to protect everyone, take care of them."

"We'll figure this out," Curtis said, and because he couldn't handle the fragile look in Jace's eyes, he looked back at the drawer and reached in, checking the corners just in case. No journal appeared. He pulled out the bits of paper. A couple of receipts, a bookmark, and one Post-it with a 613 area code phone number on it. Written beneath the number it said: Mann.

Wait.

Curtis frowned.

"What is it?" Jace said.

"Just a sec," Curtis said, pulling out his phone. He opened a search window and typed in the phone number and the name.

The university website was the first hit.

"Any idea why Matt would be talking to a sorcerer? Professor Mann?" Curtis said. "He's a poetry and literature professor at my university. Big into history and mythology. He's also one of Malcolm Stirling's spies, but he's not a willing pawn by any means. He helped us with the whole knife thing last year and managed to do it under Malcolm's radar. As far as I know, that was the first time they'd met."

Jace took the piece of paper. "Sorcerers," he said.

"Sorcerers?" Curtis repeated.

"His dreams. Sometimes when Matt woke up, he'd say it. 'Sorcerers.'" He looked at Curtis. "You think this Mann guy might know what Matt was doing?"

"I think it's worth finding out," Curtis said. And he knew just the person to ask.

SIX

The Families are in trouble?" Denis raised his glass, barely hiding a smile or his fangs. "*Dommage.*" Tallest and stockiest of the vampires Luc had gathered, Denis's visceral dislike of the Families almost remained cloaked in his sly humor.

Almost.

"Well, it's more the great-grandson of Malcolm Stirling who is in trouble," Luc said, conceding the man's antipathy with a dip of his chin. "Potentially. He's not responding, and no one is quite sure where he is. And there was a murder at the last place he was seen."

"Stirling's great-grandson," Catharine said, her honey-colored eyes flicking to him, as though Matthew Stirling's involvement made the topic slightly more interesting. Her long, chestnut hair remained loose tonight, falling over her shoulders, and she wore a simple garnet V-neck sweater and charcoal slacks, and yet she seemed as elegantly put together as when he'd seen her with her hair braided and in a gorgeous gown.

To her left, Étienne shifted forward in his seat. Of the three, he showed the most consideration of the news, though the lean, almost pretty man always seemed easier for Luc to read than the others. Something almost youthfully elfin about Étienne led to an earnestness that struck Luc as quite un-vampire like. "Missing or on the run?"

"Fair question. He is a Stirling. Perhaps he did the killing and is now in hiding." Denis's shrug made it clear he didn't care much either way. "One of these days, the Families will overstep enough and be in real trouble. I wouldn't say no to a world where the Families weren't at the top of the Accords."

"Alas," Luc said, "they are. They have more power than we do." He thought of Curtis, remembered his face as Luc had told him what they could—and couldn't—be. "And we, after all, could only rule half the time."

"But twice as well," Denis said. "At least."

"Now you sound like Renard," Étienne said.

"Étienne," Catharine chided gently, though a hint of fang belied her seriousness. "There's no need to be cruel."

Denis laughed, waving a hand. "No, he's right. I apologize. Any time I sound like our former *Duc*, I give you permission to warn me."

"Although," Étienne said, "technically, Renard was a wizard, too."

"It would be marvelous to change the subject," Catharine said. She sipped her wine.

Denis raised both hands. "I surrender."

Luc leaned back in his chair. They all had a point. The Families were by no means benevolent rulers. Renard had indeed wanted them destroyed. But Renard had been a wizard in life, had used magic to retain much of his ability when he became a vampire, and had thought nothing of using others to achieve his goal. He'd intended to flay a bound demon alive to increase his power even more, for some purpose they'd yet to understand.

Luc regarded the three others in turn. He'd gathered them in his office—the office of the former *Duc* in question, Renard—both to bring them up to speed on what had happened and also to take their measure. Part of him longed to simply ask them outright to help him investigate, but such a command would not be well received, and since ascending to the dukedom himself, he was determined not to repeat the mistakes of the past.

Renard had run roughshod over these three, despite their now sitting here as examples of charm, poise, and control, and Luc knew how much more the virtue of having control over most aspects of one's life mattered when one was immortal. He'd lived in the shadows, eked out a living from the edges for longer than he ever cared to dwell on.

No. I will not be that kind of leader.

But he *could* ask questions.

"What do we know of Matthew Stirling?" he said, spreading his hands and making the first offering of information as a way to be clear he wasn't demanding, only requesting. "I've met him once or twice, and while trusting a Stirling is, of course, out of the question, his attitude toward his great-grandfather and the Stirling Family as a whole was decidedly less than warm."

"Not surprising," Catharine said.

"Cynthia has mentioned him," Étienne said, then he paused. Luc took a moment to recall the connection. Cynthia Windsor was the elder sister of Mackenzie Windsor, and one of Curtis's friends among the Families. When Cynthia had been diagnosed with terminal cancer, Mackenzie had not wanted to lose her sister and had found a lone vampire to turn her into one of his kind. But first, Miss Windsor had researched rare magics to ensure Cynthia would retain as much of her magical power as possible after the change, making Cynthia Stirling a warlock, a rare vampire with magical ability.

Like Renard had been.

"What does she have to say?" Luc said. For a beat, Étienne continued to hesitate. Why? It might be loyalty. Étienne had developed an almost paternal relationship with the coterie Luc had allowed Renard's castoffs to form, and Cynthia Stirling was their leader.

"Matthew Stirling helped Mackenzie's sister access some of the Stirling Family library, likely for spells related to Cynthia's transformation," Étienne said. "She was particularly impressed by the risk he took, and also mentioned he asked no questions. She believed this was out of love for her sister at the time, but it's my understanding they are not a couple now." He glanced at Luc. "Both she and her sister owe Matthew Stirling a great deal."

"So it's possible they would help him," Catharine said. "Or that he'd reach out to them."

"I'll keep an eye on Cynthia, to be sure," Étienne said, with clear reluctance—at least to Luc, who noticed the way he rubbed his fingers against his thumbs when he attempted to obfuscate his emotions.

He cares. In another time, Luc might have filed the notion away as a potential weakness or something to exploit, but instead he found himself impressed with how he had taken on the role of protector over those who'd been so badly treated.

I have changed. The thought, not entirely unwelcome, still gave him pause.

"Thank you," Luc said, meeting Étienne's gaze long enough to convey his gratitude. "There will be no repercussion to Cynthia if she has none of the blame in this death."

That seemed to mollify Étienne, so Luc turned his attention to Denis.

"Did Renard have any dealings with him?"

Denis shook his head. "Nothing I can recall from his records." Denis, as their archivist, had been going through Renard's papers, accounts, and even his digital trail, as had Luc himself, but the former *Duc* was by no means a meticulous keeper of record, and more than a few things seemed to be missing.

But still. Given Curtis's concern for Matthew Stirling, it mattered. Not only because anything affecting the Families would likely affect them all, but *because* Curtis cared. And Luc wanted to make sure Curtis knew he was taking him seriously, even if he had arrived with little belief any of the others in the office would be able to offer anything.

"I appreciate your willingness to indulge me enough to check in with your coteries on the matter of Matthew Stirling," Luc said. "If nothing else, trouble for the Families has a habit of being trouble for us all, no?"

"True enough," Étienne said.

Catharine met his gaze for a moment, and she telegraphed her amusement via a twinkle in those stunning honey-colored eyes. She always gave him that look when he gave them his orders in the form of requests. As *Duc*, he could demand much of these three. He *would*, if it came down to it, or if ignorance began to extract too high a price, or if a true lead was required to put rest to this situation before any more chaos resulted. But he'd promised himself such a move would never be his opening play with these three.

Changed indeed. He couldn't help but imagine what Anders might say, and aimed a small smile of his own back at the Lady Markham.

It was time to change the subject.

"Speaking of Cynthia, how is our newest coterie?" he asked Étienne.

Étienne held out his delicate hands, smiling. "They're quick learners, and we were right to put Cynthia Windsor in charge."

The warlock. Luc forced his gaze to remain neutral, but it occurred to him in the moment they couldn't seem to take a single step these days without coming face-to-face with magic.

Luc listened with half an ear as Étienne spoke of the coterie of castoffs. More fallout from the leadership of Renard, who'd apparently turned others en masse, then cast them aside if they showed nothing more than average promise with any of the vampire graces. To hear Étienne tell it, they were handling their new status well, though, and Étienne did appear to be the right man to handle their number. The downtown territory he and the others had carved out for them was large enough for their group not to arouse suspicion or step on the toes of the other powers of Ottawa—most especially the demons, who held a great deal of the Byward Market as their territory—but didn't encroach too much on any of the areas they all preferred to hold themselves.

"Most importantly, none of them have shown any signs of acting out," Étienne said. "After how long they had to hide, and with Renard's coterie willing to destroy them on a whim, I believe they recognize the privilege in their new position."

"*Parfait*. Grant them formal territory," Luc said, giving the final permission Étienne needed to make it happen. "It's been long enough, and—as you say—they have behaved."

"*Merci*," Étienne said with a pleased smile.

All in all, it was a successful meeting.

So why did he feel a kind of dread?

"Thank you," he said to them, and then, to Denis, "Could you stay a moment?" Another request which was truly no such thing.

Catharine and Étienne offered polite farewells and nodded to Denis.

Once they were gone, Luc rose with his wine, and Denis joined him on one of the long couches Luc had had brought into the large office. Redecorating Renard's space had been a labor of love, and now the place boasted an understated elegance of finery, with turn-of-the-century French Canadian furniture, much of his made by his Levesque ancestors, and all of it lovingly restored and cared for.

Denis put his glass on the side table, ensuring he used one of the coasters. Luc fought off a small smile. They might both be monsters who needed the very lifeblood of humanity, but marking an antique with condensation would never do.

"Have you had any luck with the former *Duc's* offices?" Luc said.

Denis took a moment to reply. "Some," he said carefully, then added, "I don't want you to get too excited. I'm not sure it's a breakthrough. I'm as certain as possible we've tracked down the last of his properties, and though some were already stripped by the time we got to them, at the last we found documents making it clear he was absolutely the one who requested the Marsyas Blade." He paused. "And paid a small fortune for it."

"Do we know who he bought it from?"

Denis waved a hand. "The black market the Families run is a tangled knot of their kind. Kingston was the previous stop, and before that, Halifax. But where it came from over the Atlantic? There's no record Renard bothered to keep. If I had to guess, I'd offer England, which seems to be where the boat—the *Villaseñor*—involved travels to most often, but it's not exclusive to that route, so…" He shrugged. "Much like his tendency to turn others and then cast them off if they didn't measure up to whatever it was he was looking for, I'm afraid he didn't leave much in the way of a clue to his motives."

"At least with the knife we're completely certain Renard wanted it for something important. It was a lot of effort to go to."

"Yes." Denis picked up his glass again. "He was already powerful. The thought of him with more?" Denis sipped. "Have I mentioned lately how grateful I am you came along and destroyed that Family detritus?"

Luc smiled. Flattery was a staple of vampire politics, and unlike Étienne, Denis played it well. It would be too easy to take Denis at face value. "It's been implied often enough, I'd say." Given how much Denis distrusted the Families, Luc wondered if it would bother Denis to know Curtis had technically struck the last blow against their former *Duc*. It wouldn't do to enlighten him, either way. To some degree, Luc's position as *Duc* rested on the others believing he had taken Renard down. It *was* true—Curtis couldn't have done it without Luc and Anders and their triad bond—but there was no reason to cast any shadow of mitigating circumstances among the other vampires.

"Renard was also reading up on history," Denis said. "Local history, which struck me as…*odd*. Renard would have seen most of it—he was born in Quebec when he lived, but he existed here in Ottawa once he was turned, and as far as I can discover, he never left."

Luc frowned. "Local history."

"Specifically personages. He had a rather impressive record of the genealogies of the Families."

Luc considered. "Know thy enemy?"

"That's what I thought. Didn't Renard's warlock castoff mention something of a grudge with the Families?"

"Denis," Luc said, and Denis dipped his head in deference. Renard had kept a former vampire, Lavoie, trapped in a magical prison for decades. The Lady Markham had taken her in and made her a part of her coterie once Renard had been defeated. Indeed, Lavoie had managed to aid Luc in that regard, somewhat. She'd told him things he hadn't known about Renard. Calling her a castoff was not untrue—Renard had imprisoned her despite her being a former member of his coterie—but it was *unkind*.

As a former castoff himself, Luc didn't like the word.

"*Je m'excuse*," Denis said. "Suffice it to say, Renard had multiple orders for rare books, most of them about history or genealogy, and he'd been collecting them for some time. There were titles he was still tracking down as well, but they didn't arrive before you ended him."

"I wonder what he hoped to learn," Luc said. "Perhaps I should speak with Lavoie myself."

"I'm told she's more…coherent these days." Denis finished his wine, and Luc wondered if he'd meant the comment on Lavoie's mental state as a compliment or not. "I'm afraid that's about it. I'll have a précis sent to you, as always. You may see something I missed. And perhaps your wizard friend might, as well."

Luc fought off a small smile. Denis had a habit of referring to Curtis and Anders as his "wizard friend" and "demon friend." He never went as far as to be outwardly uncomfortable, but it was a verbal tell Denis wasn't entirely sure how to categorize what Luc had with Curtis and Anders.

Then again, this evening had proven Luc didn't either.

"No doubt," Luc said, and rose. Denis followed suit, and they shook hands.

Once Denis had left, Luc decided to travel one more avenue. He pulled out his phone and tapped the contact, waiting.

The Lady Markham answered on the first ring.

"My *Duc*?" Catharine said with the soft tones of an inquiry.

"I'm sorry to trouble you again," Luc said. "But I wonder if it might be possible to speak with Lavoie. Perhaps tomorrow night?"

"Of course," Catharine said. "I shall arrange it. At my home?"

"Thank you," Luc said.

"I will confirm a time by email."

Luc thanked her again and hung up. He went back to his desk and pulled out the laptop from the drawer. His discussion with Denis reminded him of some of his own business issues. A vampire needed income as much as the living, and most of his own finances depended on a variety of names and businesses he used to trade in antiques. There was an eighteenth-century French game board with unique squares of tortoise shell he needed to ensure would arrive on time for inspection before it was forwarded on to the interested buyer of antique chess sets. He brought up the rest of his records and noted a few more items of interest had been listed by both his procurers and potential customers.

Mostly, his people handled these things themselves, but they kept him in the loop, and he spotted a request for a "regards" ring and shook his head, equal parts amused and disappointed in the client. An acrostic of gems, the style of ring had been popular in the late nineteenth century and was named for the stones, in order: ruby, emerald, garnet, amethyst, a second ruby, a diamond, and a sapphire. He'd always found them tacky and overtly obvious. So typically *English*. Still, he had a source likely to work, and he sent a note to the agent in question.

Then, after a moment, he added another link to a seller of beautiful French *souvenir* rings, more beautiful and meaningful to his mind, and often more expensive. The buyer might not know the history of the coin rings, and upon enlightenment might prefer something classier.

Luc tried to move on to the rest of the requests, but soon his attention drifted, and he knew the mundane work would not be served by his distraction. He eyed his phone, but there was nothing yet from Anders or Curtis. The hour was growing late. If Curtis was still awake, he'd let Luc know if something had happened.

His determination lasted only a few minutes, and then he found himself unrolling the sleeve of his shirt to expose the triskelion on his forearm. The tattoo session had been a present from Anders, and they each bore the same mark. Curtis had woven magic into the design while it had been inked onto their skin, and it acted as an amplifier to their bond.

Luc pressed two fingers against the mark.

Both Anders and Curtis were awake. He felt a small wave of amusement from Anders, and then a burst of frustration from Curtis. He lifted his fingers. Neither of those things felt like a good sign.

Luc closed his laptop and slid it into his briefcase. He could work from home tonight.

SEVEN

Anders spread the map over the kitchen table and then went straight to the coffee machine to set up a pot. Curtis had come home alone. Apparently he'd managed to convince the werewolf to stay in Merrickville in case the Stirling kid checked in and he'd gone straight to his room, asking Anders to grab a map.

With zero flirtation. Curtis hadn't so much as checked out his pecs or arms. What was the point of a sleeveless V-neck shirt if it didn't get him eye-groped? Instead, a coolness ran between them. Grudgingly, Anders supposed it was understandable, what with how they'd started the evening and all, but he still didn't have to like it.

He itched to fix it. Or at least fuck it. Instead, he found himself smoothing the map on the table like the most important thing in the world was for it not to have any creases. When he caught the faintest whiff of scorched paper, he pulled his hands away. He hadn't meant to conjure heat.

The map looked almost ironed.

What the fuck is wrong with you, you freak? He scowled.

"You okay?"

He turned. Curtis was standing at the entrance to the kitchen, pendant in hand. A vibrant blue stone hung from the silver chain. He'd seen Curtis use it before.

"Fine," Anders said. The coffee machine was still gurgling, but he got a mug anyway.

"Right," Curtis muttered under his breath. Anders clenched his jaw. Curtis had to know Anders could hear him.

This fucking *sucked*. Why had Curtis gone and made what they'd already had so fucking *complicated*? Why couldn't he understand what they had was already good enough and—

Fuck it.

"Listen," Anders said, turning, but Curtis was already winding a hair around the crystal and saying stuff in whatever language it was he was using. Latin or some shit. He'd gotten all focused and had that look of complete control on his face.

It was a good look. It made Curtis seem a little older, and not just a little bit dangerous.

Hell, Anders knew full well Curtis could be the most dangerous of them all. Soft hazel eyes, short brown hair, and a face more technically cute than handsome, there was an "Aw shucks" quality to Curtis that Anders loved to see unravel. Curtis letting go, preferably while Anders was inside him? Hottest fucking thing ever.

But when Curtis used magic, bending the world around him to his will...

Well, it ranked a close second. Or maybe third, if he counted seeing Curtis on his knees in front of him.

Yeah, definitely third.

And now his dick was getting hard. Again. Hell, he'd been half-hard ever since he and Luc had told Curtis they couldn't be what Curtis wanted, and if *that* didn't underline the point they were completely wrong for Curtis, what would?

But damn, he'd love to fuck him right now.

"It would be great if you could let me concentrate," Curtis said, not looking away from his pendant and going right back to muttering in whatever language it was he was speaking to make his magic work. The statement came with a shit-ton more cool, frustrated detachment.

Fuck.

Anders turned and stared at the coffee machine until it finally gurgled to a halt. He poured himself a cup, and then, considering, put the kettle on the stove for Curtis. When he turned around, his more X-rated thoughts had settled down.

Well, as much as they ever did. One more glance at Curtis, and the thrum of power vibrating up his arm from the tattoo bond they shared, and he was pretty much back where he'd started. Partly it was Curtis's fault, though. He was biting his bottom lip in concentration.

He did the lip-bite thing when he was trying not to groan during sex, too.

Anders turned away again, aiming his gaze at the kitchen counter, which only made it occur to him he should really do Curtis against the countertop before they moved. Or maybe on it. Both, then. Just to be thorough. They'd managed most of the other rooms in the house, and it would be a missed opportunity not to check this one off, and much better a memory than the times this room had blown up in their faces.

Come to think of it, Luc might like that, too, he thought.

Curtis blew out a little breath of annoyance his way, and Anders sipped his coffee, trying not to grin. He wasn't made of willpower. Besides, Curtis's pendant wasn't moving.

"Everything okay?" Anders said.

"Hair is a connection, but it's not as good as blood," Curtis said. He rolled his head back and forth, then shook his shoulders. He palmed the pendant, then let it drop once more over the map and tried again. The effort Curtis was putting forth sent a breeze against the hairs on Anders's forearm, spreading out from the tattoo, and he forced himself not to shiver.

The kettle began the barest whistle—Anders could hear it long before Curtis would—and he pulled it off the oven ring, not wanting to disturb him.

Curtis frowned. "It's like there's something between us."

"I'm trying not to bother you," Anders said, annoyed now. "But you're being all hot and fuckable over there, making those faces and biting your lip…"

"No," Curtis said. Now he sounded pissed off, which wasn't fair at all. Fuckable was a compliment. "Not you. Although if this is you trying not to blast lust at me, you're kind of sucking at it. I meant Matt. I can almost barely feel the connection, but…" He seemed to struggle for words. "This is so frustrating."

Anders swallowed more coffee. It wasn't like he had any ideas. This was a magic thing. He didn't do magic.

"I'm going to try and break it," Curtis said.

Anders lowered the mug. "Break what?"

"The…whatever…is between me and Matt."

Anders frowned. Magic wasn't his thing, but Curtis sounded hesitant, and indecision wasn't something he was used to feeling from the wizard. "Are you sure?"

"No, I'm not, but it's late, I want to go to bed, and I can't get around it any other way, so I'm going to try smashing the crap out of it…" He took in a breath and then snapped out a few more unknown words in a rapid-fire rush. Anders tensed, waiting, and put down his coffee. A burst of satisfaction blinked between them, and Anders let out his breath, relieved.

Then the crystal shattered in a visible blast of icy cold, and Curtis flew bodily away from it.

Anders moved demon fast, but in the time it took him to cross the kitchen, Curtis almost hit the floor. He managed to catch Curtis's head in one arm, stopping him from bashing it against the stone floor. Pain and shock telegraphed between them, and Anders stared at Curtis's right hand. It was covered in a layer of ice already halfway up his forearm.

"I hate this kitchen," Curtis said. His teeth were chattering.

"Fuck." He felt cold against Anders's chest. The demon brought heat to the surface of his skin, trying to warm him.

Curtis's eyes rolled back into his head, and he passed out.

"Curtis?" Anders said, giving him a little shake. Nothing. He eyed the ice on Curtis's forearm, gripping it with his own hand.

The cold burned his skin with sharp, biting pain. At the best of times, demons didn't like cold, and this wasn't the cold of regular ice, but something conjured and directed. It *fought* him. He drew on the well of power of borrowed soul in his chest and burned back at the cold, not quite the open flame of hellfire, but barely shy of it. The ice melted, though it pulsed once or twice, and it didn't stop until he opened Curtis's pale fingers and the remnants of the pendant and chain dropped to the kitchen floor.

Even unconscious, Curtis shivered. Anders pulled him into his lap and wrapped his arms around him as tightly as he dared, radiating heat.

They were still sitting together, Anders wondering what the fuck he should do, when Luc came through the door in a rush.

"What happened?" he said. He'd obviously felt whatever had hit Curtis.

"Magic," Anders said. "He was trying to find the Stirling kid, and he said there was something in the way, and when he tried to break it, his crystal blew up and tried to freeze him solid."

Luc knelt down on the floor beside them, and Anders nodded to the fragment of pendant and chain. "Don't touch that fucking thing." A ring of frost had formed on the floor beside the remnants of the chain.

Luc avoided it. He reached a hand and put it under Curtis's chin. After a few seconds, he looked at Anders.

"I'll run a hot bath. Stay with him until it's ready."

Anders nodded.

He wasn't going anywhere.

❖

When Curtis finally stirred in his arms, Anders exhaled a long sigh of relief. They'd been submerged in the bath for nearly twenty minutes, Anders using his own power to keep it steaming. Curtis was cradled against his chest in the large tub, and Luc sat on the edge, watching. It wasn't like he could add bodily warmth.

"What happened?" Curtis said. He lifted his head a bit. "Wait. Why are we in the bath?"

"Your necklace went Popsicle in the kitchen," Anders said. "Tried to ice you."

"Oh," Curtis said, then after a moment. "Oh. Right. I remember." He shifted, sitting up and lifting his arm out of the water. The skin of his hand and wrist was now pink with warmth. It hadn't been when they'd pulled off his clothes to get him into the tub.

"Did someone attack you, *lapin*?" Luc said.

"Not actively." Curtis shook his head. "I think I triggered a kind of ward. I've never felt anything like it before. Someone cut Matt off from scrying. I didn't even know that was possible. I mean, Matt's been teaching us all sorts of stuff about divination magic at Craft Night, and there are ways to *protect* yourself, sure, but it was..." He stopped, blinking. "It was ice."

Anders waited, but Curtis didn't continue. Instead, he started to frown. Worry flared around the room between them.

"Hey," Anders said, nudging his bare shoulder. "Use your words."

"Sorry," Curtis said, coming back to himself. "It's just, it did *start* to work. I got a connection to Matt. The spell was obeying the law of constancy. The hair was enough. But...remember when I found Faris's body in the woods last winter? A scrying connection doesn't mean Matt's alive. But I was thinking...*Matt's* the expert at divination among the Craft Night group. If anyone knew how to hide from a location attempt, it would be him."

"You're saying Matt's the one who froze you out? Your so-called friend tried to kill you?" Anders said. That wasn't good.

"It wouldn't be on purpose." Curtis didn't look happy about it, though. "But ice and cold are kind of his thing, so if he'd set up a barrier to protect himself from scrying, ice is what I'd expect it to be like."

Anders shared a glance with Luc and could tell he was on the same page.

"If he is actively hiding from you, should we revisit the notion of him being responsible for the...for Aaron?" Luc said.

For the murder, Anders would have bet Luc had almost said.

Curtis bit his lip. "I don't want to believe it."

"If he was working with the wolf, getting behind him wouldn't be such a big deal, right? That Aaron guy would have trusted him." Anders traced his finger along the back of Curtis's neck. "Stick him, easy." He tapped Curtis's neck.

Curtis shuddered. "I don't know."

Anders would have bet Curtis did know but didn't want to think it. Also, now Curtis was awake and talking, it was hard not to notice they were skin-to-skin in the hot water. He and Luc had gotten his clothes off before they'd lowered him into the water, and having Curtis leaning against him in the bath often led to doing more...

"I'd like to get out of the bath now," Curtis said.

Shit. Probably wasn't a coincidence after where Anders's thoughts had been going.

"You're feeling warm enough?" Luc said, after glancing at Anders.

Yeah, Luc was likely feeling it, too. Anders cleared his throat and tried not to move as Curtis shifted against him, sitting up. Anders's cock was half-hard. Again.

"Yeah," Curtis said, and now he was standing.

Luc wrapped Curtis in one towel, and once Anders got his cock a bit more under control, he got up and wiped himself off with another, then burned enough heat to the surface of his skin to dry the rest. By the time he'd hung one towel and wrapped himself in another, Luc had Curtis dried off and gotten him into one of the fluffy white bathrobes.

"Bed," Luc said.

Curtis raised his chin. "There are still some things I could try, and I need to—"

"Nope," Anders said. "He's right. Bed."

"I didn't even tell you about Professor Mann yet," Curtis said, blowing out an annoyed breath. "And I need to phone Kenzie. And Jace. Let them know not to try tracking down Matt with magic themselves—I had you to warm me up. Neither of them has a handy demon."

"I will contact Miss Windsor and Mr. Parsons," Luc said. "You need to rest. You're barely on your feet."

Curtis tried to stare them down, but the fatigue and dark smudges under his eyes gave him away. His shoulders slumped, and he nodded. "Okay. You'll call them right away?" he said to Luc.

Luc nodded.

Anders crossed his arms. "You need me to tuck you in?"

Curtis took a step back, and all three of them tried not to react. Anders clenched his jaw.

Fuck.

"I need you to reach out to Professor Mann," Curtis said after a moment. "For some reason, Matt had his number."

"I can do that tomorrow," Anders agreed. A visit with the burly professor was no hardship. And if there was time after the Q&A, he could use some of the toys the professor kept on hand for Anders's visits. Or he could make them part of the Q&A. He smiled, his dark mood not brightening, exactly, so much as looking forward to having an outlet. He was *definitely* in the mood to make someone squirm.

"And David, too," Curtis said.

Anders's smile soured. "I thought we'd agreed to leave him out of this."

Curtis sighed. "You know what? Forget it. I'll call David in the morning myself. Good night." He turned on his heel and left them standing in the large bathroom. He even closed the door behind him, which did nothing to stop the irritation flaring along their bond.

"He's pissed at us," Anders said. "He didn't even try to touch my chest."

Luc rolled his eyes; then, with the tiniest flare of something Anders couldn't quite discern before it was gone, he reached out and ran his fingertips through Anders's chest hair, with just enough pressure to offer a pleasant scratch of his fingernails.

"Better?" Luc said.

Anders laughed. "Thank you. I'd hate it if me in a towel was losing effectiveness."

"Hardly. You are as alluring an image of masculinity as you are stereotypical."

"Aw, sweet talker."

"Be patient with him. He's hurt. We hurt him," Luc said, his expression returning to seriousness and sorrow. He shook his head, then pulled his phone from his pocket and scrolled through the contacts. "I believe I'll go make those calls he requested before I earn any more ire."

"Suck-up," Anders said.

Luc smiled enough to show fang. "Perhaps. If you ask me nicely." Beneath the humor, there was genuine care. And not just a little bit of horny appreciation.

Anders grinned right back, feeling his world returning back to balance. Sporting nothing but a towel always worked in his favor. It wasn't even the first time this week, come to think of it. There'd been a guy at the Y last Friday. He did so love the young government crowd. So tightly wound, overworked, and so very willing for a quick and dirty release.

Come to think of it, said gym was twenty-four hours, and he'd put out a lot of heat tonight. He needed a recharge.

"I'll be back later," he said.

Luc nodded, already dialing. "Be back before sunrise, would you?"

EIGHT

Despite what Curtis had said to Luc and Anders, his arm and hand still felt chilled, as though a draft had found him and was determined to stick with him even under the covers, so before climbing into his bed, he'd taken a moment to write *validum* on his arm in red calligraphy ink, dried it, and invoked the word three times under his breath, willing his magic to empower the scrolling text.

It worked to stave off the chill, and Curtis put his head down on the pillow thinking he'd never get to sleep. Murder. Matthew. Nearly dying in the kitchen. Again. Why was it always the damn kitchen? Who could sleep with all that rolling around in their head?

The next thing he knew, Luc was touching his shoulder.

"Lapin?"

Curtis opened his eyes, blinking in the near dark. A glance at his clock told him it was pre-dawn.

"Mm?" he managed, sitting up on his elbows.

"I've spoken with both Miss Windsor and Mr. Parsons. Miss Windsor asked me to pass on to you she was turned away at the Stirling chantry, though they questioned her first as to whether or not she knew where Matthew was. She believes Matthew's absence is not a secret any longer. The werewolf was less coherent and had little to offer beyond having still heard nothing."

Curtis's eyes were adjusting now, and he could see Luc's face. God, the man was gorgeous. It was like looking at the cover of a fashion magazine sometimes. The cheekbones and the perfect dent in his chin. Those lips, which he knew could kiss like the sole goal of kissing was to make someone feel cherished and needed and…

He said he doesn't love you.

"Thank you," Curtis said, taking a breath.

"You're welcome." Luc hesitated, his dark eyes catching for a moment on something beyond Curtis's shoulder before returning to meet his gaze. "I spent part of the night looking into Aaron Young. There wasn't a lot of detail in the archives—Renard didn't care much for the affairs of werewolves—excepting the coywolf's possession of his gift. He was a known prognosticator. At least, Renard knew. At one time, he had the coywolf under observation, but ultimately noted him as 'insufficient.' An ominous word which speaks of whatever Renard's plans might have been, but not one to clarify it much. However, if Renard knew of the coywolf's knack, it would lead me to suspect others did, as well."

"I'll ask David about him. See what he knows," Curtis said.

"That's a good idea." Luc turned his head. "Sunrise is approaching. I need to go."

"Luc?" Curtis hadn't meant to stop him and was annoyed with himself for reaching out to touch his shoulder.

"Yes, *lapin*?" Luc waited.

Damn it. Now he needed something plausible beyond *I just wanted to touch you*. He thought quickly. "Thank you. I know you'd rather stay out of all this Family stuff."

"Your friends matter to you," Luc said, leaning forward and kissing his forehead. "So it matters to me." Luc pulled back and regarded him. "Denis also discovered Renard was looking into the genealogy of the Families, including the Stirlings. It's likely unrelated, but I'll be seeing what he gathered tonight. Denis is organizing it for me."

"Renard hated them," Curtis said. "I mean, didn't...I've forgotten her name. The one he had trapped on the island by the bridges? Didn't she say as much?" He rubbed his eyes. He was usually better with names.

"She did," Luc said. "And her name is Jennifer Lavoie. I intend to speak with her, as well."

"Right. Jennifer. The cat lady vampire." He'd only met her the once, but Luc had told him how she'd had a whole pack of cats at her beck and call, even before she'd been folded into Lady Markham's coterie. It was a rare and unusual grace for a vampire, let alone one who hadn't been in a coterie at the time.

Luc nodded, and they were silent for a beat. Then Luc leaned forward, kissed his forehead again. Was it just Curtis, or was the man doing as much hesitating and awkwardness as he was? Then again, it was Luc. Impossible to tell. Awkward on Luc was still suave on anyone else.

"Go back to sleep. I'll see you tonight," Luc said.

"Will do."

When he woke up the next time, weak sunlight eking its way through his curtains, Curtis felt a faintness in his connection to Luc and knew the vampire was, once again, asleep. He took a deep breath, touching his forehead with his fingertip where Luc had kissed him, remembered the feel of Anders's body as the demon had held him in the hot water of the bath, then rolled his face into his pillow and yelled inarticulate rage noises into the cloth.

These two men would be the death of him. If whatever else was out there didn't kill him first. Why, why, *why* had he fallen for those two when he could have fallen for someone...

What?

Someone alive and in possession of a soul, maybe. Was that too high a bar?

Technically, both Luc and Anders shared some of his soul, he'd been told, but surely finding a man in possession of a soul of his very own who also thought he was attractive couldn't be beyond reach, no?

Honestly, the soul thing was negotiable if the person in question was willing to actually say what they felt.

This was getting him nowhere.

Besides, the last person with a soul he'd slept with had tried to betray him, too, come to think of it. Malcom Stirling's chauffeur, Ben. Fellow Orphan, possessed a soul, they'd had sex before Curtis had learned Ben had literally stolen from Curtis's father's grave so he could attack Curtis in his kitchen.

"Souls are overrated," Curtis said, staring at the ceiling.

Okay, enough self-pity. Curtis reached for his phone and sent a text to David asking him if he had time to meet today.

❖

His mind still gnawing at the problem of how to redirect his own wayward emotions, it struck Curtis as he stepped through the door and spotted David Rimmer at his usual table at the back of the coffee shop that this was fast becoming "their" coffee shop. He paused at the counter to ask for a tea, knowing full well it would be less than stellar, and tipped a toonie anyway. A dab of honey and some milk would make it passable, and when it came to tea after a near-death magic experience, even passable was better than nothing.

David smiled as Curtis approached, and tension melted from Curtis's shoulders. Something about the broad, stocky blond man—even in a plain black button-up and jeans—made everything feel a bit more surmountable. Or maybe just mountable. David was, after all, an incubus as well as a police detective. And while the latter wasn't by any means positive in general in Curtis's books, he happened to know David truly wanted to make the world safer, especially for those on the wrong end of the supernatural. Combined, the whole basically made him sex on a stick.

And gave him access to handcuffs, to boot.

"Hey," Curtis said, sitting, trying to banish the X-rated thoughts. "Thanks for coming."

"It's fine," David said. Then, after a moment, "What did Anders do?"

Curtis blinked. "What?"

"You look upset," David said.

"No, it's fine." Curtis shook his head and picked up his tea, sipping. He smoothed his expression to something he hoped said "No comment."

"I don't believe you. You look…defeated. That's not like you." David sipped his coffee, his eyes soft with concern. "What did Anders do?"

Curtis put the cup down. "It's interesting you assume Anders did something."

It was David's turn to smooth his features. But he still raised his eyebrows meaningfully. Man. Was this how he got criminals to confess? There was a whole "just tell daddy and I won't have to be disappointed in you" vibe happening, and Curtis did not want to disappoint.

"Fine. Anders did something. Or didn't do something. But it wasn't just him, it was…You know what? It's not important." Curtis looked at his tea, squaring his shoulders. "Also not why I wanted to meet with you."

David smiled, and now it was less Disappointed Daddy and straight up DILF. "Well, I'm glad you do. It's been a while, and honestly it's nice to catch up without some emergency looming."

Wait. Curtis hesitated. *What?*

David caught it. Curtis supposed detectives had to be capable of reading body language and that sort of thing.

"Oh," David said, a tiny smile tugging at the corner of his lips. It was charming. Of course. "Unless I'm wrong, which is unfortunate, but what's the looming emergency?"

Curtis stared down at his tea. *Unfortunate?* What was happening? He looked up again, and David was still regarding him with those tell-me-everything hazel-brown eyes.

"Matthew Stirling," he blurted, because as much as the man was DILFy sex on a stick, that was so not the important thing right now.

David shook his head. "What about him?"

Whoa. Now *that* was interesting. David Rimmer didn't already know? "He's missing," Curtis said. The Stirlings knew, according to what Mackenzie said to Luc, and while David wasn't completely under the thumb of the Families any more, Curtis was surprised they hadn't looped him in to help look for Matthew.

David let out a short breath. "You're sure?"

"I am." Curtis realized David might be out of the loop on more than one front. "And Aaron Young was murdered."

David paused. "Aaron Young." It didn't seem to register.

"He's a...He was a werewolf. Or a part-coyote version of a werewolf? I'm not sure what the difference is. But he was with Matt when Matt went missing. At Aaron's place. We did a spell to see the last thing Aaron saw, and it was Matt."

"So you think Matthew Stirling killed him and is in the wind?" David said, so plainly and without surprise Curtis almost shivered. He'd never get used to the way anyone associated with the Families took murder as a matter of course.

"No, no, not like that. He was running away, trying to get away from something," Curtis said. "We had to leave the body with the other wolves, but Taryne was going to examine it." He paused. "Do you know Taryne?"

"I do," David said. "So Matthew Stirling is missing, and he was last seen at the scene of a murder."

"When you put it like that, it sounds awful," Curtis said. "We're worried about him."

"We?"

"Me. My friends." Curtis considered for a moment, knowing the Stirling family inheritance was generally kept a secret, and Matthew probably would like it to remain so, but deciding David needed to know if he was going to help. Assuming he would help, given Matthew was part of the Families, even if he didn't really want to be. "The thing is, Aaron was prescient. And…so is Matt."

There was the slightest twitch in David's impeccable jawline, but that was it. "You're saying Matthew Stirling can see the future?"

"It's an inherited thing," Curtis said. "One of the Stirlings at any given time has the ability. It passes down the family line. All the major Families of Ottawa have inherited gifts, actually—not just the Stirlings. But Matthew's gift? It's very powerful and accurate. The Stirlings obviously don't like other people to know, but given someone managed to get the jump on Matt and Aaron, it seems relevant for you to know about it."

"It does." He paused for a moment. "How do you kill someone who can see the future?"

"Right?" Curtis said. That was the million-dollar question.

"When was this?" David said.

"We're not one hundred percent, but around three days ago now. At least, that's the last time anyone heard from Matt for sure."

David nodded. "And the next day, suddenly I'm missing my shadows."

"Your shadows?" Curtis was lost.

"The Knight Family pets."

"The…? Oh." The sorcerer cops. Dale's Family spies. Right. They looked at each other, and Curtis asked the question he didn't really want to ask.

"So I'm guessing them not looping you in about any of this…?" He waved a hand.

"They think they can't trust me," David said, and he shrugged. "Which is fair. I was never exactly in their good books at the best of times, and these days even less so. Since Ethan and Tyson."

David Rimmer had formed his own pack of demons, a trio, the bare minimum required. David was in much the same situation as Curtis, Luc, and Anders. David had another incubus, Ethan, and a rare male wrath demon, Tyson. Officially, it meant he'd become off-limits to the Families as a controllable—and thus useful—detective. They could still ask him to do their bidding and even apply pressure, but no longer could they simply demand it of him in exchange for his ongoing freedom to exist under their protection.

"I'd kind of hoped they'd asked you to help look for him,"

Curtis said. "Which now I've said it out loud makes me sound sort of mercenary, but I'm worried about Matt."

"Well, I can help *you* look for him," David said. "And I can check to see if there's any investigation on the books. You know, it's possible that could be where my shadows went. It's rare, but I have seen the Families hand sorcerers actual orders before, rather than demanding they tell them everything they see."

"Thank you," Curtis said. "I can text you Matt's phone number and his license plate and stuff. He rides a motorcycle. And I've got Aaron's address and everything."

"Do that." David took another swallow of coffee, then eyed him. "And, Curtis…" He paused, glancing away, and Curtis hadn't seen David do the hesitation thing before.

"What is it?" Curtis said, not sure if he was worried or nervous or something else.

"Well, maybe next time, we could get together with no looming emergency?" David regarded him with a frank smile. "If you'd like, I mean. Because I'd like to explore that."

"Oh." It was so frank and forthright, Curtis felt heat spreading up his neck. He didn't know what to say.

David stared down at his coffee cup. Wait. Was *David* blushing? Did demons blush? Anders never blushed. David cleared his throat. "I realize there are limits to what that might mean, but…" He looked back up at Curtis, and his gaze did something funny and twisty deep in Curtis's stomach. "I enjoy your company, and I would like to see where it might go, if anywhere."

"Right," Curtis said, parsing David was, unless he was completely mistaken, asking him…what? To go out on a date? He might not know whether or not a demon could blush, but he knew full well when his own face was burning, and heat from his neck was spreading fast.

"Would that be okay?" David said.

Curtis swallowed some of his tea. Would it?

His phone pinged. Mackenzie. *You free?*

"I—" Curtis had to clear his throat to speak. He looked up. "I think I'd like that," he said, and the twists in his stomach grew tighter for more reasons than he could put a finger on in the moment. "To catch up, at least, and after…" They could totally figure the rest out from there, right? Start with a *friendly* thing. Or maybe…

"Great," David said, polishing off the last of his coffee and rising.

Curtis rose, too, though his tea was still half-full.

"I'll check in with you. Send me those details as soon as you can, and I'll get back to you if I find anything. And given this is the Families we're talking about, be careful," David said, and then he hugged Curtis, squeezing him nice and tight. Curtis couldn't help but inhale. David smelled like coffee and woodsmoke and maybe even chocolate, and it was really, really nice to be hugged like this. He wondered if David had a hairy chest like Anders or a smooth one like Luc, and then David was letting go and Curtis was even more off-balance than before.

Lust demons were so unfair. And he also felt a little bit *off* about the whole potential date thing, especially given his first reflex was to measure David up against Luc and Anders.

But Luc and Anders don't want you like that, he thought, watching David leave the coffee shop, which was very pleasant. Great ass, amazing thighs. David turned and caught him looking. He winked at the door, offering a confident little smile that went right back to the twisty bits in Curtis's stomach.

A date with David Rimmer would be one hell of a thing, that wink said.

Curtis exhaled, feeling a bit more stable. He'd always known David thought good things of him. And he seemed willing to put it out there, unlike Luc and Anders with their "we don't want you" speech.

Except you know they do.

"Men are the *worst*," he said, groaning at the ceiling in frustration. The blue-haired barista raised a fist. "Preach."

Curtis smiled and sat back down, pulling up Mackenzie's text and tapping on his phone. *Very free. What's up?*

Feel like some tea? she replied.

Curtis eyed his half-finished cup of not-so-great coffee shop tea. *Absolutely.*

❖

Curtis found a spot to park off Somerset and crossed the street. He'd never been to Artistea before, but from the name alone, he was game. From the outside, it looked like a house, but it had been thoroughly remodeled to be a café and gallery both. Local art lined every wall, not quite crowded, but certainly full, and the sets of tables and chairs were charmingly mismatched. There were even couches against the far wall. The place felt a little bohemian and random, and it struck him again how Mackenzie Windsor seemed so very different from the rest of the Families. Matthew, too.

Thinking of Matt chased the small smile from his face, and he rubbed his wrist, shivering with remembered cold.

He found Mackenzie sitting in the back corner. She had her hair up, held with the usual knot and polished sticks he knew were wands, and she had a couple of books open on the table in front of her, alongside a teapot and a cup.

"Hey," he said, approaching.

She glanced up. "Hi." She had dark smudges under her eyes.

He sat beside her and glanced at the books she was reading. They seemed pretty old, and at a glance, he saw some semifamiliar runic combinations—they reminded him of the work he'd done to ward the house at the construction site.

"I'm trying to figure out a way around the scrying block Luc told me about," she said.

"Ah," Curtis said, letting out a breath. "About that."

She looked at him.

"I'm wondering if maybe it was Matt who blocked me."

"*What?*"

"Ice is his thing, and he's an expert at all sorts of divination, right?" Curtis said quickly.

Mackenzie blinked. "Oh." She rubbed her eyes beneath her glasses. "Sorry. For a second, I thought you meant…the other thing."

Curtis winced. Aaron's murder. "No," he said, then wondered if he should be considering it. No. Matt was not a murderer.

"Ice. You're right." She lowered her hand. "It could be him. I didn't even think of that. I barely slept last night."

"And she's been here for a couple of hours already," a man said, arriving with another teapot. "You struck me as someone in need of an Earl Grey," he said to Curtis.

Curtis stared at the server. He had hazel eyes and was handsome, in an ever-so-slightly coiffed way that made Curtis think he spent more time preparing his look than he wanted anyone to know. Short hair, artfully tousled. Just enough scruff to be almost be a beard.

He realized he was staring. "Uh, yeah. Earl Grey is great." It was one of his favorite blends, frankly.

"Curtis, this is Leo. Leo, this is Curtis," Mackenzie said. Then she smiled at him. "More Lady Grey for me?"

"Coming right up, dancing queen." He winked at her and left. Curtis stared at her. "Dancing queen?"

"Long story," she said, but she blushed. "Leo's a muse."

"Sorry?"

"Sloth demon," she said. "They feed on inspiration and imagination, and they sort of spark new ideas if you hang around them. We met a while back. I come here when I feel like I'm hitting a wall. He's helped me before, and I figured if I needed, I could ask him to try again."

"Oh." Curtis looked across the room in time to see Leo step back behind the counter. "Sloth." He frowned. Leo looked all graceful and elegant as he moved around opening jars of tea and pouring boiling water into teapots.

"What?"

"I guess I thought it would be more like, I don't know, lying around? Napping?" He paused. "Or, I don't know, skipping your morning run because you were too tired from having your hand nearly frozen off."

Mackenzie eyed him. "As a random example."

"Listen, I am at one with the way of the nap," Curtis said.

"I'll ask him if he can feed on dreams, too, next time it comes up," she said.

Curtis checked his teapot. It wasn't quite brewed enough. "So is it working? Any ideas?"

"No." Mackenzie shook her head. "Although what you just said... You really think Matt warded himself?"

"If he did, then it means he doesn't *want* to be found." *If he's still alive.*

"I want to believe it's him hiding from his family, but you're right. It could be all of us he's hiding from." Mackenzie sank back into the couch. "I don't understand why he wouldn't come to us."

Unless he killed Aaron. "Do you know anything about his trip to London?" Curtis said.

Mackenzie rolled her head to the side. "He took Jace there last winter. A getaway."

Curtis winced. "Apparently not. He'd been dreaming about London. Y'know, *dreaming.*"

She groaned out loud and rubbed her eyes again, pulling off her glasses entirely. "So he's been keeping secrets from us all for months."

"People do that."

Oh, good. Leo was back. Curtis eyed him. The guy was a ninja. He put down a teapot and picked up Mackenzie's old one.

Mackenzie lowered her hands and aimed a particularly friendly smile at the server. "You say it like an accusation." Was Curtis imagining it, or was Mackenzie *really* comfortable with this guy? They seemed to be teasing each other, and it struck him as playful, despite Mackenzie's obvious fatigue.

"I'm pretty sure most of us have been guilty of keeping a secret." Leo tapped his lip with one finger. "Sometimes right in our basements."

Curtis's eyes widened. *Ouch.* Mackenzie had hidden her sister in her basement once she'd helped her become a vampire. And she hadn't even told her mother about it.

Mackenzie narrowed her eyes, but she was still grinning at Leo. "Why do I come here?"

"You like my tea," Leo said. "And you also think—" He stopped.

Curtis watched as the teapot Leo was holding slipped from his fingers and crashed to the wood floor. It didn't shatter, but the lid popped out and sprayed leftover tea and tea leaves in a small arc.

"Leo?" Mackenzie said.

Leo started to shake his head, his mouth opening. He took a single step back, then started to sink, as though he didn't have it in him to remain standing

Both Curtis and Mackenzie rose, getting to him as he dropped to his knees on the floor, not even seeming to notice his jeans were in the puddle of leftover tea.

"Leo?" Mackenzie said again.

"Marlowe," Leo said. "Something happened to Marlowe. I...I can't feel her."

Curtis looked at Mackenzie over Leo's head. Who the hell was Marlowe?

Mackenzie shook her head.

"She's gone," Leo said. "She's gone."

NINE

A nders stretched, reaching out in both directions and coming up with nothing but sheet and blanket. He cracked one eye and checked the clock. Not even nine. He considered going back to sleep but then noticed a yellow piece of paper stuck to his clock. A Post-it Note. He pulled it off and looked at it.

Professor Mann, it said. Nothing else. And it was in Luc's handwriting.

He groaned. Right. That.

His sense of Luc, faded almost to nothing now the sun was up, was as usual, but he could barely feel Curtis at all, which meant he'd already left the house, ignoring their advice to take it easy, which he supposed he should have seen coming. He considered touching the tattoo on his forearm, the three-colored triska-whatever-the-fuck, to get a sense of Curtis, but instead he got out of bed and made for the shower.

After a lot of hot water, he felt awake enough to make it down to the kitchen for coffee, and while it brewed, he grabbed his phone and sent off a text to Mann.

Anders enjoyed Mann. The professor had a buttoned-up professional vibe he maintained at the university, but once the office door was locked and a particular drawer was *un*locked, the fun was anything but buttoned-up. Rope, cuffs, usually gags—the office walls were not particularly soundproofed, after all—and an expanse of hairy and inked skin to explore had made for more than a few enjoyable afternoons. When it came to enjoying his BDSM tastes, Anders knew Mann generally had a lot more takers for his dominant side rather than being the submissive, and Anders was more than happy to step up to the plate when Mann was in need of letting go.

There was just something about taking a big, stocky man to that place, especially someone as strong and cultured as the professor.

He had been taken aback when he learned Mann had also been a sorcerer and a spy for Malcolm Stirling. He hadn't thought Mann had been using him on that level, and he'd been furious at first. But Mann had promised his arrangement with Anders had had nothing to do with Curtis, and after a prolonged—and very enjoyable—question-and-answer session, Anders had come to believe him.

Heavy on the coming.

Anders drank his coffee and decided to grab some breakfast on the go, checking his phone before he grabbed his keys. No answer from Mann yet.

He smiled. If Mann took much longer to reply, he'd have to make the professor apologize for the oversight.

He got behind the wheel, considering which of the objects in Mann's hidden toy box might be up to the task and remembering the way he'd twisted in the thick rope during their question-and-answer session.

Definitely rope, he thought, and pulled the SUV out of the drive.

❖

Something was wrong. After riding the elevator most of the way up the tallest tower on the university campus, Anders found himself standing at the door of Professor Jeffrey Mann, face-to-face with a note attached to the door.

Due to family emergency, Professor Gillian Rodger will be handling all of my classes. Lecture notes are online.

The note on the office door in the tower listed a different office number, and that was it. No date when Mann would be back, and no contact information.

Anders frowned and tried the door handle. It was locked. Glancing to the left and right to make sure there were no other people around, he tried again—this time putting some of his demon strength into the attempt, not that snapping the mechanism inside the door handle took particularly much effort. University budgets sure as hell didn't set aside shit for door locks.

Their loss. His win.

Despite it being a private office, the barrier of residency didn't do much to stop Anders, either. He'd been invited in multiple times by Mann for impromptu or planned play sessions. Even without a current pass, the room remembered.

He closed the door behind him, then took a look around. Of immediate note was that Mann had emptied the single locked cabinet where he kept a few specific toys at hand—Anders knew the bottom drawer usually contained a length of rope, a ball on a strap Mann could convincingly pretend was nothing more than a stress ball, and lube in an unlabeled bottle.

If Mann had cleaned out even those tamest of sex toys, Anders didn't think he was planning on being back any time soon. He turned in a slow circle and had to admit to himself he hadn't exactly paid much attention to what made up most of Mann's office on his visits.

Mostly he'd been eager to tie the burly man up, gag him, and enjoy some playtime. Part of that wasn't his fault. Mann's rare opportunities to play with his submissive side tended to mean they got right to it, and giving Mann a release while tied up and in that headspace put a particular edge in the taste of the man's soul, one Anders enjoyed the fuck out of.

He was careful not to overfeed, though. He hadn't wanted to take too much from Mann, and leave him prone to acting on impulse. Mann hated most of the snobs of academia with a fiery passion, and once they'd both come, and the rope and gags were removed, he'd often mention how their rough rutting had been what he'd needed to put a faculty meeting or a series of emails behind him.

Anders closed his eyes and tried to remember what he'd seen in Mann's office the last time he'd been fucking the professor over his desk. Had there been a statue or something on the bookcase? He didn't think it had always been so empty.

No, not a statue. It'd been a hammer or something. An old one. Probably not a reproduction, given how much Mann liked history.

He sighed, opening his eyes, and started going through the drawers of the desk and the filing cabinets, but all he found were academic papers or conspicuous empty spaces. The whisky was gone, too, which was another sign Mann wouldn't be returning soon.

Where the fuck did you go?

Anders pulled out his phone and tried dialing Mann's number again. It went directly to voicemail, and he hung up.

They'd most often played here, in Mann's office. But there had been one occasion, when Anders had called in a particularly hungry mood, where Mann had invited him to his home, and Anders had learned Mann had many, many more interesting toys to play with there. Including a fully equipped basement playroom, complete with sling.

It had made for a memorable night.

Which he hoped translated into remembering the way.

He paused at the door long enough to take a photo of the sign there and text it to Curtis, adding *I'm going to check out Mann's house* before hitting send.

Then he waited.

And waited.

And waited.

No grey dots. No reply.

He could be busy. It could be no big deal.

Or he could be ignoring you because you broke his fucking heart, you asshole.

With a growl, Anders headed for the elevator.

❖

Mann's home was deserted as well. Or at least, no one answered the door of the small home in the Glebe. Anders was convinced he had the right place—how many other Glebe homes would possibly have Celtic knotwork carved above the front door, let alone one that made his skin itch and jump as he approached? As a sorcerer, Mann had access to very little magical ability, but Anders knew he used what little he had in every way he could.

In fact, Anders had gathered Mann's confessions in exactly how many different ways he used his low-watt magic after learning Mann had been spying on Curtis at the university for Malcolm Stirling and the whole Stirling branch of the Families. In two words, Mann said for a sorcerer, the true path to using their magic came down to *storage* and *patience*. Mann stored magic in the symbols of his tattoos, for the most part, feeding them with the dregs of power he had on a daily basis and letting them build up over time. He could later release the magic from his inked symbols in a crisis, to protect himself.

He could also use truly enchanted items, like all sorcerers, but to Anders's knowledge—and Mann's sweaty, teased confessions—he didn't own any of his own.

Anders eyed the carving and considered his options. For all he

knew, the carving up there was the same as Mann's tattoos: a giant
fuck-you of magic filled up with an eyedropper's worth of power every
day for a year or something like that, and perfectly willing to blow up
in his face if he touched Mann's front door.

God, but he hated magic sometimes. It didn't seem to have
anywhere near the same limits as his own demonic gifts, or even
vampire graces. Having Curtis in his corner had opened Anders's mind
somewhat—funny how you quickly didn't mind something powerful
when you could use it for your own means—but he still thought of
magic as something you kept far away from unless you had no choice.

He grunted at the Celtic knot, then took a walk around the side
of the house, crossing into the backyard. Of course, he found a similar
carving over the back door, though it didn't have the same potent
buzzing hum effect on his skin. Perhaps it wasn't as "charged" as the
front door. Taking a breath, Anders reached out and touched the door
handle, curious.

The pressure of residency was there, and it was more than the
usual. He'd not be able to force his way in.

Plus side? Mann was alive. His home's ability to protect itself
from unwanted demons and vampires was still there, which meant, at
the very least, Mann still breathed.

Which was something.

Specifically, it was something pissing him off, given Mann hadn't
answered his damn phone or any of his texts.

Anders tried again, but once again, there was no answer. He
considered burning a handprint in the man's door to work off some
annoyance, but decided against it.

"May I help you?"

Anders turned. A man had stepped out onto the back porch of the
neighboring house and was looking over the fence into Mann's yard.
With warm, dark brown skin and streaks of silver and grey in his short
black hair, he looked like he might be in his fifties or sixties, or older
still, but very well preserved.

"Looking for my friend Jeff," Anders said, making sure to use
Mann's first name. "Have you seen your neighbor recently?"

The man frowned, crossing his arms. "You're a friend of Jeff's?"
He sounded skeptical.

"Jeff and I go way back," Anders said, forcing a smile and
relaxing his posture and doing all the shit Curtis said made him look
less intimidating. He lifted one hand and willed his allure to the surface.

It was possible the neighbor might be into dudes, and if he was, it would smooth things over easier.

The neighbor's gaze, however, remained sharp. Not into dudes, then. Still, the power would nudge the man's attitude a notch regardless, drawing on a desire to at least be friendly to Anders, unless the man had the willpower of a saint.

"If you go way back, you'd already know," he said.

Well, shit. Mann's neighbor was a fucking saint, then. Anders sighed, trying for something a bit more contrite. "We haven't spoken in a little while, but I've known him since before he had the tattoos," Anders said, hoping the neighbor at least knew of Mann's ink, which the professor tended to keep hidden under crisp dress shirts at work. "He hasn't returned my calls, and I'm worried is all."

"He had a family emergency," the neighbor said, finally softening a trace. "I'm not sure when he'll be back. He did say I could leave a message and he'd get back to me when he could, though. Did you leave a message?"

"Yeah," Anders said.

"Then he'll get back to you when he can." The neighbor finally smiled, and Anders forced himself to return the gesture.

It was too bad the man wasn't reacting to his allure. He had a great smile. Good mouth. It'd look good around his cock.

"Thank you," Anders said, waving and making his way back around to the gate.

The neighbor watched him go, every step of the way.

Fucking dead end. He'd have to tell Curtis and Luc he couldn't find the professor.

A dark thought occurred to him. A coywolf got murdered, and now Mann was missing alongside the Stirling kid. Did it mean his most reliable fuckbuddy was involved with the murder somehow?

He didn't know. He blew out a breath, pausing when his phone buzzed in his pocket. He pulled it out and grimaced. A text from David Rimmer.

Need to speak to you.

As if the day couldn't get any worse.

TEN

Curtis drove, acutely aware of the demon in the back seat of his hybrid. Beside him, Mackenzie aimed most of her attention Leo's way, talking to him in a low, even voice that didn't much seem to be reaching the muse, whose eyes had been flicking left and right since his declaration in the tea shop. He'd barely managed to tell his coworker— the only other employee in the place, an older woman with greying hair tied back in a long braid and wearing a loose, floral print dress— that he had to leave, his voice had been so strained and stuttering, and Mackenzie had leapt into action there, too.

"There's a family emergency," she said, looping her arm through Leo's. "We'll get him home. But can you handle things here?"

"Of course," the older woman had said, putting her hand on Leo's shoulder. "I'll call in Woody and Eku. We'll assume you won't be here until you tell us otherwise, okay?"

To Curtis, it seemed like Leo had conjured a nod in response from the dregs of what was left of his willpower, and then they were outside, and since his car was closer, they piled in.

Mackenzie had managed to get an address from Leo, and that had been the last he had spoken.

"It's just up here," Curtis said, eyeing his phone in its holder and the GPS map showing his destination at hand.

"We're almost there," Mackenzie told Leo.

He didn't respond.

"Leo?" Curtis said, glancing in his rearview. "We're going to need your help here."

Leo's red-rimmed eyes flicked up to meet his gaze in the reflection. He managed another quick nod. His hands were twisted together in his lap, clenching his fingers so tightly they were white. He looked nothing like the cool and coiffed man Curtis had met less than an hour ago.

Curtis eyed Mackenzie, but she gave him a firm nod. "He'll be okay."

Curtis hoped so, because from the looks of it, while the house they were heading into was small, clean, and might even boast what he imagined could be a beautiful and colorful garden at some point over the next few months, right now everything about the place was reminding him of the cabin where they'd found Aaron Young's body.

He turned off the car, and they got out, Mackenzie having to help Leo stand.

Curtis pulled out his glasses and slid them on, concentrating to feed a little of his own power into the lenses he'd enchanted with Mackenzie and the other Craft Night group members over the last months since he'd had to barter away his original pair. He spotted what looked like faint wards over the door, a simple glamour to make someone not truly take notice of the place, but not strong enough against a wizard to have much impact.

"All I spot is a basic 'no thank you, solicitors' glamour," Curtis said, pulling the lenses off again. Using them for too long often gave him a headache, even with this newer pair, which he'd much improved from the original, thanks to the help of Mackenzie and the others.

"Leo, do you have an invitation here?" Mackenzie said, squeezing Leo's shoulder.

He nodded and approached the front door with halting, hesitant steps. When he reached out to touch the handle, he gasped, pulled his hand back, and started openly weeping.

For a moment, Curtis thought he'd missed some magical trap with no visible aura, perhaps, but then he realized the truth and reached past Leo to touch the door himself.

No sense of residency pushed against him. The little house offered absolutely no resistance to him entering. Which could only mean one thing.

Whoever had lived there was dead.

❖

It didn't take them long. The interior of the small house, which was as tidy and pretty as the outside, had a simple floor plan. A living and dining area inside the front entranceway, a kitchen behind, and a small bathroom made up the entirety of the ground floor. The most unusual thing Curtis spotted was an easel, painting supplies, and a variety of canvases taking up most of the space where a dining room table might normally be, probably set up there to take advantage of the sunlight through the larger rear windows facing the backyard.

Apparently, Marlowe liked to paint birds. At least four of the finished canvases showed long-haired brunette women with their faces turned away from the viewer, in a variety of flowing dresses, with what looked to be crows flying around them, or landing on one shoulder, or in one case, landing on an upturned palm.

Pretty. Ethereal, even. But they made him shiver nonetheless in the silent, empty house.

They went upstairs and saw two bedrooms and another bathroom along with a small laundry room not much larger than a closet. Here the canvases turned more to floral designs, though Curtis spotted another woman-dancing-with-crows at the end of the hallway.

They found the ashes in the larger bedroom, scattered over and inside a pile of clothing crumpled to one side of the bed. A pair of glasses lay to the side of the pile, arms open.

"No," Leo said, a long, extended whine of a word, as he fell to his knees beside what was left of Marlowe. "Marlowe. No..." Tears streaked his cheeks, and he made no move to wipe them away, looking up at Mackenzie with such grief in his eyes Curtis had to catch his breath. "*Why?* She was a painter, an artist. She never hurt *anyone.*"

"Leo, I'm so sorry." Mackenzie knelt carefully beside him and put her hand on his shoulder again. "Is there anyone I can call?"

"They'll be coming," Leo said, finally wiping at his face. "They would have felt it. Like me."

"Your pack?" Mackenzie said.

Leo nodded, his breath hitching. "I don't...I don't understand. Marlowe was gentle and kind." He shuddered, and Mackenzie tugged him into a hug.

Curtis regarded the room, giving them a modicum of privacy. Despite being the main bedroom, it didn't have a lot of space. The bed was pressed to one wall between two windows, the wooden headboard painted a bright yellow, which was the color accenting much of the otherwise white room. The bedside tables were small and contained a few candles as well as lamps, and about a dozen books altogether. There were more paintings—florals, mostly—and a small vanity sat opposite a wardrobe, with what seemed to be simple makeup, a hairbrush, and...

Wait.

Curtis crossed over to the vanity and looked down. A ceramic bowl caught his attention. Shallow and glazed with a deep yellow finish, it held less than an inch or so of water in it, and there was a sort of hum he could feel more than hear coming from it, like an echo of power.

"Leo," Curtis said, touching the edge. "Is this a scrying bowl?"

Leo, who still hadn't risen but seemed to be getting himself back together, looked at him, a frown marring his forehead, like he couldn't imagine why Curtis would be asking him about the bowl when his packmate lay ashen at his feet.

"Yes," he said. "Why?"

Mackenzie glanced at Curtis, then back at Leo. "Marlowe could scry?"

"She has a gift for—*had* a gift for it," Leo said, swallowing. He finally stood up. A sad, humorless laugh escaped him, and he looked at Mackenzie. "She'd use the bowl to help her paint, especially in winter. She liked to go looking at flowers wherever they were blooming in the world. And she could see the future sometimes, too. In fact, the day you and I met, she told me I'd be meeting someone special, and to watch out for a girl with magic hidden in her dark hair." His expression shifted as he finished speaking and glanced back and forth between Curtis and Mackenzie. "Why does that upset you? You're both worried now." He tilted his head. "No, you're *frightened.*"

Curtis hadn't realized muses could read his emotional state. He filed away the fact even as he took a breath, wondering how much he should say, or if he should say anything at all.

But Mackenzie decided for him.

"This is the second person who could see the future who's been murdered in the past few days," she said. "It can't be a coincidence."

"What?" Leo said. "But *why?*" Then the reality of what Mackenzie said—and then the inherent paradox Anders had noticed back at Aaron Young's house—seemed to occur to Leo. "No. It doesn't make sense. Marlowe always knew when she was in danger. When *any* of us were in danger. She'd see it playing out in front of her, like a painting in her mind, she said."

"I don't know," Mackenzie said.

Curtis, though, was looking at the ashes and realizing something else. "Matthew," he said.

"Who's Matthew?" Leo said. He seemed more focused now, more together.

"He's a friend of ours," Mackenzie said. "He…" Her voice trailed off, and she looked at Curtis, mouth dropping open.

"He can see the future," Curtis said.

"I think you should warn him," Leo said, looking down at the ashes again, the tears returning.

"I'll try," Mackenzie said, pulling out her phone and dialing. After a short wait, she shook her head at them. "Voicemail." She paused. "Matt, it's Kenzie. I need you to call me when you get this." She bit her lip, then kept speaking. "Matt. People who have similar tattoos as you, similar skill sets as you and Aaron? Well, what happened? It's not just Aaron. Call me." She tapped the screen, ending the call.

"Marlowe!" a voice called from downstairs, panicked and worried, and Leo took a shaky breath and finally rose from his crouch.

"Come upstairs," Leo called. "It's…bad. And I have friends here." He said the latter almost as an afterthought and then moved a little in front of Curtis and Mackenzie, running a hand through his unkempt hair. Curtis saw a rippling wave from his hair on down, which restored itself to its tousled-on-purpose style. The wrinkles in his clothes fell away, too, and Curtis also noticed the redness in Leo's eyes and the tears of his sorrow were both absent.

"I'll need to introduce you," he said quietly. "Please be patient, this will be…hard."

"Friends?" the voice said, two new figures coming through the door. One was a tall, muscular woman with dark brown skin, dressed in a black leather jacket and a dark burgundy button-up shirt with grey suit slacks. Her hair was styled in a bob made up of smaller braids, which flattered her sharp chin but did nothing to soften the glare she aimed at Mackenzie and Curtis.

The second person through the door, another woman, was much smaller of frame and one of the palest white people Curtis had ever seen. Her head was completely shaved, and she had intricate floral tattoos across the skin of her skull, and full sleeves of ink—also mostly flowers—visible from wrist to shoulder in the sleeveless yellow sundress she was wearing over leggings.

This woman didn't glare, instead casting her gaze around the room until she spotted the ashes and let out a low, pained cry, her hands rising to her mouth.

"Marlowe?" she said, looking at Leo.

He shook his head.

"I'm so sorry," Mackenzie said.

"Who are you?" the first woman snapped.

"They're my friends, Cor," Leo said, in a much firmer voice than Curtis had heard him use before. "This is Mackenzie Windsor, and this is Curtis Baird." He turned back to Curtis and Mackenzie. "Kenzie, Curtis, this is Cora, and this is Mel. They're two of my packmates."

More muses, then. Curtis smiled at the two women as best as he could manage, given the situation. Also, when had he told Leo his last name? Never. Never was when. Crap.

"Hello," Mackenzie said, her voice tight. "I'm sorry to meet you like this."

"You're wizards," Cora said, still not losing the angry tone or her glare.

"That's right," Mackenzie said.

"Why are you here?" Cora crossed her arms.

"They were with me when I felt Marlowe die," Leo said. "At Artistea. They drove me here, Cora."

"And? Why are you *still* here?" Cora said. This seemed to be aimed more at Curtis, and he wasn't sure how to answer.

"Cora," Leo said, but the taller woman raised one hand to him.

"Leo, I've smelled *her* on you before, so I can understand her, even if she is a Windsor." Cora didn't so much as glance at Mackenzie, and Curtis fought off a wince on her behalf. But then Cora's dark eyes were blazing in his direction. He nearly took a step back. "But this one? His reputation alone. What were you *thinking*?"

"Wait," Curtis said, blinking. "I have a reputation?"

Cora snorted. "People die around you, Orphan. Demons die around you. Vampires die around you."

Curtis felt the words like a physical blow. Was *that* what people said about him? Was that what they thought he was? Some kind of death magnet?

"I…" He didn't know how to finish the sentence. He wanted to deny it, of course, but he recalled the demons who'd attacked him in his home shortly after he and Luc and Anders had first formed their bond. He thought of Renard and his coterie who they'd fought at one of Renard's cottages. He thought of a trail of dead demons he'd followed last February, trying to stop a murderer, and—hey, just for good measure—the murderer himself.

All dead.

Then Aaron. And now Marlowe.

Cora raised one eyebrow, challenging him.

He didn't speak.

"There's a spell we could do," Mackenzie said, breaking the tense silence. "We might be able to see what happened, but…" She took a short breath, putting a hand on Leo's forearm. "It will replay all around us. If you let us cast the spell, it might be better if you don't watch, Leo."

"There's no way we're letting you magic Marlowe's ashes without us being here." Cora shook her head.

At the word "ashes," Mel let out a tiny sob. Cora turned to her, her expression softening, and took her hand, squeezing it once before letting go.

Mackenzie looked at Curtis. "You've done a Memento Loci before, right?" she said. "We know exactly when this happened, so it would work."

He nodded, still shaken from Cora's revelation of his reputation as Mr. Death Man. Memento Loci replayed the events in an area, but unless you knew the specific time you wanted to witness, you could easily miss the mark, and the attempt would pour so much magical energy into a location a subsequent spell wouldn't be able to sense anything other than the previous magic itself.

"Do you want to lead?" he said, finding his voice again. In most things, when they worked spells together, he let Mackenzie take the lead, and he did his best to support her with extra magic, allowing her to borrow some of his strength. She'd been raised as a wizard and had much more knowledge than he did, as well as precision and finesse he was still working to achieve.

"I'm not very good at illusions," she said. Her magic tended to earth, where his aligned with air. Neither was particularly gifted with illusory magic—or, rather, Curtis hadn't been, before he'd joined his bond with Luc and Anders. Something about the demon's ability to shapeshift and his facility with hellfire seemed to empower Curtis's previously weaker fire magics, of which illusion was one.

"I can," he said, and he took a moment to touch the triskelion on his forearm, to focus his connection with Anders before calling the magic forward. It came to him like a hot wind, swirling around inside him, as eager as ever to be released.

He spoke the words to guide the magic into the spell he wanted, and heard Mackenzie repeating them in kind. Her own magic was more solid, less flighty, and complemented his efforts, grounding him and creating a structure much faster than he was used to.

He reached into the past, remembering sitting at the table with Mackenzie, remembering Leo arriving with the tea, and then holding on to the moment the teapot began to fall from his hand and moving his attention backward to the time he'd first arrived at Artistea.

That, he hoped, would be enough lead time.

He released the magic, and around the five of them and the ashes that had been a sixth, the past returned.

❖

Without Anders directly beside him, the image of Marlowe that Curtis's spell recreated remained translucent, but still clear enough to see. A lightly tanned white woman, she was no taller than Mackenzie, and to Curtis's eye, shared an aesthetic. Chunky glasses, her long dark hair pushed out of her face with a headband, and dressed comfortably in jeans and a loose-fitting black cardigan over a simple white shirt, she appeared to be in her bedroom without an immediate purpose, smoothing down her cardigan.

"I think she just came back from a run," Leo said. "Her hair is still a bit wet."

Curtis regarded the illusion, still holding on to the spell rising from his skin in waves of heat and light to create this image of Marlowe in front of him, and realized Leo was right. Her hair was still damp at the edges.

"Did she do that every day?" Mackenzie asked. Her voice held a measure of distraction, and he could detect a flow of warmth coming from her—helping him with the spell—and he wrapped it into his own efforts.

"Usually," Mel said, voice breaking on the word. "Look at her. She has no idea she's in trouble."

Curtis couldn't disagree. The illusion of Marlowe was fiddling with attaching a bracelet now, not a care in the world, and—

She paused, turning her head just slightly.

"Wait, look," Cora said.

Marlowe straightened, holding the fiber bracelet in one hand, and slowly turned toward the door, frowning. Curtis glanced that way, waiting.

No one came.

A moment later, Marlowe's whole body jerked, and she reached up with one hand to the back of her neck, then stumbled back a step, her illusion now directly over the pile of ashes, and then, with a swiftness that made Curtis gasp, her body flared with the blue-white flames of hellfire and crumbled into ashes almost between blinks, the illusory glasses falling and bouncing until they merged with the real ones sitting on the floor where they'd fallen.

Curtis let the spell dissipate, a sick feeling in the bottom of his stomach.

Mel was weeping again, but Cora seemed more angry than anything else.

"I don't understand," Cora said. "What happened to her?"

"Did something hit her in the back of the head?" Leo said.

"A needle," Curtis said.

"You saw a needle?" Cora turned to him, frowning. "How? You were in front of her."

"I didn't see it," Curtis said. "But there was another murder, a lycanthrope. He was stabbed in the neck from behind with a needle. The way she touched her neck, it made me think it might have been the same thing."

"You mean like a dart?" Leo said. "But there's no window behind where she was standing. No one came in the room. How did someone shoot her?"

Curtis shook his head. He didn't know.

"Why her?" Mel said, wiping tears from her cheeks. "Why our Marlowe?"

"The other victim," Mackenzie said, and Curtis realized they'd only explained this to Leo, not Mel or Cora. "He had a knack. He could see the future."

A silence met her words, only broken when Curtis's phone rang. He pulled it out, wincing an apology, and then froze at the name on the screen.

Malcolm Stirling was calling him.

"I think I'd better take this," he said, showing the screen to Mackenzie and then stepping out of the bright little bedroom with the ashes of a dead muse.

❖

"Hello," Curtis said, holding the phone to his ear and stepping into the waning sun of the day, wanting to hold on to as much of the warmth as he could while talking to the head of the Stirling Family, who was— in most ways—the head of the Families as a whole.

"Mr. Baird," Malcolm Stirling said, in his dry, direct way. "Malcolm Stirling. Do you have a moment?" The question was perfunctory at best, intimating in no uncertain terms that Curtis should either have that moment or drop everything to make that moment happen with haste.

God, but he hated this man.

"I can talk," Curtis said. "What's on your mind?" He imagined he knew full well. Matthew's disappearance had to be the reason he was calling. Malcolm Stirling barely tolerated Curtis, and even then only because the rules of the Accords meant he had no choice but to do so, given the bond Curtis had made with Luc and Anders *technically* counted as a coven, thanks to the Law of Three.

"I believe you've met my great-grandson, Matthew?" Stirling's voice never lost its polite edge, but the words had an added weight of something else this time. Was he gloating? Letting Curtis know he was aware of how often Curtis and Matthew had not only spoken, but spent time together working magic?

No. Curtis wouldn't assume anything. He had no idea how much Malcolm Stirling knew about how often he and Matthew saw each other, not to mention meeting up with Mackenzie and the others at their Craft Night discussions to learn about magic or having gotten all their help to enchant the new pair of glasses for himself. And he wasn't about to volunteer.

If this was a bluff or a fishing expedition on Malcolm Stirling's part, there was absolutely no need to make it a success.

"We've met, yes," Curtis said.

The response earned a stony silence, and Curtis forced himself to let it play out rather than filling it.

"I thought so," Stirling said, and Curtis closed his eyes to avoid growling at the man. *Get to the freaking point, you manipulative fossil.* "I'm afraid Matthew is missing. No one has heard from him in a couple of days, and I would very much like to find him. We're all worried, as you can imagine."

"Yes," Curtis said, though it definitely took imagination to picture Malcolm Stirling actively emotional about the great-grandson he treated as little more than a useful prop and a tool to see the future.

"If you hear from him or have any idea where he might be, it is paramount you let me know."

To Curtis's surprise, this time Malcolm Stirling *did* sound emotional, a strain in his voice adding an edge to the usually cultured and careful elocution. Could Malcolm Stirling actually *care* his great-grandson was missing? Matthew had no love for the old man, and Curtis had assumed the feeling was mutual, after having met Malcolm once or twice and finding him disturbingly reminiscent of any number of movie villains obsessed only with holding on to their own power, like a Tarkin or a Snow.

Heck, Malcolm Stirling could cosplay either of them and wouldn't even have to stretch his wardrobe much.

"Mr. Baird?" Stirling prompted, snapping Curtis out of his thoughts. He needed to reply and he needed to reply the right way, because Stirling wouldn't accept anything else.

"If I hear from him," Curtis said, "I'll let him know you're worried." He took a moment to consider, but decided it was worth making an attempt to fish for some information himself. "I assume you've tried scrying for him?"

"Indeed." Stirling's reply was curt. "Unfortunately, we have not succeeded on that front."

Not succeeded. Curtis wondered if that was old-rich-stuffy-dude for "someone lost a hand to frostbite" or not.

"I'll keep an eye out," Curtis said.

"Do." Stirling hung up on him.

Curtis exhaled. The door opened behind him, and he turned, seeing Mackenzie step out.

"How are they?" he said.

"Confused. Angry. A mess." She zipped up her jacket, shivering. "More of their pack have checked in, and Leo thinks you should maybe be gone before they all get here." She winced with apology.

"Did you know I was Mr. Death Man?" Curtis said. "I didn't know I was Mr. Death Man."

"You're not." Mackenzie shook her head. "But I don't think this is the right time to break their assumptions. Do I want to know what Malcolm Stirling wanted?"

"Malcolm Stirling called to tell me Matt was missing, and to ask if I knew where he was." Curtis raised his eyebrows. "And this will sound impossible, but he actually almost sounded like a human being with actual real feelings who cared."

"That's…" Mackenzie shook her head. "I don't even know what to say about that. Or the Memento Loci. I wish there'd been *something* useful."

"Me, too," Curtis said. He took a breath. "She just…died." He shivered. "No more paintings."

"You saw that, too?" Mackenzie said. "The murders?"

Curtis frowned. "What?"

"The woman in the paintings, with the birds—it was Marlowe. And she was surrounded by murders of crows." Mackenzie took a deep breath. "She could see the future, and Leo said she used her gift to paint…" She lifted one shoulder. "Too bad she didn't paint her murderer for us."

Curtis recalled how in the paintings, the woman was always turned away. And she'd been stabbed in the back of the neck. "She didn't see the murderer," he said.

"Neither did we," Mackenzie said.

A drop of rain hit Curtis on the forehead, and he glanced up, noting the clouds rolling in. Looked like they'd be in for another rainy evening. "Can I drive you back?"

"I'm going to stay here with Leo," Mackenzie said, stepping back under the door as the rain picked up. "We'll order a ride back to Artistea for my car later. Call me if you hear anything, will you?"

"Of course."

ELEVEN

Anders didn't like many people, if he was being honest. There were a lot he tolerated if he had to, and even more it was sometimes fun to fuck with (or just fuck), but the list of people who could call him and get him to show was the shortest list yet.

David Rimmer wasn't even on that list. Not really. Maybe by proxy, what with how Curtis seemed to like him so much. He and David Rimmer definitely didn't see eye to eye on what passed for justice, or doing what was necessary, or...anything really. Other than wanting Curtis to be happy.

And it bugged the ever loving shit out of Anders how much David seemed to care about that, too.

He didn't let any of his thoughts show on his face, though, as he opened the door to the café, shaking off the worst of the rain from his jacket and glancing around for David's blond hair.

When he caught sight of him and realized he shared a booth with Ethan and Tyson, Anders had to stifle a groan. Three-for-one on people Curtis wanted him to be nice to?

Whatever this was, it was going to be tedious.

He stopped long enough to get a black coffee. The guy behind the counter kind of fumbled his way through getting it as fast as possible for him, but he didn't say a word, which was nice and probably meant he'd snarled at the kid before. It was hard to keep track. But until he snarled at them, they always asked him stupid questions like, "What kind of roast do you want?" or "Do you need room for dairy?"

Coffee in hand, he had no excuses left. He sat down in the booth beside Tyson and gave David his best impression of someone who was glad to see him.

"So," Anders said. "Who's dead?"

David frowned. "What?"

"You called me. Who's dead?"

David shook his head. "That's not why I called."

"Oh." That was surprising. He took a swallow of his coffee. "That's good, then."

"There are furies in Ottawa," David said.

Furies. Wrath demons. In Ottawa. Anders put his mug down. "And there it is." He eyed Tyson. "This your fault?"

"Me? They don't give a shit about me." Tyson laughed. It wasn't a pleasant laugh. It was sort of bitter and partly a snort, and maybe Anders would have felt bad for him if Tyson hadn't nearly gotten Anders and Luc and Curtis all killed that one time.

Okay, probably not even if he hadn't.

Tyson was a fury, too. Demons who could feed on wrath and anger, furies were almost always women, and Anders had heard they weren't generally receptive to the rare men born among their number. Not that he'd met many. In fact, Tyson had been the sum total of all the furies he'd ever spoken with.

"And?" Anders waited for someone to tell him why he should give a shit.

"Where furies go, things get bad," David said.

Oh. He supposed it made sense, what with them being creatures who fed on wrath. Anders frowned. "You mean they're here to piss people off?" Anders, as an incubus, could fan the flames of lust in people who were wise enough to recognize how hot he was, and he knew first-hand that a fury could do a similar thing, only with someone's temper instead.

"No, not like that," Tyson said, with a patronizing tone Anders didn't like one bit. "Furies don't go places to cause trouble, though they can, I guess, if they want to. Most likely, it's the other way around."

Anders stared at him until he looked away. "Explain," he said.

"We furies feed a lot like you do," Tyson said, swallowing and looking back up again. "Only with wrath. Sure, I can draw out anger easy enough as long as there's some there to start with, but it's not the same."

Anders started to get it. He could use his allure—and he did—to find willing partners and nudge the evening along to a good place, but he didn't feed as well on lust he'd willed into being. It was like trying to breathe in oxygen from his own exhalation: It could be done, but it wasn't as good, and it couldn't last forever. The lust he fed on had to come from whichever man—or men—he was with at the time, and the more of it that had been there before he started, the better. He could definitely make what they were already feeling more *insistent*, but if there wasn't an initial spark there to begin with, it wouldn't be satisfying.

So if Tyson was saying furies were the same, they could use their influence to get people mad, but people had to already be mad for them to feed well.

And they could make mad into something worse.

He frowned again. "So they go around hoping to find, what? Angry people?" He supposed it was no different than stepping into a bar or loading up a hook-up app in theory, but where did angry people gather on a regular basis? Homeowners associations?

"Kind of," Tyson said. "Sometimes you just…want to go."

"What do you mean?" Anders didn't get it. Unless… "Are you saying they're here because they know something is going down?" Anders said. "Something that's going to, what, piss off a lot of people?" That wasn't good. He turned to David. "Do we know what they know?"

David eyed Tyson for a second. Tyson shook his head, his lips drawn into a thin line. "They might not know themselves."

"What?"

"It's sort of like feeling a storm," Tyson said. "Even when on the horizon everything looks clear, but you can tell something is building. Like air pressure, maybe."

Anders took another swallow of his coffee, needing a second. What was the word Curtis used to describe the dead coywolf? "It's like being prescient, then."

Ethan frowned, but David and Tyson both nodded at him.

"That's a good word for it, yes," David said.

"So we've got a bunch of furies in town because something's about to hit the fan. But you think they don't even know what the something is?"

"It's possible." Tyson shrugged. "I think I can feel something, too. There's this anger in the city, but it's not regular people—or not just regular people. It's something else."

"So you think the furies are here because some group of *us* is pissed off?" Anders couldn't imagine a single scenario where wizards or vampires or demons or any of the other non-vanilla human types getting in touch with their furious side would be a good thing.

"Or going to be," Tyson said, his grey-blue eyes focusing

somewhere between them, rather than meeting Anders's gaze. "It might not be now, it might be soon."

The future. That kept popping up, didn't it? One dead prescient, another on the run, and now this…

The Stirling kid. The future-seer who'd run away from the dead coywolf. Why did his gut say this had something to do with him?

"You think this has anything to do with the Families?" Anders said, turning his attention back to David.

"Maybe," David said, but he lifted one shoulder, like "maybe" was pushing it. "I'm no expert, but in my experience, wizards prefer to bind or control us demons rather than calling us in. It doesn't track to me."

"Right." Anders knew David used to be under the thumb of the Families, but he'd wiggled free when he joined up with Ethan and Tyson. He should probably trust David's gut on this one. But some part of Anders insisted he consider David wasn't in the loop with the Families any more. The moment he'd gotten free of them, he'd become someone they wouldn't trust the way they used to.

"I wanted you to know there were furies in town, for whatever it might mean," David said. "Pass it along to Curtis," he said. "And Luc, of course."

That last bit seemed like an afterthought. Anders struggled not to bristle. "I will. And if you hear anything else, let me know."

"You, too," David said.

Anders eyed Tyson. "Where are they?"

He blinked. "The furies?"

"Yeah."

"Mostly in the Market. They rode in yesterday. It was…" He swallowed. "Well. I certainly felt it."

"Rode?"

"Motorcycles," David said. "They have a club."

Furies on motorcycles. Fantastic.

"How much notice do you get?" Anders turned back to Tyson.

"Notice of what?"

"Of the shit hitting the fan. This 'something pissed off is going to happen' thing. How long before the fucking rage storm you think is rolling in?" Anders leaned forward. "Are we talking days or weeks or what?"

"Oh," Tyson said. He frowned into the distance between them, like he could see something in the air Anders couldn't. "I…I don't know. I mean, it's different now, now we're..." He gestured to Ethan and David.

Right. Tyson had been flying solo, and basically enslaved to a fucking warlock vampire through one of those bindings David had mentioned, and hadn't had a pack of his own until he'd hooked up with Ethan and David. If a fury flying solo was anything like what Anders had experienced as an incubus without a pack, it meant what gifts Tyson had before he'd joined with them wouldn't have been operating anywhere near peak.

"Okay," Anders said. "If that changes? You tell David. And me. Immediately."

Tyson frowned—Anders imagined he didn't like taking an order from him, but fuck his feelings—but he grudgingly nodded. Good enough.

"Well," Anders said. "This has been..." He shrugged, then picked up his mug. "A thing that happened."

"I think it's going to be bad," Tyson said. Ethan reached across the table and squeezed his shoulder.

Anders looked at David. David met his gaze, one eyebrow rising with heavy meaning. He'd seen it, too. Ethan and Tyson barely tolerated each other most of the time. If Ethan was *comforting* Tyson...

Well, fuck.

TWELVE

"Silver."

It took Luc a moment to connect the voice on his phone, which had come from a private number that didn't show an identity, with an individual. Anger had hardened the usually softer tones of Taryne Rhedey, the lycanthrope druid.

There was, upon reflection, only one thing to which she could be referring.

"Aaron was killed with silver?" Luc said, settling back into his chair.

"Colloidal silver," Taryne said. "Mixed with a heavy dose of what I believe might have been phencyclidine, delivered through a forced injection to the back of the neck. At a guess, I'd say whoever killed Aaron used an epinephrine injector."

"I'm afraid I don't know what colloidal silver or phencyclidine are, but the delivery method makes this sound very much like a targeted attack," Luc said.

"Yes." Taryne's anger hardened her voice. "Colloidal silver is a liquid with particulates of silver, touted to be a health aid by woo-woo homeopaths and snake oil salesmen, and can cause long-term health issues in regular humans. But for a lycanthrope with canine blood, it suppresses the wolf and all but destroys the healing response until its metabolized out of the system. Combined with the dose of tranquillizer, it stopped Aaron's heart. He would have lost consciousness quickly and then died soon after."

Luc took in the information, considering. "How common knowledge is colloidal silver's effect on werewolves?" He'd certainly never encountered the knowledge, but that didn't mean much. He'd spent a lot of his time as a vampire alone, limiting himself to those nights of the full moon when the other coteries, covens, and packs were busy renewing their bonds.

Which hadn't translated to much in the way of an education.

Taryne let out a tiny snort of amusement. "I'd say most anyone likely knows the effect of silver on a wolf. It's folklore, and it's accurate, to a degree. But the liquid? It's hard to say. I certainly wouldn't put it past the former duke to have made it a point to learn of anything with efficacy against my kind. The Families would also know, and for similar reasons."

His thought so as well—especially the latter. It was the sort of specific knowledge the Families gathered to maintain the upper hand. Though one thing did surprise him, still.

"If the delivery was, as you say, from an injection device, would that not mean Aaron's killer would have to have been directly behind him?"

"That's right."

"Forgive me, Miss Rhedey—"

"Doctor."

"Of course. I apologize." Damn. Not the first time he'd done that, and it annoyed him he'd allowed the slip again. "Forgive me, Dr. Rhedey, but it's my understanding lycanthropes have similar senses to my own, if not better in the case of scent." Was he wrong? He didn't think so, but if he was correct, then something didn't add up.

"That's right," Taryne said, then seemed to realize where he was going with this. "So who would Aaron allow to get so close to him?"

"Exactly," Luc said. Unfortunately, the only person he could immediately think of would not bode well for Curtis's mood, nor for overall peace in the city.

"Matthew Stirling was with him at the time of his death," Taryne said, proving once again as sharp as he knew her to be. "And Aaron knew and trusted him."

"Yes," Luc said. He forced himself to sound skeptical on Curtis's behalf, but the truth was, to his mind, Matthew Stirling was more and more the suspect of choice. Matthew Stirling had magic. Magic was a most unpredictable power, and not always obvious in its use. Matthew Stirling was also prescient, and who better to murder another individual who could see the future than someone else with more skill utilizing the same gift?

"It would mean both Jace and I have seriously misjudged him," Taryne said, sounding not quite convinced herself.

"How well did you know him?" Luc said. His own interactions with Matthew Stirling were limited, but his experiences hadn't given him any reason to assume the worst.

"We met perhaps a half dozen times?" Taryne's sigh was one of frustration. "He seemed to be genuinely helping Aaron with his control, but..." She made another noise of annoyance. "The truth is, I don't *want* to believe it, but I also can't see another avenue to explore just yet."

"It is perhaps telling the murder weapon was *not* magic," Luc said. "Matthew Stirling is an accomplished wizard."

"Even flicks have been known to carry guns," Taryne said, surprising Luc by using the more pejorative term for those who wielded magic. "And for all we know, it could have been an enchanted needle of some kind."

"I suppose that's true." With a cool jolt, Luc remembered that last year, Curtis and his wizard friends had found just such an item—an enchanted syringe fashioned of a burnished, bronze-colored metal. To the best of his knowledge, the item had been locked in a safe in Curtis's bedroom ever since. Since enchanted items could not be destroyed, it was safer to have it out of anyone's grasp, especially given anyone with even the smallest gift of magic could wield the full power of a truly enchanted item.

Including a coywolf like Aaron himself, with his magical knack for seeing the future.

Should he tell Taryne about the syringe? No. First he would learn if the syringe had been disturbed. If it hadn't, then there was no reason to even mention it.

"Well. We'll keep investigating. I wanted to let you know what I found and to thank you for calling me," Taryne said. "I hope I can count on you to keep me up to date on any new information you might find yourself?" She paused. "Assuming you intend to keep looking for the killer?"

The first question sent an unexpected wave of something not unlike guilt for holding back the information about the syringe, but it was the second question that truly gave him pause. In truth, were it up to him, Luc wasn't sure he *would* keep investigating. A dead coywolf was not truly his concern, and the farther they kept away from it, the less likely he, Anders, or Curtis were to get caught in any fallout.

But with Matthew Stirling missing—not to mention being everyone but Curtis's prime suspect—he knew full well Curtis would not let this go, and as such...

"I intend to keep looking," he said. "And I will keep you informed of any relevancies."

Now the pause came from the other end of the phone, and he wondered if Rhedey had heard what he hadn't come out and said. "I appreciate that," Taryne said. "I know our people tend to stay out of each other's way for the most part, Mr. Lanteigne, but were it up to me, this sort of…cooperation…would not be so rare."

Luc smiled. "I believe we are on the same page, Doctor."

"Good night, then," she said, and she hung up.

Luc took a moment, listening to the rain strike his office window and considering the time. Neither Curtis nor Anders had been home when he'd woken an hour before sunset, though they'd both left him messages—Curtis telling him he'd headed out for his meeting with David Rimmer, and Anders looking for the sorcerer he knew—and he hadn't heard from either of them since, but no doubt they'd call or text when they had a moment.

Luc tapped the screen of his phone back to his contacts and considered calling Curtis directly to update him about the colloidal silver injection. Instead, his finger drifted to Denis's name, his curiosity getting the best of him.

He answered on the second ring.

"*Duc?*" Denis's calm carried a hint of curiosity.

"Denis," Luc said. "Do you have time to speak?"

"I do," Denis said. "Your office?"

Luc rubbed his chin, hiding his amusement. None of the coterie heads seemed to enjoy speaking on the phone. He often wondered if it was a dislike of the technology or of not being as capable of reading those they were speaking with, given only tone of voice to work with. "If you'd like," Luc said.

"I'll be there in forty minutes."

❖

"Colloidal silver." Denis nodded slowly. "I'm aware of it, yes. I believe it can be used to even the odds in a fight with a werewolf, though I've never had the need or opportunity to do so." He tilted his head. "Is this about the dead coywolf?"

"It is," Luc said.

The two of them were seated, and Luc had chosen to join Denis on the other side of his desk rather than stay behind it. The positioning being more cordial than formal would, he hoped, afford Denis a bit more comfort that this was in no way an interrogation.

"My understanding is enough can even force them back to their human form," Denis said, lifting his wine glass and taking a sip. "But again, I've never seen such a thing unfold."

"Did Renard have any plans for the werewolves?" Luc said.

Denis lowered his glass. "Not that I'm aware of," he said, and he paused, considering. "Though I suppose we know the weapon he intended to use was effective on them, given how Wheeler used it."

"True," Luc said. Before his death, Renard had procured a blade capable of transferring the abilities of supernatural creatures through a kind of dark necromancy Luc didn't entirely understand. In the hands of another wielder of magic, the blade of Marysas had stolen the lycanthropic form of a werewolf and bonded it to the wizard in question. Wheeler had become a *loup garou*, murdering others and attempting to forcibly take leadership of the Mitchell Family. "But we still believe Renard intended to use the blade on Tyson, to gain access to his demonic power."

"That's the picture the paper trail paints," Denis said. "First he learned how to bind a demon, then he tracked down Tyson and bound him. Then he researched methods of power transfer, learned about the blade, and spent no small fortune to have it brought to Ottawa." Denis paused. "The notations of which lycanthropes had magical ability, though…"

"Including listing Aaron Young as *insufficient*," Luc said.

"Yes, I was thinking about that," Denis said. "Do you think it could relate to his desire to find unusual graces? He turned so many vampires, but once he learned of their abilities, if they had nothing of note to offer, they were cast aside."

"I hadn't thought of it, but I see what you mean," Luc said.

"It strikes me that Renard was seeking something. Some specific ability or grace, perhaps." Denis lifted one hand. "And also arming himself with a way to take that ability for himself once he found it."

"The knife," Luc said. It made sense. And it reminded him again of the other piece of necromancy he'd encountered. "Did his research—or yours—ever uncover anything about an enchanted syringe?"

Denis's eyes flicked to the side, and a small line marred the skin between his eyebrows. "I don't believe so, but I'd have to check again."

"When you have time," Luc said. "I can follow up on that myself. Such an object was found in the possession of one of the Mitchells, but we have it locked down now."

"The coywolf was killed with an injection of silver, then?" Denis said.

"Yes." Luc affected a sigh. "To be honest, Denis, I am not sure this has anything to do with the former *Duc* at all, but I cannot quite shake the feeling his hands touched this in some way."

"Renard hated the Families," Denis said. "He wanted them deposed from their position at the top of the Accords, and, of course, to place himself there in their stead." He scoffed. "Everything he did was to that end. If killing a coywolf would have gotten him even a single step closer to his goal, he would have done it."

"I'm meeting with Lavoie tonight. It's possible she will know more."

"Likely," Denis said. "If there's anything she mentions I might be of help with, don't hesitate to call."

"Thank you," Luc said, realizing he'd taken more of Denis's time than he'd intended when he saw the hour. "I'll leave you to your evening."

Denis shook his head, smiling just enough to show a hint of fang. "I can almost forget you're my *Duc* sometimes, you know." He quirked a single eyebrow. "You're so *polite*." He held out a hand.

Luc shook it. "I see no reason to make any of our lives more complicated—or difficult—than necessary."

Denis paused, mid-grasp. He seemed to hesitate. "In that case, may I offer some advice?"

"Please," Luc said, surprised at the offer.

"You seem intent on building relationships with the other powers of the city," Denis said. "The werewolves and demons especially. I'm sure you already know Renard did a lot of damage in that regard. The demons will not forget what he did to one of their kind, even if they don't care about the individual fury Renard bound. There was no love lost between Renard's coterie and the werewolves, either, especially those with business in the Market. And while the Families might take any help you might give them, I wouldn't expect much in the way of gratitude, nor reciprocation."

"I don't doubt you are correct. Perhaps I should endeavor to keep my expectations low," Luc said.

Denis offered a small nod and then left the office.

Once the door closed, Luc checked his watch. He needed to get moving himself. Lavoie—and the Lady Markham—would be expecting him soon. He'd have to fill in Curtis and Anders when he got home.

THIRTEEN

"F or as long as you mean me no harm, you are welcome in my home for this evening, Luc Levesque," Catharine said, stepping back from the front door of her elegant home enough for him to pass. He noted she'd used his birth name—the name he used among the vampires as their *Duc*—not the name he'd been using for the past few decades.

He crossed the threshold, Catharine's residency parting for him and pulling back but hovering on the edge of his senses like a cold draft inching along the corners of a room. If he moved against her, the protection would return in an instant, but he didn't believe he would need to.

Or, at least, he hoped not.

"I have summoned Lavoie," Catharine said. "She is in the back parlor."

"Thank you," Luc said, walking down the hall of the home he'd only been in once before. He noticed movement from the corner of his eye as he passed the study where he and Catharine had spoken on his previous visit, and saw Anna, one of Catharine's coterie, pouring herself a glass of something from a decanter.

She glanced up at him, her palest of blue eyes as striking as ever.

Catharine had once admitted to Luc that Anna had a grace for knowing where interesting things would occur, a foresight Catharine no doubt used to maneuver herself into favorable positions over the centuries.

He wondered if it boded well for the conversation he was about to have with Lavoie that Anna was here.

The parlor at the rear of the Lady Markham's home was as tidy and elegant as the rest of it, with comfort balanced among the antiques. To either side of the fireplace, paired chairs were arranged for intimate conversation, one with a backgammon board between, the other with a green, felted surface he believed might be suited for cards. Lavoie sat there, waiting for him.

At first glance, Lavoie showed no sign of being the same woman Luc had first met trapped in a mystical prison beneath a small island. There she had been only a voice in the dark, blurred from burns and holding on to her mind with a tenuous grip. Only able to feed owing to her grace to bond with felines, subsisting on what blood they could spare for her, Lavoie had existed on the edges between collapse into despair, unbridled fury at Renard, and a single, shining shred of hope that the ever-weakening bars of her cell would, in time, give away completely.

Here and now, Lavoie rose from her chair the moment he entered the parlor, her smile warm and inviting, and she bowed to him deep enough to show true respect, without a trace of fear or furtiveness.

No, this Lavoie was nothing like the one he'd first met. This Lavoie was whole.

As he bowed in return, he couldn't help but notice the lack of her veritable crowd of cats. Lavoie's accompaniment appeared to be a single feline, a slender and sleek black cat with one white paw. Unlike her, it remained seated on the second chair at the card table, not deigning to show the slightest notice of his arrival.

"My duke," she said. Her accent was a familiar one to Luc, of a French he remembered spoken by nearly everyone around him, but she spoke in English.

"It is good to see you," he said, surprised to find he meant it. So many had been damaged and left to the wayside by Renard—Lavoie and Tyson chief among them—that seeing her vibrant and animated like this seemed the first good omen he'd encountered in days.

"Thank you," she said, with a small tilt of her head. She'd put her long chestnut hair up in a simple knot, and her white blouse and tan skirt seemed designed more for comfort than elegance, though around her neck she wore the beautiful antique cameo with the profile of a cat he'd seen her wear before. "Lady Markham said you wished to speak with me."

He nodded. "I did, and I'm afraid the topic is an unpleasant one."

"Renard," Lavoie said, and the word was heavy with disgust. The cat issued a low growl as well. Lavoie scooped it off the second chair to hold it, almost unconsciously.

"Indeed," Luc said, gesturing to the seats for them to sit. "I was hoping you could tell me more about Renard's original plans, and if you know of any enchanted objects he might have desired?"

Lavoie's gaze drifted to the middle of nowhere while she stroked the cat's back, as though she seemed to need a moment to find a place to begin. Luc understood the sensation—when he turned his mind to memories found many decades in the past, it sometimes felt like a physical effort just to get to them.

"I believe I told you once how he'd tried to destroy the Families," Lavoie said. "In 1916."

Luc's eyes flicked up. "The fire." Lavoie had indeed mentioned the previous year how she and the rest of Renard's coven of warlocks had been caught in the great fire in 1916, when the parliament buildings had been destroyed, with only the library spared by its large reinforced steel doors and a healthy dose of luck, and how Renard had been trying to get something from the library itself.

"Yes," Lavoie said. "After the fire, he was furious he hadn't gotten what he wanted from the library. He'd been so close—those were his words. 'I was so close.' That's what he said when I finally dragged myself to him, burned and..." She shook her head, as though dislodging the memory were a physical act. "Well. You recall my previous state. He'd bound us—all his former coven—and I had no choice but to return to him, even though I hated him for leaving me for dead when he'd misted away. I remember realizing just how much he hadn't cared at all, about the rest of us, or the ones we'd lost. And it was all right there, in what he said when he saw I'd survived."

Luc frowned, and Lavoie stroked the cat.

"Not 'we were close,'" she said. "Only 'I was close.' Always 'I' with Renard."

"Ah, of course," Luc said, understanding.

"It wasn't a small setback," Lavoie said. "Whatever he'd intended, this derailed all of it. And he was furious. He'd had to rely on all of us to create even half the kind of magic we'd had when we were still mortal. As warlocks, the magic was less." She eyed him, and he nodded. He'd known that already—wizards who were turned into vampires usually lost all their magical ability, but there were ways to carry some of it beyond the change, which Renard had ensured was the case with his former coven-turned-coterie. "And with so many of his warlocks dead after the fire, he didn't think he had enough remaining for his plan."

"I assume he never told you exactly what the plan was?" Luc said, knowing enough of Renard to be certain, but still needing to confirm.

"No, only he would depose the Families," Lavoie said. "Perhaps destroy them. He certainly intimated he intended them to feel what it was like to lose what they'd had, like what the French covens of the city had suffered here under the British, and the Families."

"As he had," Luc said.

Lavoie rubbed a finger under the cat's chin. "I could never understand that about him," she said. "I was no one before my magic came to me. At best I could have hoped to marry better than my poor start, and have better bread at every meal." Lavoie shook her head. "But after my magic came, the Families allowed me—us—to be a coven." She paused, looking at Luc with wonder in her eyes. "Everything I'd known about the world was wrong, and with the others in our coven, I did the most amazing things. I had a home, and those other Orphans were a family. It was better than I ever could have imagined for myself, even with the Families—the Stirlings, specifically—having so much more than us and ruling over us as an Orphan coven."

"And Renard chafed against that imbalance?"

Lavoie snorted. "He railed against it. He was furious. He'd been of a much higher birth than the rest of us, wealthy, inherited, but found himself on the bottom rung of the supernatural world by virtue of being both an Orphan and French. And he *hated* it." She sighed. "And he devoted himself to finding a way to have more power."

"Which led to becoming a warlock?"

She nodded. "Eventually. He waited until after Claudie died— she was the first of our Orphan coven to pass. When I look back now, I know he used our grief and loss against us. Her death was a long, painful one. Her lungs." She took a moment, then met his gaze again. "I don't know where he found the vampire who turned him, but the first thing Renard had us do after he became a warlock was to destroy her."

"So none would have sway over him," Luc said. A vampire's sire had an edge of dominance over any of its progeny.

Lavoie smiled, though it held no mirth. "But of course, that left only *him* to turn us, which…"

"Put you further under his control."

She stroked the cat again. "We all used the rituals he'd uncovered to hold on to as much of our magic as possible, though he'd also ensured the same rituals would bind us even more to him. When we presented ourselves to the duke who'd ruled before Renard, we were stronger. The Families couldn't touch us, for we were no longer of their kind."

"And Renard became the new *Duc*," Luc said.

"Yes," Lavoie said. "That's when he threw himself into the archives. Wanted to learn everything he could, and eventually he learned something he believed would allow him to have his revenge on the Families." She never stopped stroking the cat, and it rolled onto its back to give her access to its stomach. "You need to understand, the rest of us, his coterie? We could barely *disagree* with him, let alone argue or resist. His will was incredible. He had more freedom and power than ever, but all he cared about was gathering more."

"I recall," Luc said.

"I believe he was going to try again," Lavoie said. "When the fire happened in 1916, he was furious, but I recall...or I think I recall..." Her voice drifted off, and her hand stilled until the cat wrapped both front paws around her wrist and tugged at her hand, which made her smile and come back to the present. She resumed her attention to the feline and then looked at Luc directly. "It was after I was burned, when he first put me in the cell as a lesson to those around him not to fail. He stood there, and he told me he'd simply get what he needed and wait for the next time to try again." Her light brown eyes never moved from his gaze. "I remember him saying now he was a vampire, he could do that. *Wait for the next time.*"

Luc took in her words, then leaned forward slightly in his chair. "You believe he'd been working since 1916 on this plan of his? For an opportunity that would arrive, one he could take?" He heard the wonder in his own voice. "Over a *century* to have his revenge?"

"Yes, but I don't think he had a choice," Lavoie said. "If it was something he could have done whenever he wanted to, he'd have done it. Renard would never have waited to hurt the Families, not if he had the opportunity to act."

Luc had to agree.

"But he never told us his plan. I only know he wanted to get into the library for something. A book, I believe. And after he discarded—" She swallowed. "After he was through with those of us who'd survived the fire, we weren't part of his plan any more. Our power wasn't how he intended to succeed."

"So then his attention turned to enchanted items of power," Luc said. "After his first attempt failed."

"I believe so," Lavoie said, still stroking the cat. "I don't recall him wanting or needing anything more than whatever was in the library the night of the fire."

"Binding Tyson's demonic power to him must have been part of his second attempt," Luc said. "And creating more vampires, looking for rare and unique graces..." He thought about the necromantic blade Renard had brought into the city, the one a power-hungry killer had used to steal the abilities of demon and werewolf alike. "And other ways of gaining power."

"Yes," Lavoie said.

"Thank you," Luc said, rising. "You've been a great help."

"Have I?" Lavoie's soft smile spoke of her disbelief, but she rose, depositing the cat on the chair, where it sat and blinked green eyes up at him in what might have been rebuke for the interruption of its pampering. "I feel like I've told you vagaries and theories and things you already knew."

"No," Luc said. "No, I believe you've done more than that." He regarded her. "Renard was threatened by me. When he learned of me—of my triad—he decided almost immediately to destroy us. He came at us with everything he had. He tried to destroy us in our home, tried to break our triad. We were a threat he refused to ignore."

Lavoie's head tilted, then her eyes widened in understanding. "Vampire, demon, and wizard."

"Blood, soul, and magic," Luc said. "Thanks to my triad, we all wield power touched by vampire graces, demonic gifts, *and* coven magic. We're different. Renard was trying to gather power much like what we already have."

Whatever Renard's plan had been, Luc had wondered for months now if it might be possible he, Anders, and Curtis could enact it. Thanks to Lavoie, Luc was quite certain he had more of the answer.

Somehow, unless he was wildly mistaken, it might very well be his triad had the power to destroy the Families.

FOURTEEN

A nders pulled his SUV into a parking spot on York, not wanting to bother to play parking roulette to find something closer to the Market, grimacing when the wet, cold April wind hit his face. He should have brought the "big damn hero" knitted hat Curtis had given him

Once he was on foot and in motion, he wondered if he was chasing his own tail. If Tyson was right, even if the furies did feel something bad about to happen, they'd probably not be able to give him more specifics than that.

Not helpful.

He shoved his fists into the pockets of his jacket and trudged on anyway. Doing something was better than sitting at home while Luc and Curtis were out there doing their thing. Besides, there were a couple of hook-up spots close enough he could swing by after.

Assuming he could even find the damn furies in the first place.

Once he'd crossed King Edward and gotten to the Market proper, however, he found he didn't have to worry on that front. At least half the parking spots on both sides of the road were taken by motorcycles, and even if he hadn't been looking for them, there'd be no way he'd have not noticed the group of women standing on the sidewalk in front of the bikes.

"Huh," he said to himself, waiting for the light to change and taking in the sight of them.

For the most part, they wore riding gear, the vast majority of them in black, though one woman on a shiny green trike wore a jacket that matched, and given the way the other women were standing around her while she sat on the three-wheeler, he got the distinct impression of someone in charge.

Okay then.

The light changed. Crossing the street, he started to be able to make out facial features on the women not wearing their helmets, but he didn't see a particular pattern to their body types or size or even height. He'd assumed furies would look like bodybuilding Valkyries or something, but in reality, some of these women looked like they'd be at home in a courtroom, or picking up snotty-nosed kids from daycare, or running a bakery or some other shit like that. One or two of them were what he'd imagined. He spotted one tall, broad-shouldered woman with short, dirty-blond hair in particular take notice of him before the others, but for the most part the only thing they seemed to have in common was their leathers, the back of their jackets all having some variation on the same quartet of words—*Bold Streets Biker Club*—and what looked to be a flaming axe design of some kind.

The one who'd spotted him said something he didn't catch, even with his predator hearing, and now most of the group was looking his way.

Anders did his best to slow his approach, pulling his hands from his pockets to look as nonthreatening as he could, and turned his attention to the woman on the trike.

Curvy, with a head of dark blond curls, and sharp blue-grey eyes that seemed amused at his approach, she leaned one arm across the handlebars of her trike and raised one eyebrow in question when he got close enough. "You the welcome wagon? Here to tell us to enjoy Ottawa?" She had the faintest lilt in her voice, like she was from the American South or something.

The dirty-blond one took a single step to put herself between the woman on the trike and Anders, and Anders took the hint and stopped walking where he was.

"No," he said, shaking his head. "You don't need my permission to go wherever the fuck you want to go."

That made the woman on the trike laugh, and she leaned back in the seat. "Then who are you?"

"Anders," he said, and deciding it was worth some of the effort Luc always suggested he make, he held out one hand, giving the dirty-blond a "may I?" glance before she pulled back just enough to let him take one more step and offer the handshake to the woman on the trike.

She took it. "Aurora," she said. "These are my ladies." Her head tilted in question. "I'm guessing you're *that* Anders?"

"Depends on what you mean," Anders said, though he was pretty sure she'd done her homework. Her gaze had a way of pinning a guy down, and she didn't strike him as the sort to lead "her ladies" somewhere before knowing everything she could about where they were going.

Her lips turned up in another amused smirk. "You, a vampire, and a wizard offed the last duke of the city, I'm told. A warlock no less. And saved one of our kind in the process, even?"

"Ah," he said, nodding. He wondered if he should point out that at the time they were mostly saving their own skin, and while they had thought they were also trying to free Tyson from the former duke, at the time they'd had no idea he was a fury. They'd thought he was a sorcerer. Better not. Her assumptions made him look better. "Yeah," he said. "That'd be me."

"Nice," the dirty-blond woman said, and for the first time, she didn't look like she wanted to shove him into oncoming traffic. He'd take it.

"Cari isn't a fan of warlocks," Aurora said.

Anders eyed the dirty blond—Cari—and she gave him a little nod, like she was impressed.

"I can understand that," Anders said. "Guy was an asshole."

Cari actually *smiled* at that. Huh. Look at him. Making friends with other demons. Luc would be proud.

"Well, Anders, if you're not here to welcome us to the city, I'm guessing you have another reason for dropping by?" Aurora said, and he turned back to her.

"The fury I helped save, Tyson," Anders said. "He said you tend to go where there's going to be…trouble, and that's how you choose where you go."

Aurora's pink-tinted lips turned up in a genuine smile. "Sometimes. Sometimes it's as simple as going where we're invited."

Invited? Anders blinked, taken aback. "You saying someone asked you to come to Ottawa?"

"If they did, would it be your business?" Her smile didn't dim in the slightest, and she still sounded more playful than pissed off, but he couldn't be sure. Also, he'd already admitted it *wasn't* his business.

"No," he said, grudgingly. What would Luc or Curtis do here? They'd probably say something polite and charming. Then again, he got the distinct impression these furies weren't the easily charmed type. He took a breath, deciding he'd do this his way.

Blunt.

"We've had a death recently," Anders said, figuring if these furies didn't know already, they'd be able to find it out soon enough. Especially if they'd been "invited" by anyone who had connections. "I'm—*we're*—trying to help track down who the killer is, and mostly I'm hoping your arrival has nothing to do with any of that."

Another demon, a Black woman with dark brown eyes and impressive shoulders standing beside a sweet-looking Kawasaki, let out a snort. "What, because we're furies, we're murderers?"

"No," Anders said, shaking his head. "Can't have been you. You weren't here when the body hit the floor." He shrugged one shoulder. "But murder does tend to piss people off, or be done by angry people, and I thought it might have been what brought you here."

"Let me get this straight," Aurora said, her lilt increasing. "You're worried about some murder."

"That's right," Anders said. "A coywolf. The Families might be involved, too, and there are multiple people who should have seen it coming—psychics, I guess, including the dead coywolf—but they didn't. I know how that sounds, but just take my word on it."

"You want me to take your word," Aurora said, shaking her head, and now the amusement had given way to an outright snort of disbelief. "You are the *strangest* incubus I've ever met."

Anders let out a snort of his own. "Believe me, I'd rather hunker down and let it pass me by, but…" He lifted one hand, palm up. "It is what it is."

"And if I told you we had nothing to do this murder, you'd believe me?" Aurora's eyebrow rose again.

"I'd want to," Anders said, matching her less-than-convinced tone. He regarded the women, most of whom were looking at him right now, and decided he liked them. "Look, I don't know if that trick of yours to know when bad things are coming is something you rely on, but this killer seems to have figured out a workaround against you fortune-telling types."

"Wait. You're not here to grill us, you came here to *warn* us?" Aurora said, and unless she was an amazing actress, Anders would bet real money he'd surprised the shit out of her.

"In part," Anders said, though he hadn't really thought of it that way until just then. "But mostly I'm hoping you're not here to make a bad situation worse."

"Well," Aurora said, taking a breath and exchanging an amused glance with Cari before she turned back to him. "I definitely can't promise you that. But I will tell you this, Anders-who-came-to-warn-us. We feed on *righteous* anger. It's kind of our whole thing." She waved pink-polished nails in a little circle in front of her face, then smiled enough to show teeth. "So I can *definitely* tell you we don't side with most murderers. There's no wrath to be had there. I can't speak for every fury out there, but my crew? We try to stick with those who have every right to be angry." She licked her bottom lip. "It tastes better."

"That's who invited you?" Anders said, frowning a little. "*Those* who have every right to be angry?"

Aurora just smiled, one side of her lips rising more than the other. "It was lovely to meet you, Anders." Her Southern belle drawl sounded as sweet as one of Curtis's favorite ice creams, but he knew a dismissal when he heard one.

He was outnumbered, surrounded by furies, and had just received the nicest "go the fuck away" of his life.

Anders nodded. "Same," he said. "Can I give you my number before I go? Just in case."

That seemed to surprise her again. "In case what?"

He lifted one shoulder and did his best to sound like a man who wanted to help. "You never know." At least that much was true.

"Cari," Aurora said, nodding to the taller woman.

Cari pulled a phone out of a zipped pocket on her motorcycle jacket, unlocked it, and handed it to him. He keyed in his information and handed it back. Then he shoved his fists back into his jacket and left them there without any further bother.

Unless he was completely off the mark, the arrival of the furies was on purpose, not what Tyson had suggested after all. They hadn't come here because they'd caught the idea the city was going to offer up a buffet of pissed-off wrath. No, they'd been invited.

But by who?

Those who have every right to be angry.

In a place like Ottawa, that was a long fucking list.

Time to go home.

FIFTEEN

Curtis was almost home when the music he was listening to cut out for a second and the automated voice of his phone took over.

"Call from Rebekah Mitchell. Do you wish to accept?"

"Yes," Curtis said. Maybe Rebekah had heard from Matt.

A click announced the connection.

"Rebekah?" Curtis said.

"Hey, Curt." Crap. Rebekah sounded nothing like someone who'd heard from a missing friend and was calling to let him know everything was all right. No, she sounded like she had another bomb to drop on him.

"What happened?" he said.

"The pawn shop got robbed," she said.

It took Curtis a second to realize what she meant. "Wait. As in Wheeler's pawn shop?" It was a dive of a place, far enough off the Market to not qualify as being anywhere, really, and run by the Mitchells.

"Yeah."

"Crap," he said, and she laughed.

Wheeler's front appeared to be nothing more than a typically trashy pawn shop, but the rear ran a brisk trade in procuring items of a more mystical or rare nature for the movers and shakers of Ottawa's supernatural community. Curtis, Luc, and Anders had gone head-to-head with the shop's eponymous namesake last February.

It hadn't ended well for him.

"That's one way to put it," Rebekah said. "I'm at the shop now. My mother sent me to let me take a look, and I'm trying to figure out what's missing."

Curtis pulled into his driveway and idled. Luc wouldn't be up yet, but it wouldn't be long. Anders's SUV wasn't there, which meant he hadn't gotten back from Professor Mann's house yet, either. Curtis hadn't answered any of Anders's texts all day, which felt petty. Did he really want to be there when Luc woke up or Anders came home?

Hell no.

"Do you need help?" Curtis said.

"Honestly? I wouldn't mind. I'm short-handed. I called Kenzie and the others. She told me, by the way, about the other murder, the muse. Everyone's coming, but I'm not going to turn you down."

Curtis waited a beat. Matthew Stirling missing. A dead psychic coywolf. Professor Mann missing, too. A dead muse. And now Wheeler's Pawn Shop broken into?

What the hell was going on in this city?

"I'm on my way."

❖

Rebekah Mitchell's cherry red Camaro was parked at the curb, and as luck would have it, Curtis pulled his hybrid in behind just as Mackenzie's car pulled into the parking lot. He turned off the engine and eyed the storefront. It still looked dingy and uninviting. He forced himself to get out of his car, then told himself it would be polite to wait for Mackenzie to join him.

Truth was, he wasn't looking forward to heading inside. The last time he'd been there, he'd ended up trading magic for information with a murderer bent on using necromancy to increase his power through truly evil means.

"Are you okay?" Mackenzie said, frowning as she walked up.

"Just remembering how the first time I was here I had to trade my first glasses away," Curtis said, which was at least partly the truth. They'd needed information from the original owner, and he'd asked for Curtis's glasses in exchange, claiming he'd heard about them, and they were a clever bit of magic. Curtis had enchanted the lenses to reveal magical auras. He'd done it on his own, which had impressed Mackenzie and the others, given his lack of formal magical schooling, and wearing them for any length of time had given him major headaches, but it had been worth it at the time.

Those glasses had helped him avoid the other supernatural beings of the world—or, in the case of Luc and Anders, find two other beings currently on their own. Without those glasses, his original plan of finding two other Orphans like himself and suggesting they form a coven of their own would never have happened.

Except he hadn't found two other Orphans. He'd found a vampire and a demon, and the three of them had decided to try forming a bond anyway.

For all he knew, those original glasses were still in that pawn shop somewhere. He'd only belatedly realized Wheeler had likely wanted the lenses to make sure Curtis couldn't use them to see any traces of what he had been doing.

Still, in the end, there Curtis was, standing outside with Mackenzie Windsor, staring at a magical pawn shop and wondering if he never should have made those glasses in the first place. That was better than Wheeler could say, what with being dead and all.

And if he hadn't made those glasses, he never would have found Luc and Anders, which frankly had felt like a massive mistake for the last few days.

You'll come up with something. When this is all over, you'll sit down with them and figure out exactly what to do.

Assuming they were all still alive.

"He's gone," Mackenzie said. She probably meant Wheeler. Curtis figured she thought that was what was holding him there.

"Right," Curtis said, nodding. "Sorry."

They headed to the door together. Curtis knocked, and a few seconds later, Rebekah appeared from the darkness beyond the doorway and let them in.

The interior of the store looked quite a bit different from the last time he'd seen it. Someone had given the place a massive cleaning, for one, and instead of random junk, bottles, and old electronics haphazardly strewn about, the place had been reorganized, and the two long glass-topped counters now shone, with a selection of jewelry and watches and smaller, more valuable items locked inside them.

Curtis frowned, realizing something was already off. "Wait, if there was a robbery…" He pointed at the glass case of rings and necklaces and other bits of gold.

"Not the front of the store," Rebekah said, shaking her head. "The back."

"Oh no," Curtis said.

"Oh yes," Rebekah said with a tired smile. "Come on through." She led the way to the rear of the store. "As an added bonus, not only are things missing, but the man we had running the place is gone, too."

They walked through into the back room, which still felt like stepping into another world. It was nearly the size of the store's front itself. A sturdy wooden desk formed an island in the middle, with a computer, banker's lamp, and comfortable modern ergonomic chair, around which rows of storage shelves—many of them full of lockboxes—were arranged in tight, neat rows.

That the lockboxes were ornately carved and included bind runes and other magical protections probably wouldn't be obvious to anyone not already in the know.

At the rear of the room, by the fire door, a small kitchenette area offered a microwave, fridge, and even a small single oven range.

Curtis didn't see anything out of place, but there *were* gaps on multiple shelves.

"Who was running the store?" Mackenzie said, looking around with the same, unsure expression he imagined he was sporting himself.

"J.D. Domecillo," Rebekah said. When both he and Mackenzie shook their heads, she said, "They're one of my Family sorcerers."

"And they've gone missing," Curtis said, tilting his head.

"It's not just J.D., either," Rebekah said. "According to my mother, my grandfather's driver didn't show, nor did her assistant."

"It's not only them," Curtis said. "My contact with the police said his sorcerer shadows weren't following him this morning, and Anders can't find Professor Mann." He crossed his arms. "Is it possible they, I don't know, *organized*?"

"Like what, a sorcerers' union walkout?" Rebekah said, one sharply shaped eyebrow rising. "I mean, I wouldn't blame them, but it's not like the other Families are going to be okay with them taking off. I'm not even sure my mother will be able to stop the rest of our Family from smacking them down once they find them." She let out a frustrated breath. "If only they *could* unionize or something. The Families treat them like crap."

"Sorcerers can use enchanted items," Mackenzie said, looking at the shelves. "I've seen a sorcerer use my wands. If J.D. took things, there's every chance they intend to use them."

"What's missing?" Curtis said.

"Nothing like a weapon so far, if that's what you're thinking," Rebekah said. "It was my mother's first thought, too." She pulled out the desk chair and sat. "Unfortunately, J.D. wiped the computer before they left." Rebekah turned and smiled at them, a cocky, amused smile. "Fortunately, yours truly knows the value of a private automatic backup, and I've been working through it. Wheeler might have run this place on the hush-hush in his day, but my mother refuses to let anyone put anything in one of our boxes without knowing what it is."

"Sounds wise," Mackenzie said.

"She's no fool," Rebekah said. "Of course, Wheeler didn't leave the most complete records, so we've got stuff here with no idea who left it or even what it is, though usually we know who it was for. She had J.D. working through it all, but when she got a call the shop was closed this morning from one of the cousins, she sent me to check it out."

"You specifically," Mackenzie said.

Rebekah smiled, but it was wan. "I know, right? A day pass from my mother? Rare treat."

"She knows you'll be able to see exactly what's going on here," Mackenzie said.

"Exactly. I was just starting to go through the manifest J.D. was making to check each shelf when you got here. So far, the first thing I've noticed missing was in the reference stack there." She nodded at one of the shelves, which held a variety of books of various sizes, mostly leather-bound.

"You mean one of the books got taken?" Curtis said.

"I think so," Rebekah said. "There's a gap on the top shelf," She nodded again, and Curtis looked, seeing the gap where it looked like a book had been removed. "Here we go." She clicked on the computer, and a printer Curtis hadn't noticed tucked beside the shelves against the wall spat out a single piece of paper. "Can you start with that, Curt? Kenzie, I'll print another page for you if you'll start with the back lockboxes? Don't touch them, they're warded, but once we know which boxes are missing, we can cross-reference."

"Sure," Curtis said, picking up the paper. It listed titles and names, and he headed to the bookshelf.

A knock sounded from the front of the store, and Rebekah looked up. "That'll be Dale and Tracey. Your list is printing, Kenzie," Rebekah said, nodding to the printer, then rising and heading to the front of the store.

Mackenzie went to get the paper, and Curtis started checking the titles against his list, starting with the first book and working his way along. The manifest was very organized, noting which shelf each book would be found on, but the books seemed to be organized by some sort of subject or category system he didn't grasp. Still, it didn't take him too long to realize which book was missing from the shelf, not least because it stuck out.

"*Blank?*" he said.

"Pardon?" Mackenzie said from the back of the room.

"According to this list, the missing book is 'Leather-bound volume, circa 1800s, *blank.*'"

"Someone stole a *blank* book?" Mackenzie said. "Also, why would someone store a blank book here? It's not cheap to rent space here."

"Good question," Curtis said. He checked the list, which had names beside all the entries and... "Oh crap," he said.

"What is it?"

"Renard," Curtis said. "It says here the blank book was being held for Renard. He ordered it but hadn't paid for it yet." He drew his finger along the line and sighed. "Delivered by Duane Faris. Crap. Crap crap *crap.*"

"What did you find?" Rebekah said.

Curtis turned. Rebekah was back, with Dale and Tracey in tow, and her dark brown eyes met his gaze with what looked to be real concern, which was fair. Because Renard. He stared at the paper, willing the name to change.

It didn't.

"You okay?" she said when he didn't answer right away.

"Sorry, yes, I am, I just..." Curtis took a breath. "The missing book was one Renard brought into the city, delivered by a werewolf runner. And according to this, the book was blank. Renard never picked it up."

"Renard," Dale said with a frown, shaking his head.

"The former vampire duke," Tracey said. "Before Curtis's coven deposed him and Luc became the new duke."

"That's the one," Curtis said. "Deposed" was a nicer word than "destroyed," Curtis thought. And the group didn't know it had been specifically Curtis himself who'd done the final *deposing*, albeit fueled by rage from Tyson the fury, who'd jacked him so high up with anger his magic had nearly emptied himself, Luc, and Anders from the inside out.

Not to mention tearing Renard into tiny wisps of bloody mist.

"Blank," Rebekah said, coming to look over his shoulder at the printout. "Who was the last person to categorize it?"

Curtis checked the paper. At least all the other information was there. It had been placed into storage on behalf of Duane Faris—who'd been killed last winter—by the former owner of the pawn shop, Wheeler—also dead now—and intended for Renard—three for three. But the last person to handle the book in any way was...

"J.D. Domecillo," Curtis said.

"So the sorcerer who vanished with a bunch of stuff is the same person who said the book was blank and had no value," Mackenzie said. "Does that seem likely to anyone?"

"Why didn't I make them let me come here and look at everything?" Rebekah said, groaning. Curtis understood her frustration. Rebekah's ability to pierce magical veils and illusions would have let her note anything unusual in the book. Or in anything else in the pawn shop. "I told them I should do an inventory, but they wanted me at their endless damn meetings. I had to go to my mother to even get the computer set up."

Tracey put a hand on Rebekah's shoulder. "I take it J.D. is gone?"

"And took a bunch of things," Rebekah said, nodding. "We're figuring out what's missing."

"I'm not surprised they didn't let you come here," Dale said, surprising Curtis by speaking up and offering his opinion.

Rebekah glanced at him. "You aren't?"

"Ten to one even your own Family has stuff here they don't want you to know about," Dale said, lifting one shoulder. "There are whole rooms in our chantry I'm not allowed into, and they're grooming me to take up my father's position when my great-grandfather retires as coven head. I bet whatever is in our library is under some serious protection magic and illusions and whatnot. But if you so much as took a glance through a window..." He waved one hand. "You'd see exactly what was there."

"Right," Rebekah said, looking around the room again, as though hoping to see something important right there and then. She blew out a noisy sigh. "Well, when we're done with these lists, we're opening every lockbox we've got a key for so I can give everything a good coat of looking-at. To hell with their damn privacy."

"I've got something missing from this shelf," Mackenzie said, and the group turned their attention back to the rear of the room where she stood. "Box four is gone." She traced her finger across her printout, then looked up at Curtis, her eyes widening behind her glasses.

"What?" he said, feeling something like doom settling over his shoulders.

"'Glasses, enchanted by Curtis Baird,'" Mackenzie said, reading the paper. "'Found in the possession of Jerry Wheeler. Stored by J.D. Domecillo.'"

"J.D. took my old glasses?" Curtis said. "Why would—?" He stopped turning back to Rebekah as the obvious connection struck him.

"I *really* don't think the book is actually blank," she said.

"A sorcerer could use them," Curtis said. "They're enchanted." He frowned, realizing he had an opportunity standing right there to connect a few more dots. "Dale, did your Family call off the sorcerers who usually keep an eye on David Rimmer?"

"The demon detective?" Dale said. "Not that I know of. Why?"

"David said they weren't around," Curtis said. "He wondered if maybe your Family had sent them to look into Matt's disappearance, rather than asking him, but is anyone else seeing a pattern here? Professor Mann is gone. J.D. is gone. The Knight sorcerers who watch David Rimmer are gone."

"I didn't see our driver in our garage," Tracey said, frowning. "And come to think of it, I think my aunt said something about her assistant not showing up this morning, either."

"Matt isn't the only missing person here," Curtis said, turning to Mackenzie. "I think all the Family sorcerers are gone."

"Gone *where*?" Mackenzie said. "And why? They might be able to hold out for a little, but they wouldn't be able to hide from the Families long if they make a concerted effort to look for them. They don't have the power."

"I don't know," Curtis said. "But Matt had Mann's phone number, and as far as I know, they only met when I introduced them last year. None of this feels like a coincidence."

"No," Rebekah said. "It doesn't." She sat down at the computer. "Let's see what else is missing."

Curtis waited for the pages to print, but his mind was entirely on the two missing objects they'd already identified. Something Renard wanted, which Faris had brought him, and the glasses he'd enchanted, which Wheeler had taken from him. He agreed with Mackenzie. If that book was really blank, he'd eat it.

"Here you go," Rebekah said, handing him another printout, and he headed back to the shelves.

SIXTEEN

L uc felt Curtis arrive, and he lifted his gaze a moment before the front door opened.

"Hey," Curtis said in a tight, clipped voice. His gaze traveled past Luc, and Luc felt Anders approach from behind. "Good, you're both here. I have a lot to tell you." The same awkward, cool distance from before had returned in full, and it made Luc's fingers twitch with the desire to touch Curtis. To do *something* to make it right.

Not that he could.

"Us, also," Luc said. "But why don't you go first? I'll make you some tea. You look tired."

"Sure." Curtis took a deep breath, and the three of them headed to the kitchen, Curtis in the lead. Anders aimed a short-lived grimace Luc's way, no doubt due to Curtis's obvious frustration with the both of them.

What a mess. They needed a return to normalcy.

By the time they were seated around the table, however, Luc had to admit he hadn't found a path in that direction. Curtis cradled the tea Luc had made for him but hadn't taken a sip. Instead, he stared at the liquid.

"So, there are furies in town," Anders said.

"What?" Curtis said, looking up. "Like Tyson?"

"Like a whole biker gang of wrath demons," Anders said. "Lady biker demons."

"I…" Curtis shook his head. "I take it you had no luck with Professor Mann all day?"

"Fuck no. He's in the wind."

"Crap," Curtis said.

"What did you learn?" Luc said, giving Anders a small shake of his head. Curtis had no love for wrath demons—and Tyson in particular—and Anders's usual delivery method of simply dumping everything out in a verbal onslaught wasn't the tone he wished to create here.

"Right. Well." Curtis's frustration and annoyance drove Luc out of his chair to put some distance between them. "There's a lot. God, this morning feels like forever ago. Okay, first, I reached out to David—who, I might add, was man enough to ask me out on a date—and I learned the sorcerers—"

The thought of Curtis dating the handsome blond demon made Luc's chest clench in a mix of pain and regret and something darker and more possessive. And, were he to be honest with himself, fearful. Something equally complex and ugly radiated from Anders along their bond.

Curtis broke off, frowning, and his gaze snapped across the table between the two of them. Luc had to work to maintain the eye contact, and Curtis snorted.

"Wow. Really? You're *jealous*?" Curtis said. "I mean, I kind of knew Anders would be jealous, but more out of spite than actual... y'know, *feelings*."

"Hey," Anders said, scowling.

"You have no right," Curtis said, shaking his head. "Not after your whole 'we can't be that for you' thing."

Luc forced a deep breath into his lungs. "It's not jealousy you're sensing, *lapin*."

Curtis scoffed.

Fair enough. "Not entirely," Luc qualified. "It is fear." The admission hurt less than he'd imagined it would.

Curtis blinked, but the line between his eyebrows, the one carved there by frustration and anger, didn't fade. "What are you afraid of, exactly?"

Luc forced air into his lungs, an old habit of deep breathing to set his voice to a calmer tone before an admission.

"David can offer you things I cannot," Luc said. The ongoing surge of panic and fear and protectiveness and possessiveness tightening Luc's chest did nothing to help keep his voice even.

"You do love me," Curtis said, touching his own chest like he could feel every single one of Luc's fears and doubts. Then again, Luc knew he very well might. Their bond practically announced their feelings to each other as easily as one might hear a melody on a nearby radio. "Both of you," Curtis said. "I can feel it." He shook his head, looking less moved and back to angry now. "So...why won't either of you *admit* it?" He faced Anders.

Anders stared down at the tabletop.

"*Lapin*," Luc said gently, and when Curtis turned back to him, there was such frustration and sadness in the wizard's eyes that Luc found himself doing the last thing he'd intended to ever do.

He told the complete truth.

"When I wake up, my first thoughts are of you. The two of you. When I see someone intriguing, I wonder what Anders might say. When there is a voice in my head telling me to do what is right? That voice is yours, Curtis. You are the architect of this freedom we all share, but for a while now there have been others with whom I might still have freedom—an easier freedom, even—but I wouldn't have the joy of sharing this with you. And that's the problem." He leaned forward. "I could have formed a coterie of my own by now. I had the opportunity— Cynthia Stirling and those Renard threw aside—but I didn't. I would rather be with you and Anders."

"Same," Anders said. "David, Tyson, and Ethan would have taken me. They offered."

"Well, then...?" Curtis frowned, but Luc raised a hand to stall his questions.

"You need to understand the reality, Curtis. I can only share the night with you—and at that, only part of it. You sleep. Your life happens in the day, and like your upcoming graduation, I will miss much of it. I can't meet you for coffee after your classes like David can. I can't share a meal with you. I would show you all the wonders of the world if I could, but I can only show you the half that happen when the sun is gone. What *anyone* else can offer you? I can only give you half."

Curtis took a long moment with this, then looked at Anders. "And you?"

"I'm not gonna say it all pretty, but it's the same shit. You're great. I'm a demon. He needs blood, I need to fuck. We're both monsters, and I know Luc gets it, but sometimes I don't think you really do. And yeah, maybe he's a lot easier to tolerate now he's been around us. But as much as us three are good together? I can't be your boyfriend either. I can't fuck only you guys any more than Luc could drink from only us, because we'd kill you, and so...I can't give you that stuff." Anders shrugged, then scowled. "Neither can David, by the way. I thought he knew that, but in case he still doesn't get it, you need to hear it."

Curtis looked between the two of them, his eyes wet. Luc would do anything to see the look of pain and frustration pass. Neither of them had wanted to hurt Curtis, but there they were, doing it again.

"Wow," Curtis said. To Luc's surprise, he shook his head, a small smile turning his lips at the corners of his mouth. "So, I get it. It's not you guys don't love me, or even each other, it's that you're clueless."

Luc blinked.

"What?" Anders said.

Curtis held up one hand. "At what point did I ask *either* of you for a closed, monogamous relationship or an incredibly outdated notion of either of you becoming some sort of boyfriend-cum-fiancé?"

Luc glanced at Anders. Anders's mouth was open, but no noise was coming out. It was a sight that might have brought him more joy had he not been sure he was sporting a matching expression.

"Seriously," Curtis said. "Have either of you even *met* me?"

"*Lapin,*" Luc said, but Curtis met his gaze with such an annoyed glare he didn't dare say another word.

"Okay, let's go back to the only *actual* thing I asked. Do you guys feel the same way about me I feel about you? Because, as you put it, when I wake up, I'm thinking of you guys. I'm happy to say the words: *I love you.* Both of you."

Anders made a little noise that could have been him choking on some saliva. For his own part, Luc managed a nod.

For some reason, their reactions made Curtis laugh. "Love isn't some finite resource I have only enough of for one other person, which I kind of thought would have been obvious given I *already* told both of you I loved you. My heart doesn't work that way. But *come on*, it was *never* going to involve wedding bells and vows of monogamy or a sunlit picnic. I'm not deluded. I know who you are. And, to be clear, I know *what* you are." He eyed them both with such a direct gaze Luc squirmed in his chair. "As for not being able to give me what I want? How did you define *what* I want? For crying out loud, I'm queer. The last thing I care about is what other people define as a valid relationship. They can keep that crap right along with their two-point-five babies and their designated anniversary presents. I want the freedom to have you two, not to have what other people think is okay." He waved one hand, like he thought he was getting off track, and blew out an annoyed breath. "All I wanted was not to have to worry about admitting that sometimes all I want most in the world is to snuggle up on the damn couch between the both of you and show you the best movies you never knew you missed, because I love doing that for both of you." He paused. "Also going to the NAC to watch Shakespeare and Shaw with you." He pointed at Luc. "And dancing my butt off at Chances with you." He pointed at Anders. "But *also* doing crap *on my own* when I feel like it because I don't want either of you attached to my hip, except for when I do, which doesn't, by the way, have to only be on the full moon or when we're about to face whatever certain death is heading our way in any given week, usually in this freaking kitchen!"

The last three words had come at a near yell. Luc stared at Curtis. Curtis lowered his hand, panting. "Okay. I'm done."

"So…" Anders said.

It was the most meek-sounding word Luc had ever heard Anders mutter, but it was more than Luc had. He eyed Curtis, at a complete loss.

"So," Curtis said, rubbing his forehead with one hand. "We take some time, and we discuss—like the adults we're all supposed to be but apparently only I am—what that means, and we decide as a group if what we all want is within the range of what we can do and live with. But I'm telling you both, I'm there. I've been there a while."

"And David?" Anders said.

"David is great," Curtis said, and it made Anders visibly twitch. "And, okay, yes, incredibly sexy, and maybe someday I would like to climb that. But you two? If you need some sort of loaded word for it, then fine. There are details to work out, but…" Curtis shrugged. "I'd like you two to be my lovers, or partners, or whatever word you need, to understand I love you two. If that's what you want, too? I'm telling you right now, again, I'm down for it."

"*Oui*," Luc said. The knot in his chest untangled with an almost visceral sensation of release. The hours Curtis and Anders were awake and the sun was set? He wouldn't trade them for the world. It didn't need any more consideration. He'd been, as Curtis had said, a deluded fool. "*Je t'aime, lapin. Et lui, aussi.*"

Curtis smiled at him. "Yeah?"

"Why is he looking at me?" Anders said. "What did he say?"

"I said yes. To both of you."

"Of course you did." Anders grinned at him, then turned his attention back to Curtis, rubbing his chin. "So when you say you're down for it…Are we talking, 'down on your knees' down, or…?"

"Anders," Luc said. Could he not manage even five minutes without saying something insufferably crass?

"Oh no. Given how you two nearly screwed this up completely?" Curtis said. "The ones spending some quality time on their knees will be you."

Anders raised his eyebrows. "Is that so?"

"You'll find I'm a benevolent sort," Curtis said. "I treat my boy toys well, but there *will* be groveling."

"In that case, fuck yes," Anders said.

Curtis beamed at them.

"You're both the densest, but I guess you'll do," he said. "Okay. As awesome as that is, let's get back to the problem at hand, because a lot has happened and I—"

"Nope," Anders said, standing up and tugging Curtis up onto his feet with a fistful of Curtis's shirt. "The problem at hand can wait."

"Anders," Curtis said, but Luc rose as well, stepped in behind him, and wrapped his arms around them both, hands loose at the small of Anders's back.

"He's right, *lapin*. Do you remember our first time together? Before we knew you were a wizard trying to trap us in a binding?"

"Vaguely," Curtis said, his voice catching as Anders leaned down far enough to kiss his neck.

"Well," Luc said. "It's shameful we've let that memory fade. Perhaps we could…" He leaned close to Curtis's ear, nuzzling. "*Remind* you."

"That…would be okay."

❖

Luc and Anders led Curtis to the closest room—Anders's, which not so coincidentally had the largest bed. Anders took hold of Curtis's shirt, tugged it off, and tossed it over his shoulders without looking, making Curtis laugh. While Anders got to work on his own clothes, with similarly exaggerated flinging of every removed article continuing to amuse Curtis, Luc covered Curtis's laughter with a slow, lingering kiss, tracing along his smooth, exposed stomach.

"Fewer clothes," Curtis said, tugging Luc's shirt free from his trousers.

Luc stepped back to obey, and while he wasn't about to use the same dramatic flair, he took his time, unbuttoning slowly and seeing the flush rise along Curtis's neck at the more suggestive pacing of his disrobing.

Grinning, Curtis unzipped his jeans and was already out of them before Luc had finally slipped the shirt free of his shoulders. Luc considered which of Anders's surfaces might be the least risky, and he settled for draping the expensive shirt over the back of Anders's desk chair just as Anders surprised him by wrapping both strong arms around him from behind.

"Hurry. The fuck. Up," Anders said, fumbling with Luc's belt. His voice rumbled in Luc's ear, and the warm breath against his neck tickled.

Curtis laughed again, now standing only in his rainbow-striped boxer briefs, an already intriguing bulge telegraphing that his amusement had in no way tempered his arousal.

"Fine," Luc said, lifting his hands to let Anders have full access to his belt. "If we are in preference of alacrity."

"We really fucking are," Anders said, yanking the belt free and all but shoving Luc's trousers and his underwear down with his other hand.

Curtis raised one hand. "Now, I believe there was something about you two on your knees?"

Luc stepped out of the puddle of trousers, exchanged an amused look with Anders, whose eyes were already darkening at the play of arousal in the air, and sank slowly to his knees, Anders doing the same beside him.

"Yeah, I think I could get used to this," Curtis said, stepping forward and sliding one finger under the waistband of the overbright underwear he wore. "Though, as I recall in my fuzzy, fuzzy recollection..." He slid his underwear down, releasing his cock to stand almost fully to attention. "Weren't you both trying to kill me at the time?"

"Perhaps you'll settle for a *petit mort*?" Luc said.

"Just one?" Curtis said, standing directly in front of him.

"Challenge accepted," Luc said, and he took him fully into his mouth, gripping his thighs to hold him completely in place while he took advantage of one of the lesser-praised but truly inspiring gifts of being vampire.

The lack of need to breathe.

Curtis gasped, and Luc felt rather than saw Anders shifting to the other side of Curtis, and when Curtis gasped a second time, this time with a barely audible "Oh!" he didn't need the press of Anders's palms over his own to know he'd taken up position where he could use his tongue.

They hadn't done this since that first night, and while he slid his mouth along the full hard length of Curtis's cock, Luc decided that had been a *terrible* oversight.

Curtis writhed beneath their shared grip, and Anders's attention became noisier, as did Curtis's response to their paired assault on his control. Luc felt the jolts of Curtis's leg muscles and picked up his pace, not relenting in the slightest, and when Curtis laid one hand on his head, running his fingers through Luc's hair with increasing desperation, Luc couldn't help but smile around his efforts.

Keeping his fangs retracted was becoming harder with every buck of Curtis's hips, but he persevered. After all, Curtis had been correct. He and Anders had very nearly ruined this.

They owed him a few orgasms.

At the very least.

"O-Okay," Curtis said, in a breathy, hitched voice. "Bed now. *Please*."

The last was borderline pleading, and Luc settled back on his ankles, letting Curtis's wet length slap up against his stomach and smiling up at him, biting his bottom lip and pressing bodily back against Anders's attention. Anders used both hands to give him access, and the little growling noises he made voiced agreement enough with Curtis's request.

"As you demand, we'll obey," Luc said, with an amused tilt of his chin. "At least as long as you ask so…*nicely*."

❖

As the air in his bedroom cooled the sweat on their skin, Luc closed his eyes and listened to the sounds of the two heartbeats beside him, as well as their breath, both slowing now their delightful exertions had passed.

"Well," Curtis said with a long exhalation. "At least that's dealt with."

Luc shifted just enough to kiss Curtis's temple. "You make us sound like an item on your to-do list."

"To-be-done-by list is more like it," Anders said, rolling onto his side and rising up on one elbow. Luc would have laid good odds the position was at least in part chosen because Anders was well aware the effect it had on the musculature in his hairy chest and thick arms.

Sure enough, he noticed Curtis's gaze drawn to Anders's physique once more.

"Your mastery of the single entendre continues to be unparalleled," Luc said, deciding this was a one-upmanship he could indulge in, moving into the same position and regarding them both in turn.

"Oh, please don't ruin this with words," Curtis said, though his attention was now journeying the length of Luc's body. "You were both being such adults for a while there." He looked at each of them, a fond—and decidedly self-satisfied—smile on his handsome face, and then shook his head, the smile slipping away. "Okay. Enough, Mr. Sexy and Sexier. Even if I wanted another round, four is my limit. We need to focus."

"Hey, Mr. Sexier always focuses better after fucking," Anders said, with a wolfish grin. "Hit me."

Luc decided to let the self-nomination pass and gave Curtis a small nod of encouragement.

"Okay," Curtis said. "You said you couldn't find Professor Mann?"

"No, he's gone," Anders said. "And he's not at home, either. Told his neighbor and his students he had a family thing, but that's a lie. Pretty sure he has no real family."

"Other than the Stirlings," Curtis said.

"Who he hates," Anders said.

"Right." Curtis nodded, then took a deep breath, which made his lean chest rise and fall rather enticingly, to Luc's gaze. Then he rubbed his eyes with one hand. "Okay. So. Next thing. There's been another murder."

"What?" Luc said.

"Don't give me 'what?' I tried to tell you I had stuff to talk about, but then you got all emotive and then there was the mind-blowing sex." Curtis lifted himself up on his elbows. "A muse, a sloth demon named Marlowe. I was with Mackenzie and Leo—sorry, Leo is another muse, one of Marlowe's pack—when it happened. The important thing is, this muse who was murdered had a gift for seeing the future."

"Another present?" Anders said.

"Prescient," Luc corrected absently.

"Whatever."

"Right," Curtis said. "So, given Matt can see the future and Aaron could see the future, and this muse could see the future, I'm starting to think the reason Matt is hiding isn't that he's done something wrong, it's that he's trying to stay ahead of someone who seems to be targeting people like him."

People who can see the future. A jolt ran through Luc, and he sat up.

"Something I said?" Curtis said.

"Anna," Luc said. "I must go."

"What's Anna?" Anders said.

"One of Catharine's coterie. She has a premonitory grace." He slid off the bed, hunting for his trousers, and pulled his phone free from the pocket.

"Pre-what-now?" Anders said, though he, too, sat up.

"It's another word for seeing the future," Curtis said.

"Can you two just pick one?" Anders said.

"The point is," Luc said, "if someone is targeting the prescient, she may well be in the line of fire." He scrolled for Catharine's number and hit the icon to call.

"Do you still think Mann had something to do with this?" Anders said.

"I don't know," Curtis said. "But that's another thing. Multiple things, actually. David said the sorcerers who were usually watching him were gone, and Rebekah's Family had a sorcerer running Wheeler's Pawn Shop, only they're also gone and they took stuff with them, including a book Renard wanted and my old glasses, and the others said they were all missing their Family sorcerers today, so I'm thinking it's not just Professor Mann who took a hike."

A book Renard wanted. That caught Luc's attention, but in his ear, the phone rang once. Twice. Three times. At the fourth, it clicked over to Catharine's voicemail.

"So the sorcerers ditched, and robbed the wizards on the way out?" Anders chuckled. "Nice."

"Yeah, except they also stole a bunch of other stuff, and since they're sorcerers, if it's enchanted, they can use it," Curtis said. "She's going to email me the whole list. Probably already has."

Catharine's voice began apologizing to Luc for missing his call and telling him to leave a message.

"You mean like that knife," Anders said, sobering now. Luc could understand. That knife—the very blade of Marysas—had killed multiple demons.

"Like the knife," Curtis said. "I just wish I knew where they were so we could freaking ask them what they're up to. I don't suppose you have some of Mann's blood handy for a locator spell?"

"No," Anders said.

The tone finally sounded.

"Catharine," Luc said. "It is Luc. I have reason to believe Anna might be in some danger. When you get this call, ensure she is safe, or head there as soon as possible, then return this call."

He hung up, then reached down for his boxer briefs. "Denis should have Anna's night address," he said. "I'll check on her myself."

"Wait," Anders said, tilting his head. "Does it have to be blood? You used a hair for that Matt kid."

"Well, blood is the best, but hair, fingernails…" Curtis shrugged one shoulder. "Anything that was once a part of someone continues to be so as far as magic is concerned. It's the law of constancy."

"Whatever. I'll be right back," Anders said, sliding off the bed and leaving the room. Despite Luc's own rising anxiety and his attempt to button his shirt as fast as possible, he couldn't help but admire Anders's broad back and thick thighs as he exited.

"Do you know what was stolen?" Luc said, finally finishing with his shirt and locating one of his socks. The other seemed to have vanished…no, there it was.

"From the pawn shop?"

"Yes." Luc nodded, tugging on his socks.

"I'm still waiting to hear back," Curtis said. "Rebekah will let me know, though it's probably worth knowing one of the missing items was a probably-not-as-blank-as-it-looked book Renard wanted and had delivered but never got to pick up."

"Pardon?" Luc frowned. He zipped up his trousers and was looping his belt even as he started across the room. What had Lavoie said? *After the fire, he was furious he hadn't gotten what he wanted: a book. He'd been so close—those were his words. "I was so close."*

"You know my glasses, right?"

"Yes," Luc said absently. He needed to keep moving, but this couldn't be a coincidence. He shook out his trousers.

"Well, they were also missing, so we think—" Curtis had sat up now, swinging his long legs over the edge of the bed, but Anders returned, still naked, and Curtis paused, frowning at the scrap of green camouflage pattern cloth Anders was holding.

"Here," Anders said, tossing the cloth to Curtis.

Curtis caught it in one hand. "A bandana?" he said, raising one eyebrow.

"A cum rag. It's got Mann all over it."

Curtis dropped the cloth.

"What?" Anders said. "Won't that work as well as blood?"

"I have to go," Luc said, grabbing his keys after zipping up his trousers. "Once I'm certain Anna is okay, we'll gather again and finish catching each other up. Curtis, Renard was attempting to gather books on the city's history and the genealogy of the magical Families, and Lavoie believed he needed something from the Parliament Library when he made his first move against the Families back in 1916, but..." He shook his head. "I'll explain later. I must go and make sure Anna is safe."

He left.

SEVENTEEN

Luc's Mercedes covered the distance between their home and the address Denis had supplied quickly, mostly thanks to a disregard for speed limits. Luckily, no police turned up, and he pulled into a home only three streets away from where Catharine herself lived. He'd tried both Catharine and Anna twice more on the drive over, having gotten the phone number of the latter along with her address from Denis, but to no luck.

He parked the car without much care and, after a glance to ensure no mortal eyes were on him—a feat made easier by the tall hedges and private yard of Anna's home—he used his vampire graces to cross the distance to Anna's front door between blinks.

He reached for the doorbell, then hesitated as the faint scent of something caught in his nose.

He forced air inward, allowing his predator senses to sharpen, and this time the clarity of what it was sharpened into an instinctual panic.

Smoke.

He pressed the doorbell and followed with three sharp knocks on the door.

"Anna!" he called out, when there was no answer.

He stepped back, looking up at the roof of the building and allowing his vision to sharpen as much as possible. If there was smoke visible on the outside of the building, it might already be too late, but if not...

No sign yet.

Luc kicked the door, putting the strength of his grace behind it, and it flew open, the lock shattering and taking splinters of wood and the door's frame with it. He spotted the smoke at the far end of the revealed simple, neatly organized entrance hall, still faint and swirling but starting to seep in from behind a closed door.

The rear door of the house, visible through an opening at the other end of the hallway, lay ominously open.

Merde. He had no choice, but this would not be easy.

Luc forced himself to take a step, and the residency of Anna's house snapped into being to resist him, pressing hard against his chest and weighing him down as though he was attempting to walk at the bottom of a lake, its thick surface of mud sucking at his feet rather than the actual wood floor on which his foot landed.

His muscles already ached from the effort of a single step.

I am the duke of this city and I have more power than any other vampire I have ever encountered, Luc thought. *I am not just vampire, I have the power of a demon and the magic of a wizard. I* will *enter this home.*

A second step accomplished. A third. The fourth trembled, and the smoke seeping from beneath the door grew thicker. The smoke itself wouldn't be a danger to Anna. Their kind didn't breathe.

But fire devoured their flesh with eagerness.

"Anna!" he yelled, straining against the barriers of protection. Both hands shook, and a numbness was spreading up from his toes and fingertips. Residency abhorred his kind, fought the uninvited with a magic as ancient as the very notion of *home*.

I should have brought Curtis. A wizard's power was reduced by the law of residency, but Curtis *could* still enter, albeit with nearly no access to his magic. Could he get his phone out?

But no, even if he called, Curtis couldn't possibly arrive in time.

Perhaps I can borrow it from him. He shoved the cloth of his sleeve aside to touch the tattoo with one finger, drawing deeper on their bond.

Yes.

Another step. Another. Another. Pain replaced the numbness, and he snarled past it, dragging himself forward.

"Anna!" He bellowed the name as loud as he could. At least he knew Anna still lived. Residency would fail the moment she ceased to exist.

Another step. Another. His vision blurred with the effort, and his gaze traveled the length of the entrance hall to the smoking door. The reality of his situation made him curse the saints and tabernacle and every other trace of religious iconography he could call to mind.

He'd never make it.

He tried anyway.

Midway through another slurred and shaking step, the pressure released, and it was only through his vampire graces he recovered his balance before falling over entirely. As it was, he was carried forward three more steps before he regained his composure.

On the tail of which was swift regret. For if the power of residency had vanished, then...

He shook his head, determined to at least see the scene of the crime before it went up in flames entirely. Now free to use his abilities, he moved with full speed to the door, crouched low, and opened it, prepared to fling himself back from what could be a lethal outpouring of flames.

None came. Instead, he found himself in what appeared to be a library or study of some kind, a room lined with bookshelves on every wall except for the door he'd come through, two windows, and a fireplace—the logs of which had been spilled onto the floor to begin the blaze already creeping up the closest shelves of books—but his attention was drawn immediately to the figure of a woman on the floor, face turned away from him, her long brown hair splayed out, her arms tucked beneath her as though she cradled something against her chest.

Anna's figure. Not ashes.

She lives? Confusion and relief warred, but he went to her side and saw her lips moving. Despite the crackling of the ever-growing fire, he heard her voice, speaking in the faintest of whispers, repeating the same words over and over.

"Come in, Duke. Come in...come in, Duke..."

She'd *invited* him. The residency hadn't failed. She must have heard him calling her name.

Her lips were the blue of a bruise, and her cheeks were sunken, but he couldn't see any cause of her distress.

With a sudden whoosh, the second window's curtains were ablaze, and Luc knew he had to act. He had no time to waste putting distance between her and the flames already spreading. Luc gathered her up in his arms as another curtain of flames erupted up another shelf of books, and within a grace-fueled moment he had carried her out onto the front lawn. He set her down on the grass, and under the moonlight, her skin had taken on an odd, grey cast in the short time she'd been out of the house.

Also, he finally saw what it was she gripped tightly in her arms, pressed to her chest.

A book, bound in what appeared to be simple brown leather.

Anna's repeating whispers had stopped. Her eyes remained closed. Something was clearly wrong with her, but Luc couldn't see any reason for her state. Certainly, he noted no obvious wound, no stains on her clothes...

Wait.

Something born more of instinct than logic made him tilt her head to the side and brush her hair away from the back of her neck. There he found a single red mark against the greying skin, around which small tendrils of black visibly spread outward from the puncture mark.

"Anna!"

Luc glanced back, and saw Catharine, the Lady Markham, standing behind his car. A blur of motion brought her to his side, and she knelt on the other side of Anna from him.

"She's been attacked," Luc said. "Injected with something at the back of her neck. I don't know what it is..."

"Her skin," Catharine said, her voice tight with anger and worry. "It's hawthorn. We need to get it out of her blood, and fast."

"Get her into my car," Luc said, pulling out his phone as Catharine effortlessly lifted the prone Anna. The book slipped from her hands, and Luc caught it with his free hand.

Catharine's eyes lingered on the unmarked leather for a beat, then she followed him to his car, both of them moving with vampire grace as the sound of the call connecting clicked against Luc's ear.

When this was over, he'd need to feed. The hunger already pulled at his chest from battling Anna's residency and moving at the speed he'd been using.

"What's wrong?" Curtis said, instead of a greeting. "I felt you earlier, and there was this pressure—"

"Anna has been attacked—poisoned—and we need to cleanse her blood," Luc said, cutting Curtis off. He tucked the book under his arm long enough to open the rear door. Catharine placed Anna inside, closed it, then appeared by the passenger side in another blur of movement. "We're on our way home to you now. Can you do it?"

"I—" Curtis hesitated. "Maybe? I can try."

"Good enough." Luc slid behind the driver's seat, put the book beside him, and started the car.

As they pulled out of the driveway, flames licked the exterior of one side of Anna's house, the glow lighting up the trees lining the edges of the property.

❖

"Tell me what it was," Curtis said, meeting them in the driveway and walking alongside them as Catharine carried Anna's ominously still form to their front door. There was no sign of Anders, Luc noticed. He gripped the leather-bound book in one hand, but Curtis didn't so much as spare it a glance.

"Lady Catharine, you and Anna may enter our home this night, as long as you intend us no harm," Luc said quickly and then turned to Curtis as they stepped through into the house. "Hawthorn."

"Oh, that's…that's good," Curtis said, jogging past him into the house. "Put her down right there in the circle and don't scuff it," he called out as he started up the stairs to the second floor. "I'll be right back!"

Luc saw a large circle had been drawn on the wood floor of the entrance hall, out of what appeared to be salt, and beside it lay Curtis's athame and a single, stoppered bottle, the cork already removed. Catharine laid Anna down inside the circle and smoothed some of her hair away from her face, but it came away in a clump in her hand, crumbling into ominously dry and brittle dust.

"Curtis!" Luc called, turning to the stairwell. Curtis was already there, however, running down the stairs and holding what looked to be a handful of twigs of some kind.

"Coming," Curtis said breathlessly, skidding at the bottom of the steps and then dropping to his knees in front of Anna. Her lips were cracked, and her skin had begun to flake.

They were losing her to the poison.

Curtis shoved the bottle into Luc's hand. "Hold this," he said, and then he turned back to Anna, lifting the athame, then shaking his head. "Where's the wound?"

"Back of her neck, like the others," Luc said.

"Turn her head," Curtis said.

Catharine did so, and more desiccating skin and hair flaked away from Anna's form beneath her touch. Catharine made a small noise of pain and worry, but if it contained any words, Luc didn't catch them.

Curtis began speaking with the calm, controlled voice he used when conjuring his magic.

Luc didn't think it was Latin this time, but something else, and he watched in silence as Curtis lifted the twigs high into the air, touched them to the blade of the athame, then lowered the dagger until the tip nearly touched the now inch-wide, fetid, rotting wound on the back of Anna's neck.

A single drop of liquid beaded from deep within the opening, then rose to the surface and leapt from Anna to the tip of the blade.

Curtis repeated his command again and again, raising and lowering the blade, and each recitation pulled another drop from inside the wound onto the athame, where it pooled at the tip and along the edge, growing wetter and more visible with every added drop. To Luc's senses, only the faintest hum seemed to be moving through their bond. Whatever this spell was, it did not seem to be taxing Curtis to maintain it. Curtis continued, his voice never slowing.

Luc watched Anna for any sign of recovery, but he saw none. He lifted his gaze to Catharine, but her attention was solely on Anna, the gentle curve of her jaw set in a clench and her honey-colored eyes roiling with anger.

When no more liquid came from the wound, Curtis moved the blade carefully away from Anna and Catharine, holding it out in front of him, and nodded at the bottle in Luc's hand, still whispering words of magic.

Luc held it out, and Curtis angled the athame over the opening, then spoke once more.

The liquid leapt from the blade's tip and into the bottle. It wasn't much.

Curtis exhaled. "That's all I could get," he said, his voice softer now, less certain than when he'd wielded his power. "Is it...was it enough?"

Luc looked at Anna's papery, dry body and wondered. The degradation seemed to have ceased, but to go so far toward the brink of her final death, he wasn't sure.

"It will be," Catharine said, in a voice like iron, and she lifted her own wrist to her mouth, biting down with her fangs fully extended, then lowering her wrist to the lips of Anna's form without so much as a wince of pain. "In time."

Curtis bit his bottom lip, looking at Luc with widening eyes.

"Thank you, *lapin*," Luc said.

"We got lucky. I had some hawthorn," Curtis said, lifting the twigs. "Mackenzie suggested it for some anti-vampire warding on the new house. Having it in hand meant I could...well, whatever. You probably don't care how it worked, but the law of sympathy is pretty basic magic." Luc watched the flush rise up Curtis's neck and knew this stream of speech was as likely from nervous relief he'd succeeded as anything else.

Catharine, for her part, faced him. "I owe you, Curtis Baird," she said, and Curtis flinched a trace away from her, which Luc could understand.

A promise from a vampire often sounded suspiciously like a threat.

"I have more blood," Luc said, after a glance at the still-unmoving Anna. If they were to speed Anna's recovery, it would likely take more blood than either of them could spare from their own flesh. "I will fetch it for you."

"*Merci, mon Duc*," Catharine said, still pressing her wrist to Anna's lips. "I will not forget I now owe you as well."

Luc dipped his chin, acknowledging. He glanced at the hall side table where he'd placed the leather-bound book. He believed he already had a way to call a favor due, but it could wait. He went to fetch the blood.

EIGHTEEN

"Penny for your thoughts?" The man across from Anders eyed him with a slight frown.

"Sorry," Anders said, though the wave of whatever-that-had-been echoing through his bond with Curtis and Luc had been intense for a few seconds there. Pressure and frustration or anger or...?

"You seemed a little lost for a second." The smile he was aiming Anders's way seemed a bit more fragile than a moment earlier, and Anders realized his confidence was flagging.

Aw. It made Anders want to ruffle the guy's hair, and definitely made him feel like he'd made the right selection.

"I'm fine, really," Anders said, giving his forearm a quick squeeze on top of the table. Anders enjoyed the bar, finding the crowd here more to his liking than many of the other options out there for queer men. The men who came here tended to be a bit older—often in their forties, like he himself appeared to be—and there was often less in the way of preening.

Well, not counting the powerlifters and other muscle types, who preened as much as any crowds of dance-obsessed, high-fashion twink types, just in a different way. But when the bar hosted one of its Bear nights, Anders rarely found himself struggling for company.

Also, there was just *something* about a shy, burly man. And the one sitting across from him had it in spades. Even better, he was from out of town, in the city for a conference on justice reform or something. He was a paralegal, which Anders was pretty sure meant he was smarter than a lawyer but paid and respected less, and the whole package worked for him. A plain white dress shirt, open at the collar now, showed off enough curls of dark hair to advertise what was bound to be a very enjoyable chest, and he'd rolled up the sleeves, too, revealing visibly veined forearms Anders would bet Luc would have enjoyed enough for both of them.

If only he could remember his name. He wanted to say Thad, but it didn't seem right.

"Hm." The paralegal picked up his bottle of beer and tipped back another sip, smiling around the opening. He put the bottle back down. "So you're not going to tell me?"

"Tell you what?" Anders leaned back in the booth they shared and allowed his allure to the surface of his skin. Heat spread between them, and Mr. Paralegal's Adam's apple bobbed, even though he wasn't drinking his beer any more.

"Whatever you were thinking about," he said, though his voice was a little huskier now.

"How about I tell you what I'm thinking now?" Anders said, letting one eyebrow creep up.

"I think I can guess," he said. His gaze flicked around Anders's face, and he bit his bottom lip. "I did tell you I'm only here through the weekend, right?"

"You did," Anders said. "But you didn't say if your hotel was close by."

Another swallow, and this time, the man cleared his throat audibly. "Do you know the Lord Elgin?" he said. "I walked here."

Anders grinned.

❖

Two orgasms and a surreptitious check of the man's wallet while he was in the bathroom to learn his name later, and Anders left *Shad*—cool name, definitely better than Thad—dozing in his hotel bed. He pulled out his cell in the elevator, tapping Luc's name and enjoying the deep heat the double draw of Shad's soul brought to his whole body.

"Luc Lanteigne." Luc answered after only one ring.

"Hello, Luc Lanteigne," Anders said, dropping his voice as low and gravelly as it could go. "What are you wearing?"

"I won't dignify that with a response," Luc said. "What is it?"

"You're no fun." The elevator opened on the ground floor, and Anders started heading for the outside. "Checking in. Felt something funny, earlier."

"Hours ago," Luc said, and he laughed. "And you call *now*?"

"What?" Anders said, rolling his eyes. "I could tell you handled it. What was it?"

"Anna," Luc said. "I was right to be worried, but we got to her in time. Curtis saved her life."

"Saved her life? Anna's already dead." Anders snorted. "Like you."

"You know what I mean," Luc said, and though Luc was trying to sound annoyed, Anders could tell he was smiling. "You seem to be in a good mood. Did someone pay you a compliment?"

"I met a hot paralegal from Halifax, and then I fucked the hot paralegal from Halifax. Twice." Anders winked at the two silver-haired women in the lobby who'd gasped at his pronouncement and kept walking. "You'd have liked his arms. Veiny. His thighs, too."

"He sounds delightful," Luc said dryly. "Are you on your way home?"

"I can be," Anders paused outside the hotel entrance, considering the short walk back to where he'd left his car in the bar parking lot. "Is something up?"

"Beyond two dead, someone trying to kill Anna, Curtis's missing friend, and the murderer still at large?" Now Luc definitely sounded amused with him.

"Don't forget the biker furies," Anders said, grinning.

"How could I?"

"I'll be home soon," Anders said, hanging up. He rolled his neck to the left and right as he walked, making it crack and pop, and had to resist the urge to run the flat of his palm along his chest. It always felt so good to be *full*. The heat of a freshly acquired sliver of soul made a hot shower seem tepid by comparison.

Okay, two slivers, but in fairness, Shad had begged for the second round, and Anders hadn't got the impression Shad asked for things for himself very often, so how could he deny the man?

He was whistling by the time he got to the bar parking lot but stopped when he saw a tall blond figure leaning against his SUV.

Well, shit.

"David," Anders said, crossing the pavement. It might have been the copious sex of the night still aiming his thoughts, but Anders couldn't help but notice the way the blue Henley and leather jacket combo was working very well for David Rimmer.

What had Curtis said? *Okay, yes, maybe I'd like to climb that.*

"I figured you still hit this place on Bear night," David said. "Saw your car, didn't find you inside, so I waited for you. From your strut, I take it you had a good night."

"I'm not strutting. You could have called," Anders said, not sure he liked where this was going.

"I did call. I called Curtis, but I got his voicemail," David said.

"He's probably sleeping," Anders said. "The three of us…" Anders allowed a slow smile to spread across his face, and—okay, *fine*, he'd been looking forward to this moment with David in particular—lifted one shoulder. "We all came to an understanding about being together. It was what Curtis wanted. To be *boyfriends*, or whatever. Then we celebrated. So he was tired."

David's jaw worked, his only tell. "Boyfriends?" he said.

"Well, as much as we can," Anders said with another careless shrug. "You know."

"I do," David said, heavy with meaning.

Right. *That*. Sore point.

"Well." David shook his head. "It explains your strut."

"Fine," Anders said cheerfully. "Maybe I was strutting."

"Look," David said, pushing off the SUV, "can you let Curtis know I've had no luck with Matthew Stirling's motorcycle or phone? Also, I managed to take a look at his banking information and there's nothing since Young's murder. No debit activity, no credit cards, nothing."

Anders nodded. "I will." David had been helping them out? Well. Now he *maybe* felt a little bad for bragging about the whole Curtis-and-Luc-and-him thing. He cleared his throat and tried to even things up a little. "By the way, I talked to the furies, and I'm pretty sure they were trying to tell me they were invited here."

"*Invited?*" David frowned. "By who?"

"Believe it or not, they didn't tell me," Anders said.

"Really? But you're so charming."

Okay, now he felt less bad. "Figured you might make better headway on that front. Or Tyson."

David took a deep breath. "I'll see what I can dig up." He rubbed the back of his neck with one hand. "That can't be good. The furies, I mean."

"They did say they prefer righteous wrath," Anders said, shrugging. "That's better than nothing, right?"

"Do you have any idea how many people in this city have every right to be pissed off?" David said, gaze unblinking, and okay, maybe they were talking about the furies here, but Anders thought maybe they were also talking about each other.

Anders pulled out his keychain and unlocked his SUV. "Yeah, fair enough." He eyed David. "You should head in," he said, nodding to the bar. "Still got an hour before closing, right? You still prefer ginger cubs? There's a new bartender."

"Don't be an asshole," David said, shaking his head and stepping away from the SUV toward the sidewalk instead of the bar. He didn't sound particularly pissed off, though, which was new. Maybe he was finally letting some of his baggage go after all these years?

"For what it's worth," Anders said, wondering why he was saying anything at all, let alone to David, who'd done next to nothing over the years before he'd found Luc and Curtis to make Anders's life even a fraction less difficult, "I think...I mean, I get it now."

The words stopped David in his tracks. His expression shut down, the annoyance from a moment before vanishing, replaced by an icy *nothing* that made Anders wonder if he should have said anything at all.

"For what it's worth," David said, his voice even and hard, "you were right about how I couldn't have had what I wanted with...him." The hesitation before the word "had" been slight, but it had been there. *Chad.*

Looked like neither of them were willing to say the name of the man David had loved, Anders thought. Normally, being right made him feel great. Not so much this time.

"For the record? You don't deserve them," David said, turning and walking away. "They're *way* better than you."

"Please. I'm fucking *amazing*," Anders said, raising his voice to make it carry enough. David didn't so much as slow down, though he aimed a one-finger salute over his shoulder.

He supposed that was the best he could expect from David, really. Seduce and screw a demon cop's love-of-his-life to break them up just *once*, and they didn't tend to let it drop.

❖

Back at the house, Luc was waiting up for him, sitting in the living room on one end of the couch, apparently flipping through an old-looking book. Whatever it was, it had his forehead lined with concentration and maybe some frustration.

"Did someone spill salt in the entrance hall?" Anders said, aiming a thumb over his shoulder.

"Curtis's spell," Luc said, rising and closing the book. "He drew the toxin out of Anna in the entranceway." Luc tapped the back of his neck with his free hand. "Same delivery method as the coywolf, but this was a strong tincture of hawthorn, not silver. Quite toxic to vampires."

"Killer did their homework," Anders said, not liking the sound of that. The last thing he wanted was a needle full of holy water squirted into his head. "Did she at least see who tried to kill her?"

"She's not mobile or vocal. She'll need a lot of time and blood to recover to the point where she can speak," Luc said, shaking his head. He tapped the book absently with one hand, and Anders eyed it. Nothing was written on the brown leather cover.

"What's that?"

"A book. Anna was holding it when she was attacked."

Anders rolled his eyes. "I know it's a book, Luc. What's it *about*?"

"Ah, well," Luc said. "See for yourself." Luc handed it to him.

Anders flipped it open to a random page. Only nothing was written on it. He flipped a few more pages. They were all the same. "It's blank."

"Indeed."

"You were reading a blank book?" Anders stared at him.

Luc shook his head. "I was trying to discover if there was *anything* different about it on any page."

"Fun," Anders said. He frowned at the book. "So, it's, what, a journal? She was thinking of starting a new one when she got jabbed?" Anders said, closing the book with a snap. "Dear Diary, today I'm going to nearly die."

"I don't know, but Lavoie mentioned something about a book earlier," Luc said, glancing up at the ceiling above them. "When he wakes, Curtis is going to take a look at it. By the time Anna and Catharine left, it was already quite late to begin with. He wants to attempt to find that missing sorcerer, Mann, in the morning as well, so I thought it best to let him sleep. I turned off his phone."

"Which explains why David couldn't reach him," Anders said.

"Oh." Luc eyed him. "Does David have news?"

"Fuck all, more like. The Stirling kid hasn't done anything David could track, so he's still in the wind, assuming he's alive. And not the killer."

"Given the other targets, I'm inclined to agree with Curtis now," Luc said.

"You're only saying that because we're all gooey and cuddly now." Anders snorted. "I told David."

"Told David...?"

"About us three being all gooey and cuddly now."

"And enjoyed it, I'm sure," Luc said.

"Maybe."

"Hm." Luc raised one eyebrow. "Gooey and cuddly. Is that what you and your paralegal called it?"

"No, no, that was more grunty and sweaty," Anders said, waving a hand and shrugging. Then he eyed Luc, noting the slight shadows under his eyes and the way his shoulders were set. He looked...hungry. "Speaking of, did you manage to slurp anyone? You've got your needy look."

"*Needy* look?" Luc's lips turned up in a small smile, but Anders thought it might have bothered Luc he'd noticed.

Huh.

"I've known you long enough," Anders said. "You need a bite. If you put it off, you'll only get cranky, and you're barely tolerable as is."

"Of course," Luc said, and he did his stuffy sighing thing. It used to annoy the shit out of Anders, only now it wasn't as annoying somehow, which was probably down to the whole boyfriend thing, and fucking strange, really.

Anders crossed his arms. "I'm serious. Go bite someone. Needy and cranky Luc is my least favorite version of you."

"Gooey and cuddly, needy and cranky..." Luc shook his head. "You're nearly poetic tonight."

"But am I wrong?" Anders said.

"I had some of my emergency supply," Luc said.

Anders grimaced on his behalf. His *emergency supply* was literally bottled blood in a mini-fridge. "You know I've heard you complain drinking from a bottle isn't nearly as good as from a person," Anders said.

"This is true," Luc said. "But needs must. With Catharine and Anna here, I didn't want to leave Curtis alone in the house."

"I thought you said they left?" Anders turned around, frowning. He hadn't heard anyone else beyond Luc—and Curtis's soft snores—and his hearing was usually up to the challenge.

"I did. No, they left as soon as Catharine could move Anna safely." Luc rubbed his eyes. "But you're right. Now they've gone and you're home..."

"Yeah, yeah," Anders said, waving toward the door. "I'm good. Go find a nice bite. Or two. Treat yourself. I think it's men's night at Sintillation. You know Kavan only gets the hottest dancers. Go nibble a stripper or two."

Luc chuckled, passing by him and scooping up his keys. They both knew Luc would never deign to visit a strip club.

Anders looked down at the book once he'd gone, flipping it open again. Still blank. He carried it with him to the kitchen and pulled a beer from the fridge, cracking the bottle open and tipping half of it back before he turned the book around on the counter. He ran his fingers over the inside cover but couldn't feel anything in the binding that might have been hidden beneath it. He shook it, but nothing fell out. It didn't have one of those built-in ribbons or anything, and he even sniffed it.

Smelled like leather and book.

Well, that was pointless.

Annoyed, Anders gave up, finishing the beer and leaving the bottle on the counter, then taking the book and heading upstairs. He stripped down and showered in his bathroom under a hot spray, leaning into the jets and luxuriating under the pulsating heat as he washed the remnants of Shad away, then toweled off. He considered his own bed for a few seconds, then shook his head.

Gooey and cuddly, after all.

He took Luc's blank book with him across the hall to Curtis's bedroom, where he placed it on Curtis's desk, then he slid under the sheet and blanket beside the sleeping wizard, who didn't so much as stir.

You don't deserve them. They're way better than you.

I'm fucking amazing, he'd said. And he meant it. He was amazing. He was a demon with access to a soul, he'd never been more powerful, and it only took a glance into a mirror to remind him he was the hottest thing around, even before the whole conjuring hellfire thing.

Truth was, though, it wasn't thinking he was better than Curtis and Luc that made him want to—what had David called it? Strut. No, he wasn't strutting because he thought he was better than them.

Anders had been strutting because Luc and Curtis thought *he* was good enough for *them*.

NINETEEN

Curtis had almost finished making a simple breakfast of eggs and toast when Anders strode into the kitchen in his boxers, likely drawn from Curtis's bed by the promise of coffee, the scent of which wafted from Anders's plain, no-frills coffee machine Curtis had flicked on once he'd gotten the toast buttered.

"You made me coffee," Anders said, eyeing the almost full carafe and stretching his arms over his head, which gave Curtis some time to admire what it did to the muscles in the demon's hairy chest and arms. Of course he caught Curtis ogling, and one eyebrow rose teasingly. "Enjoying the view?"

"You know I am," Curtis said. "Coffee, eggs, and toast. I wanted to get started early tracking down Professor Mann, and I needed to catch up with you before I go."

"Luc was here when I got home. I heard about..." Anders frowned. "I want to say Annie?"

"Anna." Curtis shook his head, because of course Anders didn't remember her name. He divided up the eggs and toast and carried them to the small kitchen table while Anders poured himself a cup of coffee and followed.

"Right. She got stuck in the back of the neck, you saved her life— unlife—whatever, but she's not up for talking." Anders took a healthy swallow of coffee.

"Yeah," Curtis said. "It'll be a while." He scooped up some egg and decided it wasn't bad. He was no chef, but he'd been trying to do better. Adding some chives and pepper to some eggs wasn't much, but it was a step above his usual go-to bowl of cereal.

"I bumped into David last night," Anders said. "He has no leads on the Stirling kid. Said he hadn't used his cards or accessed any accounts, and all that other shit." He lifted one shoulder. "I told him about the furies, tried to play nice."

Curtis paused, toast halfway to his mouth. "What does that mean?"

"What?" Anders ate some egg. Looking down. Not at him in the slightest.

Fabulous. "Anders?" Curtis said. "*Tried* to play nice?"

"I told him about us." Another half-shrug. "I think maybe it stung him a little."

Curtis leaned back in his chair, staring at Anders, who finally paused eating long enough to look at him. The dent in his nose, the angular chin covered in rough dark stubble, and his heavy browline always struck Curtis as best encapsulated by the word "lug," but the furtive little glances Anders kept giving him seemed almost *bashful*. Despite imagining the worst of Anders's delivery of the news to David, Curtis couldn't help but be charmed.

Because unless he was mistaken, this rough-and-tumble, sex-on-a-stick demon had been *bragging* about him.

Yeah, he was charmed.

The thrum of attraction, contentment, and something else—pride, maybe?—sang across the table through their bond.

"I'll call David later," Curtis said, deciding not to press any further. "I saw I had a missed call."

That earned him another glance from Anders, and Curtis grinned into his next bite of egg. "You're funny when you're smitten," he said after swallowing. "It's a good look on you."

"You teasing me?"

"Maybe."

"You sure that's a good idea?" Anders said with a little growl, putting his forearms on the table and leaning forward. Okay, it was a *very* good look on the demon. "You were up late. Maybe I should drag you back to bed."

"We both know there'd be little to no resting involved." Curtis laughed, then shifted in his chair when Anders doubled down on the leaning thing with a curl of his lips, up higher on one side of his leering smile than the other, in the way he had of making Curtis feel edible. "Also, murderer on the loose, remember? Runaway sorcerers armed with who knows what?" Curtis said, attempting to convince himself as much as anyone else.

Anders grunted. "Fine, fine." Then he snapped his fingers. "Oh, and Luc gave me that book. I put on your desk."

Curtis shook his head. "Right. Also on the to-do list."

"Am I on the to-do list, too?" Anders grinned and popped more toast into his mouth. How he made it look sexy was beyond Curtis. "Luc said you'd want to give it a once-over. Annie had it, he said?"

"Anna," Curtis corrected absently. "Wait. Come to think of it, did Luc say *how* Anna got it?" He frowned. "If it's the same book, it was stolen from Wheeler's. I can't believe I didn't think about that last night."

"Luc said you were wiped." Anders scooped up the last of his egg on some toast. "And he didn't say anything about where it came from, no. He was all 'vampire need blood, blah blah!'" He wiggled two fingers in front of his mouth.

"Your impression is uncanny."

"You know Ducky." Anders popped the last bit of toast into his mouth and crunched it noisily around a broad grin.

"I'll take a look at the book before I go," Curtis said, hurrying to eat the last of his breakfast.

They went back to his room once their plates were in the dishwasher, and Anders handed him the book from Curtis's desk, where Curtis apparently hadn't noticed it that morning when he was tugging on his pajama bottoms and his favorite Transformers T-shirt, the one with Grimlock looking coyly over one shoulder to tell everyone he "liked big bots."

Curtis picked it the book, opened it, and flipped through the pages. They were blank.

"Brown leather," Curtis said, remembering what Rebekah's printout had said about the book. "Leather-bound volume, circa 1800s, blank." He went to his desk and picked up the glasses he'd enchanted to see magical auras, sliding them on, and empowered the lenses.

He reminded himself Anders was standing right beside him, which meant his power would already be more than usual, and then opened his eyes, turning his head to look at Anders.

Curtis saw the golden yellow light around Anders where his aura interacted with the passing currents and energies of the world, revealing him to be a demon. Other demons were a kind of blue-purple color, the same shade as hellfire, but since forming their triad, Anders's flames had turned the brighter color.

A friend had explained the color change had something to do with Anders sharing some of Curtis's soul, a thought Curtis tried not too hard to dwell on.

Once he was sure he had the lenses aligned and his focus was holding steady, Curtis looked down at the book and opened it to the first page.

"Oh," Curtis said.

"What do you see?" Anders leaned over his shoulder.

"Nothing," Curtis said, frowning and turning page after page. "It's still blank. But..." He frowned, though, trying to focus on the edges of the book itself. There. A shimmer along the edge of the leather. "There is *something*. It's definitely enchanted." He lifted the book off the desk and stepped to the window, deciding to let sunlight hit the pages, just in case, and something moved across the page, too fast for him to track.

"Wait," he said. "For a second there..." He frowned, but now the page was blank. "I could have sworn I saw something." He traced it with his finger, but it remained blank and smooth.

"I didn't," Anders said.

Curtis stepped back once, then twice.

There.

A mark had appeared near the top corner of the page. Curtis lifted the book to look closer, but the mark slid off like liquid, vanishing.

He lowered it again, and the mark returned.

"What the hell?" he said, squinting at it. It looked like...*what*? A cupcake? No, it was too pointy on the top, unless those pointy bits were supposed to be candles?

"I still don't see anything," Anders said.

Every time he tried to move the book to look closer at the tiny marking, the marking would move, sometimes right off the page.

Curtis exhaled and then tugged off the glasses. "I'll need to really sit down with this. Or maybe I should call Rebekah. It's her Family's store the book was stolen from, and she's far more talented at seeing veiled magic than I'll ever be."

"You want to give it back to the Families?" Anders didn't sound convinced.

"No, I want to understand what the damn thing is." He scowled at the book.

"Hey," Anders said, giving his shoulder a little squeeze. "You're fine."

"Sorry." The book felt like yet another reminder of how often he was working with nothing but instinct and what shreds of knowledge he'd managed to gather on his own or from his Craft Night friends. Anders had probably picked up on his frustration. He handed the book to Anders. "I'll call Rebekah later. First I want to try and find Professor Mann."

"Time for the cum rag?" Anders grinned.

Curtis winced, but unfortunately, the demon was right. It was time for the cum rag.

His phone rang, and he checked the caller ID. Mackenzie.

"Hey, Kenzie," he said, answering and giving Anders the little nod he used to let him know he could listen in.

"Hi, Curt," Kenzie said. "You know how yesterday we wondered how many of the sorcerers might be missing?"

"Yes," he said.

"Well, I just got off the phone with Dale, and he was the last of the group to check in. It's official," Kenzie said. "They're *all* gone. Malcolm Stirling has definitely noticed, and he's called a coven head moot. Tonight. And it's all hands on deck. I'd say it probably means Stirling is going to order all the Families to start looking for them with everything they've got at their disposal."

Which meant methods both mundane *and* magic, Curtis figured. The sorcerers likely wouldn't be able to hide from the Families for long. Which meant...

What?

He had no idea. But if every sorcerer had gone underground for a reason, Curtis wanted to know what it was.

"I was just about to start looking for Professor Mann," Curtis said. "If I can attune my pendant to him, did you want to ride shotgun?"

"Absolutely. I'll head to your place right now. Oh, and I have the list from Rebekah for you. Everything that went missing."

"Great. See you soon," Curtis said, and hung up.

"You're going to make me sit in the back?" Anders said, frowning and crossing his arms. He didn't look happy about it. "What's the point of being boyfriends if I don't get shotgun?"

"Blow jobs."

❖

Curtis parked his hybrid in the visitor parking area of the apartment complex and turned off the car.

"Something's off," Anders said from the back seat.

"What?" Curtis said, turning to face him. Anders was sort of glancing around left and right, and he grunted, shaking his head.

"Anders?" Curtis said again.

"Those buildings," Anders said. Gripping the back of Curtis's chair, he crouched down to look past him through the windshield at the trio of apartment towers. His frown grew, and then he grimaced and looked away.

Once Curtis had aligned the pendant to Professor Mann via Anders's cloth, it had landed on their map of the city more or less where these three buildings stood. An apartment complex near Hurdman, the area struck Curtis as more serviceable than stylish. It wasn't much to look at, but being close to the Transitway and the train would at least make living there convenient, Curtis supposed.

At least on the days the train decided to run.

But he didn't see anything off, unless you counted planter boxes filled with nothing but weeds, or the neglected circles of grass growing inside the drop-off/pick-up points in front of the towers.

"What are you seeing?" Mackenzie said. She'd greeted Anders politely when she'd arrived at the house, and Anders hadn't seemed too put out by her impromptu joining them on their trip, but she'd been pretty quiet on the drive over. Her confusion now made Curtis think she didn't see whatever it was the demon was seeing, either.

"It's hard to look at the towers," Anders said. "It's…" He shook his head. "I don't know why." He stared at the floor of the car. "I know they're there. I know it's where we're going, but I can't look at them."

"Oh," Mackenzie said, her eyes widening. "It's a ward."

"A ward?" Anders said. "Like the things Curtis is doing at the new house?"

"Yes," Mackenzie said. "It's a pretty basic one, though if you're determined to head there, you end up with what you're feeling now, like you want to look but can't quite make yourself do it."

"Your chantry had it, I think," Curtis said. "The first time I went there."

Mackenzie nodded. "That's right. It's designed to keep those of us who are more or less than human from getting too close."

"More," Anders said from the back seat, crossing his arms and raising one eyebrow. "I'm more than human, right? That's what you meant?"

"Of course." Mackenzie pinked.

"But wait. Why isn't it working on us?" Curtis said.

"And how do I make it stop?" Anders grumbled, rubbing his eyes.

"It'll wear off if you persist," Mackenzie said to Anders, then she turned to Curtis. "I think we already wore it out for us with the pendant."

"Ah," Curtis said, understanding now. "That explains it."

"What?" Anders said.

Curtis had had a hard time getting a reading with the replacement pendant Mackenzie had given him when he'd first let it swing over the map on the kitchen table. He'd assumed it was his magic acting as it sometimes did; the elemental powers he could wield tended toward favoring air and didn't always like the more grounded tools when he tried to use them, so when Mackenzie had arrived, he'd asked her to give him a hand, and they'd worked the pendant together until the quartz had stopped swinging and held itself pointing at a slight angle to these towers. But it had taken more effort than usual and longer than he'd expected.

"It wasn't me having a hard time locking on to Professor Mann," Curtis said. "It was the ward trying to keep my pendant from paying attention."

"Oh," Anders said. After another quick look at the buildings and another twitch, he asked, "Which tower? I'm ready to start *persisting*."

Curtis didn't know. He eyed the three towering apartment blocks, and realized how much more work they had ahead of them.

Mackenzie gave him a small smile of support. "If we go to that little patch of grass in between the parking lots, we should be able to use the pendant to figure out which building right away."

They got out of the car. At least they wouldn't need the map now.

They started for the grass together, but Curtis paused after a couple of steps, turning to see Anders standing still at the edge of the parking lot between two of the numbered signs on their little poles. He hadn't left the paved surface.

"Anders?" He went back. Anders's fists were clenched at his sides, and he gave Curtis a small shake of his head.

"Something is pushing me. Like residency, but much fucking stronger."

Curtis glanced at Mackenzie, and Mackenzie shook her head. "I don't know. Apartment towers aren't chantries, and we're not even at the entrance yet. An individual apartment might do this, but not out here."

Curtis pulled out his enchanted glasses and slid them on, taking a moment to center himself before opening his eyes and drawing a sliver of magic into the lenses to spark off the power.

The parking spot signs rippled with a soft silvery light as the energies of the world brushed past them.

"It's the signs," he said, walking slowly around the closest sign, which was nothing more than a number on a pole, as far as he'd noticed when he'd pulled his car in, but now… "Oh," he said, pointing.

Something had been scratched into the metal on the rear of the sign. His glasses caught the faint, barely discernible shimmer of magic in the air above the various lines. "It's a bind rune," he said, then moved to the next sign. "There's another one here, too." A quick scan of the parking lot indicated all the signs were shimmering with the silver light the lenses used to show him the patterns of magic.

He pulled his glasses off, blinking to adjust going from seeing auras to back to normal, and crouched low behind one of the signs. Mackenzie joined him.

"On the plus side, I think this means we're on the right track to find Professor Mann," she said.

"Absolutely," he said. "This is subtle."

"Doesn't fucking feel subtle," Anders said. He was still on the inside of the barrier the signs created. "Did your pendant wear these out for you, too?"

"No," Mackenzie said, pointing at the scratches. "This is specifically anti-demon." She glanced up at him. "Sorry."

"Can you break it?" Anders said, swallowing. He'd taken a step back from the line the signs formed around the edge of the parking lot. "Or is there a way to go around it?"

"It's etched in metal," Curtis said, shaking his head. "And there are a lot of them. It'll be fine when I drive you back out again, but I don't see an immediate way to get you across the threshold otherwise, so—"

Anders held up one hand, interrupting him. "You're *not* going in there alone."

"Anders," Curtis said, pointing at Mackenzie and not bothering to hide his annoyance. "I'm not alone. She's literally right here."

"Hi." Mackenzie waved at him.

Anders let out a deep, frustrated sigh, then held out his hands. "Give me the keys, then. I'll wait in the fucking car."

Curtis tossed them over, and Anders snatched them out of the air.

❖

"So," Mackenzie said. "Are we going to tell him those runes were familiar?"

"You think Matt did them, too?" Curtis said.

She blew out a breath. "They're a lot like the ones he showed you how to make for your house, aren't they?"

"Yep," Curtis said. "I should probably tell Anders, but he's already pretty iffy on the Matt-is-innocent front."

Mackenzie shook her head. "Matt didn't kill anyone. If anything, someone is killing people like him." Her voice rose with every word.

"I know," Curtis said softly.

"Sorry," she said, and they dropped the conversation.

Once they were on the small grass space between the various parking lots, Curtis pulled out the pendant and cloth, closing his eyes and willing the stone to draw on the essence in the cloth again.

Okay, fine, the cum. It was dried freaking sperm, why was he trying to fool himself?

Beside him, Mackenzie said, "You've got it."

Much easier this time. Which put point to Mackenzie's theory they'd already worked their way through the "nothing worth looking at" ward. Curtis opened his eyes watched the pendant move in a slow circle, warping into an oval, and then a back-and-forth rocking, and then—alongside a kind of mental tug between Curtis's eyes—the pendant froze in the air, pointing about halfway up one of the buildings.

"Hold still for a second," Mackenzie said, and Curtis obeyed, doing his best not to move while she crouched behind him on the thin grass, lining herself up with the pendant and—he realized—doing her best to guess which floor the crystal was aiming for.

"I'm going to say nine or ten floors up," she said.

Inside the building, they looked for a list of residents but instead found a display where you had to key in the person's name to get their code. They tried typing in Mann's name, but the only match was a "Tiffany Manning."

"Do we wait for someone to leave, or—" Curtis started, but Mackenzie stepped up to the second door and pressed her hand against it, closing her eyes and whispering something he didn't quite catch.

The lights above them flickered, and the door buzzed and un-locked.

"I didn't think that could work," Curtis said, surprised. "Didn't residency fight you?"

"It's a lobby, Curt," Mackenzie said, shrugging and holding the door open for him. "Do you feel any residency?"

He blinked, realizing she was right. He'd felt no sense of pressure against him when he'd come through the front doors of the apartment building. Huh. Lobbies didn't do residency.

You learned something new every day.

"Once we're in the elevator, use the pendant again," Mackenzie said. "I'll press nine and ten, and we'll see which one the pendant prefers."

"Got it," Curtis said. "Then we follow it to the right door."

"Right." They stepped into the elevator and Mackenzie pressed the two buttons.

Curtis pulled out the pendant and cloth again, and Mackenzie tilted her head.

"What's on that, anyway?" Mackenzie said. "Sweat? It doesn't feel like blood, but there's still a pretty strong connection."

"You *so* don't want to know," Curtis said, closing his eyes and attuning the pendant again.

TWENTY

Fifteen minutes later, they stood in front of door 1010, the pendant pointing at it with no hesitancy whatsoever.

Curtis let his magic release, and the pendant fell loose again.

Mackenzie knocked, and it wasn't long before the door opened.

It took Curtis a moment to realize he was looking at Professor Mann. He was used to seeing him in a crisp white dress shirt, dress pants, and some form of tie. The white tank top and faded jeans didn't say "professor."

Instead, they said "badass."

Or maybe it was the tattoos. In fact, Mann had two full sleeves, a riot of mostly Celtic or Nordic symbols inked right up and across the front of his shoulders to meet at the incredibly detailed tattoo of Mjölnir just below the hollow of his throat.

Also, Professor Mann hit the gym pretty damn hard. He had *guns*. Guns covered in ink.

Holy crap.

"Mr. Baird, Miss Windsor," Mann said. He didn't use a particularly welcoming tone of voice, and his eyes went straight to the pendant.

"Uh," Curtis said. He slipped the pendant into his pocket, pushing the bandana out of view.

Mann tracked the movement, scowling openly now. In fairness, Curtis imagined he wouldn't be pleased himself if he'd learned someone used magic to track him down. He hoped he hadn't seen the cloth.

"Professor," Mackenzie started, but Mann held up his hand. She stopped.

"Who else knows where I am?" Mann's already deep voice was rough. "Did you tell anyone I was here?"

Curtis shared a quick glance with Mackenzie, not sure how

truthful they should be, but he opted for honesty. "No one. I mean, Luc knew I was going to try scrying for you, and Anders is here, but he's waiting in the car thanks to whatever you did in the parking lot." Curtis felt more foolish the longer he spoke. "No one else knows. We didn't know where we were going ahead of time, not really."

"How did you find me? The pendant?"

"The pendant," Curtis said.

Mann stepped aside, opening the door, but he didn't invite them in, which was telling.

Crap.

They went inside. Curtis felt the apartment pressing at him the moment he crossed the threshold. Unlike the lobby, the law of residency very much existed in the apartment and would work against him. If this was Mann's place, using magic here would be harder.

Not impossible, though. What residency this apartment had didn't strike Curtis as particularly strong. Curtis didn't think Mann had lived here long—or maybe it was more of a case of "not often." Either way, the knowledge he'd still be able to throw around a spell if he needed to was comforting.

Mann closed the door behind them and locked the deadbolt.

Okay. Also not great.

Mackenzie exchanged a glance with him, her eyes wide behind her glasses, and he tried to give her a confident nod in return.

When Mann stepped past them, Curtis spotted a series of runes burned into the wood in a circle around the spy hole on the back of the door. They were similar to the runes Curtis had used to create both pairs of his enchanted glasses. Even a sorcerer, using those runes, might be able to make a similar effect happen through the spy hole, which was clever, but added itself to the growing list of things that didn't exactly bode well.

"Have a seat," Mann said, more gruff than polite.

There was a small two-seater couch and a pair of chairs and not much else in the apartment's main living area. Curtis could see through to the kitchen, but all the doors in the small hallway were closed. The walls sported the same neutral-nothing color of apartment buildings everywhere. It barely looked like someone lived there.

Curtis sat on one side of the couch. Mackenzie took a chair.

Mann himself didn't sit.

"Why are you here?"

Okay then. Curtis was used to Mann being refined and educated.

This grumpy, almost prickly version of the professor was hard to reconcile.

"We realized all the sorcerers have gone missing," Curtis said. "You among them, obviously. And some people have turned up dead. Honestly, at the start, I was worried about you—your name came up when I was looking into a murder." He was stretching the truth there a bit, but Matthew had Mann's phone number. Close enough.

Mann crossed his arms. "You're not working with Malcolm Stirling?"

"Absolutely not," Mackenzie said. "But there's going to be a coven head meeting with all hands to follow, so I'm pretty sure they're going to start looking for all of you."

"And given we're talking about Malcolm Stirling and the other coven heads…" Curtis shrugged. "It seemed like a good idea to try and track down the missing sorcerers ourselves, before they did."

For the first time, Mann's demeanor softened. He even smiled, a flush of white teeth amidst his dark beard.

"I've never had cause to complain about your judgement," Mann said.

"Look," Curtis said. "Matthew Stirling is missing, and someone is out there killing people—anyone with a gift to see the future."

"Like Mr. Stirling himself," Mann said. Matthew had told Mann last February about his inherited gift, when they'd been tracking down a different murderer.

My life has too many murderers.

"Right," Curtis said, reining in the errant observation. "And he had your number. Can I ask why he was calling you?"

"He had some history questions," Mann said, after enough of a hesitation Curtis believed the answer, but was pretty sure it was carefully stated not to really tell them much of anything.

Okay. New tack, then. "Will you tell us what's going on with the sorcerers? Why you've all taken off? Why you're hiding here?"

Mann's smile faded, and what little of the familiar Curtis had seen in his former professor was once again gone, replaced by something closer to menacing. "What happens if I say no, Mr. Baird?"

Crap.

Curtis blew out a breath. "If you say no, then…we leave, I guess." Mackenzie frowned at him, but he shook his head.

Silence stretched.

"Is Matt with you?" Mackenzie said, breaking it.

"No." Mann shook his head. "Not any more."

"Not *any more*," Curtis said. "You've seen him. When?"

"Last Wednesday."

Curtis sighed. Before Aaron's death. For one brief moment, he'd hoped Mann was about to tell them Matt was okay. Now they were back to not knowing.

But Mackenzie leaned forward. "What lessons?"

Mann regarded her. "Pardon?"

"You said he wanted history lessons. It wasn't official business from Malcolm Stirling, I don't imagine."

"No, it wasn't." Mann snorted. "Malcolm Stirling doesn't bother with many of us peons unless he wants a report."

"So, what did Matt want to know?" Curtis repeated Mackenzie's question.

For a moment, Curtis was convinced Mann wasn't going to answer. But then he finally crossed the small living room and sank into the other chair, glancing down the hallway.

"What do you think, Carol?"

Curtis blinked, and looked behind him. There was a woman in the hallway. He hadn't seen her there before. Had she been listening the whole time?

Mackenzie was biting her bottom lip. So she hadn't noticed the woman either.

How had neither of them seen her? Well, obvious answer: magic. The woman wasn't very tall, looked to be in her fifties or perhaps her sixties. She wore her steel-colored hair in a long braid, and a simple coral peasant blouse and comfortable-looking grey slacks. Around her neck, a black stone with tiny golden striations hung on a gold chain.

"I think anyone who'd rather Malcolm Stirling didn't find us can't be all bad," she said. "But I don't know them."

"I owe these two a debt, Carol." Mann rubbed his beard.

"I'd still say it's too risky." Carol shook her head, though she almost looked apologetic as she did so.

"Look," Curtis said, leaning forward. "I don't know what you're all trying to accomplish right now. Is it a strike or something?"

Carol laughed and Mann snorted.

Okay. Not a strike, then.

"But someone is out there killing people like Matt, and we want to make sure he's not next," Curtis said. "I'm not here—we're not here—to do anything to mess with your plans."

"Assuming your plans don't involve those murders," Mackenzie said with a coolness he'd never heard her use before.

Both Carol and Mann stopped at her words. Mann looked almost *offended*.

"Young Mr. Stirling wanted to know about sorcerers and about the Accords," Mann said.

"*Jeffrey*," Carol said, but Mann didn't seem upset by the mild rebuke.

Curtis frowned. "I don't get it." Surely someone who grew up with the Families would already know about sorcerers, and the Accords were just the rules all the various supernatural beings held to when they bumped into each other—rules which left the wizards in the top dog position among the vampires, demons, and the rest of the not-quite-human. Or at least, that was Curtis's understanding of it.

Mackenzie seemed equally nonplussed. "Was it something specific?"

Mann turned to Carol, who sighed and joined Curtis on the couch. She had a very pretty smile, and the lines around her eyes made Curtis think she smiled often. "What do you know about us?"

"Sorcerers, you mean?" he said, taking an educated guess.

She nodded.

"I'm not part of the Families," Curtis said. "I'm an Orphan. But my understanding is sorcerers are kind of like me. You pop up at random, not in the magical bloodlines, only with a more limited amount of personal magic to draw from."

Carol's smile grew a trace sad, but she nodded. "And our position in the Accords?"

"Well," Curtis said, feeling like he was on shaky ground here, "I know the Families adopt sorcerers much the same way they do Orphans, to some degree, because they are magic." He swallowed. "But I also know they don't tend to treat them as much more than, uh…" He spoke multiple languages, but somehow the only word coming to him was *flunky*, and he groped for another one. "Lesser."

That didn't make anyone smile, sad or otherwise.

"But," Curtis said, looking at Professor Mann and remembering the last time they'd had a discussion about sorcerers, "I also know sorcerers have enough power to work with truly enchanted tools." He'd seen Mann demonstrate that first-hand with the very same wands Mackenzie currently wore through her braided hair. "And I know you've stolen some from the Mitchells."

He wished he'd taken some time before this discussion to look at the list Mackenzie had gotten from Rebekah.

"You're correct about sorcerers, more or less," Carol said. "Though I won't speak to any potential theft." That came with a winsome little smile Curtis didn't believe for a second. "Now, did you ever wonder how we came to be?"

Mackenzie frowned. "I'm sorry?"

Mann's smirk was almost triumphant. "I told you. Young Stirling wasn't an ignorant one-off. There's no way the Families would teach their own anything about us. You owe me a whisky."

Carol laughed. "Fair enough."

"I'm sorry," Curtis said. "I'm not following. Ignorant about what? And what do you mean, 'came to be'? I thought…I mean, aren't we all born with our magic?"

"We are," Mann said. "Some of us with much less than others, as you've said, and the Families with the lion's share, Orphans like you notwithstanding—who they *also* snap up as little more than servants, yourself being a rare exclusion."

"Okay," Curtis said, still not getting the point. Though he had to agree. He'd only met a few other Orphans, and they'd been treated terribly by the Families who adopted them. Wheeler had felt so ill-used by the Mitchells he'd turned to necromancy to attempt to overthrow them, and Ben, who was Malcolm Stirling's driver and errand runner, had been tasked with trying to seduce Curtis into joining the Stirling family, way back when Curtis and Luc and Anders had first formed their triad.

Hell, Ben had been ordered to kill Curtis if he didn't agree. Hadn't worked out for him, and Curtis was no fan of the man, but even considering all Ben had done, he'd seen how cowed and under Stirling's rule the man was. Some days, he almost felt sorry for him.

"You're saying there's something more about sorcerers than being born with magic?" Mackenzie said.

"There were no sorcerers before 1816," Carol said.

"*What?*" Mackenzie's voice was just shy of a laugh, like Carol had told a particularly terrible joke. And if it was, Curtis didn't grasp the punchline.

"Can we play catch-up for those of us who didn't grow up knowing they were magic?" he said.

"Before the Accords," Mackenzie said. "You're implying there were *no* sorcerers before the founding of the Families and formal peace between the wizards, demons, and vampires." Her tone made it clear she didn't think this likely. "And then, what, *suddenly* there are sorcerers?"

"Can you bring any to mind?" Mann said. "From before the Accords?"

"No, but, sorcerers aren't—" She bit off whatever she'd been about to say.

Curtis remembered Anders referring to sorcerers once as "low-watt bulbs," and he'd pretty much had to admit the descriptor was apt. Mackenzie was blushing, and both Mann and Carol were waiting for her to finish her sentence. But what could she say that wasn't rude?

Curtis decided to rescue her.

"So, Matt was asking about the Accords? About how sorcerers started...uh, popping up around then?"

Mann nodded but didn't say anything else.

Why would Matt care about when sorcerers began being born? Sorcerers weren't a threat. He looked at Mackenzie, and she seemed equally befuddled. She shook her head, and the light caught on the two wands she wore crossed through her braided hair.

No threat wasn't technically true, was it? Because these sorcerers could be a threat, given they had access to truly enchanted objects.

"Does this have anything to do with what was stolen from Wheeler's Pawn Shop?" Curtis said.

Mann's expression closed.

"That's a yes," Curtis said. "There was a book," he started, but Mann rose from his chair, cutting him off.

"I'm afraid that's all I have for you," Mann said. His demeanor had returned to "biker enforcer" rather than "former professor." Or maybe it was the ink. Curtis was really struggling with the whole tattooed daddy bear thing happening.

"Oh. Okay." Curtis stood up as well.

Mann led them to the door. Carol waited beside the couch.

"Do you know if Matt's okay?" Mackenzie said, a note of pleading in her voice. "Can you tell us that, at least?"

Mann softened. "To the best of my knowledge, he's alive. But you have to stop looking for him. He believes it's dangerous."

"*He* believes it's dangerous?" Mackenzie shook her head. "*Matt* does?"

"You bring death," Mann said, lifting one shoulder.

"That wasn't comforting." Curtis stared at Mann. "If you meant it to be, I mean."

Mann put his hand on Curtis's shoulder. Curtis resisted the urge to flinch, but only just. How had this man gone from being a favorite professor to a threat?

"What did you use to attune your scrying pendant?" Mann said.

"You, uh, left behind a"—*Don't say cum rag. Don't say cum rag.*—"bandana. With Anders."

"May I have it back?"

Well, crap. Giving Mann back the bandana would effectively close off his ability to track Mann down again if he wanted to. Unless Anders had another cum rag lying around he was sure belonged to Mann.

But Curtis handed it over. It hadn't felt like a request.

Mann slid it into his back pocket after a quick glance.

"Please," Mackenzie said again.

"Believe me," Mann said. "I've said enough."

He squeezed Curtis's shoulder and winked.

Actually *winked*.

"It was good seeing you again," Curtis said. He didn't want to go, but they were obviously being dismissed.

Mann closed the door behind them.

"What the hell?" Mackenzie said.

"Come on," Curtis said.

Once they were outside the apartment buildings, he stopped her.

"He winked at me."

"What?"

"Mann. At the end there. When he said he'd 'said enough.' He winked at me."

"Clear as mud." Mackenzie exhaled. "And the sorcerer woman, Karen. I didn't recognize her."

"Karen?" Curtis said, frowning. "I thought it was Claire…" But even as he said it, he shook his head. "No, that's not right."

"Wait." Mackenzie stared at him. "Who?"

"The woman. The woman with Professor Mann…" Curtis shook his head. It had been a woman, right? Why couldn't he picture her? Or was it a man? "What's happening?"

Mackenzie put a hand to her throat. "Oh, no. No no *no*. Obfuscation. The necklace. Black jade. He…She? It was an obfuscation. Enchanted on the necklace." She pulled out her phone, and Curtis watched while she pulled up something on the screen and then groaned. "Damn it. Right there on Rebekah's list. Black jade pendant." She turned back to the door, taking one step, then stopping. "Do you remember what room they were in?"

"Sure, it was...I...no." Curtis couldn't even remember whether or not they'd taken stairs or used an elevator at all, let alone what floor they'd been on. "I remember what they said, though."

"Yeah," she said. "It's like that. That's a pretty rare enchanted piece of bling they had there. Dates back to before the Accords. But..." She eyed the door they were standing beside, then pulled out her phone and snapped a picture of the address on the door's front. "That might help. If I wasn't standing right here, I wouldn't even be sure this is the right building. If only Bekah was here. I'm pretty sure the necklace wouldn't affect her."

"We could come back here with her, if..." Curtis patted his pockets. "The bandana is gone. Crap. I gave it back to him, didn't I?"

"Yes."

"Who *was* the other person?" He couldn't even remember what they looked like. "Kenzie," Curtis said, biting his bottom lip.

She eyed him, one eyebrow rising. "You have 'I don't want to say it' face."

"Because I don't," Curtis said. "You know how there was no one in the room with Marlowe during the Memento Loci spell?"

"Yes," she said, frowning, and then shook her head. "Oh, you're wondering if an obfuscation charm would affect a Memento Loci?"

"It wouldn't?" Curtis said.

"No," Mackenzie said, and Curtis felt real relief. He hadn't wanted to believe Professor Mann would be involved in the death of Aaron or Marlowe or the attack on Anna, but he'd had to consider it. "We'd have seen someone, and then forgotten the specifics about the person wearing the charm all over again," Mackenzie said. "Memento Loci replays things exactly as they appeared..." Her eyes widened. "Oh. Oh *damn.*"

"What?" Curtis said, but she was already scrolling her phone again.

"Right there," Mackenzie said, using her thumbs to make the text bigger on the screen.

Curtis leaned over to read it.

Mantle, shrouding. Enchanted by Abraham Stirling, stored on behalf of Malcolm Stirling. Stored by Benedict Lister.

"Does shrouding mean what I think it means?" Curtis said.

"Invisible," she said. "It means invisible. No wonder they couldn't see the attack coming."

Curtis's phone buzzed, and he pulled it out of his pocket. A text from Anders.

stop standing there talking and COME BACK TO THE FUCKING CAR

Two bursts of his car's horn sounded from the parking lot.

"Let's get back to the car," Curtis said, fighting off a smile in spite of himself. "Anders is worried."

TWENTY-ONE

Anders clenched his jaw as they got back into the car, Curtis in the passenger seat and Mackenzie in the back behind him. He'd taken the driver's seat.

"Well?" Anders said, grinding the word out.

"Give us a second," Curtis said. "There was a lot, but they used magic to mess with our memories."

"*What?*" Anders turned in the driver's seat to stare at him. This was why he hadn't wanted him to go in alone, for fuck's sake.

"'I've said enough'?" Mackenzie leaned forward, but she wasn't talking to him. She was talking to Curtis. "He barely said *anything.*"

"Give me a second." Curtis sat back in the passenger seat and closed his eyes. "This is so weird. I usually remember everything so clearly, but all I can remember is what they said, but not much else."

What the flying fuck happened in that damn building?

"Who's *they?*" Anders said, in his best demon-is-out-of-patience voice.

They both finally paid attention to him.

"Sorry," Curtis turned in his seat. "Professor Mann wasn't alone. There was someone with him, but they used some sort of magic, and we can't remember what they looked like."

Anders sighed. "Fucking magic."

"Right, well." Curtis cleared his throat. "The guy who was there with Professor Mann, the other person, they didn't like what Mann said at one point. Mann said Matt asked about sorcerers and about the Accords, and the other guy was all '*Jeffrey.*'"

"I don't get it," Anders said. "Who cares about sorcerers or the Accords?"

"They do," Mackenzie said, still facing forward in the passenger seat. "Matt too. That's what he'd been talking to Professor Mann about. But we don't know *why*."

"Is this the sort of thing you could ask your mother?" Curtis said.

Mackenzie sighed. "No. She and I…" She glanced at him. "Since she found out about Cynthia? It's been awkward. I don't think she trusts me right now, and she's the new coven head, so I *can't* trust her. Not with how much Stirling loves his truth spells. And besides, there's the moot tonight. We won't have any time alone."

"Right," Curtis said.

"You said you could remember what they said," Anders said, turning sideways in his seat. He was pretty sure this was the girl who'd kept a vampire in her basement, so really, he couldn't blame her mother much for not feeling the love. "What did they say? Exactly."

"Mann saw Matt last Wednesday," Mackenzie said, holding up one finger. "Matt has been asking Professor Mann about sorcerers, and how they came to be." She raised another finger. "And the other man… Woman? Ugh. The other person said there were no sorcerers before the Accords." Another finger. "And I think he called us ignorant, but he said he owed us." She lowered her hand. "Am I forgetting anything?"

"That's everything they said," Curtis said. "But was it me or did they both get squirrelly when I mentioned the book?"

"Yes," Mackenzie said.

"You told him we had the book?" Anders said, about to remind Curtis sharing information was best when other people did it in their direction, not the other way around, but Curtis held up a hand, so he bit his comment back.

"No," Curtis said. "I asked if the sorcerers had anything to do with the stuff that got stolen from Wheeler's."

"Which they did," Mackenzie said. "Because that's how the person with Mann messed with us—there's a pendant missing from the pawn shop, and she was definitely using it."

"Oh, and we're pretty sure the killer is using one of those items, too," Curtis said. "A mantle to turn invisible, basically."

"Mantle." Anders shook his head, because did these people *ever* use English?

"Like a fancy cape," Curtis said. "Malcolm Stirling had it stored there. And Ben was the one who stored it."

"Ben as in 'seduced you, fucked you, tried to kill us' Ben?" Anders remembered the tall blond with the goatee who'd quite literally grave-robbed to take a shot at making Curtis leave their triad back when they'd first gotten together. First he'd tried seducing Curtis away, though, which hadn't worked, obviously, given Curtis had access to him and Luc, and what scruffy goateed fucking Orphan wizard could measure up to him *and* Luc? Or just him, even.

"Yes." Curtis's ears turned pink. "Ben. They said they had nothing to do with the murders, but the point is these sorcerers can use enchanted stuff to…I don't know, be a threat."

"Oh fuck," Anders said. *Be a threat.* The damned sorcerers. Why hadn't he considered *them*? Because no one did. That was why. They barely had any power, and the wizards…

Fuck.

"What?" Curtis said, frowning at him, eyes wide.

"The Families treat sorcerers like shit," Anders said.

"Well," Mackenzie leaned forward. "I mean, I know my mother does her best to…" She trailed off at his look, because come on? *Really?*

"Fine," she said. "Yes. Yes, they do."

"What is it?" Curtis said.

Anders stabbed the power button to start Curtis's ridiculous car. He wasn't sure where they were going to go next, but he definitely wanted to have anything enchanted back in hand. That book, for one thing. "They have every right to be pissed," Anders said.

"The sorcerers?" Curtis said. "I guess so, yeah."

"Well," Anders said, trying to put the car into reverse. Only he couldn't. His hands wouldn't move. Magic. Again. "Oh, *for fuck's sake.* I can't even *drive* out of this goddamn parking lot?"

"It's the wards," Mackenzie said, in a tiny soft apologetic voice that made Anders want to growl at the sky. *Of course* it was the fucking wards.

"Swap with me," Curtis said, undoing his seat belt and opening the door.

Luckily, that Anders *could* do. They traded places, and Anders tugged his own seat belt down after two tries of it catching behind him. Curtis watched him but didn't say anything until they were out of the parking lot.

"What did you mean about the sorcerers being pissed?" Curtis said.

"It's more about how they're pissed." Anders took a breath. "Their anger is righteous." That was the word for it. *Righteous*.

"Oh no," Curtis said. He glanced at Anders, and Anders could tell he'd made the same connection, even without the thrum of worry now coming off him in a pulse.

"Sorry, I don't follow," Mackenzie said.

"A pack of furies rolled into town," Anders said. "Bikers."

"Biker wrath demons," Curtis added.

"And they made it sound like they were invited," Anders said, meeting Mackenzie's frown in the rearview.

"Wrath demons," Mackenzie said.

"Wizards and anger don't mix," Curtis said.

"Same with sorcerers, I figure," Anders said. At least it seemed like the worst-case scenario, so it felt like a good bet. "Either way, the fury I spoke with, Aurora, she said her pack preferred *righteous* anger. So, I'm thinking your missing, pissed-off sorcerers? They've got demon backup, and their backup probably jacks up their magic."

"If it works the same way for sorcerers like it does for wizards," Curtis said. "Which…Does it? Kenzie?"

"Pretty much," the woman replied, though Anders would have laid even odds she was more guessing than sure. "Though on a sliding scale, if you get what I mean."

Low-watt bulbs could only burn so bright before they'd pop, in other words. Anders grunted, and silence followed for a few blocks. He bounced his left knee, thinking. "Why would blue eyes care about when sorcerers started popping up?"

"Blue eyes?" Curtis frowned, though he didn't take his gaze off the road. "Oh. Matthew. I don't know."

"I didn't even know they hadn't always been around," Mackenzie said, "which Professor Mann said was ignorant, right? Matt didn't know, either?"

"That's right," Curtis said.

"But it's important?" Anders said.

"I don't know," Curtis said. "Any chances it would be in the books in your library, Kenzie?"

"No. I've read all the books in my family library," Mackenzie said. "There are a couple on the Accords, but I don't remember any mentions of sorcerers in them."

Anders blinked and nearly asked her if she was sure, but Curtis shook his head. Apparently, he believed her. He supposed she did look like a big reader.

"Are you going to head home, Kenzie?" Curtis said after another silence.

"I have to," she said. "Prep for the coven moot. I don't think it'll help, but I'll try those books on the Accords again." She sighed. "I wonder how long the sorcerers will be able to hide if the covens really decide to go looking for them."

"Not long, I'd bet," Anders said. "I bet your Families have little boxes full of their hair or blood or whatever, to make sure they can always track them down."

"Anders," Curtis said, but Anders noticed Mackenzie didn't argue. After a second, Curtis seemed to notice it, too. "Really?" he said, glancing in the rearview.

"Maybe," she said in a voice that said *absolutely*, lifting one shoulder.

"Wow." Curtis tapped his hands on the steering wheel. "You're right, though," he said to Anders. "We're on a ticking clock here, and I don't know what to do next, other than try to figure out that blank book."

"First we go back home," Anders said. "If you're saying any enchanted thing is a weapon in the hands of the sorcerers, I want everything we've got at hand or locked up. You still got the syringe thing?" They'd picked up some sort of necromantic needle from one of the big gun wizards last February, and Curtis had been sitting on it ever since. The last thing they needed was to find out whatever the hell it did the hard way.

"It's in the safe," Curtis said. "But I get your point."

"Speaking of the book," Mackenzie said. "Did you want me to call Rebekah?"

"Yes," Curtis said. "If she can get free, she could take a look at it."

"I don't know how, given the moot," Mackenzie said.

"I know. But just in case."

"Okay," Mackenzie said. "It's from the same time period, right?"

"Sorry?" Curtis said.

"The blank book. It's from the same time as the Accords?"

"I think so," Curtis said.

"Wait," Anders said. "How long ago are we talking, here?"

"The Accords?" Curtis said.

"1816," Mackenzie said. "Not exactly recent history."

Anders grinned. "That's perfect."

"It is? Why?" Curtis eyed him, though he had a half-smile, like he could tell Anders was on to something, which he *hoped* he was.

"*Recent* is a relative term," Anders said, giving Curtis's shoulder a little nudge. "We happen to know someone who's been twenty-eight for a *very* long time. In fact, we fuck on a regular basis."

"You think Luc might know?" Curtis said, but his smile grew.

"Maybe. I mean, he had a lot of time flying solo and hiding from everyone like I did, but he's Lucky Ducky now, so even if he didn't see anything or notice anything, I'm pretty sure the fucking duke can ask the rest of the bloodsuckers about it."

"He has access to vampire records," Mackenzie said, sounding hopeful.

"It's possible one of the other vampires was around then, too, right?" Curtis said. "I get that impression from Catharine, at least. I mean, they're immortal. And I'm told they keep good notes."

"It's worth a try."

"We just have to wait for him to wake up," Anders said.

"Sunset," Mackenzie said, sighing. "Still a ways off. Still, gives us time to check in with everyone else, and for me to hit the library just in case."

Anders glanced at Curtis, who looked straight ahead and kept driving. Luc had been waking up almost an hour before sunset most evenings since their bond, sometimes as much as an hour and a half, which this time Curtis had been smart enough to keep from the rest of his wizard friends, which just went to show he *had* learned enough from him and Luc not to share any of their unique strengths they'd gotten since they formed their triad, even with his best friends.

Good move.

"We'll be home soon," Curtis said.

TWENTY-TWO

L uc looked up when he heard Curtis and Anders coming down the stairs. They didn't often come to him before the sun had set properly. He tended to use this time for himself, especially since he couldn't cross past the top of the stairwell near the kitchen, given the last rays of the sun were often streaming through the kitchen windows and into the hall.

It likely didn't bode well they weren't waiting for him.

Sure enough, Curtis's face seemed apprehensive, and Anders looked positively dour.

"I take it you had an eventful day?" Luc said. "Any luck finding your professor?"

He sat at his desk, his computer open with mundane work. He'd showered already and had partially gotten dressed, though he'd yet to put on socks or his belt.

"Yes and no," Curtis said. Luc listened as he explained both the finding of the sorcerer professor and the subsequent loss of the specifics of his whereabouts, thanks to magic stolen from the Mitchell-operated pawn shop.

"But it's not only him we have to worry about, I think," Anders said, once Curtis was done relaying everything he could recall about the conversation he and Mackenzie had with the professor and the mysterious "other" with him.

"How so?" Luc said.

"Remember when I said the furies came here with an invitation?" Anders said. "I think it was the sorcerers."

"*Merde*," Luc said.

"This all has something to do with the Accords, and how sorcerers weren't around until after then." Curtis bit his bottom lip. "So...um... can you tell us anything about that?"

It took Luc a moment to realize what Curtis meant. "You mean what I know of the original Accords?"

"Yeah. Like..." He and Anders had sat on Luc's bed while he'd been talking, and now he leaned forward. "Were you, uh, *there*? Or was that, um, before..." He waved a hand in a vague circle.

"I was already vampire then," Luc said.

"Told you," Anders said, bumping shoulders with Curtis.

"You did not," Curtis said. "You said he *might* know." But Curtis was looking at him in wonder, and he couldn't help but enjoy that. "I've given up on this guy ever telling me what his job is," Curtis said, bumping shoulders again with Anders. "But I've always wanted to know...how old *are* you? You've said some things. Like, you remembered Canada's centennial, but if you were around when the accords happened, my guess was way off."

"I was made a vampire in 1759," Luc said.

"Wow." Curtis's eyes widened. "I mean, holy *crap*. I've always had a thing for older men, but..."

Anders snorted.

Luc smiled. "I was twenty-eight at the time. The French vampires, still loyal to *la Reine*—the Vampire Queen, in France—were attempting to hold against the British wizards and vampires, and while we prevailed against the latter thanks to those turned *en masse* for the fight, such as myself, the former..." He shook his head, remembering the noise and blood and yelling, and not wanting to conjure more of those awful moments. "Well. The *Première bataille de Québec* was not won. Within the year, I was on my own. Within four years, the French vampires were all but scattered in Québec, and it took another century for them to restore the *lignage* in what would become Canada."

"I..." Curtis stared at him. "I don't even know how to conceptualize that amount of time."

"You don't have to. And neither do we. It's different for us. Our sense of the now is stronger, our memories hold less sway over us. Distance tucks them away, perhaps, but leaves them accessible to us, like drawers in a card catalog."

"A what?" Curtis said.

Luc opened his mouth, then closed it. He wasn't entirely sure whether or not Curtis was joking with him. He shook his head. "It isn't relevant. It doesn't matter. You asked about the Accords."

"1816," Curtis said.

"The year without summer," Luc said, allowing his mind to wander back over the centuries to that year, pulling open the correct drawer and remembering.

"What?" Anders said.

"The summer was very cold," Luc said. "I was in Montreal by then. Snow in June."

"You're kidding," Curtis said.

"No." Luc shook his head. "It didn't stay, but it was bitterly cold. I remember the worry about all the crops, and it wasn't as easy to find people wandering alone at night because of the chill, so it was a lean time for me. And eventually, I heard about the Accords." He looked at the other two, who both seemed immersed in his every word. He was used to that from Curtis, but even Anders's dark brown eyes were locked on his.

"I'm afraid I don't have a lot of details. As I said, I was alone—my sire had…" He shook his head. The less said about the vampire who'd made him, the better. "I'd never been introduced or claimed after the battle, so I was at risk, and at that point in my life, I'd only barely begun to build my legitimate enterprise, so my attention to the other powers of the city had been mostly in aid of learning to avoid them."

Curtis nodded.

"But even I heard about the Accords. A deal struck between the vampires, demons, shape-shifters, and wizards—a formalizing of bonds and of territories. Unprecedented and building on the Law of Three, designed to 'bring a calm.' "

"Calm," Anders said, grunting. "I can just imagine what kind of calm the wizards wanted."

"Ah, but they were different then." Luc drew on another drawer of memory. "The wizards of the late 1700s weren't like the Families of today. They were scattered, though the seeds of what was to become the Families were there, I suppose. But at the time, they were more like you, Curtis."

"Orphans, you mean?"

"Yes. Wizards finding each other, creating covens, and more than a few marrying and having children. There were perhaps a dozen covens back then in Montreal, and they squabbled, often ending up on the wrong side of each other's ire. The French wizards got along no better with the English wizards than the French and English vampires did."

"That's one thing we demons never bothered with, at least," Anders said.

"True," Luc said, though he'd never truly considered that before. He'd never known demons to align themselves in a patriotic or nationalistic sense.

"So before the Accords, the wizards weren't really in charge?" Curtis said.

"The truth was, none of the supernatural groups were in charge," Luc said. "Or at least, that's how it felt to me. I knew certain areas of the city to be demon territory or claimed by the wizards or werewolves, but it certainly never felt like the wizards ruled, no." Luc considered. "If anything, we vampires had the slight advantage—but more in the sense of long-term planning, as it were."

"Says the man who took centuries to find two friends," Anders said.

"Hush, you," Curtis said, nudging him. He glanced back at Luc. "But after the Accords, it changed?"

"Over time," Luc said. "The Families strengthened their bonds, their power grew over generations with their children, and soon it rivalled the vampires', then surpassed it in many ways." He tried to find a specific moment in time where the balance had tipped, but he couldn't. "It was nothing immediate or drastic. The Law of Three already had power, but the Accords reinforced it, built it up into its own force—three of a kind, working together, bound to each other, could gain status and power of their own. I was glad of it, honestly, since it meant were I to find two others capable of joining me..." He smiled at the two who had, eventually, become just that to him, albeit two hundred years later, as Anders had noted.

"I can't imagine being alone all those years," Curtis said.

"I can," Anders said, and for the first time in Luc's long existence, he heard a sympathy for Luc himself in the man's low, rough voice. "And I don't know how you did it."

"I had some wealth," Luc said. "And once my enterprise took off, I grew to have a lot of wealth. It shielded me enough, most of the time."

"Still," Anders said, shaking his head.

"Okay. This is fascinating, and I could talk about it forever, but I'm not seeing what this has to do with the sorcerers. Hey, when was the first time you met a sorcerer?" Curtis said.

Luc paused to consider. "I believe I met one the first year I'd come here—the year the city changed its name to court the Queen."

"Beg your pardon?" Curtis said, shaking his head.

"1855," Luc said. "The name changed from Bytown to Ottawa. The citizens thought it would raise the chances of the city being selected as the capital."

Curtis stared for a second, and Luc could tell he was about to ask more questions about the history, so he raised his hand. "But you asked about sorcerers. There was a man I met on the train. A soldier, I believe. His blood tasted of magic, but only barely so."

"So when you say 'met on the train,'" Anders said, leaning forward on the bed, "you mean you fucked him and drank from him, right?"

Luc nodded and waved a hand in dismissal. "Of course. Though as I recall, he fucked me."

"Okay." Curtis closed his eyes, and through their bond his concentration sent a cool brush across Luc's senses. "Accords happen, sorcerers happen...Families get stronger." He opened his eyes. "Please tell me one of you is seeing something I'm not."

"I'm sorry, *lapin*," Luc said. "If Renard saw some opportunity with the Accords, I don't see it."

"I mean, other than busting them?" Anders said, lifting his shoulders. "Breaking away from the Accords, I mean? Can someone do that?"

"Perhaps," Luc said, though he didn't see the fallout being of particular use. "Though to what end? The Families would remain as powerful, and what does a vampire gain by not renewing their bonds on a full moon but *less* power?"

"And a target on their back," Curtis said.

Anders shrugged.

Curtis's phone pinged, and he pulled it out to read the screen. "Mackenzie says Rebekah might be able to meet us, but only if we come to her. The coven heads are meeting at the Château Laurier, and she might be able to slip away once they go into private discussions." He looked up and likely saw Luc's confusion. "The book. I want her to take a look at it. I caught something earlier with my glasses—there's a mark moving around when I move the book, but it's tiny and I couldn't make anything useful out of it."

"What time?" Luc said, nodding at Curtis's phone.

"Oh, uh..." Curtis looked down, and then tapped on the screen with his thumbs, typing a text. A few moments later, another ping denoted the arrival of the response.

"Coven heads are all meeting at nine, so Mackenzie thinks Rebekah might be able to get free around ten-ish."

"That gives me time to speak with Catharine," Luc said. "I'd like to know how Anna came into possession of it."

"Oh," Curtis said. "Right. That. Do you think Anna stole it, not the sorcerer the Mitchells had working there? Or…Wait, do you think she's working *with* the sorcerer who stole it or something?" Curtis shook his head. "I never got around to asking anyone where Anna got it."

"You've had a lot on your plate," Luc said.

Curtis sighed.

"I will attempt to ascertain how Anna came into possession of the book and let you know," Luc said. He regarded the other two. "Where are you meeting with Ms. Mitchell?"

"Some place called Sacred Ground."

Luc raised an eyebrow.

"I think it's a coffee shop not, like, a church or anything," Curtis said.

"One would hope. You two have something to eat, and a rest. I should be able to speak with Catharine and still meet you both in the Market before Ms. Mitchell arrives."

❖

Luc had never been sure if the Lady Markham's title was self-declared or some nod to a position she might once have held in her living, breathing days, but he couldn't deny her presence had a regality, even when she was faced with the distasteful.

Which, he believed, was the position she found herself in as she opened her door to him standing there.

"*Duc*," she said with a tilt of her head.

"How is Anna?" he said, deciding to start with a less-than-gentle reminder of her being in his debt.

Her lips turned up in the smallest of a smile. "She still sleeps, but she is improving."

"I need to speak with you about the former duke's plans, and—I believe—your involvement with the theft of a particular volume." He didn't look away from those honey-colored eyes of hers, and to her credit, she didn't blink.

Nor did she try to deny the accusation.

"Of course," she said, and paused after opening the door. Her gaze lifted to him, and she said, simply, "Come in, Luc Levesque."

Luc schooled his reaction carefully, but the blanket invitation—and the sense of her home's residency parting completely from him, like a sheer curtain tugged away in the wind—had been entirely unexpected.

"We can speak in here." She stepped away and gestured to a doorway, leading him through into the parlor. "Here," she said, pouring a finger of port into a snifter and handing it to him before pouring another for herself. She nodded to one of the two overstuffed leather chairs to either side of the backgammon table, and he took a seat.

"Please," she said. "Ask your questions." Her directness was in such a contrast, he couldn't help pausing to regard her.

"You are in a different mood than I expected," he said.

"Anna," she said, the name spoken plainly. "I owe you. If this is the price, I'll happily pay it."

"Fair enough," Luc said. He didn't believe she was lying. "Perhaps we can begin with how Anna came to possess the book? It is my understanding it had been stolen from the Mitchell family," Luc said after taking a single sip of the port.

"Yes." Catharine tilted her head, cradling her own glass. "It goes back to Anna, and the former duke, and Lavoie. I've told you before of Anna's grace, yes?"

"You said she knew when places would be *interesting*, I believe," Luc said.

"Places or things. For her, a shine grows as events of note approach." She smiled. "She likens it to being a corvid."

"*Events of note* sounds rather euphemistic," Luc said, turning the glass in his hand.

"It is." Catharine's tone softened. "I suppose a more accurate phrasing would be anything from trouble to catastrophe. The greater the shine grows before the event itself happens, the worse the outcome for some—or all—of the people involved."

"How did she even manage to see the book?" Luc said. "It was my understanding it was locked away in the rear of the Mitchell Family's pawn shop, where they store and ward objects."

Catharine lifted her glass and took a sip. Delaying, perhaps, or giving herself time to think. Either way, Luc wondered how honest her next words were going to be.

"For some time, I have been in contact with a few individuals of lesser power among some of the Families," she said.

Luc raised an eyebrow. "You have spies in the Families."

She affected a sigh. "I wish I could claim that level of success, loyalty, or infiltration. No, I have…" She waved a hand. "*Contacts*. And from them, I received requests as much as they offered information, but after you freed Lavoie and she joined me, she suggested I extend my reach among the Families, and I saw the value. But these are people on the outskirts, *Duc*, they are not of consequence to the Families."

"Lesser power," Luc said. "You mean sorcerers."

She nodded.

"All the sorcerers have gone into hiding."

"Yes," Catharine said. "I've been told. And none of them are speaking to me right now, including the one who allowed Anna to take the book three months ago."

"Three months ago. She's had the book that long?" Luc said.

"Yes."

"So this was before the other thefts," Luc said. When Catharine tilted her head in ignorance, he saw no reason not to enlighten her. "Before the sorcerers fled, the one working at the Mitchell pawn shop absconded with multiple items. Enchanted items."

"Ah," Catharine said. "Which they can use."

"Anders believes they've also invited furies to the city for some purpose." Luc regarded her. "You don't know why they might have done so, or gone into hiding in the first place?"

Catharine shook her head. "I do not. If I had to guess, I'd assume an attempt to gain some freedom from the Families, but I can't imagine they'll have any success. Their power against the Families—even with the aid of wrath demons?" She sipped her port. "They wouldn't stand a chance."

Luc believed her. Or perhaps he wanted to. "What is the book's importance?" he said. "Curtis tried to examine it without success."

"I'm afraid I don't know that, either. Only that Anna saw more shine on that bound volume than she's ever seen before," Catharine said. "She believed it would spell disaster, and Lavoie believed it meant something to Renard if he'd gone to such lengths to acquire it."

"And then someone tried to end Anna. For the book?" Luc said.

"I assume so. I never should have let her take it back to her home," Catharine said, with real regret. "But she thought if she could be alone with it, she might be able to glimpse more. Believe me, I don't know who tried to kill her, and I don't know why the other murders happened, either." She lifted her glass. "My assumption is someone is trying to permanently censor anyone with knowledge of the future."

"To stop them from upsetting a plan of some sort," Luc said.

"Of some sort."

"Renard's plan," Luc said.

"As I say, I assume so." Catharine took another sip of port but didn't disagree.

"But we don't know what part this book was to play in his plan exactly," Luc said, frustrated.

Catharine shook her head. "Lavoie only knew getting access to the Parliament Library was important to Renard, and she believes this book could have been why. You can ask her again, but I don't believe she held anything back from either of us."

"Nor do I," he said, considering. "Whatever Renard's plan might have been, there is one we know about Renard for sure. He *hated* the Families. I can't believe any plan of his wouldn't include some sort of revenge—or worse—against them. If Anna says this book spells disaster, I can't help but think any disaster is aimed at Malcolm Stirling and his lot."

"Indeed," Catharine said. "As a mortal he was an Orphan, like your Curtis. They denied him any real standing. His entire coven was of a similar bent." She paused. "As a warlock and holding the dukedom, he had *more* power, but I never had the sense the man was satisfied."

"No," Luc said. "He bound a demon to himself for even more power, and no doubt he intended worse with the tools he was gathering." Marysas's knife had been capable of flensing the ability of one supernatural being and transferring it to another. Renard had died before he'd been able to use the knife, and they'd assumed he'd intended to take Tyson's power rather than have to control him through a binding.

But what if that *hadn't* been Renard's end purpose for the necromantic blade?

"You said the sorcerers made requests of you," Luc said, putting down his glass. "What requests?"

"Names, mostly," Catharine said. "History."

"Genealogy," Luc said. "Of the Families, especially?"

Catharine tilted her head in mild surprise. "That's correct."

"Denis found much of the same topic in Renard's files. Do you recall any specifics?" Luc said.

"Yes," Catharine said. "Anything to do with the Stirling family and the previous coven heads, but they also wanted to know about Malcolm Stirling's son, specifically when he had moved out of the Stirling chantry, and if it coincided with the grandson moving in." Catharine paused. "There were similar questions about Jonathan Mitchell, actually, and then his daughter, Kendra."

"And his granddaughter, Rebekah?" Luc said.

"Yes," Catharine said with another small tilt of her head. "That's right."

The inheritances. From what Luc recalled of Curtis's explanation of Rebekah's gift to see through any magical illusion, she had inherited it down her familial bloodline, from her mother. The same had happened with Matthew Stirling, he believed, who'd inherited his prescience in much the same way.

And now Matthew Stirling was missing—with someone attempting to kill him, most likely—and they'd arranged for Rebekah Mitchell to sneak away from the covens to meet with them.

And Curtis was bringing the book with him.

Merde.

Luc rose, and Catharine watched him, tracking his expression closely. "Thank you," he said, already reaching for his phone. "I believe you've been very helpful."

TWENTY-THREE

Curtis waited while Anders tapped the fob to lock his SUV, and then joined him for the long walk down from the parking garage level where they'd finally found an empty spot. The stairwell stank of urine, and the garbage crunched underfoot.

"You okay?" Curtis said. A thrum of something *tight* came from Anders, and he didn't think it had anything to do with Luc's phone call or what he'd told them.

"Remembering the last time I was here."

Of course. This was the same parking garage where Anders had nearly gotten killed by a *loup garou*.

"Oh," Curtis said. "Right."

They stepped out onto the sidewalk, and Curtis held the messenger bag containing the book against his side. He felt exposed, and he glanced up and down the street, seeing a typical enough night in the Market, really: people in fairly nice clothing heading to and from the bars, restaurants, and clubs, often in groups, laughing or talking loudly. It was cool, but at least it wasn't raining, which was nice for a change, and the moon was even popping out from behind the clouds now and then.

Still, something felt *off* to him. He frowned at some fresh graffiti, not sure what was getting under his skin.

Well, other than the fact he was now pretty sure the murderer they'd been chasing was *invisible*. Didn't exactly help his mood.

"Where did Ducky say he'd meet us?" Anders said.

"He's going to go right to the coffee shop," Curtis said, snapping out of his odd mood and nodding across the street to Sacred Ground. "Mackenzie suggested it. She said Rebekah goes there often enough it wouldn't look strange if anyone watched her go."

"Okay." Anders seemed to be scanning the street to either side of the small coffee place for something, and whatever it was, he seemed satisfied. He nodded. Curtis almost asked him what it was, but then the light changed.

They crossed the street and went inside, making a line for the empty booth farthest in the back. Anders reached for his wallet once they'd claimed the space, but Curtis shook his head. "I'll get it."

It looked like the kind of place where the baristas would make suggestions or offer options. No need to traumatize them with Anders's usual reaction to anything other than black coffee.

And, of course, at a glance it appeared the tea selection was crap.

"What can I get for you?" asked the barista, a stocky dude with deeply tanned skin and a Gatineau accent.

"May I get a venti dark roast and a hot chocolate, please?" Curtis said, eyeing the chalkboards and deciding he didn't have it in him for coffee shop tea tonight.

"Need room for cream in the coffee?" the barista said, with a helpful smile and a quick bit of eye contact, and Curtis congratulated himself on judging correctly and leaving Anders in the booth.

"No, thank you," Curtis said.

"Jet fuel it is," the barista said, and Curtis laughed. Okay. He could see why Rebekah liked the place.

After tipping well, he slid back in the booth with drinks in hand, passing the dark roast to Anders, who took a swallow and nodded. Curtis's hot chocolate was scalding, so he managed only a sip.

A shiver ran all the way up his spine and he twitched, putting down the cup.

"You good?" Anders said, frowning at him.

"Someone walked over my grave," Curtis said, managing another sip of scalding hot chocolate. He checked his phone. Nine forty. Rebekah was fairly sure she could sneak out to them around ten, which meant sitting and waiting until then.

Super.

Luc arrived a few minutes later, joining them in the booth. A second barista had come out from the back, a tall, kind of butchy Black woman with a gorgeous short fade, and the two employees were chatting lightly behind the counter, wiping and cleaning things. Only three other people were in the shop: two women on the stools looking through the front window and chatting, and a man sitting and scrolling his phone while he drank at one of the tables.

As privacy went, it wasn't the worst. He pulled out his glasses and slid them on. Luc gave him a small nod of appreciation and Curtis gave the room a once-over. Nothing. Everyone in the room—well, at least, not those sharing his booth—read as normal human beings.

He pulled the glasses off. "We're good," he said quietly.

"I've learned a few things, perhaps," Luc said. He told Curtis how Catharine had plants in the Families—sorcerers, again—and how the book hadn't been stolen at the same time as everything else J.D. Domecillo had taken from the shop, but rather months beforehand, and how Renard was interested in the inherited abilities of the Family magical gifts.

"I think we also need to consider that whatever gathering of ability Renard was attempting for his plan, the three of us might somehow qualify," Luc said, gesturing at Curtis and Anders before lowering his hand back to the tabletop. "He wanted demonic, vampiric, and magical ability. We have that."

"Right," Curtis said. They'd considered it before, but only as why they were a threat to Renard in the first place: They had what he wanted. But adding in he wanted it so he could do something to the Families and…well, yeah. Didn't it mean they might be able to do whatever it was he was going to do?

"Before she arrives, I wish to be clear," Luc said, checking his watch. "You trust her, Rebekah Mitchell?"

Curtis leaned back in the booth and fought back the urge to answer flippantly, because if Luc was right, if the three of them somehow had the power to do whatever it was that bastard Renard had been intending to do, then he needed to seriously think about how much he could trust *anyone* from the Families, given Renard's plan had to involve hurting them in some way.

And as much as he didn't want to admit it, that included Rebekah Mitchell.

But on the other hand, Renard had been interested in the inherited abilities running down the Family bloodlines, apparently. Rebekah Mitchell had her Family gift, just like Matthew Stirling. Curtis couldn't help but believe it made Rebekah a target, and his first instinct was to *warn* her.

"Rebekah knows better than most what the Families are really like," Curtis said. "You remember how she and her brother were treated. And her mother had to do some pretty hard things to keep Rebekah out of their line of fire for as long as she managed." He looked at Luc and

Anders in turn. "But if you're asking what I think you're asking? I don't think she'd tell Malcolm Stirling anything. I think she cares about Matt too much to do that."

"Enough to take risks on his behalf?" Luc said.

Curtis exhaled. "We've seen her take risks before, for her mother and her brother and her grandfather, too."

Luc tipped his head, conceding the point.

"Well, I like her," Anders said, lifting one shoulder. "She's a no-bullshit type. And great taste in cars."

Curtis chuckled, and Luc dipped his chin again. "I trust in your judgement."

"Really?" Anders said, grinning.

"I was speaking to him," Luc said, pointing at Curtis.

The door opened, and Curtis looked up and saw Rebekah. She was dressed up fancier than he'd ever seen, in a kind of black jacket-and-skirt combo that hugged all her curves, her braids gathered up to hang between her shoulder blades. She gave him a small nod before stopping at the counter, where both baristas greeted her warmly and with clear familiarity—especially the stocky dude, who, unless Curtis was severely misreading, was flirting up a storm.

"Look at you," the stocky guy said, waving a hand in front of his face like he was trying to cool down.

Rebekah flirted right back, ordered her drink, and joined them in their booth once she had it in hand.

"Thanks for coming," Curtis said, tugging the messenger bag strap over his head to pull it free and sliding over to give her room to sit beside him.

"I usually step out once all the shaking hands shit is done," Rebekah said, rolling her eyes. "But they'll expect me back in fifteen or twenty, at most, once they get down to real business."

"Hopefully this won't take long," Curtis said, unzipping the bag. "So, we got that missing book, and you were right. Not blank. Only all I could see with my glasses was this little scribble that sort of moved around on the page depending on how I held it."

"So, should I ask how you got the book?" Rebekah raised her sculpted eyebrows. "Or do I want to know?"

Curtis laughed, which he imagined was answer enough. He handed the book to her.

"Right," she said dryly.

"We believe this volume in some way related to the previous

duke's plan to do real harm to the Families," Luc said, keeping his voice pitched low. "I don't think we can understate how deeply Renard's antipathy went."

Rebekah paused, having barely lifted the cover open the tiniest bit. She glanced at Curtis. "Well, let's see."

She opened the book and frowned, then looked at Curtis. "It's blank."

"You might have to hold it up and try moving it around," Curtis said. "It was the same when I looked at it. It's a little fiddly."

Rebekah lifted the leather-bound book, and almost immediately, her dark brown eyes snapped to the page again. Curtis leaned forward.

"You see something?"

"It's a picture of Parliament, I think," Rebekah said, and she turned the book in the booth, until she was holding it almost upright. "Or part of it. Yeah. It's the library."

Curtis thought of the tiny little scribble he'd seen on the page, the shape of which had been rounded, with spiky bits on top and...

Not a tiny cupcake. The Parliament Library. Huh. Rebekah had a keen eye for architecture.

He put on his glasses, and after taking a moment to draw power into the lenses, he opened his eyes and...

"It's absolutely the library," he said, leaning over to get a better look. No tiny scribble now, though still drawn in simple black ink on the creamy pages, the round building was unmistakable. Rebekah tilted the book his way, and the image started to slide off the edge of the page again. She tilted it back, and Curtis stopped up short as realization hit him.

"Oh. Of course," he said.

"What?" Anders said, eyeing him across the table.

"The library *is* that way," Curtis said, pointing in the direction he was almost sure led from here to Parliament. "It's like the book is a window or something."

Rebekah tilted the book one way, then the other, nodding. "You're right."

"Renard wanted to retrieve this book from the library in 1916," Luc said. "Before the fire destroyed every part of Parliament *except* the library. That cannot be a coincidence."

"Is it the same on every page? Because I don't get how a picture of the library is useful," Anders said.

Rebekah turned the pages, and as she did, the image of the library seemed to zoom in, a tiny bit at a time, until near the end of the book Curtis saw something on the side of the building now, barely visible.

"What is that?" he said. It *almost* looked like a tree, only the way the black ink lines moved and shifted, it appeared to be in motion, and while it contained branches off a single large trunk, there were no leaves.

"I don't know," Rebekah said, squinting at the image. "But it's right up against the library wall, isn't it?"

"Perhaps we need to take a closer look," Luc said.

Curtis nodded, pulling off his glasses. The book appeared blank to him again. Rebekah, though, leaned closer to the image, shaking her head. "I think he's right, but I don't have time to walk to Parliament and back before I'm missed." She sighed, closing the book and handing it back to him. "I'll pass the message on to Dale, Tracey, and Mackenzie, if I can get them alone. We'll try to sneak off and meet you there after the moot ends, if we can."

"How long is that?" Luc said.

Rebekah shook her head. "I don't know. Usually midnight, at least. Malcolm Stirling sounded like he wanted everyone to start looking for the sorcerers, so once they're done eating, I'm betting he'll send everyone on their way, but Alastair Spencer didn't look jazzed about it, and I think Katrina Windsor might also have some doubts about forcing the sorcerers' hands, whatever they think they're doing."

"We can at least go look," Luc said.

Curtis bit his lip. He'd rather have the rest of the Craft Night group with him if he was going to check out something magical, but Luc was right. Waiting seemed like a bad idea. At least right now the movers and shakers of the covens were busy.

"Okay," he said.

Rebekah eyed the book, then sighed, rising with her coffee. "Good luck. And be careful."

Curtis nodded, and she left.

"We'll wait a few minutes in case someone is watching her," Curtis said.

Anders grinned at him.

"What?"

"You're thinking all sneaky-like." Anders shrugged. "It's hot."

"Paranoid self-preservation is hot?" Curtis said.

"The hottest." Anders winked.

They waited a few more minutes in silence. Finally, Curtis tucked the book away in his messenger bag again, and they left the coffee shop. Outside, the cooler night air was refreshing and chased away the scent of coffee. Curtis turned to head toward Parliament, but Anders reached out and touched his shoulder.

"Wait," he said, a thrum of tension reverberating among their bond.

"What is it?" Curtis said.

"Company," Anders said. He was looking straight ahead down the sidewalk, and Curtis followed his gaze. All he saw were three women, which didn't seem particularly threatening, though they *were* wearing motorcycle jackets…

Oh.

Motorcycle jackets. Motorcycle gang.

Were these the furies?

"I'm afraid we need that book," one of them said, a curvaceous woman with curly hair and an *almost* pleasant Southern drawl.

It didn't sound like a request.

TWENTY-FOUR

*F*uck.

Anders slowly slid a half-step ahead of Curtis on his left, and Luc did the same on his right. The twist of a smile on the curly-haired fury's lips—Aurora, he remembered—faded a trace.

"Anders," she said by way of greeting. "We have no quarrel with you or yours." Said in her laconic, Southern belle voice, it even sounded sincere. Hell, it might very well be. She and her crew did say they were about righteousness.

"Friends of yours?" Luc said mildly.

"The lady in the middle is Aurora," Anders said, without breaking eye contact with the fury. "She's the pack leader I told you about. And the tall one to her left is Cari." He flicked his gaze to the last of the three, a lean Black woman smiling at him with what appeared to be amusement at his introductions so far. "I didn't get your name, but you had a sweet ride, if I remember right."

"Yolanda," she said. "Thanks."

"And that's Yolanda," Anders said, with exaggerated politeness. "Ladies, this is Curtis." He aimed a thumb at Curtis, then pointed at Luc. "And the handsome one over there is Luc, the Duke of Ottawa." He stressed the last a little bit. Vampires were faster than demons, and Luc wasn't just some random vampire, he was the damned duke. For once in Anders's life, maybe Luc's position was going to be an advantage he could use. Aurora had to know making a move against Luc—or anyone he cared about—would be a fucking *terrible* idea, especially if she cared about her people the way he thought she did.

He saw her pause, eyes flicking to Luc and back, and decided he'd been on the mark. "It's nice to meet you both," she said, and fuck if it didn't sound like she meant it. "I'd like to think we could be friends."

"Okaaay." Anders drew out the word, crossing his arms. "Then maybe you don't try to take our stuff?"

"Technically, it's not *your* stuff," Aurora said.

"We know. And I intend to give it back to the Mitchells," Curtis said, though it was the first Anders had heard of turning it back over. "I know it was stolen from their shop."

Cari snorted, shaking her head as well as earning a quick glance of annoyance from Aurora, and Anders frowned.

"You didn't mean the flicks, did you?" Anders said.

"I'm afraid we don't really have time to get into it," Aurora said.

"Why the alacrity?" Luc said. "Surely we can discuss this? And perhaps not on the street where *anyone* might see us?"

"Anyone who?" Yolanda said, her smile widening enough to show teeth.

Anders glanced around, and... *Well, fuck me.* The entire street was empty. Wait. No. He saw two more women in motorcycle leathers at the other end of the closest intersection, and then four more behind them, where the street met King Edward. How had they chased off all the normals? He eyed the furies, and Yolanda lifted one shoulder in a "What can you do?" gesture.

Anders could use his allure to attract the lustful attention of people, and he could reverse it to make himself less noticeable and less interesting—a complete lack of anything arousing led to him sort of blending in and not drawing attention. Did the furies have something like reversed allure, too?

He didn't know.

What *was* the opposite of wrath, anyway?

"Why do you want it?" Curtis said. Anders wanted to give him some credit for not confirming he had the book, but he was the only one carrying a bag, so it was likely moot. Had the furies followed Rebekah, or had someone else guided them here?

"Look," Aurora said. "None of us want this to be difficult."

"I'll bet," Anders said.

"But we need what you have, and we're going to take it," she said. Grudgingly, he had to admit her delivery came off cool and collected.

The sound of an approaching motorcycle made Anders glance over his shoulder long enough to see the inbound fury. Or he assumed a fury rode the motorcycle.

"You'll hand your bag over to Victoria, and then you'll leave," Aurora said.

"Look," Curtis said, holding up one hand and sounding a bit shaky. "I don't want to fight. Really. I'm kind of squishy, and I'm nowhere near as fast as any of you. How about a counteroffer?"

The pulse of preparedness through the bond alongside Curtis's words, however, was nothing at all like the uncertain, desperate tone he was projecting. Apparently, Curtis had a plan. Anders did his best not to so much as twitch.

"No offence, wizard." Aurora was already shaking her head, her curls swaying. "But there's nothing you—"

"*Necto!*"

The burst of magic lashed out from Curtis ahead of them, and Aurora, Cari, and Yolanda were dragged down to their knees with grunts of pain as the binding took hold. A half-second later, Cari and Yolanda toppled over onto their sides, outclassed by Curtis's magic. Aurora, though, managed to remain on her hands and knees, and waves of heat radiated visibly in the air around all three of them as they drew on their demonic power to fight against Curtis's binding.

"You two run," Curtis said, hand still outstretched, concentrating. "Now."

"We're not leaving—"

"Now," Curtis snapped. "They want the *bag*, not me, Luc. Call me when you've got it somewhere safe. *Understand?*"

This was his plan? Leave him here and run off with the book? This was a *shit* plan.

Anders started to open his mouth, but then Luc reached past him and actually took the damned bag from Curtis.

"I understand," Luc said. The motorcycle was almost there.

"I sure as fuck don't," Anders growled, but Luc shook his head and grabbed Anders's shoulder.

"We run. Now," Luc said.

Fuck.

"Go," Curtis said, and then with a flick of his wrist, he was chanting something else and the temperature started to drop around them, fast.

Demons hated the cold.

"Anders!" Luc said, and Anders took one last look at Curtis, who was lifting both hands, twists of frigid wind forming like tiny tornadoes in his palms, and then despite every part of him not wanting to do this, he drew on his demonic speed and took off with Luc.

The motorcycle chased after them, leaving Curtis behind as well as all the furies Anders had spotted, minus the three Curtis had slammed into the ground. The world around them seemed to move slower and slower when Anders moved like this, and he wondered if it was the same for Luc or not.

He also wondered what the *fuck* they'd done by leaving Curtis back there.

"I'm holding you back," Anders said. "You can go faster." *And I can get back to Curtis.*

"We need to get out of their line of sight for a moment," Luc said, the words slurred and drawn out as Anders's perception adjusted to the speed they were moving.

Out of their line of sight? He didn't get time to ask, however, as Luc snatched his jacket and pulled them both bodily down an alley, Anders nearly tripping over his feet at the burst of speed Luc had fed into the move. And the speed Luc already displayed was *nothing* compared to the blur of motion that followed. Anders could barely keep track but…

Suddenly he was holding the book. Luc had shoved it into his hands.

"Hide it under your jacket, tell me to keep going, then shadow-walk out of here," Luc said rapid-fire, the bag already over his shoulder again.

Anders stuffed the book under his jacket, and wanted to scream. Now what Curtis had said made sense. *They want the* bag. Fuck. He hated this plan, but he could already hear the motorcycle coming.

"Go!" Anders yelled, allowing all his frustration to come out in a bellow. "You're faster than me!"

Luc winked and was gone.

Anders didn't use quite as much of his power this time to move fast, knowing he'd need more of it in a moment. Next up, he had to find himself a natural shadow, which, at night in the Market with the clouds coming and going, wasn't in easy supply. Too many streetlights where he was. But the moon was up, so if he could get to Confederation Park…

Two furies were up ahead of him, and he allowed himself a moment to flip them off. "You're too late. You'll never gonna catch a fucking *vampire*," he snapped, then he deked them out when they lunged for him, their fingertips lit now with the blue-white of hellfire.

Okay, so now he'd pissed off two furies. Maybe not his best move, but if it meant he got to work out some of this frustration, it would be worth it.

Except the book inside his jacket wedged under his damned arm made it too awkward to throw down, and he needed them not to notice it. He slid between them and kept running.

One gave chase, but the other seemed to think she could catch up with Luc. Fat chance.

He got to the bottom of the steps that led up to the park, still amazed no other people were around. How the fuck did the furies empty out the whole damn Market? He didn't have time to worry about it, though. He leaped up from the bottom of the stairs to the top in one go then, finally, seeing the trees, he dove for the first dark corner of the park he could see, glanced up for the moon, which was close to the edge of a cloud, and lit the hellfire behind his eyes to see where the shadows offered him entrance.

The fury hadn't made it to the top of the steps yet. He could do this.

A moment later, the sound of his footsteps, his own heavy breathing, and the demon scrambling after him was replaced by utter silence, and the world had shifted into a featureless blackness entirely made of shadow. His motion became intent, rather than muscle, and he brought more hellfire up behind his eyes to "see" around him, revealing the inky black shapes making up the shadows cast by an entire world without light.

Other demons appeared, too. Figures made of blue-white hellfire slid around from shadow to shadow off in the distance, but not many, and—as far as he could tell—not the furies pursuing him, Luc, or Curtis.

With a flare of blue-white, the fury chasing him appeared through the same shadow he'd used, and Anders allowed himself a moment's amusement at the visible hesitation in the figure when she turned his way.

No doubt she'd never seen a demon who burned with the bright gold of having a soul. It had been like that since he and Luc and Curtis had created their bond in the first place, and here, deep in the shadow, it made him larger, brighter, and more imposing than any other demon he'd ever glimpsed while shadow-walking.

Still, the fury cautiously drifted toward him before he raised one hand and drew on his power, flaring brighter and hotter than her by far. If she wanted a fight on the shadow side, he was perfectly willing to burn her to ashes right here, right now.

She leaned away, and then she slipped off back toward the Market in the flowing way of all movement on this side of the shadow.

Yeah. I didn't think so.

He lowered his hand, watching to make sure the fury's particular blue-white spark vanished before he moved on. Once she'd crossed back into the real world, he took stock. He needed to go somewhere safe. Preferably somewhere Curtis and Luc had never been, because if they'd been caught or captured, and the furies really wanted to know where Anders might be, they might not be above getting rough for the answer.

Fuck fuck fuck. Worst plan ever.

He turned to face the river, which to his demon sight in the shadow world was a rippling blackness edged with the golden-white of his oddly soul-fired senses, and leaned.

The world flowed around him.

On the other side of the river, it took him a little time to find the only nearby space he'd thought of that neither Curtis nor Luc would know, and he hoped the trees would be within the light of the moon— though if they weren't, then he'd just have to find another tree or large enough rock to work with—but he was in luck, and the opening was wide enough.

He stepped out in a small backyard, beneath the tree in question, pausing to look at the leather-man statue he'd placed there for the very purpose of navigating to that spot during a shadow-walk. Out of habit, he rubbed the stone crotch for good luck, then dug into his pocket for his keys.

The house wasn't much—a tiny, post–World War II bungalow— but it was the only place he could think of.

He'd left them both behind. They'd told him to, but…

"Fuck!" he yelled, balling his fists and pulling the stupid book out from under his goddamn jacket, flinging it onto the tiny kitchen counter. Then he pulled out his phone and took a deep breath. Luc might have stayed ahead of the demons long enough to get away, assuming he'd had enough blood in his tank and the demons hadn't cornered him in some way. But Curtis…

They want the bag, not me.

Yeah, but if they kept you to try and trade? What then?

He shook his head and tapped the icon to call Curtis.

It rang once. Twice. He closed his eyes, jaw clenching. *Come on, come on…*

"Hey." Curtis sounded out of breath.

"Are you okay?" Anders nearly growled the words, he was so angry.

"Yeah, I'm fine. Just a bit winded. Threw around some magic." He took a shaky breath on the other end of the phone. "I felt a bunch of stuff from you and Luc, and it mostly felt like smugness, so I'm guessing it worked. Did it work? Did he give you the book?"

"He did, and it did, and I am really pissed at you right now," Anders said.

"What? *Why?*"

"They could have captured you and tortured you until I handed over the book, Curtis," Anders said, rubbing this face with one hand. "Or killed you."

"Oh," Curtis said. "Well…they didn't?"

"That really doesn't make me feel better."

"I can tell. Look, I don't know if they'll try and follow me. I *think* they all went after you and Luc, and the first three left once I got all Canadian Winter on their asses, but I don't know for sure I'm not being watched. Maybe I shouldn't join you until—"

"You get in your car and you get the *fuck* over here, *now*," Anders said. He was *not* letting Curtis wander around by himself after pissing off a bunch of furies.

There was a long pause. "Or," Curtis said, with what Anders really hoped wasn't fucking amusement, "I could come over there now. Wherever *there* is?"

"You haven't been here before. I'm in my office," Anders said.

"I'm sorry, your *what*?"

"My office. Where I work." Anders rubbed his eyes again. "It's a little house on the Gatineau side."

"I get to see where you work?" Now Curtis sounded positively delighted, as though they hadn't just played fucking hot potato with some demons over a stupid goddamn book that could have gotten them all killed. "Finally! What's the address?"

Anders shook his head and gave him the address. Then he looked down at the book again, swallowing. "I'll call Luc," he said.

"I'm on my way."

TWENTY-FIVE

Judging he'd not need to keep up the chase much longer—and being aware at some point, even his own powerful graces would falter—Luc led the three furies, including the one on the motorcycle, to the edge of the Market and then allowed the speed he'd been drawing upon to leave. The world around him sped back up, including traffic on Sussex, and finally, a few pedestrians, unlike the oddly empty streets near the coffee shop and much of the interior of the Market itself.

The first demon to arrive simply stopped, watching him. She had short, dark hair, and though she was breathing heavy from her run, she didn't back down.

Another demon appeared beside her, almost between blinks, and the motorcycle pulled up as well. The woman riding it flipped up her helmet visor.

"Hello," he said, allowing his fangs to slide free to give her a good glimpse of them. "I am the city's duke. And you are?"

"Hand over the bag," the one on the motorcycle said, apparently not in the mood for polite introduction.

"*Bien sur*. Victoria, was it?" he said, sliding Curtis's bag off his shoulder. "Though if you appreciate the bag, you could purchase one of your own. I believe Curtis found it at a gallery on Bank Street."

The helmeted demon snatched the bag out of his hand and then paused at the feel of it. She opened it up, and he saw her nostrils flare once she looked inside.

"What is it?" the first demon said.

"It's empty," Victoria said. Her eyes had darkened almost completely, and she aimed a glare Luc's way.

He lifted an eyebrow.

"They must have stashed it somewhere," she said.

"You should leave now," Luc said, reaching forward and taking the bag back from the fury. "So far, you have not done anything too beyond the pale to forgive. I could even venture to call this all a *misunderstanding*, but my patience has limits."

"What do we do?" the first demon said.

Victoria snapped her visor back down. It seemed to be answer enough, as the other two turned and strode off at a decent clip, while Victoria took a little longer to turn it around before zooming off, accelerating quickly and loudly.

Certainly not the subtle sort.

Luc reached for his phone, wanting to make sure the rest of the ruse had gone off as hoped for, but it rang before he could bring up his contacts. It was Anders.

"Yes?" Luc said.

"That was the *worst* fucking plan." Anders's voice heralded an impending tirade. "What if they'd decided to grab Curtis and trade him for the book? Or beat the shit out of him?"

"Did they?" Luc said. It had been his own worry the moment he'd realized what Curtis had wanted him to do by stressing the messenger bag so meaningfully, but Luc hadn't had time for a better plan of his own.

"No." Anders growled the word.

"Well then," Luc said. "Where are you?"

"I'll send you the address. It's on the other side of the river."

Luc's phone vibrated, and he quickly checked the screen. The address was unfamiliar. "What is this place?" he said, putting the phone back to his ear and starting to walk back toward the Market and his Mercedes. He kept his eyes peeled for anyone suspicious, but so far it seemed he wasn't being followed.

"It's where I work," Anders said.

Luc blinked. "I see. I'll be there shortly. I'll need to walk back to my car from the Mint."

Anders made a grunting noise and hung up.

❖

Luc nearly drove past the small home but caught a glimpse of the number above the door in time, and he pulled into the driveway just as Curtis's hybrid pulled up to park on the street—the driveway wasn't large enough for two vehicles, and there was no garage.

Luc eyed the unremarkable building and considered. Erotic massage? A brothel of one? Perhaps one of those paid online streaming pornographic options only for fanatics?

Curtis climbed out of his car and jogged across the street to join him by the time he'd gotten out of the Mercedes. Luc looked him over, but he seemed uninjured.

"Your plan was reckless," Luc said.

"He already went over that," Curtis said, nodding at the house. "But it worked, so I'm calling it a win. Come on. We can get the book and then head back over the river again. Also, aren't you curious?"

"I'm more wishing I'd worn less expensive shoes," Luc said, though he started for the door.

Curtis glanced down at his sneakers. "What? Why?"

"For whatever I might step in," Luc said.

Curtis blinked and then looked at the house again, this time not so much with curiosity as alarm. He touched the doorbell, then glanced at Luc. "What do you think he *does* in here?"

Luc didn't reply, allowing his expression to speak for him.

Curtis chuckled, and then the door opened and Anders stood before them.

"Come on in," he said. "Both of you."

The house had enough residency even with the invitation. Luc felt it as he crossed the threshold, which meant Anders spent time in this home on a regular basis. He supposed it must be during the sunlight hours, given most evenings he was well aware of where Anders was, but it still surprised him.

He looked around the interior, curious in spite of himself and every other pressing matter they had to deal with. A simple enough floor plan—the front door opened into a living area, where Luc imagined couches or a dining table were intended to exist, but where the space instead been turned into a surprisingly comfortable looking office of sorts, with three large bookcases, a desk with an impressively modern chair, and a computer with a curved, ergonomic keyboard. Behind the repurposed living area, an open serving counter revealed a kitchen beyond, and Luc assumed the three doors to their right led to bedrooms and a bathroom. The walls were painted with simple earth tones, and the whole place had a feel he couldn't quite reconcile with Anders— professional, functional, and not at all snide.

There were even frames hanging on the walls that weren't male nudes. He eyed one and frowned when he realized it was a framed document. A certificate of some sort? Or perhaps a degree? It had a calligraphy to it and was marked with a deep red metallic seal. Had Anders acquired an education at some point?

But no. He read the name written in the looping, almost overdone script, and it wasn't Anders's name, but someone named Keah Sander, who had apparently won first place in the category of "Erotic Romance."

It was an *award*.

He glanced at Anders. "Who is Keah Sander?"

But Anders didn't answer. In fact, he looked...*uncomfortable*.

"What?" Beside him, Curtis turned and looked at the framed award—then another and another. Luc noticed they all had the same name. Then Curtis turned, facing Anders.

"Anagram. That's an anagram," Curtis said, his voice rising in stunned amazement as he pointed at the framed awards. "Anders Hake, Keah Sander."

Luc blinked and felt rather foolish he hadn't noticed. He'd taken on multiple names in his centuries—including four different surnames so far, when he couldn't manage becoming his own "son"—though he'd always managed to keep some variation of Luc as his personal name whenever he needed to retire a previous identity due to the passage of years. Curtis was, of course, correct. The name was an anagram.

"Pen name," Anders said, crossing his arms. It was a rare tell, making him look wider and larger and more masculine, and yet at the same time vulnerable.

"Wait," Curtis said, holding up a hand. He crossed to the first bookshelf, which seemed to only contain hardcovers, and touched one of the spines. "Anders, these are *all* by Keah Sander. By *you*?"

"Yeah."

"You write *books*?" Luc said, trying to keep the disbelief out of his voice. "Under a woman's name?"

"Yeah." Anders shrugged. "I use my mother's picture for the author photo. She loved romance novels." This last came out even more gruffly than before, like he was daring Luc to challenge him over any of it.

Luc had no urge to do so. He was too busy trying to equate *Anders* with *romance*. Not to mention being articulate at prose.

"*This* is your job?" Curtis said. He'd pulled out one of the books. On the cover, an admittedly handsome dark-haired man who seemed to have forgotten to button up his dress shirt loomed in a doorway, with what appeared to be a trickle of blood running from the corner of his bottom lip to his chin. *The Vampire Lord's Lover.* "*This?*"

"Yeah," Anders said, repeating the word for a third time, this time with some annoyance. "What? It's a decent living, and I mean…" He tapped his chest, as though somehow who he was made some sort of point in his favor.

"But…" Curtis was staring at Anders with his mouth open. "You? I don't…I mean…You're really…"

"I'm really *what*?" Anders said, one eyebrow rising.

Curtis seemed to run out of words. He shook his head.

Luc forced a breath into his lungs and sighed. "I think you broke him." Truth be told, he was a little unnerved himself, though he didn't intend to let it show. Also, the more he looked, the more the vampire "Lord" became far too familiar—had Anders *really* written Renard into some sort of romantic hero?

"I get that a lot," Anders said. "Can we get back to the part where we got chased by a pack of furies now?"

"Right, right," Curtis said, looking at the book once more. He turned the book over, though, and a soft smile replaced his stunned expression. "She's pretty. Your mother," he said, holding up the back of the book for Luc to see. The woman there, curly black hair and light brown skin, beamed out at him, smiling with genuine joy. Luc read the text beside the picture.

Keah Sander believes in gazing at the stars, making wishes, and the power of love. He supposed it was better than *Keah Sander is the pen name of a lust demon who fucks men and draws on their souls to live.*

"She is," Luc said.

"Was. Thank you."

Curtis turned the book back over again and frowned at the cover. "Anders?" He shook his head. "This is *Renard*, right? I'm not crazy?"

It wasn't only Luc who saw the resemblance, then.

"His name is Fox in the book," Anders said, taking the novel from Curtis and sliding it back onto the shelf. "He's more of a dominant alpha type than a killer, though. But you have to admit, he was a good-looking guy, even if he was a murdering warlock who tried to wipe us out."

Curtis just stared at him.

"Perhaps *Keah* here is right," Luc said, and—yes—enjoyed the little flinch from Anders the name earned him. "We should focus on the evening at hand rather than his bibliography."

Curtis stepped away from the bookshelf. The book they'd kept from the furies sat on the desk beside the laptop, and Curtis picked it up. "Parliament Hill," he said.

"You still want to go?" Anders said.

"Do we have a choice?" Curtis said, and as much as Luc might concede the point it was their only true lead, he wasn't eager to cross the river again, not with the furies still likely on the other side.

Anders blew out a noisy sigh.

Curtis's phone rang. He dug it out and frowned, showing them both the screen reporting an unknown number before he tapped the screen to answer it. His quick nod to them both made Luc sharpen his predator hearing to listen in to the call.

"Hello?" Curtis said.

"It's me."

"Matt?" Curtis said, a mix of worry and hope thrumming through their bond.

Matthew Stirling is calling? Now? After we had a run-in with the furies. Luc exchanged a glance with Anders and saw the same apprehension drawing lines on Anders's rough brow. The timing painted a poor portrait.

"Hey, Curt." Luc hadn't spoken with Matthew Stirling much— they'd only really met during an incident where demons had attacked one of Stirling's boyfriend's pack, in fact—but the young man's voice sounded tighter and more careful than he recalled from their inter- actions.

"Are you okay?" Curtis said. "Everyone is looking for you—your great-grandfather, the Craft Night group, not to mention Jace."

"I know, I—I know."

Curtis frowned. "You *know*? What the hell, Matt? Aaron is dead. You left a *dead body* behind, and other people are *dying*—people like you, by the way—and something is happening with the sorcerers and wrath demons—"

"I know! I know all that, Curt." Stirling's calm cracked now, and Luc thought there was true grief and fear to it. If Luc were forced to wager, he'd no longer put his coin on Stirling being the murderer after all. "You need to listen to me. *Please.*"

Curtis took a breath. "Go on."

"I know people like me are dying. I've seen it a dozen different ways since Aaron."

"It?" Curtis frowned.

"My turn. Me…dying." The young Stirling's voice caught. "And you're always there. You and Rebekah and the others. From Craft Night. You come at me, and I die."

"*What?*" Curtis said. "Matt, I'd *never—*"

"I know," Stirling said. "I…I *know*, but I'm not usually wrong, Curt, but at this point…" A puff of a sigh over the line. "Look, Curt. I may need to risk it. I need you to give me that book. I know you have it, and I know you gave Aurora's people the slip."

And there it was. The confirmation of Stirling's involvement Luc had been waiting for since Stirling had ended his hiding by phoning Curtis. Anders blew out a breath, and Luc regarded him grimly.

"You sent them after me?" Curtis said. "Wait. How did you even know where I was?"

"I scried you in the coffee shop."

"What?" Curtis's voice—and the pulse through the bond Luc shared with him—cracked with betrayal.

TWENTY-SIX

Curtis closed his eyes, reining in his anger—tempers and magic, he reminded himself—and waited for the silence on the other end of his phone to end. Matthew Stirling sent the furies after him. The very person he'd been trying to prove was innocent in all this...

Wasn't

"Curt." Matt's voice, so shaky and tired and unlike his usual upbeat and amusing self, softened. "You don't understand."

"No, I really don't," Curtis said. "So if you want this damn book, you're going to need to *explain* it to me."

"I don't have time, if the coven heads—"

Curtis's phone beeped twice, and he pulled it away from his ear. The call had been disconnected.

"Crap," Curtis said, calling up his recent calls and dialing the number. To either side, he could feel Luc and Anders. Their mix of apprehension and a desire to likely say something that was going to piss him off, most especially if it included the phrase "I told you so," made it harder to concentrate as he held the phone back to his ear and waited.

It rang. And rang. And rang. No answer, and no voicemail. He eyed the screen. Full bars, full service, battery good...

"Double crap." No way was their disconnection an accident. What if the coven heads had already tracked Matt down? "Okay, let's go." Curtis tapped to end the attempted call.

"Go *where*?" Anders said.

"Parliament," Curtis said, staring him down. "Matt has to be somewhere near there. Whatever this is, that's where it's happening."

"*Lapin*," Luc began, and Curtis held up one hand because they didn't have time for this, but to his surprise, Luc shook his head, took his hand, and stepped closer to him. "No. Listen to me."

Curtis took a breath. "Okay. Go. Hit me with the 'I told you not to trust him' and any other 'I told you so' you've got stored up. It's been a good couple of days of me being wrong about people."

"*Non*," Luc said, shaking his head. "It's not that. I cannot say I told you so because I didn't. I originally may have thought Matthew Stirling might have had something to do with the murders, but he clearly does not. He is a target, as you believed all along."

Curtis relaxed a fraction.

"But..." Luc said.

And there it was.

"He is working with the furies," Luc said. "He admitted he scried you to locate that book, which we *just* kept out of the hands of furies on the other side of the river. Taking it back to them seems foolish."

"Ducky's right," Anders said. "I get you want to go help, but he didn't seem to want it. All he wanted was the book, and fuck that, you don't owe it to him. You can call Rebekah and the others and tell them to stay put, too."

Curtis closed his eyes, because the thing was, they *were* right. Both of them. Calling the rest of the Craft Night group. Keeping the book away from the sorcerers and Matthew—and, ultimately, the coven heads—was likely the safest thing for Luc and Anders and himself, but...

"What?" Luc said softly. "I don't understand what I'm feeling from you. You're conflicted."

"Honestly?" Curtis smiled, opening his eyes. "That's probably because I don't understand what I'm feeling right now."

"Say it out loud," Anders said. "That's what I do when I can't get an alphahole to cooperate."

"Alphahole?" Curtis blinked.

"Alpha protagonist who's also an asshole. Alphahole," Anders said. "It's a writing thing. Making them use their words usually helps."

"I..." Curtis stammered again, because his brain really wasn't handling the whole *my demon lover is some sort of award-winning romance novelist* thing. "Yeah, okay. Use my words. Fine. Here are the words. Renard wanted to take down the Families. This book was a part of his first plan, and we know it involved Parliament, right?"

"Correct," Luc said slowly. "Or at least, the book was there at the time."

"When the first plan failed in 1916, we know he was trying to gather power like the kind we already have—blood, soul, magic—

which somehow would offer him, I don't know, another crack at it. One he had to wait for, sure, but he was a vampire now, so whatever, right? Tick-tock means nothing."

"Yeah," Anders said.

"Wait," Luc said, frowning. "One hundred years."

"Is now-ish, yeah," Curtis said. "More or less."

"No." Luc shook his head, then dipped his chin in acknowledgement. "Although yes, you are correct. But I meant the accords were in 1816. Renard's first attempt was 1916. One hundred years."

"Oh," Curtis said, and then he took a breath, because another hundred years was... "*Oh.*"

"You think that's why the coven heads are in such a damn hurry? And your buddy with the blue eyes?" Anders said. "It's now or they've missed their shot until another hundred years from now?"

"It's already a little overdue by that clock," Curtis said. "But... maybe?"

"I interrupted," Luc said, waving his hand.

Curtis took a second to gather his thoughts. Renard's original plan. Waiting a hundred years to try again with powers like theirs. And now... "Now we've got Matt working with the furies, who we're pretty sure are working with the sorcerers—which I'm going to take the leap and say has Matt also working with the sorcerers, if you'll let me?"

Both men nodded.

"Which gets us to now. Matt wants the book because he's no fan of the Families." This was where Curtis felt a bit shakier, because he had no doubt Renard's plan was about *destroying* the Families, and he didn't think Matt would go that far, but what if he *would*?

"Then there's the murders. Whatever is coming, Matt's one of the only people who might see it," Curtis said. "And someone else—I don't know who—is trying to kill anyone with that power. I'd started to think it might have been the sorcerers—they stole the mantle to turn invisible, right?—to cover their plans, but if Matt's working with them, it doesn't make sense."

"Agreed," Luc said.

"No, they didn't steal it," Anders said.

"What?" Curtis said.

"The timing is wrong," Anders said, and he sounded angry. "Fuck. Wheeler's place got robbed *after* the coywolf got offed."

Curtis stared. "Oh my God." He was right. "So, the book wasn't all that was gone before Rebekah's inventory. The mantle was, too."

"And the murderer isn't on the side of the sorcerers, then," Luc said.

"Right," Curtis said, trying to shift the mental pieces into new positions. "So. Even discounting we think there's a murderer after Matt, Matt's got sorcerers and furies on his side, the coven heads are trying to track down the sorcerers, which they'll absolutely be able to do once they set their magic to it. Matt might be able to buy them time with his wards, but wards wear out, and then…" Curtis lifted his gaze to the other two men, and it turned out Anders had been right all along. Saying it all out loud did help. "And then the Families win. *Again.*"

There. That was what it came down to, and why he wanted nothing more than to find Matthew, figure out what the book might be able to do, and help him. What bothered him about staying out of the way, about allowing Renard's plan—whatever it might have been—to fail for the third time?

It let Malcolm Stirling and the people like him continue to go unchallenged.

"You want to break the Families," Anders said, in the quietest voice he'd ever heard him use before.

"Yes?" Curtis said, lifting his shoulder. "No? It's not that simple. I don't want to *destroy* them, but Malcolm Stirling killed my parents, and the Families didn't so much as bat an eye. It's just what they do when an Orphan shows up—force them to join a family and be one of their flunkies, or never use their magic, or be destroyed. Get in line or die." He took a breath. "The Families tried to screw us over or outright kill us multiple times. Can you think of anyone else as lucky as us three? Figuring out a way to be ourselves without being under their sway?"

Luc fell silent, and Anders shifted. He waited for them to remind him this was simply the way it was, but to his surprise they didn't. So, he continued.

"The way they treated Wheeler led to how much death?" Curtis said. "And the sorcerers have it even worse than Orphans like Wheeler and me." Curtis took a long, deep breath. "I want to believe things are heading in the right direction. I do. With Matthew and Rebekah having inherited, they're already in a position to make things better, I hope. That kind of influence they can bring to bear against the likes of Stirling, for sure. And Katrina Windsor and Kendra Mitchell are coven heads now, and they seem to be cut from a better cloth, but…" He shook his head. "Can they change it *enough*? Or am I just fooling myself?"

Neither answered him, which Curtis took as answer enough.

"I am, aren't I?" he said. "The Families won't change, or whatever change those few inside who want to improve things try to make, the rest will fight tooth and nail."

"Yeah," Anders said.

"Do we go?" Curtis said.

"Matthew Stirling seemed to intuit your arrival might be detrimental," Luc said. "Lethal, even."

"I'm not going to kill him. I'm not going to kill *anyone*," Curtis said, promising it as much as stating it. "But that's the thing about visions. Once you've seen the future, you have a shot at changing it."

"So," Anders said, reaching over and picking up the leather-bound book, "we're heading back over the river and then…" A slow smile spread across his face, and his voice got the added rumbly bass sound it always got when he was amused. "The plan is, what, fuck if we know what we're doing, but let's try to do it on purpose?"

"I wouldn't have put it like that," Curtis said, wincing at the truth of it regardless. "More like, uh…" He considered. "We keep Matthew alive, find out what he needs the book for *exactly*, try to make sure the sorcerers don't get punished, and figure out what that book is supposed to do." He shrugged. "And maybe not pissing off the furies is in there somewhere, too. For a start."

"You don't ask for much, do you, *lapin*?" Luc said, but the vampire was smiling now, too.

"Maybe we ask them to hold hands and sing in a big circle, like we're friends?" Anders chuckled.

Sing in a big circle. Curtis looked at him, and for the first time all night, he felt a surge of confidence.

"You are a fucking *genius*," Curtis said, forgetting not to swear. Magic sparked and crackled along his skin. The lights flickered above them, and a burst of wind scattered some of the loose papers on Anders's desk, but Curtis didn't care one bit. "God, I love you two."

TWENTY-SEVEN

They took Luc's Mercedes, finding a spot on Elgin to park.

Anders looked up and down the street, spotted no one in either direction, and turned back to the other two. "Is it just me, or did everyone go home?"

"Just like before," Luc said. "When the furies gave chase, the streets were oddly empty."

"Hang on a sec," Curtis said, leaning forward between the two seats and pulling out his glasses. Anders watched as he slid them on, waited for the tiny hum through their bond that meant he was using magic. Curtis scanned through the windows, his hazel eyes flicking left and right, lines forming between his eyebrows.

"What is it?" Luc said.

"Remember when a demon was killed in the parking lot last winter?" Curtis said.

"Burke?" Anders said, remembering the big, surly, and mostly silent demon who'd gone toe to toe with a *loup garou* and lost.

"Right," Curtis said. "The Mitchells sent in people to sort of close off the area."

"I recall," Luc said. "They drew symbols in the snow, correct?"

"Right," Curtis said. "Subconscious 'go-away' vibes, for lack of a better way of putting it." He pulled his glasses off. "It's that again. But…" He waved a hand outside the window. "Like, a *lot*. And not in snow, obviously, but on posters and signs and things—see those marks there, on the bus shelter?"

Anders looked where Curtis pointed, seeing what looked like any other random tag out there. The scale of it struck him, though. "You're saying someone filled the whole downtown with magical graffiti *fuck-offs*?" Anders said.

"I mean...yeah." Curtis shrugged one shoulder and put his lenses back in his pocket. "On signs, bus shelters, those posters, too." He shook his head. "Looks like they used nametag stickers. It would have taken *hours*. All day, maybe. They would have had to start early, maybe set a kind of magical timer, and even then, every single ward would need a bit of magic to..." He sighed.

"The sorcerers?" Luc said.

"Maybe," Curtis said, but his tone didn't quite match the worry Anders felt between the three of them.

"You think Matt did it," Anders said. "This is his play."

"I think it's maybe his way of trying to keep innocent people out of harm's way. These wouldn't have any effect on anyone like us. They're not powerful enough to nudge a wizard or a vampire or a demon, but designing these only to work on regular people means if Matt worked with the sorcerers, they could have used their own weak magic to empower all those..."

"Graffiti fuck-offs," Anders said.

"Sure. Let's call them that."

"In a way, it speaks well to his motives," Luc said, and Anders glanced at the vampire. It wasn't like Luc to give anyone the benefit of the doubt, but when he saw the way Luc was regarding Curtis with the gentle fondness thing he could do so well, Anders got it. Luc was trying to look for the bright sides here for Curtis.

"I guess it does," Curtis said.

"Do you think they tagged Parliament, too?" Anders said, curious. "I mean, that'd be harder, right? Cameras, guards, whatnot?"

"You're assuming there are no Family plants on the premises," Luc said.

Anders winced. "Well, fuck me. Right." Of course the Family would have had their people on Parliament Hill. Shit. How had he not thought of that?

"Except not tonight, because—" Curtis said, and his eyes widened. "Oh crap. Oh crap crap *crap*!"

"What?" Anders said, not getting it.

"The covens are in moot," Luc said, his jaw clenching. "Malcolm Stirling called them all to gather to hunt down the sorcerers, and Mackenzie said it was an all-hands kind of thing. And the sorcerers have already gone rogue. So any of the Family people normally placed on Parliament Hill—wizard *or* sorcerer—"

"Aren't gonna be there," Anders said. "Or at least, any of the ones who are there aren't going to be loyal—skipping Stirling's party, or not having been invited on account of being the runaways they're trying to find." Anders paused. "Except, also maybe furies."

"Right," Curtis said. "So, I guess now we go?" He lifted the messenger bag, sliding it over his shoulder, and offered the other two a gamey smile.

"We go," Anders said.

❖

By the time they passed the Centennial Flame, Anders would have sworn they had eyes on them, but the large fields to either side of the pathway up to the front of the seat of the government were empty, and they hadn't spotted so much as a single woman in motorcycle leathers, so even the furies didn't seem to be around.

Which should have made him feel better, not worse.

"I keep waiting for that little whistle-song thing to happen," Curtis said. "You know, from the westerns, when the gunslinger walks down the main strip?" Curtis whistled the stinger.

Anders chuckled. "I know the feeling." A drop of rain hit his forehead, and he glanced up in time to see them lose the moon behind thicker clouds rolling in.

Fucking hell. No shadow-walking, then. Couldn't one thing go well for them?

"I see no one," Luc said. "But I believe I hear..." He shook his head. "I'm losing it to the rain. But it might have been voices."

"We should head around behind," Curtis said. "That's where the library is."

They kept going. Like Luc, Anders didn't see anyone. He sharpened his vision and hearing as much as he could but ran into the same problem. All he could hear was the soft rain as it started to pick up speed into something closer to a shower.

Ugh.

He kept one eye aimed at the groups of statues as they passed them—easy place to hide, given how large the women having tea were—but again, nothing. If someone would just jump them already, he'd feel better about this whole deal.

No one did, and they made it to the rear of Parliament with not so much as a security guard in sight. The wind picked up, as did the rain, and then...

"Matt," Curtis said, with such relief it made Anders want to put a hand on his shoulder to keep him firmly planted where he was. But Curtis didn't make a move toward the slender wizard standing near Parliament in a hooded jacket.

"Curt," the Stirling kid said. "Please tell me you brought the book, because we're stuck here."

"*We?*" Curtis glanced around, and Anders did the same, and now they *weren't* alone. It should have been impossible. There'd been no people at all, but after a ripple of heat that made the rain mist and hiss, now he saw furies—maybe the entire pack of them he'd seen at the Market—each of them with a hand on the shoulder of someone else. Sorcerers, he assumed, once he caught sight of the bearded Mann in front of Cari.

"Did you know furies could do that?" Luc said in a voice barely above a whisper.

"No," Anders said.

"Oh," Curtis said, turning back to Matthew. "We. Right. What are you going to do with the book, Matt? We got cut off before."

"It's the covens." Matthew shook his head, sending a spatter of rain off his hood. "They're already wearing down my protections, Curt. I need the book to figure out the way *in*." He pulled something out of his pocket, holding it up, and it took Anders a second to recognize what the glints of the light were.

Reflections off glass lenses. Matthew Stirling had Curtis's old glasses.

"Give him the book." The now-familiar Southern lilt made Anders turn his head to find Aurora among the group. She had her hand on the shoulder of a grey-haired woman in a long raincoat. He realized the woman's eyes were closed, and she looked like she was concentrating, and unless he was mistaken, the air around them rippled with heat.

"You're keeping them angry," Anders said, confirming with a glance all the sorcerers had their eyes closed and some of them were even moving their lips. "Bumping their magic?"

"They're holding the wards up," Matthew said. "To give us the time we need to get to the Accords."

"Get to the Accords?" Curtis frowned. "You make it sound like a place."

"Give me the book, and I'll show you," Matthew said, even putting his hands together in front of him like he was pleading. "We know it's here somewhere."

"What do you want to do?" Anders said, shoving his fists into the pockets of his jacket. The rain was cold, and his hair was getting wet enough now to be uncomfortable.

Curtis frowned, biting his lip. "Okay." He looked at Luc and Anders, and the frustration in his voice was matched through their bond, a kind of tap-tap-tap against the back of Anders's neck that made him want to growl.

"You're sure?" Luc said. Somehow, his hair looked just fine even though all three of them were crossing the line from damp to wet.

"Yeah, but I'll hang on to the book," Curtis said, raising his voice at the last. He slid on his glasses first, then kept the bag on his shoulder, tugging it around and unfolding it to pull out the book, and Anders waited while he did whatever he had to do to juice up the glasses, closing his eyes, and then opening them with purpose before opening the book.

The Stirling kid took a hesitant step toward them, then crossed the distance. He joined them, and it took everything Anders had not to grab the blue-eyed little shit by the back of the neck and give him a shake.

"Now you trust me?" Curtis said, with more snark than Anders usually heard him use in a month. Nice.

"Every time I see myself die, it's not just you with me, it's Rebekah," Matthew said, all his attention on the book. "She throws fire at me."

Ouch. Anders exchanged another glance with Luc, who raised his eyebrows.

"It's blank," Matthew said. "Why is it still blank?" He reached up to touch the lenses, but Curtis shook his head.

"You have to aim the book, it's like a window." He held up the book, and while Anders only saw a blank page, he saw Matthew Stirling's shoulders slump with relief.

"There," Matthew said.

"What is it?" Anders said. He still only saw a blank page.

"It's the tree-thing," Curtis said, pointing toward the round Library. "On the wall there, between those two columns."

"Tree-thing?" Luc said.

Curtis held up the book in front of them—it still looked blank to Anders—and led the four of them over to the library. "It's not a tree, obviously, but it's sort of got the same sort of arrangement in the picture. A central trunk, a bunch of branches, but it's twisting and moving in the picture. I'm not sure what it is." He reached out. "It's just here, and—"

Curtis vanished. One second he was there, the next he touched the wall and was simply *gone*.

Matthew Stirling pressed his hand against the stone, and he vanished, too.

"Fuck," Anders said.

TWENTY-EIGHT

"It's not a tree, obviously, but it's sort of got the same sort of arrangement in the picture," Curtis said, trying to explain the ink drawing on the page of the book to Anders and Luc, who couldn't see it. "A central trunk, a bunch of branches, but it's twisting and moving in the picture. I'm not sure what it is." It didn't have leaves, and every branch split into thinner and thinner offshoots until it ended in sharp lines which faded off into nowhere. But the book was definitely showing something right there in front of him, against the library wall. He reached out one hand to where, on the page, the stone was marked with the tree-like object.

"It's just here, and—ow!"

A burst of light and heat blinded him, and he had to close his eyes against the sudden brightness. His ears popped, and he nearly dropped the book in surprise, but held on. When he blinked away the sudden shift from the dim, rainy night to this warm, bright wherever, his mouth dropped open.

He heard Matthew gasp beside him.

It was as though they stood *inside* fire, a nearly spherical whirl of golden reds and yellows moving in all directions at once but never seeming to come any closer, and yet they could breathe and didn't burn. Through his glasses, Curtis saw twists of silvery-white among the raging sphere, and it clicked what he was actually seeing.

Magic. Raw magic, not held inside anyone, not at someone's command. This was the very magic of the world around him, as loose and wild as the wind or the ocean or any other natural force at play.

And in the center of this bubble of magic, the "tree" rotated slowly in front of him, itself made of more of those bright twists of light. It wasn't thick branches growing thinner after all, though, but instead made up entirely of tiny threads of light. Those threads were woven around each other, growing into thicker and thicker "branches" as five main braids created the "trunk" and five "roots" of the tree.

Curtis looked back up at where the five branches spread off in every direction upward, until only the faintest traces of it brushed the edge of the sphere of magic, and…

Red. Gold. Silver.

Blood. Soul. Magic.

"What is this?" Curtis said, looking at Matt.

"It's the Accords," Matt said. After a moment, he slid Curtis's old glasses off, and at his small, surprised smile, Curtis did the same. The big glowing tree-thing remained visible. Wherever they were, they didn't need help to see the magic. "Or part of it. It's an old enchantment, worked here to make sure the Families have the power they want." He swallowed. "I've been dreaming about it for months and months now, my tattoo has been telling me about it for years, but…" He finally dragged his gaze away from the tree—no, the Accords—and faced Curtis. "It *takes*, Curt. It takes magic, and it feeds it into the Families."

Curtis took a second to put the book back into his messenger bag, letting everything Matt said sink in. When he looked back at the Accords, the sheer scale of what he was seeing finally struck him. Those tiny silver threads? He'd seen them before, as magical connections between wizards and their covens. And the way they were braided, how they led to the five thick roots…

"It's stealing the power from Orphans," Curtis said. "Feeding it into the Family bloodlines."

"Whenever someone is born to the Families," Matt said. "The lion's share of power from someone else—maybe multiple someone elses—is snatched away and given to them."

"Leaving sorcerers," Curtis said.

"Right."

"But not always," Curtis said. He was living proof of that. Wheeler had been, too. And Ben. And Rebekah's grandfather.

"There are still more Orphans than there are new wizards born into every Family generation." Matt swallowed. "But if they marry into the Family, then their kids get hooked into the same deal."

That explained why the Families were so keen on "adopting" Orphans and willing to kill to make sure Orphans didn't practice magic on their own. They wanted to steal the Orphans' magic, divert every last drop of it back into their own damned pipeline of power.

"How do we stop it?" Curtis said.

"I...I don't know," Matt said. "I was under the impression it needed upkeep of some kind."

"Upkeep?" Curtis blinked. "Like what? Lube, oil and filter?"

"I guess?" Matt said, and Curtis stared at him, stunned.

"You *guess?*" Curtis waved his hands. "Matt, we are standing *inside* magic right now, beside a two-hundred-year-old magic-sucking tree spell, and you're *guessing?*"

"I thought I'd be able to understand when I got here," Matt said. "It's supposed to be my thing, my inheritance—this *thing* started it, started all the inheritances—and we're supposed to use those gifts to keep it going, I think. At least, I think that's why I always dreamed about the others, so I found them, pulled them together."

"I think Renard was trying to find you all, too," Curtis said, looking back at the twisting magic. "He was looking into the genealogy of the Families. Maybe he intended to kill you all or something. Make it impossible to do this upkeep or whatever?"

"You can't kill the inheritances. If we die, they pass to the next person," Matt said.

"He had that knife," Curtis said. "He could have taken your abilities from you, one by one, if he'd known who had them."

Matt shivered. "And then he could have done whatever he wanted to the Accords."

So could I. The thought came before Curtis could stop it, but as he watched the twists of light for a breath, and then another, he realized he could feel the Accords on some level, the same way he could feel Luc and Anders and his own magic. Blood—the bloodlines of the Families. Soul—the Orphans, each a pinprick of silver light among the roiling energy. Magic—taking their potential and feeding it back. Using all three things: blood, soul and magic, to steal what they might have been and weave it into the Families. It was like the give-and-take among his triad, but without the give.

Matt took a step closer to it, and Curtis winced. When Matt reached his hand out, Curtis couldn't stop himself from moving forward and taking his shoulder in one hand.

"Are you sure you should do that?"

"I need to get a feel for it," Matt said, holding his hand close to the twisting trunk, shaking his head. "It's like it's designed to look for Orphans before they're even born," he said. "Watching the horizon for the next wizard, and then waiting to pounce if there's a…" He seemed to fumble for a good word, then finally grimaced. "Receptacle."

Closer to it, Curtis couldn't ignore the feel of the pulse and play of it, and he held his own hand out, not touching it, but wondering if he'd be able to feel anything.

It bulged toward his palm, the threads pulling away from the trunk of the tree as though he had a gravity of his own. He yelped and jumped back, but not before some of the threads had brushed his skin.

Magic *whipped* inside him, the usual sense of wind and motion he associated with his magical talent turned up to gale force. He gasped, then gritted his teeth tight, desperate to stop himself from speaking any word he could think of, from casting *any* spell, from doing *anything* to let the magic out, *now*, which it so desperately wanted to do.

"Curt! Curt!"

When had he sat down? He blinked, realizing Matt was kneeling beside him, holding his shoulders and saying his name, his blue eyes wide with fear.

"Holy crap," Curtis said.

"Curt?"

"I don't suggest touching it," Curtis said, struggling back to his feet. "I have so much magic in me right now. Like…so much." Every word he spoke came with the rushing sensation of wind beneath his skin. "I think I need out of here."

"It reacted to you," Matt said, helping him to his feet. "It didn't react to me."

"My triad," Curtis said. "This is what Renard wanted to do. I think I could pull that thing to pieces, Matt, but I don't think you'd survive. I don't think anyone in any of the Families would survive. You're all connected to it, and all that magic would have to go somewhere, have to do something." He closed his eyes, concentrating past the desire to *use* the power inside him.

"So what do we do? How do we stop it?" Matt said.

"You said the five of you could do upkeep," Curtis said. "Maybe that's it? Maybe, once all five of you have your inheritances, you can, I don't know, rewire it somehow."

"We can't wait," Matt said. "I know it. I *feel* it."

"What if you worked with the people who already have the

inheritances, then? I mean, Rebekah, for one, right? And Mackenzie's mother seems cool enough?" Curtis knew he was grasping at straws.

"I've screwed this all up," Matt said. "I had this one chance, but I don't understand enough to *do* anything..." He clenched his fists, shaking, then yelled an inarticulate noise Curtis flinched away from.

"We can't stay here, Matt," Curtis said, after Matt was done and finally unclenched his hands, panting. "If nothing else, we need to get the sorcerers somewhere safe."

"Where?" Matt said, with utter misery.

"I don't know," Curtis said, admitting the truth. "But I have kind of a plan in place. Maybe."

"That's more than I've got." Matt took one last look at the twisting tree-like Accords, then sighed. "Do you even know how we get out?"

"I'm hoping the way we came in. We walk through that." Curtis pointed at the roiling magic sphere surrounding them.

"Right."

They turned and moved back to the outer edge, and they reached out their hands together.

The light winked out around them.

❖

Curtis had to blink away the afterglow of the Accords, barely able to see Anders and Luc, still standing in the rough circle formed by the sorcerers and furies, and feeling the cool rain against his forehead again—the sensation helping to counterbalance the massive jolt of power still whirling around inside him.

"*Lapin?*" Luc's voice cut through the noise of the showers. "Where did you go?"

"Good question," Curtis said. He opened his mouth and closed it. "The Accords isn't just an agreement, it's also a spell, an enchantment, and I think we were kind of inside it. Beside it?" He shook his head.

"Something hit us," Anders said. "Like..." He patted the center of his chest, making water spray off his leather jacket. "Strong."

"Yeah, that was me," Curtis said, trying to think of how to explain accidentally picking up a bunch of extra stolen power from the magic-sucking soul tree thing. "I got too close to it, and it reacted to me, and—"

"Matt?"

They all turned at the voice. It was Mackenzie coming around the corner into view, walking with an umbrella. Behind her were Dale, Tracey, and Rebekah, all of them in hooded jackets, moving at a decent clip.

Curtis turned to Matt, and saw his eyes widen in panic. *You're always there. You and Rebekah, and the others. From Craft Night. You come at me, and I die.*

"Stay back!" Matt said, holding up both hands.

At the same moment, Rebekah yelled, "*Matt, behind you!*" and Curtis frowned, looking behind Matt on reflex.

Nothing.

Curtis looked up just in time to see Rebekah throwing fire sorcery their way, and he remembered what Matt had said. *Every time I see myself die, it's not just you with me, it's Rebekah. She throws fire at me.*

Curtis tackled Matt, and the flame went over their heads by inches, and even as he hit the ground, Curtis was trying to make sure he was covering Matt's body, protecting him from—

The yell behind him made him look up, but all he saw were odd wisps of flame in the rain, sort of *hovering*, and almost like the outline of a man's shoulders.

"Get the fuck *away* from him!" Rebekah yelled, and she sent another dart of flame streaking across the space between her and where Curtis and Matt had just been standing. This time, Curtis saw it hit its target, the outline of a man clear against the flames, though it was there and gone.

The mantle. The invisible killer. The figure twisted and was turning to run. Luc lashed out with one hand, but Curtis saw he got nothing but air.

Only Rebekah would be able to see him.

"Curt…"

Curtis looked down and saw something had been jabbed into Matt's shoulder. It looked like an allergy medication injector.

Matt's eyes were already rolling back into his head.

TWENTY-NINE

The killer was there among them. Luc moved between the prone figures of Curtis and the young Stirling boy and tried to sense the figure he'd seen backlit by the fire the Mitchell woman had thrown, but there was nothing. The invisibility he wore seemed perfect. Not even a sign of him in the rain, Luc noted, with a quick glance at the ground for footsteps among the puddles.

"Where is he?" Luc snapped.

"Trying to get away from the building," Rebekah said, then another flare of heat and flame lashed out, only this time without revealing the figure at all. The Mitchell wizard grunted in annoyance and moved toward Parliament herself. "You're quick, asshole, but you're not getting by me."

She flicked her wrists again, and this time instead of a stream of flame, it was a spray of smaller darts of fire, and amongst the tiny flares, Luc saw where the fire licked against something.

Someone.

He drew on the blood and the odd energy Curtis seemed to have brought back with him from wherever he'd been, and the world—even the darts of sprayed flames—slowed down to nearly nothing, raindrops becoming visible spheres to him as he streaked forward and struck out without holding anything back. His fist connected against pliant flesh and harder bone beneath, both crushing and folding with a wet, heavy crunch in the face of vampire strength.

He released the speed and flinched from the hail of tiny fires peppering his skin and his greatcoat—no vampire was a fan of fire—but luckily he'd been thoroughly coated by the rain, and nothing caught. He knelt down, blindly groping till he found a person beneath his hands, and he yanked at the cloth with both hands, pulling hard until, with a sudden ripple of light, Luc held a prone blond man by his collar, the hood of his long cape falling back off his forehead, and blood pouring thick and dark from the side of his mouth, where it ran into a short blond goatee.

Benedict Lister. Matthew Stirling's driver. And an Orphan, like Curtis.

Benedict coughed once with a wet, pained gurgle, more blood pouring from his mouth. Luc realized his punch had connected with the man's ribs and likely staved them in on one side and punctured his lungs, given how much of his strength he'd put behind the blow. The man's eyes filled with panic and he gurgled again, a spasm twisting the length of his body and his hands clawing at Luc's forearms weakly.

"Kenzie!"

Luc turned at Curtis's voice, hearing the desperation and fear in it. Matthew Stirling lay on the ground in the rain, and Curtis stood over him, holding something small in one hand it took Luc a moment to recognize.

An injector.

They were too late.

"What's in the needle?" Luc said, turning back to Benedict and shaking him. If they knew what he'd injected into Matthew Stirling, perhaps they might be able to save him, as they had Anna. "Tell me."

But Benedict's eyes no longer tracked him, and the wet, wretched gurgles had stopped. Luc let the man's body go.

Rebekah came beside him, panting, and she looked down at the body for a beat before offering Luc a hand. He took it and rose, seeing Mackenzie Windsor now kneeling with both hands on Matthew Stirling's chest, her voice speaking in the same calm, controlled manner Curtis had when he brought forth his magic, and her palms rising and falling and seeming to drag the slim wizard's chest up and down with them. The two others and Curtis hovered a step or two back, and Anders had given them space.

"Is that who I think it is?" Anders said to Luc, nudging the body with his boot.

"Benedict Lister," Luc said.

"Malcolm Stirling's man."

"I don't understand," Rebekah said, and Luc could hear rage in the woman's voice.

"I do," Curtis said. His eyelashes were wet with a mix of rain and tears, and his chest shook. "If Matt dies, the gift moves on to someone

else in the Stirling family. Someone Malcolm Stirling can trust to..."
He turned back to the library wall, where Luc had watched him vanish
and then return, feeling a helplessness he'd never wanted to experience
again in his life the entire time he'd been gone. "To do the lube job. I
think that's why it's overdue. He knew Matthew would *never* be a part
of it."

"*What?*" the broad man—Dale, Luc thought his name was—said.
"What are you talking about?"

"Guys, I'm losing him," Mackenzie said. "I can't...I can't do this
forever..."

"Do you need more magic?" Curtis said. "Take mine, I've got so
much right now—"

"It's not about *more*," Mackenzie said, her own face streaked with
tears now. Her hands remained on Matthew Stirling's chest, and Luc
saw they were growing pale. "Healing spells can't do this. I'm not my
mother, I don't have her way with life magic yet, Curtis."

"Duke, we're losing ground, too," Aurora said, her voice a
surprise from behind. When he turned to face her, Luc noticed her eyes,
entirely black now. She was drawing heavily on her demonic abilities.
Her hand, still on the shoulder of the grey-haired woman in front of her,
shook visibly.

The coven heads would know where they were, then. Sooner
rather than later, and given they were only on the other side of the locks,
at the Château, it wouldn't take them long to get here. *Merde.*

"If your mother comes?" Luc said, turning to Mackenzie and not
voicing the rest of his question. Could she heal Matthew? Or, more to
the point, *would* she?

"Maybe," Mackenzie said, shivering. "I—I don't know." But he
heard the truth in her uncertainty. She didn't think her mother would
try, not if Malcolm Stirling wanted his great-grandson to die.

Anders stepped up to him. "Do we go? Hasn't been long enough
for holding hands, has it?"

Luc checked his watch. "No."

"I have an idea," Curtis said. "But I'll need time, and I need you
all to help me move Matt and come with me." Luc turned but saw
Curtis wasn't speaking to him or Anders. He was looking at Rebekah
and the others. His Craft Night group.

"Come where?" Dale said.

Curtis gestured to the wall of the library, where he'd vanished
before. Dale shook his head, clearly not any more enlightened.

"They're going to break through the wards," Aurora said. "Any moment now."

Luc met Curtis's gaze. "Go. We will buy you the time you need."

Curtis exhaled and reached down, taking one of Matthew's shoulders in both hands. "Dale, help me. Kenzie needs to keep her hands on him."

"I still don't know where we're going," Dale said, but he and Rebekah and the other young woman, Tracey, were all moving to help now, and they awkwardly managed to move both the prone Stirling and Mackenzie toward the wall, Mackenzie never releasing her hands from Matthew's chest.

They backed up farther and farther until, with a final glance aimed their way, Curtis reached out with one hand to touch the wall, and all six of them vanished.

"So," Anders said. "We've got a dead body, a bunch of nearly fried sorcerers, and some wrath demons. What's this plan to buy more time, exactly?"

Luc forced a deep breath into his lungs and sighed out into the rain, holding up both hands.

Behind them, with a grunt, Aurora let go of the grey-haired sorcerer, who grimaced and stumbled forward, nearly falling to her knees. Anders caught her, and she gripped his arm with both hands, barely able to stay upright.

"Yeah," Anders said. "That's what I thought." He looked down at Benedict's body, then at the sorcerers, seeming to settle on a large, bearded man in a long grey trench coat. "Wait. Maybe I do have something."

Another sorcerer stumbled. Then another. Another.

Their circle was broken.

THIRTY

W hat the hell is *that*?" Dale said, staring at the swirling mix of blood, soul, and magic in the center of the whirling sphere of magic all around them.

Curtis could relate. "It's the Accords Capitol A. It wasn't just a deal your ancestors struck with all the other supernatural types, it's a spell. It moves magic. In fact, it steals magic for the Families, and I need you all to let me steal some magic for you."

"What?" Tracey said, shaking her head. Her wet hair hung limp against her cheeks, and her usually impeccable makeup was smeared. "Curtis, slow down."

"It's connected to all of us," Rebekah said, staring at the twisting threads. "He's right. It's taking magic from people and funneling it into the Families."

"And has been for about two hundred years and change," Curtis said.

"Bekah?" Dale said, frowning.

"I can see it," she said. Of course. She could see full well what was happening here. That was her inheritance—to see the truth of magic in any form, just like she'd seen right through the mantle the killer had been wearing.

Curtis took a breath. "Mackenzie, if I made sure you inherited, right now, could you save him?"

Kneeling over where they'd laid Matthew down, Mackenzie glanced up at him, her lips pressed tightly together, brown eyes widening with understanding. He knew she couldn't hold on to Matthew much longer, but he wouldn't do this without her permission.

She nodded.

One down. Two to go.

"What's happening?" Tracey said. "What do you mean if you made sure? *How?*"

"You five have one shot to undo this," Curtis said, pointing to the Accords. "Matthew saw it. That's why he gathered you, because he knew you five could change things some day. And it's right *now*. I wish I could give you more time, but there's enough power in that thing to move mountains—or your inheritances—if someone can access it, and I *can*, because of Luc and Anders. And if you five inherit, if you all work together, you can save Matt. And I think you can really change things."

"What?" Dale's voice was small, and barely a breath. "Curtis, the inheritance…" He looked like he was on the edge of tears. He'd never seen Dale like this, but a moment later Tracey moved beside him and took his hand, lacing her fingers with his.

"I'll be with you," she said.

"Please," Mackenzie said, her voice breaking. "If I might be able to save him…"

"Yes," Tracey said.

"O-Okay." Far, far less enthusiastic from Dale, but it would do.

Curtis reached his hand toward the Accords, biting his bottom lip and trying not to let his fingertips shake too much. Just like the last time, threads from the tree started to *bend* toward him, like seeking like, and wanting to *take* him, *use* him, *fill* him.

I am made up of magic, and I am vampire, and I am demon. You're nothing but a magic-sucking evil tree. You *obey* me.

The first thread brushed his skin, and magic burst through in a painful rush of heat and light and power scorching at him from the inside out. Curtis screamed words in English and Latin and French with as much instinct as intent, and the threads connecting Dale and Tracey and Mackenzie to their covens—to the Families—blazed white before his eyes, lightning-bright and just as quick. With every bit of willpower he had, Curtis *demanded* the Accords do what they'd been designed to do.

Take power from one person and give it to someone else.

Another lightning-bright flare of light, and the power shifted around him. This time, metaphorical thunder followed a moment later, a reverberation of power slamming back through the same paths it had left, and their cries made it perfectly clear whatever Curtis had done, whether or not it had been enough, it had *hurt*.

"Curtis!" Rebekah's voice. She squeezed his shoulder. She could see what he could see. Hell, she probably understood it better than he did. "Let go!"

Right. Right. He pulled his hand away hard, but the raging twists beneath his skin barely dimmed. He had so much power inside him right now he could barely see. Burning light existed *inside* him, behind his eyelids, and he didn't think he could hold on to it this time. It hurt deep within like some part of him was aflame, and he had an awful feeling it was maybe his soul. He blinked rapidly, trying to see, and in front of him, he saw Rebekah and Dale, Tracey and Mackenzie, and Matthew on the ground between them, all of them working together to save Matthew's life. Mackenzie's voice was loud and stronger than before, but their threads, those individual strings of magic so visible to his gaze in that space, were still connected to different parts of the Accords. Their Families.

"Is it working?" he said, then he coughed. He tasted blood. That probably wasn't good.

"Maybe," Rebekah said, her voice tense. "Kenzie almost has it, I think."

"I can see his spirit," Dale said. "It's not gone. There's still time."

See his spirit? Curtis winced, another jolt of pain inside him.

Rebekah faced him, or at least the aura of her and her thread of connection seemed to pivot his way. He could barely see anything beyond the omnipresent glare of the magic inside him. "It's hurting you," she said.

"I think...I think I took too much," Curtis said.

"I'll try to help," Mackenzie said. "If I can just...get him *back*."

Tracey put a hand on her shoulder and started speaking softly as well. A flare of magic passed between them, but Curtis watched as most of it ran back up the thread to Tracey's Family.

Tracey and Mackenzie weren't coven mates. They'd never been in the same coven. They'd worked together, yes, but all of them—Matt, Rebekah, Tracey, Mackenzie and Dale—were from five different Families, and their magic would only complement each other so far without the bond of a coven.

"I'm not getting further ahead," Mackenzie said.

"What if you were a coven?" Curtis said.

"What?" Dale faced him.

"If I shift your bonds to each other from your covens. It's the only thing I can think of to do with all this power." He coughed again, and this time he felt the blood drip off the bottom of his lip. Gross. "Especially since I think it's going to kill me if I don't do *something*."

"He's right," Rebekah said. "You guys can't see this, but...He's right."

Super. Rebekah could tell he was totally going to die, too. Great.

"Matthew, too?" Mackenzie said.

"Him, too," Curtis said, forcing down another cough. "Listen, I'm all about consent, but I don't think I can hold this and really need an answer." The pain flared again, and he very nearly swore, biting hard on his tongue to stop himself. He was pretty sure even a "crap" right now wouldn't end well. "Like, right now."

"Yes," Mackenzie said. "For both of us."

"Do it," Rebekah said.

"Okay." Tracey's voice shook.

"Yeah," Dale said.

Letting the burning, overwhelming magic free but doing everything in his power to be in command of where it went, Curtis reached out a hand and flicked his wrist, a lash of power snaking out like a thing alive, wrapping itself around the threads binding them to the Accords and their Families, and tearing them free with the barest of efforts.

The reverberation hit him a second later like a punch to his chest, and he saw a spray of blood come from his lips as he coughed—*that's probably really bad*—but he held his grip, even as the threads burned and twisted and sent arcing lances of pain up his arms. He refused to let go, pressing them into each other and demanding they obey him in a voice now thoroughly wet with his own blood until he saw the five threads, struggling in his grip, finally, painfully, find each other and connect, weaving themselves into a knot, becoming a group, becoming a coven.

Curtis smiled, opened his mouth to tell them he'd done it—

Then died.

THIRTY-ONE

Anders had barely finished explaining everything he even slightly understood about what the fuck was going on to Aurora and the other furies, as well as the laughably far-from-foolproof idea he was calling a plan, before his predator hearing picked up footsteps in the rain.

A lot of them.

"Incoming," he said, and Luc took up a position beside him, nodding once.

He eyed the furies and sorcerers, who'd spread out a bit around the open space and were doing their best impressions of people not already completely tapped out, but they all looked pale and shaky to him, so he wasn't sure how well that would ride.

If only they'd bothered to steal some damn weapons from Wheeler's along with all their protective shit.

The dark and the rain didn't make identifying the approaching figures easy, but right at the lead Anders spotted a silver-haired man walking with a cane—not that he seemed to rely on the cane to help him walk much—and won his own silent bet with himself about who would show up first.

Malcolm fucking Stirling.

More old white dudes walked along with him, as did some closer to Anders's age and even a few as young as twenty. Women were peppered about, but for the most part, Stirling had brought men to this particular meeting. Anders recognized one of the others from a dinner he'd had with Stirling once, another coven head, though he was fucked if he could remember the man's name.

"Which of you attacked us?" Stirling called out in his calm, faux-polite, I-get-what-I-want voice. "Tell us, and the rest of you won't be punished."

"Attacked *you*? The only person attacking anyone is your driver, old man," Anders shouted back, and Stirling turned to face him, but Anders was still too far away to really catch his expression. "Benny. Remember him?"

"I don't know what you're talking about," Stirling said. "Benedict has been missing for days. But someone here attacked one of the coven heads and two others."

"Right." Anders rolled his eyes. Fuck this guy. "Pull the other one."

"Katrina Windsor collapsed," said the man Anders had met before. "As did two others. Something was done to their magic."

"Let's say I believe that. So what?" Anders said with a glance at Luc, but the vampire only gave him a little nod to continue and a tiny smile that showed just a hint of his fang. Apparently, he wanted Anders to keep the lead here. In fairness, given they had exhausted furies at their back, they'd all agreed the best move they had was to try and give the furies some anger to feed on to recover, and Luc had not-so-subtly pointed out it might be best, then, if Anders did the talking.

"An attack on any coven member is an attack on the coven," Stirling said with a false politeness. "You know the rules, Mr. Hake. You attacked *three* covens."

"No, I didn't," Anders said. "I'm not really the attacking type, Malcolm. I'm more about fucking, sucking, swallowing, bondage, maybe some light roleplay now and then—you'd think you'd know that, what with being old and supposedly smart about stuff—and I promise you, the last people I'd *ever* want to fuck are any of you." He gestured with one hand, making sure to encompass their whole group. "I mean, I have *some* standards."

Luc coughed a small noise of amusement, and Anders stole another glance his way. This time, Luc shook his head. Not yet, then. Okay. More talk. He could do that. He was having fun, actually.

"Why'd you have Benny kill the coywolf, by the way?" Anders said, tilting his head. "And the muse? I don't get that part. Was it just to stop anyone from seeing whatever it was you were planning to do, or do you just, I don't know, get off on the murder of psychics?"

"I told you—"

"Yeah, yeah, you have no idea why your driver—who, for the record, you sent to try and break up our triad once before, remember?—

went out and started killing people. Totally his own thing, right?" Anders held out both hands and then shook his head, crossing his arms. "Only, that's not fucking true, is it, Malcolm? Because when have *any* of your people done serious shit like murder without your okay?"

The other coven head glanced Stirling's way, and even in the rain and across the half a dozen meters between them, Anders could see the frown there.

"He knows what I'm talking about." Anders pointed at the man.

Stirling himself still didn't respond, but his lips were a thin line, and if that wasn't rich-old-white-dude for pissed off, Anders would give up his favorite toys.

Well, maybe not Mr. Fisty.

"I know," Anders said, snapping his fingers. "You pull out one of those feathers your kind like to use. The truth-telling feathers. You can ask me if I attacked your coven heads, and I can ask you if you ordered your boy Benny out there to go kill people, including your own great-grandson, or not. We can clear this right up, right?"

"Don't you *dare* to presume to order me around," Stirling said. He started to lift his cane, the tip of which began to glow, which probably meant Anders had achieved his goal of pissing the man off, but also meant it was time for that plan of his.

"Mann," he said. "Now!"

Stirling frowned, like he barely recognized the name. Typical of the asshole, Anders thought, given Mann was one of the people he'd had spy on Curtis for over a year, but he didn't slow down on bringing his magic stick up in front of him.

Then Stirling grunted in pain, his head snapped to the left, he dropped the stick, half stumbled, and toppled over onto the rain-soaked stone with a second, airy "Oof." His hand went to his temple and came back wet with blood.

"You gave your boy an invisibility toy," Anders said. "He's not using it any more, what with being dead back there." Anders aimed a thumb over his shoulder. He cleared his throat and looked at the rest of the gathered wizards, and holy fuck were they ever the most *boring* looking people ever. So many black trench coats and dress shoes. "Anyone else tries to cast a spell or use a magic stick, you're also gonna get beaned. And you can't see the guy doing the clobbering, but I promise you, he's thic as fuck, and has years of academia *and* wrath demons fueling his rage."

A ripple of motion moved through the crowd of wizards, and they all started looking around, like somehow they'd be able to see the invisible sorcerer in the magic cape.

Malcolm shifted on the ground. His nice pants were all wet, but he didn't make a move to stand. Smart guy. No doubt Mann would club him again if he tried, whether or not Anders told him to.

"For the record," Anders said, deciding to lie to sow a little mistrust, "I don't need a feather. Benny lived long enough to tell us it was you. You asked him to off those people."

Malcolm glared up at him, but he didn't speak.

"Malcolm?" the other coven head said.

"Shut *up*, Alastair," Malcolm said.

Alastair? *That* was the guy's name? Of course it fucking was.

"You had us all looking for your great-grandson," Alastair said, and Anders gave him some credit for having the balls to keep talking after Malcolm's command. He eyed Luc, and Luc gave him another little shake of his head.

Oof. He was running out of material here.

"Probably easier to kill him if you helped Benny find him," Anders said. That earned him another glare from Malcolm.

"You wanted to stop him before he could help us," a grey-haired woman said, one of the sorcerers. She was standing with Aurora, so Anders took the opportunity to check out the fury. She definitely looked perkier now. That was good. They were still outnumbered by Family wizards, but at least the furies weren't going to pass out from exhaustion.

"I don't even know who you are," Stirling spat.

"Carol Rosenfeld," the woman said. "You had me working in your lawyer's office for the last thirty years, you useless piece of shit."

Go, Carol. Anders grinned. *Tell your boss how you really feel.*

"Do you really think this is going to end well for you?" Malcolm said, doing an excellent version of stern for a guy sitting in a puddle and bleeding from his face. "I'm giving you one more chance. Tell us who organized this attack, and the rest of you can return to your roles."

"No," Carol said, and she seemed to be speaking for everyone there. At least, no one argued, though more than a few of the sorcerers looked like they were on the edge of wetting themselves. Which, fair enough.

"We outnumber you, and we have more power than you'll ever have," Malcolm said. "We can drop you *all* with a word, and your one hidden thug won't be able to stop all of us." As he spoke, he rose slowly to his feet, his hands outstretched as though feeling for the "hidden thug."

"That's not true," Luc said, and Anders nearly groaned with relief. *Finally.*

Stirling eyed him. "I'd have thought the Duke more capable of seeing what's in front of him."

"I'd have thought a coven head would learn to look behind him," Luc said. "Because you no longer outnumber us. By quite a margin, if my ears are correct."

Malcolm spun on his heel, as did quite a few of the wizards he'd brought with him including His-Name-Is-Seriously-Fucking-Alastair.

Jace Parsons hadn't put on a jacket. Anders wondered if that was so he wouldn't ruin it if he had to shift into his big wolf form, or if he just knew how intimidating he'd look in a wet shirt, because he looked *really* fucking intimidating in a wet shirt. It clung to every curve of his thickly muscled chest, and his biceps looked like they were about to tear the sleeves.

Yeah, he'd do him.

Behind Jace were more of Jace's pack. And Taryne Rhedey, the veterinarian and druid, who maybe didn't look so intimidating beside Jace, but she did have a certain presence to her nonetheless, and was staring at Stirling like he was a bug.

It wasn't just werewolves, though. Tyson, Ethan, and David had also arrived, the three of them standing a bit apart from the dozen or so werewolves, and behind *them*, Anders saw a bunch of people he'd never met before but assumed was the coterie of Renard's former castoffs Luc had called.

"So," Anders said, clapping his wet palms together. "We invited all our friends." Then he aimed two finger-guns Malcom Stirling's way. "You don't *have* friends, do you, Malcolm?"

Stirling swallowed.

"This isn't over," Stirling said.

"That's what people always say when it's over," Anders said.

Then a jolt of pain lashed up his forearm and he grunted, nearly losing his balance. He barely kept on his feet and grabbed at the source of the pain with his free hand, realizing where it was coming from with real panic.

The tattoo. The tattoo binding him and Luc and Curtis together.

Something bad just happened. Something…

He saw Luc beside him also flinching and holding his own arm in the same place.

But he couldn't feel him. He couldn't feel Luc through their bond at all.

Or Curtis.

No.

THIRTY-TWO

C urtis grunted, aching from head to toe, and he shifted uncomfortably. He'd assumed being dead wouldn't hurt. Dying, sure, but the being dead part? Wasn't that supposed to be peaceful?

He blinked, opening his eyes, and found himself staring into the pale blue eyes of Matthew Stirling. And beyond him, fiery golds and reds and yellows and streaks of white...

Maybe they were in hell? That would explain the pain, right?

"Oh, crap," Curtis said, "You died, too?" Had it had all been for nothing, then?

"What?" Matthew said, then he laughed. He actually *laughed.* "Oh. I mean, kind of. A little. But Dale and Mackenzie did their one-two thing, and...How are you feeling? Close call for you, too."

Dale and Mackenzie. Everything came back to him in a rush, and he sat up—big mistake. He nearly vomited from vertigo, but he choked it back and threw one arm out to keep himself half upright—then he looked around. Sure enough, they were all there. Tracey and Rebekah were facing the Accords, the twisting, turning tree of magic threads still doing its twisting-turning tree of magical threads stuff, while Dale and Mackenzie were crouched on the other side of him from where Matthew was kneeling, both of them looking at him in concern.

Also, Dale's irises were a super pale grey-white now, which was new. And really, really creepy.

"Uh," Curtis said. "Hi?"

Mackenzie laughed and threw her arms around him, hugging him tight. To his surprise, he nearly burst into tears. Apparently, dying—even a little, whatever that meant—made him weepy. Who knew?

"Matt, Kenzie, Dale?" Rebekah's voice broke the emotional moment, and Mackenzie let him go.

Curtis slowly got himself off the ground. Dale reached out and gave him a hand, and Curtis tried not to stare at his newly bone-colored eyes.

Dale glanced away, though, so he'd totally failed.

"Sorry," Curtis said, assuming the eyes had something to do with his inheritance. Which was his fault.

"It'll be okay," Dale said with what sounded a bit like bravado, but he followed it up with a hug, so Curtis tried to take it at face value. "I'll get sunglasses," he added as they broke apart, and Curtis laughed.

"Or contacts, maybe?" Curtis said.

Dale smiled, and it barely wobbled, then he followed Mackenzie and Matthew to join Rebekah and Tracey at the Accords. Curtis stayed a few steps farther away.

"We can't break it," Tracey said. "The feedback of power alone would kill everyone connected to it, which might not include us any more, but…"

"Our entire families," Rebekah said.

"Wait," Curtis said. "You're not connected to it any more?"

"It was your doing," Rebekah said, but her smile told him she wasn't mad about it. "When you tied us all to each other, you untied us from our families—and you took the hit of feedback, which was the whole nearly dying thing."

"No *nearly*, he died." Mackenzie crossed her arms.

"Right," Rebekah said. "But we have the inheritances, and Matt was right. We're the ones who can change this thing. I can see how this works."

"And I understand the connections," Tracey said.

"And the bloodlines," Mackenzie said.

"And the way it transfers power from soul to soul," Dale said.

"And how it looks to the future," Matthew said. "Figures out who to take from."

"But you can't break it," Curtis said, regarding the twisting construct of power and for a second allowing himself to *loathe* it. The pain it had caused, the damage it had done, all the lives it had forced into a trajectory that led them to the Families.

"No," Matt said. "But I think we can untangle it."

Curtis faced him, and the light on Matthew's pale face underlined the dark smudges under his eyes. He'd been quite literally at death's door a few moments ago. Maybe they shouldn't rush into messing with the all-powerful soul-sucking magic tree right now?

"Yes," Tracey said, and her certainty seemed to reach them all. "It doesn't have to work this way. It would take time for everything to flow back to where it belonged. Decades, even, but...yes. We can do that."

"Tracey takes the lead," Matt said, like he wasn't so much making a decision as allowing himself to think out loud, confirming what he was thinking as he was saying it, and Curtis realized it likely that was exactly what he was doing. He could see the future. "Rebekah shows us what Dale and Mackenzie see for the connections, and I'll be able to tell you when we've done as much as we can without setting off any feedback."

Curtis saw his five friends nod slowly, and then he cleared his throat.

"I'm...gonna give you space," he said, when they all turned to look at him, varying amounts of amusement on their faces. "I really, really don't want that thing to touch me again."

"Probably best," Matt said, blinking at him. "Thank you, Curt. I mean it."

"I'll be right outside," Curtis said, pointing at the edge of the swirling sphere of magic. "You just walk through to get out," he added, given he'd brought them here without really explaining anything. "See you in a bit."

He backed up to the edge, then turned and left them to it.

❖

The rain had really picked up, but frankly, after nearly burning up from the inside out, it felt kind of nice on Curtis's skin and dealt with the worst of the blood he'd coughed down the front of his shirt. He took a single step away from the wall of the library before he saw the crowd of people—way more than when he'd left—and came to a sudden stop.

"*You,*" Malcolm Stirling said, pointing at Curtis with a finger like he was some sort of pod-person. "What did you do?"

"Uh." Curtis blinked, and he barely got the word out before Luc and Anders were on either side of him, doing their faster-than-he-could-see moving thing, and their expressions were guarded but maybe relieved and...

He couldn't feel them.

He couldn't feel their emotions, couldn't feel their presence, couldn't feel *anything* from them.

Oh *crap*. No wonder he felt weaker and wobbly. Not just from dying.

Luc gave him the tiniest shake of his head, and Curtis aimed a look back that he hoped eloquently conveyed "I'm not *that* fucking stupid" and turned to face Malcolm Stirling, because apparently the gang was all here, but no one had decided to go home yet.

God, he hoped no one could tell their triad had been broken.

"What did I do?" Curtis said. "Well, I figured out you sent Ben to kill your own great-grandson so his inheritance would pass on to someone you could control, who you'd then use to reinforce the Accords for their century check-up—though, for the record, I have no idea how you were planning on talking Rebekah into that, unless you planned to kill her, too."

Stirling swallowed. Beside him, Alastair Spencer was glaring at him, though it might have had something to do with how Jace Parsons was sort of looming over the two of them and looking all big and brawny-like.

"Yeah, I'll take that as a yes," Curtis said. "Anyway, you failed, is the bottom line. Matthew isn't a Stirling any more." He paused to glance at Jace, who looked at him with such hope it made Curtis's chest ache on his behalf. "He's fine, and he's in a new coven now."

"*What?*" Stirling said.

"Your inherited gifts are out of the Family bloodlines now," Curtis said. "I'm not sure where they'll go from there, to be honest, and..." He shook his head. "I don't care. The important thing is your great-grandson is on it, even as we speak. You don't get to steal magic any more, Malcolm."

"The Accords..." Stirling said, and his eyes widened in realization and anger, and then he was moving forward, raising his hands, and Curtis started to call a protective spell to mind but with a loud thump, Stirling pitched forward face-down into the puddles, and appearing in a ripple of light behind him, Professor Mann popped into view out of nowhere, in a hooded cape, the hood falling back, holding what looked to be some sort of big stone hammer in one strong hand.

"I won't lie," Mann said, in the same voice he used to give a lecture on poetry. "I enjoyed that."

"You will leave now," Luc said, aiming the command at Alastair Spencer in the way he had that he used to be able to back up with their combined power, but Curtis didn't think anyone else here would be able to tell the difference. Or at least he hoped not. "Two at a time. And take him with you. And the body. I imagine you all have the capabilities to handle ensuring none of this ends up on any of the cameras?"

"They're already off," a grey-haired woman said, and Curtis frowned at her. She looked vaguely familiar. She caught him looking and smiled and waved. "We handled that."

Two by two, the wizards started to leave, and Curtis noted each pair was accompanied at least part of the way by some of Jace's pack, or David or Tyson or Ethan, or the others, who he was pretty sure were Luc's vampires and...

He stopped, staring at the vampire coterie Luc had allowed to be formed by those Renard had tossed aside. A taller, brown-haired vampire looked far too much like Mackenzie to be anyone other than her sister, and he gave her a small nod of support, trying to let her know her sister was all right. But that coterie, and David and Tyson and Ethan...

He swallowed, waiting. It took time for all the wizards to go, and then the furies left with their sorcerers. Mann swung the big stone club over one shoulder and didn't seem to be about to hand back the mantle, either. Finally, the others started to move off until it was just the three of them. The rain had even washed away the blood from where Ben's body had fallen.

Only Jace remained, and he stood at the far side, leaning against the low fence that overlooked the river, not looking particularly bothered by being soaked to the skin.

"I think we should stay until they come back out," Curtis said, nodding at the wall.

"*Lapin*," Luc said, his dark eyes full of concern and dropping his voice to a whisper. "What happened to our bond?"

"I died," Curtis said, and at the look of alarm on both their faces, he held up one hand. "Just a little. Dale and Mackenzie fixed it, but it must have been enough for..." He gestured between the three of them. "Snap."

"At least the full moon is soon," Luc said.

"About that," Curtis said, and he took a deep breath. "It occurred to me, just now, seeing David and Mackenzie's sister, and..." He shook his head. *Just say it, Curtis.* "There's a coven back there who would take me in," Curtis said, pointing at the wall. "And you've got David," he said, nodding to Anders, whose eyes were wide, before turning back to Luc. "And as the duke, you could have a coterie of your own, with Mackenzie's sister's coterie."

He couldn't feel a thing from them. He had no idea of the emotional impact of what he'd just offered, but he'd already thrown their lives into a tailspin once with his offer to bind them all together into their unique triad instead of traditional groups.

They didn't have to do it again.

Luc opened his mouth, but before he could reply, voices came from behind them.

"—decades before all that power goes back to where it should have been in the first place, like I said," Tracey was saying.

Curtis turned and saw all five of his Craft Night friends had returned, looking exhausted and wet, and yet, he saw triumph in their eyes.

"You did it?" Curtis said, trying not to let his voice crack at the thought of whatever it might have been Luc was about to say.

"Matt!" Jace's booming voice interrupted his question, and a moment later a very wet werewolf had scooped Matt up in both arms and looked to be trying to eat his face.

Okay, fine, it was a really hot kiss. And Matt was *definitely* reciprocating.

Curtis cleared his throat and exchanged amused glances with the others, then turned to Luc and Anders.

"Okay," he said. "Let's go home."

EPILOGUE

The Law of Three is everything. Every full moon, for the three days of the phase, the groups of supernatural beings gather and renew their bonds. It takes three wizards to form a coven, three demons to make a pack, three vampires to create a coterie. More is safer, but three is required.

Luc Levesque, Vampire Duke of Ottawa, lifted one finger to his lips and pierced the tip with a fang before holding it out and placing it on the tongue of Anders Hake.

"My blood," he said.

Anders closed his lips around Luc's finger and then made a show of sucking on it like he'd suck on something else, even winking when Luc rolled his eyes.

Could Anders *ever* take something seriously?

Beside him, Curtis sighed at the antics, but he was smiling, hazel eyes bright with amusement.

"My blood," Luc said again, drawing his finger out from Anders's lips—the demon made a loud, smacking noise—and then offering it to Curtis, who was a lot more restrained in his taste of Luc's essence.

"What?" Anders said, lifting his shoulders once Luc withdrew his finger.

Curtis just shook his head, then held out his own finger. "Do the honors?" he said to Luc, and Luc smiled, taking the digit into his mouth, biting the tip with one fang, and tasting the vibrant something extra he always tasted in the blood of those who could do magic.

When he'd had a taste, Curtis held his finger out to Anders and said, "Suck it."

Anders laughed, and if his display had been somewhat over-the-top before, now it was a borderline farce, complete with a deep groan from the demon, before he offered up a finger of his own to Luc, almost challengingly, a wide smirk on his rough, unshaven face.

"My blood," Anders said, and they repeated the process.

Luc closed his eyes after he and Curtis had tasted the demon's blood. The connection between them *flickered*, dim and faint, but present. The tattoo on his forearm, too, no longer felt numb and senseless. He opened his eyes.

"There you are," Curtis said, smiling at them both.

It would take two more nights, of course. And they weren't done this evening, either—they'd share more blood, and Curtis would weave more magic between the three of them, and Anders would no doubt demand they enjoy a more carnal connection as well, but that was no hardship. Never had been, he could admit now.

"Did you really think we'd let you go that easily?" Luc said, seeing a thoughtful look on Curtis's face.

"You do remember the part where you both tried to tell me you weren't right for me, right?" Curtis said, crossing his arms. "Or did you forget, with all the magic and death and stuff?"

Luc just smiled.

Anders leaned forward. "You think the Families are freaking out yet? Trying to do their bonds right now and feeling their power slip away?" He raised one eyebrow. "Please tell me that's what's happening."

"Sorry." Curtis shook his head. "It won't be so quick. It won't be like that at all, in fact, which sucks but when you take that much power from people, there's no way to give it back in one big go. But over time, the sorcerers will get stronger. And there won't be any new ones, only more Orphans. Who knows," Curtis said, grinning at them, "maybe someday the wizards won't be the top of the pecking order any more. Maybe it'll be the shifters. Or one of the clans of demons. Or the *vampires*." He faced Luc, and his face an exaggerated expression of horror. "God. What have I *done*?"

"Well," Luc said. "When it happens, I'll put in a good word with the Duke of Ottawa. I believe he owes you both one."

"Just one?" Anders said.

"Yeah, what he said," Curtis said. "Pretty sure I can come up with more than one."

"And to be clear," Anders said. "One *what*? Are we talking blow job, bondage, roleplay…?"

Curtis laughed, and Luc managed to control his own reaction to a mild smile, though in truth he had a few ideas of some roles he might enjoy seeing Anders play.

Anders, though, remained undeterred. "No, I'm serious. One what? I could go get Mr. Fisty. Also, why are we still wearing clothes?" At this, he reached to grab Curtis's T-shirt, and the two started wrestling with each other playfully while Luc watched, though he decided to start on the buttons of his own shirt, so as not to tempt Anders into ripping it.

It was a fine shirt, after all, and Luc had started reading some of the Keah Sander books, and there was a *lot* of shirt-ripping. Anders's heroes and heroines alike hadn't seemed to have mastered unbuttoning.

He caught both of them watching his fingers work and decided to put a little more effort into the process, smiling at them and enjoying their rapt attention.

Outside, the full moon continued to shine. It would for two more nights, during which the three of them would spend every moment together, and throughout which no doubt Curtis would continue to indulge Anders's propensity for turning everything into a single entendre, and all the while asking Luc questions about his three centuries of existence with endless curiosity.

As his shirt hit the floor, Luc decided he wouldn't trade any of it for anything.

About the Author

'Nathan Burgoine grew up a reader and studied literature in university while making a living as a bookseller. His first novel, *Light*, was a finalist for a Lambda Literary Award. *Triad Blood* and *Triad Soul*, the first two novels in this series, are also available from Bold Strokes Books, as is his YA novel *Exit Plans for Teenage Freaks* and his first collection, *Of Echoes Born*. For novella lovers, *In Memoriam, Handmade Holidays, Faux Ho Ho, Village Fool, Felix Navidad,* and *A Little Village Blend* are shorter queer romances (often with a dash of speculative fiction). A cat lover, 'Nathan managed to fall in love and marry Daniel, who is a confirmed dog person. Their ongoing cat-or-dog détente ended with the rescue of huskies. They live in Ottawa, Canada, where socialized health care and gay marriage have yet to cause the sky to cave in.

Books Available From Bold Strokes Books

Triad Magic by 'Nathan Burgoine. Face-to-face against forces set in motion hundreds of years ago, Luc, Anders, and Curtis—vampire, demon, and wizard—must draw on the power of blood, soul, and magic to stop a killer. (978-1-63679-505-8)

Head Over Heelflip by Sander Santiago. To secure the biggest prizes at the Colorado Amateur Street Sports Tour, Thomas Jefferson will do almost anything, even marrying his best friend and crush—Arturo "Uno" Ortiz. (978-1-63679-489-1)

Mississippi River Mischief by Greg Herren. When a politician turns up dead and Scotty's client is the most obvious suspect, Scotty and his friends set out to prove his client's innocence. (978-1-63679-353-5)

Murder at the Oasis by David S. Pederson. Palm trees, sunshine, and murder await Mason Adler and his friend Walter as they travel from Phoenix to Palm Springs for what was supposed to be a relaxing vacation but ends up being a trip of mystery and intrigue. (978-1-63679-416-7)

The Speed of Slow Changes by Sander Santiago. As Al and Lucas navigate the ups and downs of their polyamorous relationship, only one thing is certain: romance has never been so crowded. (978-1-63679-329-0)

Felix Navidad by 'Nathan Burgoine. After the wedding of a good friend, instead of Felix's Hawaii Christmas treat to himself, ice rain strands him in Ontario with fellow wedding guest—and handsome ex of said friend—Kevin in a small cabin for the holiday Felix definitely didn't plan on. (978-1-63679-411-2)

Manny Porter and The Yuletide Murder by D.C. Robeline. Manny only has the holiday season to discover who killed prominent research scientist Phillip Nikolaidis before the judicial system condemns an innocent man to lethal injection. (978-1-63679-313-9)

Murder at Union Station by David S. Pederson. Private Detective Mason Adler struggles to determine who killed a woman found in a trunk without getting himself killed in the process. (978-1-63679-269-9)

Corpus Calvin by David Swatling. Cloverkist Inn may be haunted, but a ghost materializes from Jason Dekker's past and Calvin's canine instinct kicks in to protect a young boy from mortal danger. (978-1-62639-428-5)

A Champion for Tinker Creek by D.C. Robeline. Lyle James has rescued his dad's auto repair business, but when city hall condemns his neighborhood, Lyle learns only trusting will save his life and help him find love. (978-1-63679-213-2)

Heckin' Lewd: Trans and Nonbinary Erotica, edited by Mx. Nillin Lore. If you want smutty, fearless, gender diverse erotica written by affirming own-voices folks who get it, then this is the book you've been looking for! (978-1-63679-240-8)

Inherit the Lightning by Bud Gundy. Darcy O'Brien and his sisters learn they are about to inherit an immense fortune, but a family mystery about to unravel after seventy years threatens to destroy everything. (978-1-63679-199-9)

Pursued: Lillian's Story by Felice Picano. Fleeing a disastrous marriage to the Lord Exchequer of England, Lillian of Ravenglass reveals an incident-filled, often bizarre, tale of great wealth and power, perfidy, and betrayal. (978-1-63679-197-5)

Murder on Monte Vista by David S. Pederson. Private Detective Mason Adler's angst at turning fifty is forgotten when his "birthday present," the handsome, young Henry Bowtrickle, turns up dead, and it's up to Mason to figure out who did it, and why. (978-1-63679-124-1)

Three Left Turns to Nowhere by Jeffrey Ricker, J. Marshall Freeman & 'Nathan Burgoine. Three strangers heading to a convention in Toronto are stranded in rural Ontario, where a small town with a subtle kind of magic leads each to discover what he's been searching for. (978-1-63679-050-3)

One Verse Multi by Sander Santiago. Life was good: promotion, friends, falling in love, discovering that the multi-verse is on a fast track to collision—wait, what? Good thing Martin King works for a company that can fix the problem, right…um…right? (978-1-63679-069-5)

Fresh Grave in Grand Canyon by Lee Patton. The age-old Grand Canyon becomes more and more ominous as a group of volunteers fight to survive alone in nature and uncover a murderer among them. (978-1-63679-047-3)